A MOST PECULIAR PROVIDENCE

ANGELA E. HUNT

A Most Peculiar Providence, Angela Hunt

Published by Hunt Haven Press

First Edition Copyright 2026 by Angela E. Hunt.

All rights reserved. No part of this book may be reproduced in any form or by any electronic or mechanical means, including information storage, artificial intelligence, and retrieval systems, without permission in writing from the publisher, except by a reviewer who may quote brief passages in a review.

Print ISBN-13: 978-196901113-9
E-book: 978-196901114-6
Hardcover: 978-196901115-3
Deluxe Hardcover: 978-196901116-0

He keeps a quiet house on a Peculiar street,
Where the past still knows his name.
She's been running from the cold too long,
From love that only brought pain.
It's Christmas Eve and the night is thin,
Grace is knocking, let hope begin.
There's a baby breathing hope in the dark,
A small, fierce light with a beating heart.
When the world takes more than it gives,
Love says stay. Love says live.
Maybe Christmas is mercy born
In a most peculiar way.

CHAPTER ONE

In a town the size of Peculiar—four hundred and ninety-three souls at last count—folks notice everything.

Trust me. I've been the police chief here long enough to know that if you so much as sneeze out of season, three people will offer you soup, two will pray over you, and one will start a rumor that you've taken up smoking. Privacy is theoretical in a town this small.

Which is why nearly everyone paid attention to Joshua Donnelly.

I'll admit, I did too. Not because he caused trouble. Quite the opposite. Men like Josh Donnelly stick out precisely because they don't.

For years, Josh and his mother moved through their days with a rhythm so steady you could set your watch by it. Sunrise breakfast. Dishes washed before the coffee cooled. Bibles opened before the first car turned onto Main Street. Grace Egan, who lived next door and had a kitchen window positioned like a theater box seat into the Donnelly household, could've sworn to it under oath.

Grace claimed she never once saw a variation.

Not until the December morning everything shifted.

Before that day, Peculiar knew twenty-six-year-old Josh exactly as he'd always been. A little odd around the edges, in the harmless way folks call "quirky" when they're fond of you.

Josh carved animals out of fallen branches—rabbits, raccoons, the occasional tractor—and sold them at Retro Relics, Jackie Leakey's antique shop. Jackie will tell you she bought the first few pieces out of neighborly pity. She'll also tell you she tripled her money on them and never thought twice about it. Folks around here like things that are handmade and gentle, reminders of softer days. Josh's toys fit the bill.

He moved through life like a boy raised in a forest chapel, which wasn't far off. The Donnelly house sat on Church Street, a sagging Victorian surrounded by live oaks, scrub pines, and palmetto bushes that refused to be contained. Vines crawled up trunks and spilled back down like green curtains, giving the place an otherworldly look. According to local legend, the woods were full of monsters. Personally, I'd have been more concerned about snakes and spiders.

Every afternoon, after his bologna-and-mustard sandwich, Josh walked the mile to Twin Oaks Assisted Living Center. He always changed shirts first, usually into a plain white tee. And every time he reached the front door, he paused to smooth his jeans like he was about to meet royalty.

Maybe he was.

Bill Goodman—my predecessor and, depending on the day, my conscience—had taken a shine to Josh years back. Bill spent most afternoons in a recliner by his window, muttering about baseball stats and the decline of civilization. Josh listened. When Bill felt sharp enough, they played chess in the community room. One man at the far end of life, one still near the beginning, keeping each other company.

That was Peculiar.

Then came December ninth, 2006.

A northern wind swept through Florida that morning, rattling palmettos and dragging sweaters out of drawers that hadn't been opened since the Apollo moon landing. Jackie Leakey turned on the heat and fussed over her potted hydrangeas.

That's when she noticed something peculiar.

Josh Donnelly wasn't wearing his usual T-shirt. He had on a button-down. A nice one.

He moved faster too. Rinsed the breakfast bowls without lingering. Kissed his mama on the forehead. Picked up a foil-covered plate he must've prepared the night before. Then instead of taking the sidewalk route to Twin Oaks, he cut through Peculiar Park.

Jackie stood on her porch, broom in hand, and watched him disappear into the trees. She wondered if the assisted living facility had called with bad news about Bill. Around here, deviation from routine usually means trouble.

Josh reached Twin Oaks early, cheeks pink from the cold. He warmed one hand by the electric fireplace, nodded to Isabella at reception, then headed for the elevator to Bill's room.

Bill was still in his pajamas, but his eyes lit up.

"A little early today, aren't you, son?"

Josh grinned and held up the plate. "Don't you remember what day it is? You're eighty-five today. Mama made you a mini pound cake."

Bill blinked. "Well, I'll be."

"Want cake for breakfast?"

"Why not?"

Josh fetched plates and forks, then the room filled with the aromas of vanilla and butter while the wind rattled the palms outside. They talked about the cold snap, the Noah's Ark Josh wanted to carve someday, and the Rays' chances at another World Series.

Bill was halfway through a complaint about pitching when someone knocked at the door.

Isabella peeked in, worry written all over her face.

"Josh," she said, "your neighbor called. Your mama's in an ambulance. They're taking her to the hospital."

The fork slipped from Josh's hand and hit the table.

He didn't stop to clean up.

He was already running.

And that's where this story truly begins.

Josh's breath steamed as he hurried across the Twin Oaks parking lot, his mind racing faster than his feet. His mother—Margaret Donnelly—had never been anything but as sturdy as a rock. She caught the occasional seasonal cold, but she'd never spent a night in a hospital. She was the sort of woman who kept the house spotless, canned peaches every summer, and insisted on trimming her own palmettos until Josh put his foot down.

The old sedan coughed to life when he turned the key, its engine rattling like loose change in a coffee tin. Josh didn't wait for the heater. He backed out, tires crunching over the crushed shell of the driveway, and headed for Highway 90 with more speed than he usually dared. The wind barreled against the car, rattling the windows, but he kept one hand steady on the wheel and the other clenched tight against his knee.

"Mama, Lord—please," he whispered.

The road curved east toward Marianna, the sky washed in a pale blue. Josh's heart hammered with every mile. He didn't turn on the radio, but listened to the dry hiss of the tires and the sedan's wheezing engine. He couldn't listen to music when he didn't know if his mama was breathing easy or fighting for her life.

When the hospital appeared—a low, sand-colored building with big blue lettering and a crowded parking lot—Josh swung into the first open spot near Emergency. He didn't bother locking the door.

Inside, the antiseptic smell hit him like a slap, sharp and sterile. The waiting room vibrated with quiet tension—an older man rubbing his temples, a mother rocking a fussy toddler, a passing nurse wearing a look that said she was three hours past her break.

Josh approached the check-in desk, his hands trembling.

"I'm Josh Donnelly. I'm looking for Margaret Donnelly. They brought her a few minutes ago."

The woman behind the counter offered a practiced, sympathetic smile. "You can have a seat in the waiting area, sir. A nurse will come get you when she's ready."

Ready for what?

Josh nodded and sank into one of the plastic chairs. The seat was cold, so he sat on its edge, bouncing his knee, one hand clutching the other. He prayed without stopping—half-formed pleas and familiar verses melded with memories of sitting beside his mother as she read the Psalms aloud in her soft morning voice.

Two hours crawled by.

His foot tapped nonstop. He stared so hard at the speckled linoleum floor he could have counted every dot. Finally, a nurse with sympathetic eyes called his name.

"Your mom's awake, but very weak," she said. "You can walk with us. We're taking her upstairs."

Josh followed her through swinging doors to a corridor that stank of disinfectant and fear. There, on a rolling gurney, lay his mama. Her eyes fluttered open when she recognized his voice.

"Josh?" Her voice was faint and slightly slurred. Her left hand rose, but her right lay limp against the blanket.

"Mama, I'm here." He reached for her fingers, startled by how cold they were. "What happened?"

A doctor stepped forward. "Mr. Donnelly," he said, his voice gentle but direct. "Your mother had a stroke."

"Will she . . . will she be okay?"

The doctor gave the slow, careful nod Josh had seen on television but never in real life. "We won't know how much damage she's suffered or if it will be permanent until we see how she responds to the TPA."

"To the what?"

"It's a clot-busting medicine."

The words made Josh's skin crawl and for a moment he thought his legs might give out. But he forced himself to nod, to breathe, and to walk beside the rolling gurney.

CHAPTER
TWO

Out on I-10, Heather Thomas didn't notice the camper van's gas gauge until Brett muttered a curse under his breath. She leaned sideways in time to see the needle sag below E.

"Great," he said, tapping the cloudy plastic as if that might coax the needle upward.

They took the next exit—Peculiar, Florida—announced by a sun-faded sign featuring a cartoon crawfish in a chef's hat, claws open as if welcoming them to the middle of nowhere. The Interstate spilled them onto Highway 90, a cracked strip of asphalt lined with palmettos, scrub pines, and weather-beaten signs that looked older than she was.

A few miles later, they rolled into town—what there was of it. A Piggly Wiggly with half its sign burnt out. A white clapboard church with hand-painted lettering over the door. A brick schoolhouse that appeared to be hibernating. A row of tiny shops selling sea-shell mirrors and gator keychains that glinted in the sun like jewels.

Heather looked around, baffled. "Where's the Walmart?"

Brett barked a laugh. "Pretty sure you're not gonna find one here."

He steered the aging Westfalia camper into the lot beside a public park. Gravel crackled beneath the tires as they rolled to a stop.

"We passed a gas station," she said, pointing back the way they'd come.

Brett killed the engine and raked a hand through his blond hair. "Yeah. No money, no gas."

Before she could form a reply, he reached into the back and grabbed his guitar case.

Heather blinked. "You're kidding. Here?"

Brett checked his reflection in the rearview mirror, ran his fingers through his hair again, and slid out of the driver's seat, grabbing the guitar after he landed. "I'll get some cash," he said. "Won't take long."

Then he headed across the lot toward a picnic table, the sun glinting off his guitar.

Heather watched him go, her chest tightening. Brett had once sung for her, his eyes warm with affection, his voice soft and low. Lately, though, his songs were reserved for strangers who might toss him a dollar or two.

Sighing, she climbed out of the van and walked to a nearby bench, not wanting to take up space that could be enjoyed by an appreciative music lover. The bench's peeling green paint stuck to the back of her thighs as she sat.

Though the sun was shining, she shivered in her thin sweater. She leaned back as Brett set his sign near a chipped concrete fountain. A sandwich board announced *Brett Steelhawk, an American Original,* and an old hat lay beside it, ready to collect cash from those who appreciated his talent.

An old man walked a dog on a nearby sidewalk and a pair of kids coasted by on bicycles. The air smelled like cut grass and woodsmoke. The chill must have encouraged some resident to put a log on the fire.

Brett strummed a few chords, then looked around to see who might be listening. When he spotted a young couple, he launched into one of his favorites—an original song about running free and never looking back. His voice drifted across the park, as thin as the shade beneath the nearby palm trees.

Heather studied the people who passed by. No one paused. No one reached for a wallet.

She balled her hands into fists and shoved them into the pockets of her sweater. What luck, to run out of gas here.

Maybe, if Brett made enough change, she could buy a bite to eat before dinner. Maybe something more substantial than fast food.

Anything to make this situation—this slow deterioration—feel a little less empty.

CHAPTER THREE

Josh settled into the stiff vinyl chair beside his mama's hospital bed, its edges cracked from years of anxious families shifting their weight. The room hummed with quiet machinery—steady beeps, a soft whoosh from the oxygen line, the faint rattle of vents pushing recycled air.

Margaret Donnelly didn't wake. She didn't move. Her eyes stayed closed, her lashes pale against her cheeks, her breathing shallow and ragged.

Josh watched her chest rise and fall, each breath a feeble lift. Something inside him trembled, a feeling he hadn't experienced since childhood.

He leaned forward, his elbows on his knees, and prayed. "Lord, please give her strength. Don't take her yet."

Only the beep of the monitor replied.

A nurse opened the door sometime after sunset, her shoes whispering against the tile. She checked his mama's vitals, made a few notes on her chart, and looked at Josh with an understanding smile.

"Can I get you anything?" she asked.

Josh hesitated. His stomach was knotted, but a need tugged at his heart.

"A Bible," he said. "If there's one around."

Her smile softened. "I'll find one for you."

When she returned, she placed a worn blue Bible in his hands. Josh brushed his thumb over the edge, feeling the familiar ridges of thin paper. His fingers found the Psalms, which he and his mother had read for years.

He landed on one of David's laments: "But I—I am poor and needy—yet my Lord is mindful of me. You are my help and my deliverer—O my God, do not delay!"

Josh blinked until the blurred words focused.

He and his mother had been alone for so long. Two people against the world—one praying, one learning, both leaning on each other more than either of them would admit.

What would he do without her? Who would he *be* without her?

He shut the Bible and pressed it against his breastbone, willing himself to remain strong.

After a while, the tension in his belly evolved into hunger. He hadn't eaten since breakfast with Bill, and then he'd only picked at the pound cake. He slipped out of the room after taking one last look to make sure his mama was still breathing.

Downstairs, the vending machines hummed in a lonely alcove that smelled of coffee and lemon cleaner. Josh fed a dollar into the machine and pressed the button for a chocolate bar. The candy hit the tray with a thud.

He leaned against the wall, peeled back the wrapper, and took a bite. It tasted too sweet, but it grounded him.

A man sat in a nearby chair, elbows braced on his knees, staring at nothing. Considerably older than Josh, the man had oil stains on his pants and redness around his eyes. When he realized Josh was watching, he attempted to smile.

"Long night?" the man asked.

Josh nodded and walked over, then sank into a nearby chair. "My mama had a stroke."

The man exhaled with a rush of air. "My wife's upstairs. Complications from surgery." He scrubbed a hand over his face. "Doctors said the procedure was routine, but nothin's routine when someone you love is on the table."

Josh nodded at the truth in the man's words.

They talked about where they came from, about how fast life could flip, and about the strange quiet of hospitals at night.

Finally Josh said, "I'll pray for your wife, if that's all right."

The man's eyes glistened. "That . . . would mean a lot," he said. "Thank you."

The man attempted a laugh. "I'd pray for your mom," he said, "but I'm not a praying kind of guy."

Josh managed a small smile. "I can handle that part."

As Josh prayed aloud, the man wiped his eyes with the heel of his hand.

They parted ways a moment later. Josh returned to his mother's room and sat at her bedside. Her breathing hadn't changed. Her hand was still cold.

He wrapped his fingers around hers and bowed his head.

"Lord," he whispered, "help us make it through the night."

THE DRIVE HOME seemed longer than the trip to the hospital, though Josh followed the same stretch of Highway 90, took the same curves, and passed the same familiar landmarks. The old sedan's headlights cut through the early morning fog, catching the silhouettes of pines nodding in the brisk wind. He kept one hand on the wheel and pressed the other to his thigh to keep it from trembling.

The doctor's words echoed in his ears: "You should go home, son. Rest while you can. We'll call you if anything changes."

Rest? As if that were possible.

When Josh pulled into the driveway, the rising sun revealed the Donnelly house, looking as though it had exhaled its last breath. The porch light, left on out of habit, cast a weak pool of gold across the steps. Everything else—the plants, the trees, the sagging fence—lay swallowed in shadow.

A chill filled the inside of the house. The door creaked as it closed, and the sound startled him. He stood in the silence, letting his eyes adjust to the dim glow from the lamp his mother had left on in the living room.

He turned, his shoes squeaking on the worn linoleum. Halfway across the living room, his breath hitched.

On the floor lay the sewing she'd been working on that morning—a small pile of fabric squares she was turning into a quilt for a family with a new baby. The soft flannels, faded blue and yellow squares, were scattered where she'd dropped them.

Josh knelt and picked up one of the squares. When he pressed it to his face, he inhaled the fragrance of his mother—a mixture of laundry soap, peppermint lotion, and a flower he'd never been able to name.

He closed his eyes, but a knock startled him upright.

He swiped at his eyes and opened the door to find Jackie Leakey standing on the porch in fuzzy slippers and a quilted robe, her hair pulled into a messy knot. The porch light caught the worry carved deep into her forehead.

"Josh, honey," she said, "I saw your headlights. How's your mama?"

He swallowed, trying to gather the right words. "She had a stroke. The doctor says they have to wait to see how bad it is."

"Oh, sweetheart." Jackie pressed a hand to his chest. "I was afraid it was something awful. When she didn't answer my knock, I knew something wasn't right, so I marched right on in. Found her on the floor in front of the couch. Scared me half to death."

Josh nodded, his throat tight. "Thank you for checkin' on her."

Jackie shifted, creaking the boards under her slippers. "I called the ambulance as quick as I could. I didn't know what else to do."

"You did the right thing," Josh said. "Thank goodness."

She squeezed his arm, her fingers warm and oddly comforting. "You let me know if you need anything, anything at all. I can bring a casserole tomorrow, or come sit if you don't want to be alone."

"I . . . thank you. I'll let you know."

"Please do." She gave his arm one last pat, moved down the porch steps, and turned. "We're all praying for her."

Josh nodded. "I appreciate it."

He moved into the living room, the fabric square still in his hand. He set it on the coffee table and added the other quilt pieces from the floor. Then he dropped onto the old couch, its springs groaning in protest.

Sleep seemed a million miles away. So after a few minutes, Josh got up, went upstairs, and dressed for church.

At 9:12 a.m., Josh dialed Jackson Hospital. A soft-spoken nurse answered.

"Any change? Margaret Donnelley?" Josh asked, his throat tight.

The nurse tapped on the computer, then sighed into the

phone. "I'm sorry," she said. "No improvement yet. She's resting, though."

Josh dressed for church because Mama would have wanted him to—slacks, a clean shirt, the shoes he only wore for church and funerals. When he opened the front door, cold air brushed his face. A thin fog clung to the yard, catching in the arms of the palmettos. He stepped out and locked the door behind him.

He had barely taken two steps when he heard footfalls on his neighbor's sidewalk.

"Josh?"

Grace Egan, his other neighbor, was bundled up in a puffy blue coat with her hair in curlers under a scarf. She stopped at the fence between their houses, her breath clouding in the cool air.

"How's your mama?" she asked, lines creasing her forehead.

Josh steadied his voice. "She's still unconscious. It might be a while before we know anything."

Grace pressed a hand to her bosom. "Lord, have mercy. I was horrified when I heard the news."

Josh's throat threatened to close, but he pushed the words out. "Thank you for caring. I hope you'll pray for her."

"Well, of course," Grace said. "You tell me if you need anything, all right? Dinner, a ride to the hospital—anything at all."

"I will," Josh said. "Appreciate the offer."

She nodded before heading back into her house. Josh watched her go, then turned to glance at his mama's home. The narrow windows stared at him like sad eyes.

He took a breath that burned and headed toward Peculiar Community Church, a brisk walk away.

CHAPTER
FOUR

Heather lay in the back of the van, staring up at the stained ceiling she'd tried to dress up with thrift-store fabric. The pink flowers had once been cheerful, but now they looked like ghosts of themselves. Brett's snoring filled the cramped space, steady and unbothered, as if the world outside had never kept him awake. His arm was draped across his chest, his shoes still on, and the scent of cheap beer clung to him like another blanket.

Sweat beaded on her forehead in a sudden wave of claustrophobia—sticky vinyl under her spine, stale fast-food wrappers under her hip, the oscillating fan clicking above her head. She shifted, trying to get free of the tight space, but the thin foam pad clung to her skin and didn't want to let go.

Her stomach roiled again—not with hunger, but a sensation deeper and queasier. She pressed a hand to her middle and breathed through a wave of nausea.

It had been persistent for days now.

She wasn't stupid. Even without the pregnancy test, she would have known.

And deep down, she suspected Brett did too.

He wouldn't mention it—Brett didn't believe in acknowledging anything that might ruin his mood—but every time she paused in front of a restroom or pushed away a greasy sandwich, she caught him watching her, his jaw tightening. Then he would suddenly need a drink or another cigarette.

Heather turned onto her side to look at him. Even in sleep, Brett looked restless. The empty beer can beside his pillow glinted in the sunlight. Yesterday he'd made nearly forty dollars carrying groceries out to cars. Enough for a couple of decent meals . . . or for a couple of six packs and a pack of smokes.

He'd chosen the latter.

Heather exhaled through her nose, long and quiet, trying not to wake him. She wasn't angry—not really. Brett had always been Brett, charming one day and slippery the next, a boy who chased moments instead of plans. Part of her loved his impulsive nature. Part of her once believed she could keep up.

But things were different now. Or they would be. Soon.

A faint noise drifted through the cracked window—a lawn mower humming beyond the park, mingling with the screech of a hawk and the distant barking of a dog. Heather pushed herself onto one elbow and peeked out the window.

Across the street, the white Victorian house caught the late-morning light, its porch sagging, its paint dull and gray. A tall, lanky young man stepped onto the porch—dark hair brushing his collar, button-down shirt wrinkled. He moved slowly, as if his mind was miles away.

A nice face, though. He reminded her of a stray dog—scruffy, shy, but maybe the loyal sort if anyone gave him a chance.

He locked the door, slipped his keys into his pocket, and

walked down the path that cut through the jungle that passed for a yard. A neighbor called him over, and he threaded his way through the tropical plants to talk to her.

Brett shifted beside Heather, mumbling in his sleep. She lay down and studied the ceiling again, fighting a fresh wave of nausea that had more to do with fear than queasiness.

She had to tell him. Soon. But once she said it out loud, it would be real, and real meant change. And change meant Brett suggesting an action she couldn't consider. Not again. Not after the clinic.

She nudged him with her foot. "Hey! Whaddya wanna do this morning?"

He groaned, dragging his arm farther over his eyes. "Sleep," he muttered. "And maybe grab a few things at the convenience mart."

"Grab" meant *shoplift*. He always said it like that—as if stealing were no big deal.

She turned back toward the window. The young man—whoever he was—was stepping out of the yard that looked like a tropical jungle about to devour the aging house. A car sat in the gravel lot beside the property, an old sedan with faded blue paint, but he turned to walk down the sidewalk.

What would someone like him think about the life she and Brett were living?

She curled into herself, her hands tucked under her arms, listening to the mower hum and the rustle of the wind in the palmettos. Her world had shrunk to the four walls of a camper van, one thin foam mattress, and a half-dozen truths she wasn't brave enough to speak.

She stayed where she was, breathing through her fear, knowing that part of her life had already changed—and she couldn't pretend it hadn't.

Not for much longer.

CHAPTER
FIVE

Josh slipped into the back of Peculiar Community Church and took his usual seat—the left corner of the last pew on the right. Without his mother beside him, the space seemed immense. The wooden pew creaked as he eased himself down, and the faint scents of lemon oil, dusty hymnals, and flowers drifted through the sanctuary.

The sign out front had promised a sermon on "The Last Prayer of the Last Supper," words that had intrigued him earlier in the week. But now, with his mother lying silent in a hospital bed, he couldn't remember what he'd been curious about.

The choir was already singing the special, their voices woven together in a steady braid over the piano accompaniment. "Great Is Thy Faithfulness" had always been one of his mother's favorites.

He rubbed his jaw, feeling the rasp of stubble beneath his fingers. He'd meant to shave, but when he stood in front of the mirror, his eyes looked so hollow he'd turned away.

When the choir finished, Pastor Gary stepped to the pulpit. His Bible opened with a soft flutter.

He began with Judas—how the man slipped off into the night and how Jesus spoke of going away and sending a Counselor. The pastor's voice carried through the sanctuary, rich and warm, but Josh struggled to maintain his focus. His thoughts kept drifting to the image of his mother's slack hand on the hospital blanket.

The pastor finally snagged him with a single phrase: "My prayer is not that You take them out of the world, but that You protect them . . ."

The words struck like a rap on Josh's head.

His mother had spent her whole life keeping Josh out of the world—building a small, safe life for the two of them. But here he was, alone in the world she'd kept at bay.

The sanctuary blurred at the edges. He bowed his head, breathing through the sudden sting behind his eyes.

When the benediction finally came, he lingered in the pew. He wasn't ready to face the empty house.

Not yet.

JOSH STOOD and waited as the other church members filed by. His left leg twitched, wanting to run, but determination held him in place. As he stood there, resisting the urge to flee, voices carried from the line of retreating families.

"There's that man, Mama. The one who walks everywhere."

"Keep your voice down, dear."

"You know—" another woman's voice—"he'd be nice looking if he'd get some decent clothes."

"Shh! It's not polite to laugh in church."

When everyone had gone, Josh squared his shoulders and walked to the door, where Pastor Gary was sweeping the front steps. "Um, Pastor?"

"Still here, Josh?" The minister's eyes sank into soft nets of wrinkles as he smiled. "I thought Nora had chased everyone into the fellowship hall."

"I'm here."

Pastor Gary was watching him the way a father might watch a son—patient and concerned. "Josh? Something on your mind?"

For a moment, Josh couldn't answer. A tremor climbed from his chest to his voice.

"Mama's in the hospital," he finally said. "She had a stroke."

The broom slipped from Pastor Gary's hands and tapped against the railing. "I'm so sorry, son. When did this happen?"

"Yesterday." Josh cleared his throat. "She hasn't woken up yet."

Compassion flooded the pastor's face. He stepped closer, lowering his voice. "Why didn't you tell me when you came in?"

Josh forced a shrug. "Didn't want to... interrupt."

Pastor Gary shook his head. "Josh, a shepherd's job is to walk with hurting people." He paused, his eyes warm. "And an empty house has a way of shouting, doesn't it?"

Josh rubbed his thumb along the spine of his Bible, grounding himself. "I don't know what I'm supposed to do without her. We've always... been together."

The pastor rested a hand on Josh's shoulder. "You're not alone, son, even though it might feel like you are."

Josh didn't answer. His gaze drifted to the parking lot, where families were climbing into SUVs and minivans. Mothers fastened seatbelts. Fathers opened car doors. Children waved bulletins like flags. Life moved on without noticing Josh's had stopped.

Pastor Gary followed his gaze. "Josh, have you eaten anything today?"

Josh shook his head.

"Come on," the pastor said. "We'll get a bite from the fellowship hall. Coffee's probably still hot."

"I don't want to be any trouble."

"Don't worry about that," the pastor said. "Your church family wants to be there for you. Come on."

Family. The word lodged under Josh's ribs like a thorn.

Pastor Gary started toward the fellowship building, but Josh hesitated.

"Pastor?" Josh looked at the ground, unable to meet the man's gaze. "Could you pray for her? For Mama?"

"Of course I will. Right now, if you want."

Josh nodded.

And there, on the front steps of Peculiar Community Church, the pastor bowed his head and prayed for Margaret Donnelly. For healing. For peace. For the son trying to survive with his heart cracked open.

Josh kept his eyes shut, trembling, knowing that Heaven was listening, too.

I<small>N THE EARLY</small> hours of Monday morning, Josh stood against the back wall of the hospital elevator and stared at the glowing numbers as they slid downward. The air smelled of coffee, maybe spilled earlier in the day. He was going back to the vending area, where he could get a fresh cup.

The doors slid open on the fourth floor and a man stepped inside.

He was short, barely reaching Josh's shoulder, with a shock of white hair that looked as if it had lost an argument with a comb. His suit hung on him—the jacket sleeves covered his wrists and the trousers drooped over his loafers. He clutched a folder to his chest, a fat one filled with papers.

Josh blinked. The man didn't look like a doctor, and all the business types had gone home. The only folks in the hospital at this hour were late shift nurses, custodial staff, and family members holding all-night vigils.

The doors sighed shut. The elevator lurched. And the man's folder slipped.

Papers spilled across the floor—forms and reports and pink and yellow slips fluttered like startled birds. The man gasped and bent down too quickly, wobbling.

Josh dropped to one knee, gathering pages, smoothing bent corners, stacking them into what he hoped was the proper order. The chill of the linoleum seeped through the knees of his jeans.

"Oh—oh dear," the man said. "I'm terribly clumsy tonight."

"It's okay," Josh said. "No problem."

They worked in silence for a moment, Josh handing pages up, the man receiving them. When the last paper was rescued from beneath the man's shoe, Josh stood.

The man peered at him through thick lenses, his head tilted. "Thank you, young man."

Heat burned the tops of Josh's ears. "It's no problem," he repeated.

"No," the man said, frowning. "It is unusual to find a young man so polite these days. "

Josh blew out a breath and looked at the floor numbers. Third. Second. "I just—anyone would've done it."

The man didn't seem convinced. The elevator chimed and

the doors slid open, but the man ignored them. He studied Josh's face, his gaze sharp despite the heavy glasses. "What is your name?"

"Josh. Donnelly."

"Donnelly," the man repeated. "And why are you here, Mr. Donnelly?"

Josh pictured his mother's thin hand on the blanket, the blue veins like ink beneath her skin. "My mom's sick," he said. "I was goin' for some coffee."

The man's expression changed, the lines around his mouth softening. "I am sorry to hear that." He wrapped his arms around the folder. "I pray that she will get better."

Josh took a deep, quivering breath. "Thank you, sir," he said. Then he remembered his manners. "I hope you're not here because someone's sick."

"Not at the moment," the man said, "I work with children. Department of . . . well." He tapped the folder. "Paperwork. I'm here to pick up a child."

"At this hour?" Josh glanced at the papers, noticed a corner stamped with a seal.

"Time doesn't matter—I can't rest if one of our children isn't in the place where he or she belongs." The man's bushy brows rose. "The system says good is acceptable, but I want the best for our kids. Some folks disagree, but—" He leaned in and lowered his voice—"they've never been in the system. I have."

"You have?" Josh didn't know if he should smile or not.

"Indubitably. I survived, but not unscathed."

The man's smile faded. "When it comes to children, I don't keep office hours. And settling for what's good is the enemy of what's best." He stared at the elevator wall as if he could see through it into his past. "Don't you agree?"

Josh thought of his mother—of how she had stood up for

him when he'd been bullied and never allowed him to feel ashamed. "Yes," he said. "Of course."

The man turned back to him, his eyes intent. "I'm glad we met, Josh Donnelly. And I will pray for your mother."

The man stepped out, his baggy suit swishing around him. He waved and disappeared down a corridor, his folder tucked under his arm.

Josh stayed against the wall as the doors closed and the elevator carried him down. His ears burned from the man's praise. But beneath the helplessness he felt about his mother, his heart burned with a warmth he could not explain.

Josh sat slumped in the stiff chair beside his mother's hospital bed, the vinyl sticking to the back of his shirt. Morning had arrived—he could tell by the pale stripes of sunlight cutting through the blinds—but nothing else had changed. Mama's right hand still lay motionless at her side. Her breathing still rose and fell in that fragile pattern that made Josh's heart clench with every pause.

A soft sound broke the silence. Barely a murmur—like a faint attempt at breath.

Josh straightened, his heart pounding.

"Mama?"

For the first time since Saturday, her cheek moved. Barely. A small, unmistakable smile curved a corner of her mouth.

He choked on a breath. She could hear him. She was fighting.

He leaned closer, gripping her fingers with both hands.

"I love you, Mama," he whispered. "I'm right here. And I'm okay, so don't you worry about anything. You get better, all right? That's your job."

Her fingers didn't curl back, but her eyelids fluttered, as if she wanted him to know she'd heard.

A knock sounded as the door opened. Dr. Henley stepped inside, tucking a pen into his coat pocket. "Morning, Josh," he said. "Any changes?"

Josh nodded, his voice thick. "I think she tried to smile."

The doctor leaned in, inspecting her face, lifting her eyelid, checking her reflexes. After a moment, he straightened.

"That's encouraging," he said. "Very encouraging."

Josh braced himself, gripping his Bible. "What do you think about her chances?"

The doctor removed his glasses and wiped them with a cloth from his pocket. "Well, your mother's young. Forty-nine is on the good side of recovery statistics. The brain is remarkably resilient at her age. It's too early to predict outcomes, but given what I'm seeing—" He nodded. "I am optimistic."

Relief hit Josh like a warm wave. "Thank you."

The doctor offered a small smile. "Keep talking to her. Keep reading. It makes a difference, you know."

Josh nodded and wiped his eyes with the back of his hand. When the doctor left, he turned back to his mother and read the twenty-third psalm, the words swirling into the quiet room like a promise.

"'The Lord is my Shepherd, I shall not want...'"

CHAPTER SIX

Monday morning found me scowling into my coffee like it had personally betrayed me.

It wasn't the first time. Coffee and I had an understanding: I showed up on time, and it did its job. This mug had apparently called in sick.

Then the door opened.

I looked up, ready to chide Tony for being late, and stopped short.

Bill Goodman, former top cop and a living legend in Peculiar, stood in the doorway, leaning on his cane like it was an old friend who'd earned the right to complain. He moved slower than he used to, but his back was straight, his hat tucked under his arm, his eyes clear. Retired or not, he still looked like a police chief. Some things never change.

I stood. "Chief."

"Morning, Bowen," he said.

I pulled out the chair across from my desk. "Please. Sit."

He took it, lowering himself like each joint had to be

consulted in advance. I waited until he settled before I sat back down.

"So," I said, nudging my coffee aside. "What's on your mind?"

He studied his hands for a moment, then lifted his gaze. "I just had a birthday."

"Well, congratulations."

He smiled. "The Good Book says a man gets three-score and ten. By that measure, I'm living on borrowed time."

"Depends on who's keeping the books," I said.

He chuckled. "Maybe so. But it got me thinking. I don't want to burden my girls with certain things when they're busy planning a funeral or whatever it is they want to do."

I raised a brow. "You planning to go somewhere?"

"Not today," he said. "But I don't take tomorrow for granted."

Fair point. Coming from a man who'd spent half his life knocking on doors in the middle of the night, it carried weight.

"I'd be fine with being planted under an oak," he went on. "But my missus would prefer I lie next to her."

I nodded. "Sounds like Franci."

He smiled again, and the smile stayed a beat longer. "You're doing a good job, Horace. In case no one's told you lately."

I blinked, surprised and pleased by the comment. "That means a lot, sir, coming from you."

He stared at my desk as if he could see through the wood. "Have you ever done anything on the job . . . you'd rather people not know about?"

I blanched. "We've all made mistakes."

"I'm not talking about mistakes. I'm talkin' about . . . well. Maybe I should stop talkin' and let sleeping dogs lie." He looked at me and smiled. "After Franci died, I fell in love—well.

That's not quite right. I fell. She didn't. I never told the lady, but I did somethin' for her . . . and trouble is, I'd do it again. No matter what it cost."

He reached into his inner coat pocket.

When he withdrew a white envelope, sealed and marked only with my name, the air in the room shifted. He held it like it weighed more than iron.

"I've tried to live by man's law and God's," he said. "I wasn't always successful. But when I had to choose between the two, I did my best to defend the poor and the innocent. To provide justice. That's what every lawman should do, isn't it?"

I didn't know where he was going, but when a man like Bill Goodman asks a question, you answer straight.

"It is," I said.

He set the envelope on my desk.

"File this away," he said. "Or keep it in your safe. When I die—" He paused, then corrected himself. "After I die, I want you to take this letter out and read it. You don't have to publish it, and I don't know that it will change anything. But it will allow me to stand before my Lord with a clear conscience."

He looked me square in the eye. "Can I trust you to do that?"

I saw no fear on his face. No drama. Just solid resolve.

"Why, Bill," I said, trying to lighten the mood. "You got some dark secret hidden in your closet?"

He didn't smile. "The life of every man," he said, his voice rumbling, "is a diary in which he means to write one story and writes another; and his humblest hour is when he compares the volume as it is with what he vowed to make it." One of his bushy brows rose. "Know who said that?"

"No clue."

"James M. Barrie, the man who wrote *Peter Pan*. If a man like that can have regrets, I guess I can, too."

I took the envelope. "You can trust me," I said. "I'll take care of it for you."

He nodded and exhaled a long breath. "Thank you."

He stood with effort, steadying himself on the cane. I rose with him.

"I'll be getting back home," he said. He took a step, then turned. "By the way—any word on Margaret Donnelly? I heard she was taken to the hospital."

"Nothing yet. Josh will let folks know if there's a change."

"I suppose he will."

I nodded, and in that moment, I wondered if he had taken a shine to Josh Donnelly's mother. But in a town of over four hundred people, nearly half of them adult women, it could have been anyone.

Goodman paused at the door and looked back at me, his eyes wet. "God has blessed me with good health and eighty-five years, but there's a downside to that blessing. If you live this long, you will say good-bye to many of your friends."

"Good to see you, Bill," I said, extending my hand. He shook it and stepped into the hallway, his cane tapping a slow, steady rhythm.

After Bill left, I sat with my hands on the desk, the envelope parked between them like it had every intention of starting trouble. I'd spent enough years in this business to know that men don't start weighing God's law against man's unless they're somewhere they never expected to be. Whatever was in that envelope, it was the cost of a choice, maybe a payment due when a man reached eighty-five years.

As I sat there listening to the radiator tick, I had the uneasy feeling that sooner or later, I might have to earn my badge all over again.

By late Monday morning the December sun had wrapped Peculiar Park in a soft, balmy haze—Florida's version of winter. With the end of the cold snap, the air filled with the scents of pine sap and warm asphalt. Heather perched on top of a picnic table, the green paint flaking beneath her fingers, her legs swinging over the edge.

Brett sat beneath the canopy of a live oak, strumming his guitar as if the music came from someplace deeper than his bones. He always looked right with his guitar—like he was born holding it, so the world made more sense when his fingers were moving across the strings. In another life, he might have been on a stage instead of busking in a sleepy Florida town without a Walmart.

She tore open a pack of crackers she'd found in the glove box—dry, past their date, and salty enough to make her need water after two bites. She ate them anyway. They soothed the queasy feeling in her stomach but did nothing to settle her nerves.

Movement across the street caught her attention.

The old sedan with faded blue paint slanted onto the gravel parking pad in front of the old Victorian house. The engine died, and the lanky young man got out of the car. His shirt was tucked in today, but nothing else about him seemed polished. He walked toward the house like someone lost in thought, his head down, his shoulders rounded.

Heather leaned forward to see him better.

A gentle quality animated his movements, as if he'd practiced moving quietly, determined not to attract attention. Like a person who carried sadness the way other people carried car keys.

He walked down a brick path and climbed onto the slanting porch, keys dangling from his fingers. Then he disappeared into the house.

"Nice face," Heather murmured. "What I could see of it."

She wondered where he had been, coming home on a Monday morning when most people had already gone to work or school. Maybe he worked nights. Maybe he'd been visiting a girlfriend. Maybe he'd been out driving around, though she couldn't imagine anything better than being at home.

Safe. Secure. With food in the cupboard.

She pulled her gaze back to Brett, though her thoughts lingered on the dark-haired stranger.

A moment later, the sound of children drifted across the park. The elementary school must have let the kids out for recess. A swarm of them burst from a gate like a flock of bright birds—laughing, shouting, chasing each other across the sidewalk. Their voices rang through the air, echoing between the oaks.

A couple of them stopped at the sight of Brett with his guitar. His playing shifted—subtly but noticeably—and he played a folksy tune that hinted at freedom and long roads and dreams too big to name. The children ventured closer.

"What's that hat for?" one of them asked, his voice carrying on the wind. When no one answered, the kid put Brett's hat on his head and danced until Brett stopped playing and gestured—firmly—for the kid to put the hat back. He did, but not before taking a bow in front of his classmates.

Heather sighed. School kids didn't carry money—or if they did, they needed it for the school lunch. They had no idea that she and Brett were hungry.

Every coin mattered now. And every moment.

One girl waved at Heather as she ran past. Heather smiled and waved back, then pressed her palm to her belly. Was that a flutter? Probably a hunger pang, but who knew?

Brett stopped playing, realizing that no one could hear him above the squeals and shouts of the kids. He sat for twenty minutes, his arms folded on top of his guitar, until a teacher blew a whistle and herded all the kids back to school.

When the last of the children scampered toward the schoolyard, Heather exhaled and tipped her face to the sky. The breeze brushed her cheek, warm and soft.

Her eyes slid back to the house where the dark-haired man had disappeared.

She wished—for one heartbeat—that her own life was as regular as the stranger's. She wanted to walk as if she knew where she was going. As if she had someplace to belong.

But she did, didn't she? She had Brett, and they'd been together nearly three years.

She straightened her spine. She'd tell him soon.

Later today.

Tonight, maybe.

She'd find the right moment.

She had to.

AFTER SLEEPING FOUR HOURS, Josh showered and dressed in fresh clothes, made himself a sandwich, and headed back out to the car. The sleep had helped tremendously and, coupled with his mother's improvement, put a smile on his face as he headed toward the hospital.

By the time he arrived, the halls of Jackson Hospital were bustling. Phones rang. Nurses hurried down hallways in soft-soled shoes. Carts rattled as volunteers distributed flowers and cards. And inside Margaret Donnelly's room, the blinds had been opened and the sun allowed to enter.

Josh stepped in, afraid Mama might be sleeping, but she was sitting up, a tray in front of her. One corner of her mouth still drooped, but a nurse wiped her chin as Mama tried to sip from a straw.

Josh's heart squeezed. "Mama! You're up!"

She raised her left hand and he wrapped his fingers around it. Her skin felt warm and alive.

Her lips worked, struggling. "You—you doin' okay?"

"I'm doin' fine, Mama. But don't worry about me. Just focus on getting better."

The nurse offered the cup of water again, but Margaret Donnelly pushed it away. "I need to t-talk to you."

Josh smiled. "I'm right here. I'm not goin' anywhere."

She blinked hard, struggling to form each word. "Been thinkin' and d-on't w-want you . . . be 'lone." Her hand curled around his. "Y-you . . . need . . . wife. F-fam'ly." A tear spilled from her eye and slid over her cheek. "F-fill . . . house . . . with . . . love."

Josh couldn't speak, unable to push words past the lump in his throat. She had teased him about finding a wife, but never with this kind of urgency.

"I hear you, Mama," he whispered.

Her eye closed, as if talking had exhausted her. After a moment, she forced the cooperative eye open again.

"Go . . . home," she said. "Rest." Her chin trembled. "See . . . you . . . mornin'. Love you."

"I want to stay a while."

"N-no, J-Josh. G-go home."

Josh cupped her hand between both of his. She was awake and fighting. God had answered his prayer.

"All right," he said. "I'll go. But only 'cause you asked me to." His smile wavered. "I'll be back first thing tomorrow. As soon as visiting hours start."

He leaned over and kissed her left cheek, the one she could feel. Her skin was warm beneath his lips.

As he straightened, he saw the doctor in the doorway. The man stepped inside.

"She's up," Josh said, unable to stop a smile.

"I see that," the doctor said. "An encouraging sign." He studied the monitors at Margaret's bedside and jotted notes on her chart. "Your mother has a good chance of recovering significant function."

"That's great."

The doctor nodded. "We'll know more over the next few days, but yes—she has youth and determination on her side."

Josh stepped back to his mother, squeezed her hand again, and released a trembling breath. "I won't forget what you said," he whispered. "I promise."

Then, with one last look, Josh released his mama's hand and stepped into the hallway with a smile.

Josh only meant to close his eyes for a minute. The house was dense with quiet, and he hadn't realized how drained he was until he sank onto the sofa. Sunlight slanted through the thin curtains as dust motes drifted like slow-moving dancers.

The motion must have put him to sleep, then the phone rang, sharp and unexpected, in the dark.

Josh jolted upright, his heart thudding, and hurried to the phone mounted on the kitchen wall. "Hello?"

A man's voice—steady, professional, and calm—filled his ear.

"Mr. Donnelly? This is Dr. Henley at Jackson Hospital. I'm very sorry to have to tell you that your mother passed away this afternoon."

The words hit like a punch to the gut. Josh gripped the counter to stay upright.

"What?"

The doctor kept talking, his voice soft but clinical, using words Josh could barely process—*embolism . . . unexpected . . . sudden cardiac stress . . . nothing more we could do.* The phrases slid past him like water over stones.

He heard himself speaking, but the words sounded as if they came from a stranger inhabiting his body.

"Yes, sir."

"Yes, I understand."

"No . . . no, thank you. I don't—no, I don't need to come back to the hospital."

He couldn't go back. The sterile halls, the machines . . . The smell of disinfectant still clung to his clothes.

The doctor kept talking, his words slow and precise. ". . . then we can have her transported to the funeral home in Peculiar. You can meet them tomorrow morning to make the arrangements."

Josh cleared his throat. "Yes. I'll do that."

"We're very sorry for your loss."

The line clicked, and silence swam up to fill the kitchen.

Josh lowered the phone as if it weighed a hundred pounds. He stood motionless, staring at his reflection in the window—his hair mussed from sleep, his eyes wide and dazed, his face slack with disbelief.

She's gone.

If he had known this afternoon would be the last time he talked to her, he would have said so much more. He would have held her hand longer, told her she was the best mama in the world. That he loved her with his whole heart. That he wasn't ready to lose her.

But he had believed she would pull through.

He had prayed. Begged. And God had helped her, just not the way he wanted . . .

God had healed her, but not for this earth.

"Mama." Josh's voice cracked. He gripped the counter as hot tears slid over his cheeks, addressing the woman whose soul seemed as present as the wallpaper on the walls. "Mama, I know you're okay now. I know you're in heaven."

His voice trembled, and the kitchen blurred.

"But I'm sure gonna miss you."

He pressed the heels of his hands to his eyes. Loneliness pressured his ribs and made breathing feel like work.

And then, in the stillness, he heard a voice. Not aloud, but in that deep place where faith spoke louder than sound.

Your mother gave you everything she could . . . I will supply the rest.

Josh remembered his mother as she had been before the stroke—bright-eyed, an apron tied around her waist, teasing him about his messy hair and the way he tossed his dirty socks toward the hamper, but never in it.

His breath caught as a memory rose in his thoughts—comforting and familiar, like a hand smoothing his hair.

In his mind's eye, his mother's face softened in a smile as warm and steady as a sunrise. He saw her move to her desk, the place where she paid the bills and kept important papers. "Look here, Josh. If something happens to me, everything you need is in this drawer."

The memory faded, but the impression lingered, a nudge as real as a hand on his shoulder.

Josh wiped his cheeks, drew a shaky breath, and walked to the desk.

Everything he needed. What did that mean? He didn't know, but she did.

In the hush of the empty house, he sat and opened the drawer, each movement guided by a love that would never leave him.

CHAPTER
SEVEN

Heather drifted down Main Street, kicking at a stray pebble as it skittered ahead of her. Brett was at the park, strumming songs that might earn enough for ramen and a bag of apples. Since she couldn't sing or whistle, she wandered while he played. Walking kept her busy—kept her from staring too long at the hollow places in her life.

A week in Peculiar had taught her the rhythms of the town, but today the air felt heavy on her shoulders.

She wrapped her arms around her middle, her fingers settling below her ribs. She wasn't showing yet, but she could feel the tiny, growing truth inside her. She thought about telling Brett every day. Thought about choosing the right moment, a soft one.

But Brett liked soft moments only when they were about him.

The last time she'd tried—when she joked about sitting outside the church with a cardboard sign reading **Homeless and Pregnant**—he looked at her like she'd pulled a gun.

That was when she knew he wouldn't want the baby. And if she pressed, he might not want her.

She was passing the Peculiar Community Church when she noticed a cluster of people at the small cemetery. Curious—and grateful for a distraction—Heather slowed.

The mourners stood in a loose half-circle around a narrow mound of fresh earth. Their heads bowed as a minister read from the Bible. And there, near the front, stood the tall, lanky young man who lived in the Victorian house—the one who walked like his burden weighed far too much.

Today he wasn't counting sidewalk cracks or staring at the ground. Today his face was open, wrecked with grief.

He clasped his hands in front of him. His hair, dark and rumpled, ruffled in the breeze. The minister's voice floated over the group—low and steady as he offered a prayer.

When the amen faded, people stepped forward to touch the young man's arm, hug him, or murmur words Heather couldn't hear. The old man with the cane pulled the younger man into a fierce embrace, then released him and spoke for a moment, keeping his hand on the young man's shoulder. The young man nodded, red-eyed and silent, as if he wasn't sure how to hold his grief without letting it shatter him.

Heather knew that look. She'd worn it the time she ran away . . . and her mother didn't want to take her back.

The young man finally stepped forward, gave the grave one last look, and turned toward the road. He reached the sidewalk a few feet away from Heather.

She watched him turn the corner and walk toward the Victorian house. She was about to follow when someone tapped her arm. "Did you know Margaret?"

An older woman stood beside her, dressed in a navy-blue suit, her eyes somber.

"Who?"

"Maybe you knew her as Mrs. Donnelly. Were you one of her students? Maybe you knew Josh."

Heather drew a quick breath, putting the pieces together. "I didn't know Mrs. Donnelly. But I feel sad for Josh."

The old woman's gaze shifted to the young man walking parallel to the park. "You needn't worry about him. I know he's quiet, but he's solid. His mother raised him right."

Heather nodded. "I can see that. He seems . . . extraordinary."

The older woman chuckled. "That's a good word for him." She tilted her head and gestured toward the sidewalk. "Are you going my way?"

Heather was willing to go anywhere if this woman would keep talking. "Yes."

"Are you staying in town? I don't think I've seen you around here."

Heather smiled. "I'm visiting. But when I saw the funeral—and Josh—I thought I should come over."

The old woman slipped her arm through Heather's as they began to walk. "I'm Grace, Josh's neighbor, and I'll bet you haven't heard about what he did at that softball game."

Heather shook her head. "I haven't."

Grace released a throaty laugh. "People tell the story a hundred ways, but it all happened after Josh's daddy left. Josh and my Petey were playing for the Little League. Josh hit a fly ball that headed straight for Isaac Hern. Isaac took the ball on his cap and dropped like a stone. Instead of running to third, Josh ran to center field."

"Was the boy hurt?"

Grace arched her brows. "What do you think? One of the refs said Isaac's lips were blue by the time he got there, but Josh got there first, and was praying like he meant it. And then

—folks swear this part is true—Josh said amen and the boy came to."

Heather blinked. "So he was okay?"

Grace laughed. "He looked up at all those men and said, 'Did I catch the ball?' Everybody laughed and helped Isaac up, and some folks started calling Josh Donnelly a miracle worker."

"So . . . was he?"

Grace's smile faded. "Seeing as how one of the refs worked at the funeral home, I believed him when he said he first thought he was looking at a dead kid. He figured Josh Donnelly had prayed Isaac Hern back to life."

Heather forced a smile, though she was certain the old woman was exaggerating. In a small town, a near-fatal bump on the head could be big news.

"I'm glad the boy was okay," she said. "And Josh seems like a nice guy."

"He is," Grace said, looking at the spot where Josh had turned onto his walkway. "It's a shame, though, that the Lord didn't answer like he wanted with his mama."

Heather paused in respect, then frowned. "You mentioned something about Josh's daddy leaving. Where'd he go?"

The woman's brows arched. "Nobody knows. But I tell you this—nobody has missed him. Most people thought George Donnelly was a good man, but they didn't live next door. I did, and I heard him scream at Josh and Margaret more times than I can count." She pressed a finger across her lips. "He was a weekend drunk and that little boy suffered for it. I was relieved when I heard he'd left town."

Heather absorbed the horrible news in silence as Grace sighed. "This is my house," she said, pointing to a white two-story next to Josh's Victorian. She released Heather's arm. "It's been nice to chat with you, honey. Enjoy your visit to Peculiar."

Grace walked up the sidewalk, her sensible heels moving

quickly over the concrete. Heather waited until she made it safely into her house, then she looked across the street, where the travel van sat beneath the shade of a live oak.

She did not see Brett, so he must be in the camper. If he hadn't made any money, he'd be stretched out on the bunk, depressed and irritable.

Brett wasn't gone—not yet. But their relationship was dying in slow motion, and she felt every second of it.

She pressed a hand to her stomach, blinking hard.

Some losses come without warning. Some arrive before you're ready to face them. And some happen without anyone else knowing.

THE SUN HUNG low and steady over Jackson County on Tuesday afternoon, brushing the tops of the longleaf pines with the color of golden honey. Josh drove with his windows cracked, letting the December breeze drift across his cheek. It carried the scents of orange blossoms, sunbaked asphalt, and cut grass—an odd mix of fall fragrances.

The funeral was behind him—the casseroles, the handshakes, the murmured condolences from people who had loved his mama. He didn't weep until he got home, then he cried in the privacy of his room, hands over his face, shoulders hunched.

Today the ache inside him felt different. Not smaller, but softer around the edges. Because the last words his mother had spoken to him had been full of love and gentle urgency: *You need a wife. Family. Fill the house with love.*

She had believed he could. She wanted to believe he would. And for her sake, he wanted to try . . . though he had no idea where to start.

Now, with the sun warming his forearm, Josh wanted to obey her.

Last night, sitting in front of the TV, he'd been watching an old movie. Nothing was going right for George Bailey until he met an angel. Josh was wondering how a bewildered angel could possibly help, then the movie cut to a commercial.

The ad featured big-eyed, sad-looking dogs who shivered in the cold while a woman urged listeners to donate to an animal charity. The sight of those dogs, compounded with his mother's last wish, brought Josh to a decision.

He wasn't going to spend even one more night alone in an empty house. He was going to get a dog.

He reached Highway 90, flipped on his blinker, and turned toward the county line. A sign appeared a minute later: **Jackson County Animal Services, Where Your New Best Friend is Waiting.** A cartoon dog grinned from the billboard.

Josh snorted a laugh. "Mama always did say a man ought to have a dog."

A dog wouldn't fix everything. It wouldn't bring his mama back or fill the emptiness in his heart. But it would be nice to sit in the house and hear footsteps other than his own. The sound of breathing. Someone friendly to greet him when he walked through the door.

A small start, maybe. But a beginning.

The county shelter was housed in a cinder block building beyond a high school football field. A cheerful red banner stretched across the front: ADOPT TODAY! A couple of bicycles leaned against the fence while a volunteer swept the walkway.

Josh pulled in, gravel crunching under his tires. He rested both hands on the steering wheel and collected his thoughts. This wasn't like him—he didn't usually make spontaneous decisions, not at all—but this was the first small step out of the deep shadow he'd been living in.

He closed his eyes. "Lord . . . lead me to the right one."

He opened the car door, stepped into the breezy afternoon, and squared his shoulders.

He was going to get a dog. For companionship. For courage.

And because Mama had told him to fill the house with love.

CHAPTER
EIGHT

Though Josh had never been comfortable talking with people he didn't know, he figured it was easier to introduce himself to a dog than to a stranger.

A sign on the concrete-block building said the animal shelter would reopen at three, and he could see people moving around the kennels when he arrived at 2:55. He could hear dogs too—yelps, gruff barks, squeals, and whines, all tangled in a single, pleading chorus. The woman who'd been sweeping the sidewalk had disappeared.

He walked to the gate, found it padlocked, and scanned the parking lot. Four vehicles sat in the sun. Either he wasn't the only one hoping to adopt, or those belonged to people tending to the animals.

He leaned against an oak tree and told himself to be patient. He'd waited years to have a dog; he could wait five more minutes.

At exactly 3:00, a middle-aged woman in a sweatshirt came to the gate and fumbled with a ring of keys on her belt.

"Sorry," she said, not glancing up. "I was trying to get them all fed before three, but time slipped away."

Josh cleared his throat. "If, um, you want to give dogs a home, why do you keep the gate locked?"

The woman squinted through her glasses. "Because people steal dogs." She turned the key and looked at him with narrowed eyes. "Why are *you* here?"

"I want a dog," Josh said. "For company."

"Any specific breed? Age?"

He shrugged. "I figured I'd know the right one when I saw it."

She opened the gate and stepped back. "Come on in."

The woman led him down a covered walkway that smelled of bleach and wet fur, then opened a door to a long room lined with kennels. Chain-link gates rattled as dogs barked and jumped, each one hoping, pleading, to be chosen.

"You'll find basic info on the clipboard hanging from each gate," the woman said as she led the way. "If you see one that interests you, let me know and I'll bring it out for a meet-and-greet. You take your time while I start hosing out these kennels."

Josh moved down the center aisle, his eyes adjusting to the dim light. How would he know when he found the right one? He'd never had a dog before. His childhood memories were as patchy as a sponge, but he thought they might have had a cat once. It bit him, he remembered that much. Afterward it vanished, or was taken away. He frowned. Sometimes he felt like he was trying to remember someone else's life.

He passed a young puppy who yelped and wagged so hard it nearly rolled itself over. The next kennel held a hound, restless, bred to chase. The next, a pug, snored peacefully despite the clamor.

At first glance, Josh thought the final kennel held a small

bear. Then the creature raised its head, and he saw it was a massive beast with a black face and a fawn body, at least two hundred pounds of quiet solemnity.

He waved for the woman's attention. "This one—are you sure it's a dog?"

She lowered her hose and grinned. "That's Hoss. English Mastiff. Six years old, so he's almost a senior."

"Six isn't so old. Isn't that, what—forty-two in people years?"

"Big dogs age faster. Hoss is about forty-seven in human years—not ancient, but not young either."

Josh tilted his head. The dog tilted his in return, and Josh laughed. "You trying to tell me something?"

The woman dropped the hose and wiped her hands on her jeans. "Wanna take Hoss out for a walk?"

"Will he let me? Or drag me?"

She chuckled. "Don't let his size fool you. Mastiffs are gentle giants. Just don't get him riled up."

"How would I—"

Before he could finish, she had opened the gate, slipped a leash around Hoss's neck, and slapped the other end into Josh's palm.

"Let's go to the field," she said. "There's a fenced area where you can walk him or sit. Hoss likes to sit. He also likes to sleep. And eat."

Josh led Hoss out into the field, sunlight flashing off the dog's smooth coat. He expected the dog to drag him across the grass, but Hoss walked beside him as if they'd been walking partners for years. Josh made a small circle, then, on impulse, broke into a jog.

He had barely managed three strides before resistance yanked him backward. He turned to find Hoss sitting at the end of the leash, his expression serene.

"One thing about the big guys," the woman called, coming over, "you can't make them do what they don't want to do. That's why training matters."

"But he's six," Josh said. "And you can't teach an old dog new—"

"Hogwash." She waved the idea away. "You can teach any dog, if you're patient. Helps if you pick a breed that fits your lifestyle, and Mastiffs aren't runners. Are you?"

"No." Josh rolled his sore shoulder and smiled. "Got it. So what was this guy bred to do?"

"Guard a castle," she said, patting Hoss's flank. "And be a companion. They've got the protective nature of a lion and the heart of a nanny." She looked up at him. "You got kids?"

He shook his head.

"Well, if you ever do, Hoss would be perfect for them."

The dog lifted a paw and set it on Josh's sneaker. The sheer size of the dog's foot startled him.

"Where'd he come from?" Josh asked. "Did a local family give him up?"

"Came from Georgia. Overpopulated county. We take what we can."

Josh nodded, relieved. If Hoss ever got lost, he wouldn't head for a local house, thinking it was his home.

He looked at the big dog again. "You ready to walk?"

Hoss stood, obedient and slow, and followed Josh to the kennel door.

"I'll take him," Josh said.

The woman laughed. "What convinced you? The castle?"

Josh frowned, uncertain how to explain it. From the moment Hoss tilted his head, an instinctive recognition had settled inside Josh. Here was a creature who didn't need to fill silence with noise. Who wouldn't demand explanations or ask questions. Hoss would be there—solid, patient, and understanding.

Josh looked at the woman and shrugged. "Because I promised Mama I'd fill the house."

A FEW MINUTES later they reached Peculiar, rolling past the Peculiar Historical Society Museum and the post office.

Josh hesitated as they passed the Piggly Wiggly. He knew dogs weren't supposed to go inside grocery stores, but he hoped—believed—they might make an exception for Hoss. The dog's enormous dark head tilted toward the automatic doors, his nostrils flaring, tongue visible between his jowls, as if he already sensed the possibility of new smells and experiences.

And food.

Josh parked, then clipped the leash to Hoss's collar and looped the extra length over his wrist. "All right," he told the dog. "Quick in and out."

They stepped onto the welcome mat and the doors swung open with a swish. Hoss let out a low, questioning woof.

"It's okay," Josh said. "Come on. Let's see what they've got for you."

Inside, the aromas of pumpkin pies, fresh bread, and the tang of cleaning spray mingled in the air. Kelly Haviland, the main cashier, froze mid-scan. Her wide eyes tracked them as if a parade had entered the store. Behind her, Leo Wilkerson, the manager, hurried forward, arms waving and brow furrowed.

"Josh Donnelly! Josh, we can't—"

"We'll only be a minute," Josh said. "Let him pick out his food, then we'll be gone. Quick as you like."

Leo's frown deepened. "But it's against—"

"Let him be," Kelly said, waving him off. "Not every day we get this much entertainment."

Josh gave a small nod of thanks and led Hoss toward the dog food aisle. The polished linoleum reflected the afternoon light streaming through the huge windows, and Hoss's massive paws clicked over it. Josh kept his hand on the leash, but he gave Hoss slack, letting him choose.

Hoss worked his way down the shelves with serious attention—nose to bags, a careful nudge to the lower row, then a stretch to sniff the top. Josh followed, watching the small, thoughtful flick of Hoss's ears at every sound: carts rolling, a child giggling, the soft ping of a cash register.

Finally, Hoss stopped in front of a red bag. He looked up at Josh, patient and intent.

"Goliath's Choice? Is that the one you like?"

Hoss's tongue licked the air.

Josh chuckled and hoisted the largest bag onto his shoulder. He shortened his grip on the leash and turned them toward the registers.

They were halfway there when Leo appeared again, closer this time, arms flailing as he came around the end cap.

"Josh! I said you can't—"

His voice shot up, sharp enough to cut through the store.

Hoss startled hard. Panic rippled through him like a jolt. He backed up, paws skidding on the tile, head twisting as the leash tightened. Josh's balance wavered under the weight of the dog food.

"Easy," Josh said, trying to keep his voice steady. "It's all right. It's all right."

But Hoss kept backing, bigger and faster than Josh could manage. The leash jerked, the bag slid on Josh's shoulder, and for one quick, sick second Josh could see it—fifty pounds of kibble busting open across the floor, Hoss tangling them both in a mess they couldn't fix.

He let the leash slip through his fingers, giving Hoss room instead of resistance.

That was the wrong kind of room.

Hoss spun. Two hundred pounds of English mastiff clipped the end of a stacked display of Branch's Boston Baked Beans, and the pyramid collapsed with a clatter that echoed—pop pop pop —like gunfire in the quiet store.

Josh's stomach lurched.

Hoss bolted straight for him.

Josh dropped the dog food and went down on one knee, arms wide. "Hey," he called. "Hey, boy. Come here."

Hoss collided with Josh's chest, all shaking muscle and warm breath.

"I'm sorry," Josh whispered into the thick fur at Hoss's neck. "I didn't mean for that to happen."

Leo was still talking—still waving—still pointing at the spilled cans. Josh barely heard him. He kept his hand pressed to the dog's side, feeling the wild thrum of Hoss's heart, waiting for it to slow.

When it did, Josh gathered the leash, shortened it, and stood. He lifted the bag of Goliath's Choice back onto his shoulder and walked them to the register.

Kelly's smile softened as she tipped her head. "First dog?"

Josh nodded, then made himself answer. "Yes."

"You picked the good stuff. My Chiweenie can't get enough of this brand," she said, running the scanner over the bag.

Though he would have preferred to pay and disappear, Josh's curiosity nudged him into the open. "Chiweenie?"

"Chihuahua–Dachshund mix," she said, laughing.

As Josh handed over the money, Pastor Gary's words came

back to him: *My prayer is not that You take them out of the world, but that You protect them...*

He was certainly out in the world now.

He glanced down at Hoss, who watched him with an anxious, pleading look that said plain as day: *We're going home, right?*

"Yes," Josh told him. "We're going home."

Then he looked up at Kelly. "Thank you."

And as he guided Hoss back toward the doors, he found himself smiling.

CHAPTER NINE

Heather sat cross-legged on the worn passenger seat, picking at the saltines Brett had found in the glove box that morning. Brett twisted the cap off a gallon jug of water they'd filled in a Piggly Wiggly restroom. He took a long pull, then passed it to her.

"Gourmet lunch," he said, attempting a grin that didn't quite reach his eyes.

Heather drank, the lukewarm water doing nothing to wash away the paste on her tongue. Through the camper van's windshield, streaked with bug guts and road grime, she watched the grocery parking lot. Josh Donnelly's blue sedan was there, and a moment later she stopped eating mid-chew.

"Holy cannoli," she whispered. "Look at that dog."

The animal was massive—easily the size of a small pony, all muscle and fur. It moved with an easy confidence beside Josh Donnelly, who seemed utterly unbothered by the spectacle he was creating in the parking lot.

Brett leaned forward, squinting through the dirty glass.

"Man! That thing probably eats better than we do." He laughed, but she heard an edge in his laughter.

"Two forty-five. That's what I made today. Two dollars and forty-five cents from little brats throwing pennies." His jaw flexed. "Can't fill the tank. Can't buy dinner. Can't—"

". . . buy love," Heather finished, quoting the words of the old Beatles' song. The words hung in the stale air of the camper. Brett didn't respond, but stiffened beside her.

As she watched Josh Donnelly and his enormous dog climb into the blue sedan, envy twisted in her chest. The dog would soon be served clean water in a ceramic dish. A bed, even.

While she sat in a camper van eating crackers that had been in the van for only God knew how long.

She could go home. The thought arrived unbidden and unwelcome. Her father might actually open the door, would probably let her stay a night or two. There'd be food—*real* food, not soggy crackers. A bed with clean sheets. No more sleeping on a thin mattress that reeked of damp and desperation.

But then her father's face would shift to that disappointed, knowing look that said *I told you so* without words. And her mother—

No. Some things couldn't be mended. Some doors, once slammed, stayed closed.

Especially if the people behind them learned the secret she carried.

Brett crumpled the cracker package and tossed it toward the back of the van, where it landed among their scattered belongings. "Tomorrow will be better," he said, but he didn't sound convinced.

Heather watched as the blue sedan pulled away from the Piggly Wiggly. Tomorrow *had* to be better . . . because now three lives were at stake.

CHAPTER
TEN

As police chief, I heard all about the Piggly Wiggly ruckus. After we listened to the story—twice, because Leo kept circling back to emphasize particularly egregious details—my deputy and I exchanged pointed looks.

"Leo," I said, hooking my thumbs in my belt, "what exactly do you want? Do you expect me to drive over to the Donnelly place and issue Josh a citation?" I let that hang in the air for a beat, watching Leo's mustache twitch. "I'd do it, but Josh Donnelly's mother just passed. You wouldn't want to give him grief at a time like this, would you?"

"Well...no." Leo crossed one arm over his chest and twiddled the end of his mustache with his free hand—a nervous habit I'd noticed over the years. "It's —I have to think about our liability, you know, and what might have happened. What if someone with a dog phobia had been coming around the corner and seen that beast? They might have had a heart attack! And there's the issue of germs and proper sanitation—"

"Josh said it would only happen once." Kelly Haviland, the

main cashier, sidled up from register two. "I think he would have been in and out in a flash if the boss hadn't started waving his arms. The poor dog can't help being huge."

Tony Kirkpatrick, my deputy, couldn't resist a quip. "How big *was* this dog? Y'all are making it sound like he was the size of a Buick."

"He was *big*," Leo said, dipping his chin in a nod that sent his glasses sliding down his nose. "What else could have done this sort of damage?" He gestured at the fallen cans like he was presenting evidence at trial.

"Really." I caught the glimmer of amusement in Kelly's eyes and winked at her. "I can't wait to see this dog for myself."

I looked back at the manager, whose face had gone from indignant red to a more resigned pink. "Whaddya say, Leo? Shall we let this one slide?"

Leo drew a breath, then nodded. "All right. But if he brings that beast again, you'll need to enforce the law."

"Noted." I picked up an errant can of Boston Baked Beans from where it had rolled against the shelf, set it atop Leo's precisely stacked pyramid, and strolled toward the exit. Tony followed, and I could hear him snickering.

Outside, the weather had reached a pleasant seventy-two degrees, with enough breeze to rustle the palm trees around the parking lot. Not bad for December.

I couldn't help but wonder how Josh and his newfound companion were getting along. A dog that size didn't wander into someone's life without a story attached, and I was sure I'd hear it sooner or later.

In towns like Peculiar, stories have a way of spreading whether you want them to or not.

Josh sat at the kitchen table and checked his watch. Ordinarily he would have finished his bologna sandwich by this time, but Hoss was sprawled in front of the refrigerator door and Josh wasn't sure how to move him. The dog's massive rib cage rose and fell in a slow, contented rhythm, and something about the peaceful sight made Josh reluctant to disturb him. What was it the woman said? You can't make a two-hundred-pound dog do anything he doesn't want to do...

The words lingered in his mind, and Josh realized they applied to more than dogs. In the past, his mother had tried to make him do things—leave the house, talk to people, find his place in the world. She'd failed. Pastor Gary had tried gentle suggestions and invitations to singles gatherings at the church. He'd mostly failed too.

But when a woman spends some of her last minutes telling you to fill her house with a family, you have to pay attention. And a dog was family, wasn't it? Most people seemed to think so.

So today he had taken the first step. He'd gotten a dog, who was quite capable of filling at least the kitchen.

If only he would slide over...

"You hungry, Hoss?" Josh stood and opened the cupboard, searching for a bowl. The soup bowls didn't look like they'd hold enough for a mastiff appetizer, let alone a full meal.

Josh opened the bottom cabinet where his mother kept mixing bowls and baking pans. The smell hit him as he opened the door—vanilla extract and cinnamon, a fragrant remnant from years of Mama's baking. He spotted a gigantic bowl beyond the cupcake tin and recognized it as the one his mama used whenever she baked a double batch of brownies. The last time she'd used it was Christmas, two years ago.

Josh pulled out the bowl and rinsed away a layer of dust. He filled it with Goliath's Choice, the kibble clattering against the ceramic in a sound that was almost cheerful. Because the dry brown balls looked unappetizing, Josh stepped over Hoss, pried the refrigerator door open, and managed to slip his hand inside and grab the lunch meat. He peeled off two slices—one for his sandwich and one for Hoss.

He dropped the dog's slice on top of the kibble, then set the bowl on the floor, away from the oven and fridge. "Okay, boy. Dinnertime."

Hoss didn't need to be cajoled. He rose with surprising enthusiasm and hurried to the bowl, then crunched his kibble while Josh dropped his bologna onto a piece of bread and slathered it with mustard. The kitchen didn't feel as empty with the sound of Hoss's munching in the background.

Josh choked down a big bite of sandwich, the bread dry in his mouth. Okay, then. He'd done what his mama and Pastor Gary wanted him to do. He had walked out of the hospital and found a new friend—maybe a couple of them. The woman at the SPCA had smiled at him, *really* smiled, not the absent nod people give when they pass a stranger on the sidewalk. He didn't catch her name and that bothered him—he should have asked.

Then he'd gone out of his way to ask about Kelly's Chiweenie, and her face lit up like he'd given her a present. He also tried to help the red-faced manager who kept yelling about Hoss, though that encounter hadn't gone quite as well.

He finished his sandwich, brushed the crumbs into his palm, and turned to Hoss, who had scattered bits of Goliath's Choice all over the kitchen floor. But apparently he had eaten enough, because he lowered himself to the floor with a satisfied groan, then released a loud, dish-rattling belch.

Josh smiled. "Let me get you some water," he said, standing. "Then we'll go outside so you can explore your new home."

Your new home. The words surprised him as they left his mouth, but they sounded right. This wasn't only his mama's house anymore, it was becoming something else. Something different.

Someone—probably Jackie Leakey, who often kept an eye out for nice pieces of timber—had deposited a two-foot log in front of Josh's gate. He and Hoss strolled down the driveway, their shadows stretching across the gravel. Josh examined the log, running his palm over the bark, and Hoss waited behind the fence, his tail swishing while Josh opened the gate and rolled the log onto his property.

"This is good wood," Josh said, words coming easier now that he had someone to talk to. He set the stump on the walkway that led to the house and probed the surface with his fingers, feeling for rotten areas, reading the wood the way some people read books. "Jackie is always saying I need to make bigger pieces, and I need big wood to do that."

Hoss sniffed the log with interest, his wet nose leaving a dark spot on the back, then his head swiveled as he spotted a squirrel in a pine tree. As Josh rolled the log toward the house—his back straining, sweat prickling at his hairline—Hoss did what he'd been bred to do. He ran circles around the tree, barking at the squirrel in deep, resonant booms that echoed off the house. Because barking failed to make the squirrel disappear, Hoss stood against the tree trunk and warned in a thunderous voice that no further squirrel trespassing would be allowed.

When Josh, breathless from exertion and laughing at Hoss's indignant performance, dropped onto the front porch swing, Hoss gave up his chase and came to sit on the porch.

The dog's furry bulk pressed against Josh's leg, solid and reassuring. He found himself resting his hand on Hoss's broad back, feeling the dog's rib cage expand as he panted. They sat together in comfortable silence, watching the sky turn from gold to amber to rose. Josh couldn't remember the last time he'd watched the sunset. He'd spent far too many evenings watching mindless television, letting darkness fall around him unnoticed.

Two hours later, Josh had scraped the bark from the log and sanded the cut edges until they were reasonably smooth. Dust clung to his forearms and the scent of raw oak filled his nose—clean and sharp. The log was twenty-three inches long, solid and heavy. A fissure ran through one side, and Josh ran his fingers over it the way he'd traced his mother's hand in the hospital, following the landscape of veins and tendons. He could chip out the weakened wood and use the space as an accent—maybe fill it with glass beads and seal them with epoxy. He had seen a footstool made from a similar log at a craft fair Mama dragged him to. The cracks and gouges had been accented by colored crystals, turning flaws into something beautiful.

The memory hurt, but not as much as he feared it would.

He heaved the log onto the porch and whistled for Hoss, who was sleeping beneath the swing, his massive body twitching with dreams. His former owner must have trained him well, because Hoss rose and followed Josh into the house, his nails clicking against the hardwood floor in a rhythm that sounded like lively castanets.

Josh checked the dog's bowl—plenty of Goliath's Choice remained, so he tossed some pieces of chicken on top and let Hoss dig in. Josh went to the pantry and grabbed a box of macaroni, his usual Tuesday dinner. Then, on an impulse, he took a can of chicken noodle soup instead. He liked soup, and he could pour the leftover liquid over Hoss's kibble. Soup had to be healthier than lunch meat.

Darkness had engulfed the house by the time Josh finished his supper. With Hoss in the kitchen, washing the dishes and wiping the counter felt less like going through empty rituals and more like tending to a home. He turned out the lights, then he and Hoss climbed the stairs, the old wood creaking under their weight. The dog seemed to know where Josh was heading, because he displayed no interest in Josh's boyhood bedroom or his mama's room. He followed Josh into the room Josh had claimed as a teenager and sniffed the narrow bed against the wall. A moment later, Hoss jumped up and stretched out, taking up the entire length of the bed with a contented sigh.

"Oh, no. That's where I sleep." Using his sternest voice—which Josh had to admit wasn't very stern—he pointed to the floor. "See this rug? This is where you sleep. There's plenty of room and it's plenty soft."

Hoss replied with something between a grumble and a question, but pulled himself off the bed—the top half of himself, that is. His front paws hit the floor while his back end remained on the mattress.

"All the way off," Josh commanded, though he could feel his resolve weakening. "I sleep on the bed. You sleep on the floor." He knelt, clasping his hands around the dog's thick shoulders as he tugged Hoss off the mattress. When the dog was on the floor—and on top of his new owner—Josh squirmed, pushed, and pulled to free himself from the mastiff embrace, half-laughing, half-gasping.

While pinned to the floor, however, Josh couldn't help noticing the yellowed paperbacks on the lowest row of his bookshelves, their spines cracked and faded. He couldn't remember the last time he'd taken a book from the bottom row

—those were Mama's books, the ones she'd read as a girl—but this was a day for doing different things.

Once he was free of Hoss, he spotted a yellowed copy of *To Kill a Mockingbird* and plucked it from the shelf. His mother's name was written inside in looping cursive: Margaret Ann Whitley, her maiden name.

Josh peeled off his jeans and tee shirt, the evening air cool against his skin, then pulled back the blanket—his mother's wedding quilt—and slid between the sheets. The cotton was soft and worn, familiar. As the bedside lamp cast yellow light across the pages, he began to read. The words flowed over him —Atticus Finch's quiet wisdom, Scout's innocent observations —and the tangle inside Josh began to unknot.

By the time he had finished the chapter where Atticus shoots the rabid dog, Hoss was back on the bed, stretched out along Josh's side, his massive head on the pillow. Josh's left side was pressed against the wall, his right side warmed by a snoring fur coat that rose and fell with each breath. As the dog's heart beat steady and strong against Josh's ribs, Josh realized he didn't mind.

Sighing, he closed his book, tucked it beneath his pillow, and turned off the light. In the darkness, he rested his hand on Hoss's side, enjoying the simple comfort of not being the only living creature in the house.

"Okay, boy," he said. "You win."

Hoss's tail thumped against the mattress. Josh closed his eyes, warmed and wrapped in a peaceful feeling as he drifted toward sleep.

CHAPTER
ELEVEN

Yessir, Josh and Hoss made a big splash when they teamed up in Peculiar. By the middle of December they were the main topic at every dinner table in town, including the square tables of the assisted living facility. No one had a problem with Josh and his dog, except, of course, the manager at the Piggly Wiggly.

I had just finished my coffee one morning when my deputy waved for my attention. "Chief?"

"Yeah?" I looked up from the stack of paperwork I'd been avoiding—budget reports that made my eyes glaze over.

"Caller on line one for you."

I groaned, my back complaining as I shifted. "Know who it is?"

"Says his name is Cody Fisk."

I leaned back, the chair creaking in protest. I'd met Cody a few years before at a law enforcement conference in Tampa—one of those obligatory things where they served rubber chicken and talked about community policing strategies. Cody was working for the Florida Highway Patrol and lived in Tallahassee with his wife and three kids. A good guy, solid and dependable, but why was he calling? We weren't exactly the sort of men who liked to shoot the breeze on a Wednesday morning.

I picked up and punched the blinking button on the phone. "Cody! How ya doin'?"

"Hey, Chief." We exchanged a couple of good-natured verbal jabs—he ribbed me about my department's size, I reminded him about the time he'd locked his keys in his patrol car—then Cody's tone went serious. "Chief, we've been working the lot at Big Al's truck stop, which is a hop 'n skip from you. The place has picked up a couple of lot lizards, and we're getting complaints."

I grunted, the leather chair cracking under my weight. I gazed out the window at Main Street, where Mrs. Miller was walking her Pomeranian past the hardware store. "Lot lizards" were girls running from something, toward something worse, selling what shouldn't be for sale. The phrase always made my stomach turn. "Big Al is complaining, huh?"

"Yeah, but so are the drivers. I think the girls have come south for the winter, because you can't take ten steps without spotting one between the trucks or hiding in the woods. Big Al's wife—have you met Irene?—is always chasing them out of the restrooms."

I had met Irene, a mountain of a woman with a heart to match. She'd made me a sandwich the size of my head and refused payment. "So what are you doing—undercover work?"

"That's actually not why I'm calling." Cody's voice dropped and I leaned forward, elbows on the desk. "I'm calling because a couple of weeks ago Irene saw a pregnant girl begging for food. Irene tried to get her some help, but she disappeared and

Irene hasn't seen her in a while. She asked us to investigate, and I thought the girl might have wandered into Peculiar. Irene said she was young. But they all look young when they aren't painted up."

A knot formed in my stomach. A pregnant girl. "Was she turning tricks?"

"Irene didn't think so. Irene said her belly was so big she'd have trouble climbing into a rig."

I stopped to think, my fingers drumming on the desk blotter covered with doodles. While I might not have noticed a girl I'd never seen before, I think I would have noticed a pregnant girl walking around by herself. In a town this size, everyone noticed everything. Mrs. Patterson had recently called me because someone's cat was sitting on her mailbox.

"Anything unusual about this girl?"

"Just that she looked like she was about to pop. Otherwise, white, brown hair, medium height, no distinguishing characteristics."

"Except being about to deliver a baby."

"Yeah, that."

"Did you check Jackson Hospital? Someone could have taken her to the emergency room."

"We've checked—Irene snapped a picture of the girl and we sent it to all the hospitals in the county, but we got nothin'. Mind if I send you the photo? If you see her, let me know, okay?"

"Will do." I gave him my email address, the one that didn't get fifty spam messages a day, told him I'd see him around, and hung up.

I set down the phone and blew out a breath. I was getting too old for this job, though I'd never admit it to anyone, especially not Tony.

A moment later the email came through with a soft ding. I clicked on the image, my reading glasses sliding down my nose. The photo was blurred, probably taken with Irene's phone. But it was clear enough to make out a skinny-legged brunette who looked like she'd stuffed a basketball under her blue shirt. Who knew? Maybe she *was* carrying around a basketball, trying to get what she could from people who'd take pity on her. But I doubted it. Something in her posture spoke of genuine desperation.

I shook my head, feeling inexplicably weary. Where had this girl come from, and what was she thinking, hanging out at a truck stop? But I already knew the answer. She wasn't thinking. She was just trying to survive.

"Tony?" I cleared my throat, which had gone thick, then clicked print on the computer. The machine whirred to life, chugging and grinding.

My deputy appeared in my office doorway, coffee mug in hand. "Take a look at this photo and let me know if you see this girl in town, will you? The highway patrol wants to make sure she doesn't have that baby on a sidewalk."

"Will do, Chief." Tony stepped closer, his boots heavy on the tile floor, and I could smell his coffee—fresh, not like the swill I'd been drinking.

"Thanks." I stood, my knees popping like firecrackers, grabbed my hat from the coat rack, and headed toward the exit. The hat was worn, sweat-stained around the band, but I'd had it for fifteen years and couldn't bring myself to replace it. "I'm going to drive around town for a look, just in case."

Tony pulled the photo from the printer tray and studied it, his brow furrowing. "This girl doesn't look more than fifteen or sixteen."

"If she's about to have a baby, I hope we find her soon."

I settled my hat on my head and walked out into the December sunshine. The patrol car was parked out front, warm from sitting in the sun, and I slid behind the wheel. My lower back ached—it always did these days—but I ignored it.

As I pulled onto Main Street, I found myself thinking about Josh Donnelly, his enormous dog, and the way the town had taken to them. Sometimes, I thought, people needed something to care about. To pull them out of themselves.

Maybe that pregnant girl needed the same thing—someone to care.

I drove around the town center, then spotted the yellow camper van and the young couple who'd been hanging out there for a couple of weeks. Several people had asked how long I was going to let them stay in that spot, but the town fathers had neglected to include a park closing time in the city code. As long as the couple wasn't breaking the law or panhandling, I told the complainers, they could stay. Panhandling was begging; busking was performing for gratuities. As long as the guy kept singing, he was legal.

After circling the park—and noting that the young man was playing and singing for a blonde girl and an older woman, I turned my cruiser toward the lake. I hoped I wouldn't find the missing girl there—having a baby in the woods had to be the world's worst idea.

But hope doesn't stop much. Reality always gets a handhold.

JOSH FELT PRETTY pleased with himself the next day. After all, he had taken a major leap forward, and no one could say he was still living alone.

So after he and Hoss enjoyed their breakfast—kibble topped with eggs for Hoss—Josh put on jeans and a fresh shirt. He even splashed on some of the aftershave Mama had given him last Christmas. Then he hitched Hoss to his leash and together they set out for Twin Oaks.

This time Josh took the long route. The crisp air carried the scent of freshly cut grass and orange blossoms. Dew clung to spider webs strung between fence posts, glittering like diamonds in the morning light. Instead of going east, they went south, passing the Peculiar Community Church with its white steeple pointing toward a cloudless blue sky.

They walked to Twin Oaks, the building with neat landscaping and a ramp at the front entrance. Josh didn't think Hoss would be welcome in a place with so many older people, so he walked to the courtyard and peered in the window of the community room.

About a dozen residents sat in the space, some watching television, some playing cards. In a wide recliner near the window, former police chief Bill Goodman sat reading a magazine.

His eyes stinging with sudden moisture, Josh rapped on the window, then knelt on one knee and threw an arm around the dog's shoulders. Hoss's fur was thick and solid beneath his hand as the dog leaned into him. The residents gestured in amazement, leaning on walkers and canes. Several applauded. Josh wished he could save the moment forever.

If only his mother had been there to see it.

Nurse Shari raised a window. A wash of warm air escaped, carrying the aroma of coffee. "You should hear them in here," she said, laughing. "They're saying that dog is as big as you!"

Josh nodded. "I know he's heavier."

He shifted his gaze back to Chief Goodman. "Did the chief see me?"

"Oh, yes." The nurse's smile deepened, and the softness in her voice told Josh she understood what the old man meant to him. "You're the best entertainment he's had all day, for sure. Best medicine, too."

"Tell him I'll see him tomorrow." Josh stood, then gave his audience an impulsive wave. "Bye, everybody."

He should have gotten a dog years ago.

THE NEXT DAY, Josh and Hoss took another walk. Josh didn't think they walked more than a mile and a half, but when they were still a block from home Hoss sat on the sidewalk with a thump that seemed to vibrate the ground.

"Come on, boy." Josh tugged on the leash, the leather pulling taut in his hand. "You know we still have a way to go."

In answer, Hoss stretched out his front paws and lowered himself to the sun-warmed concrete, officially down for the count. Josh grimaced. *You can't make a 200-pound dog do anything he doesn't want to do . . .*

If the dog needed a rest, fine. After all, they'd had another big day, taking a walk by the Wiggly and through the town square.

He turned when he saw movement from the corner of his eye, heard the shuffle of feet and the metallic click of walkers on pavement. A line of Twin Oaks walkers in stretch pants and sun visors came into view. Josh stepped off the sidewalk onto the grass as the young woman at the front of the line called a greeting. "That must be Hoss the ginormous dog. I was wondering when I'd meet him."

Josh nodded.

"Looks like you've worn him out." Her smile was gentle, not mocking, and some of the tension left Josh's shoulders.

The second woman in line—wearing a purple tracksuit and thick-soled sneakers—frowned as she passed Josh and Hoss, her walker wheels squeaking. "What'd you do, try to run him? The dog looks like he'd have a heart attack if you tried to make him run." She shook her head, her gray curls bobbing. "Poor thing."

The next woman—short and round with enormous glasses—shied away, pressing herself against the opposite side of the sidewalk, her eyes wide with alarm. She muttered something about being afraid of pit bulls and clutched her fanny pack like a shield.

One by one the walkers moved past Hoss, some admiring, some fearful, some confused, and Bill Goodman brought up the rear. The former police chief stopped dead in his tracks, his tripod cane planted on the sidewalk, his eyes wide behind wire-rimmed glasses. Then he tipped his head back and released a belly-laugh that echoed off the nearby houses.

"That *is* a dog," he told Josh when he was finally able to catch his breath. "He looks so much bigger up close. Where'd you find him?"

"At the shelter."

"Well, you found a friend and a half. What's his name?"

"Hoss."

"Any relation to the Cartwrights?"

Josh blinked. "Huh?"

"Never mind, son—you'd have to be as old as me to get that joke." The chief's eyes twinkled, his crow's feet deepening. "It's a good name. So how are you two getting along?"

"Fine, but the Piggly Wiggly will never be the same." The words came easier now, almost like telling a story.

"What happened?" The chief leaned forward, genuinely interested, his hands trembling on his cane.

"We knocked over a pyramid of baked beans."

The chief chuckled, a dry, wheezing sound that spoke of too many cigarettes and too many years. "I would have loved to see that." His face sobered. "I miss seeing you, son. I know things are different with your mama gone."

"Thank you. I'm—we're okay. I miss her, though."

"Of course you do. What are you doing with yourself these days?"

"I was thinking about working on that old shed in the back yard. Mama was always after me to fix the leak in the roof—"

"You should leave that old thing alone." The chief shook his head. "You don't really use it, do you? Aren't most of your tools in your garage?"

Josh nodded. "Yeah."

"Then I'd let it go."

"Mr. Goodman." The young woman at the back of the line —young and efficient, with her hair pulled back so tight her face looked stretched—folded her arms across her uniform. "The others are leaving us behind. You wouldn't want to miss the start of Bingo, would you?"

"Who would want to miss that?" the chief said. "Never fear, I will make certain the train arrives on time."

He turned to Josh, one weathered eyelid dropping in a conspiratorial wink. "I think it's about time you got yourself a haircut, dear boy. Now that you and Hoss are getting so much attention, you don't want to go around looking shaggy. You might frighten the women away."

Josh lowered his head, his cheeks heating, and reached up to touch his hair—it *was* long, curling over his collar. He thought of Kelly at the Piggly Wiggly and his face grew hotter.

"Now excuse me while I take my leave, or Nurse Ratched will haul me in," the chief said, his voice as dry as autumn leaves. "You mind how you go, Josh. Come see me again, will you? You can bring the beast. If they let Mildred Solomon's daughter bring that snippy little Chihuahua she calls a therapy dog, I've every reason to believe they will let Hoss through the door."

Josh smiled. "Yes, sir. I will."

The chief hurried away, catching up with the group, and the tension in Josh's shoulders eased.

CHAPTER

TWELVE

Heather spied from the van, her breath fogging the glass of the back window, as the guy with the shaggy hair talked to the old man with the cane. She'd been half-dozing when the parade of old folks shuffled past and the commotion pulled her from the fog of nausea.

Her mouth tasted like something died in it. She had awakened with Brett's arm around her, his breath warm against her neck. Then uncertainty crashed in. She still hadn't told him about the baby.

Now, watching the scene on the sidewalk, an odd feeling stirred under her ribs. Josh Donnelly had nodded at each person who passed, his shoulders hunched like he wanted to disappear but his face open and earnest—and all the while that massive dog lay sprawled on the concrete, panting in the sun.

Everyone in town seemed to like the young man. The old ladies had smiled and waved. The volunteer at the front stopped to chat. Now the old man with the cane was laughing. The young guy's face went pink, but he was smiling too.

Josh Donnelly was polite to everyone, she noticed. And patient. The dog certainly adored his new master, looking up at him with droopy eyes.

Brett stirred behind her, his hand finding her hip under the sleeping bag. "What're you looking at?"

"Nothing." She kept her eyes on the window. "Just people."

He pushed himself up on one elbow, his hair sticking up. "That dog is a monster."

"He seems sweet, though." She sighed as the old man with the cane finally walked away, the nurse herding him like a wayward sheep. Josh Donnelly remained on the sidewalk with his dog, looking almost happy. "Everyone seems to really like that guy."

"Yeah?" Brett yawned, exhaling a wave of morning breath. "Good for him."

Heather remained quiet, watching until the dog finally rose. Josh and his dog walked away, heading toward the old Victorian house.

Brett groaned and sat up, the sleeping bag falling away from his bare chest. "We need to figure out where we're playing today. The park isn't working for us. We gotta get some gas if we're ever gonna get outta this Podunk town."

Heather's stomach clenched. Gas required money, which had been in short supply since they landed in Peculiar. Every day Brett had played in the park and they'd barely made enough for a few groceries.

She cut off that train of thought before it plunged her into despair.

"What day is it?" she asked, her brain still fuzzy from sleep.

"Wednesday. I think." Brett scratched his neck, frowning. "Or Thursday? I don't know. Does it matter?"

"The old folks." Heather sat up, ignoring the way her head

spun with the sudden movement. "That parade of old people. They came from that retirement home."

Brett looked at her, his blue eyes still sleepy. "So?"

"So they're not at work during the day. You could set up in front of their building, maybe on the sidewalk. Play there, maybe even go inside. Old people love music, right?"

Brett's face lit with the smile that had made her fall for him. "That's not bad, babe." He cupped her face in his hands. "See? You're not as dumb as you look."

She forced a smile and filed it away with the other small cuts, the ones that didn't bleed unless she visited them later. "You think they'd let you play inside?"

"Only one way to find out." He was already pulling on his jeans, running his fingers through his hair. "It's a shot, right? Better than standing beside a picnic table."

Heather hugged her knees as he transformed from sleepy boyfriend to Brett Steelhawk, ambitious musician. He looked up. "You comin' with me?"

She thought about it. "Maybe later. I need to clean up first."

"Okay." He didn't push.

Brett grabbed his guitar case, climbed out of the van, and walked down the street without looking back.

Heather crawled to the front of the van and sank into the passenger seat, her stomach twisting. Through the window, she could still see where Josh Donnelly had stood.

Some people had a gift.

THE NEXT MORNING, Josh got up, rubbed Hoss's ears, and told the dog to follow him downstairs. After saying grace and eating breakfast, Josh sat and watched Hoss finish his meal. "What should we make today?" he asked. "I was thinking about some blocks."

Hoss ate the last of the kibble and licked the inside of his bowl, the scraping sound oddly soothing. When he finished, he stood and looked at Josh, a droplet of milk balancing on his whiskers like a pearl.

Laughter bubbled up from somewhere deep in Josh's gut. "Then again, maybe we'll go see the old chief first. You can entertain him a while."

He remembered what Bill Goodman had said about dogs being allowed to visit the ALF, and hoped the former police chief was right.

They walked to the retirement home, then strode into the building, the automatic doors whooshing open with a blast of climate-controlled air. Josh said hello to Isabella at the reception desk—she was reading a paperback romance, her finger marking the page. The lobby was unusually quiet, but a strong baritone voice came from the community room.

Josh turned to Isabella. "Is that who I think it is?"

She grinned. "Who else sings like that?"

"Hoss and I will go in and listen for a while."

Isabella's jaw dropped when she peered over the counter. "I don't think—"

"Chief Goodman said some of your visitors bring dogs. And Hoss is well-behaved. If he makes any trouble, I'll take him home."

Sighing, Isabella sank back into her chair and waved them by.

Josh led Hoss down the hallway, his sneakers squeaking on the linoleum, until he reached the community room and took a seat near the window. Without being told, Hoss sat by Josh's chair, then lay down and rolled onto his side.

In the community room, Mrs. Ledbetter was distributing

butterscotch candies from her purse. Morning light streamed through the wide bay windows, backlighting the open area set aside for speakers and performers.

At eighty-five, Bill Goodman had retained his intellect, his thick hair, and an amazing baritone that filled the room like warm honey.

Every Thursday morning, his health permitting, Goodman grabbed his karaoke machine and stood to bless his neighbors at the ALF. The karaoke machine began another song, the instrumental track filling the room, and the Chief picked up his microphone. "There's a land beyond the river," he sang, looking into the eyes of his fellow residents, "that they call the sweet forever. And we only reach that shore by faith's decree . . ."

Josh propped his elbow on the table and tried to remember the first time he met Chief Goodman. The former chief had been part of his life for as long as he could remember. At one point, Josh had hoped to call him Dad.

But though Chief Goodman had always been fond of Josh's mother, after a while Josh realized they weren't likely to marry. When he grew older, he sensed an awkwardness between them, a formality that frayed his mother's smile during the Chief's visits. He couldn't understand why, but she always seemed relieved when he left.

Josh waited until the Chief finished his brief concert—three hymns and a patriotic medley that had several veterans sitting at attention in their wheelchairs—then he told Hoss to stay while he walked over to say hello.

"Josh!" The chief tossed him a smile as he packed up his karaoke machine. "I didn't see you come in."

Josh shoved his hands into his pockets. "You sounded great. You always sing songs I've never heard."

"That's because you're young." The chief picked up his

machine and grinned, but a wistful note entered his expression. "Most churches don't sing the old hymns anymore." He nodded toward the window. "Am I mistaken, or have you managed to sneak your beast past reception?"

Josh grinned. "Isabella didn't have the heart to stop me." He offered to carry the karaoke machine, and the chief accepted his help. They were walking toward Hoss when Isabella tapped the microphone.

"May I have your attention?"

Josh turned, along with everyone else in the room.

"Ladies and gentlemen," Isabella said, smiling at the young man who stood next to her, "Today we are in for a double treat. This is Brett Steelhawk, and he's going to sing for you now. Would you please give him a warm welcome?"

Every eye in the room turned to the blond man with the guitar. Wearing a worn blazer, Brett gave them a broad smile. "Mornin', folks."

He opened the battered guitar case and took out an acoustic. He strummed a chord. "Any requests?"

Bill Goodman sank into a chair and winked at Josh. "Do you think he knows 'In the Sweet By and By?'"

Josh chuckled and sat beside him. "I doubt it."

A woman who'd been playing checkers raised her hand. "Do you know any Elvis songs?"

"My specialty, ma'am." The singer strummed his guitar again, then broke into a simple rendition of "Love Me Tender."

"Something more lively," the woman interrupted. "How about 'Blue Suede Shoes?'"

Josh chuckled, enjoying the gentle hum of people who were still eager to enjoy life.

"How about something for the ladies?" Brett said. He played a chord and launched into "Can't Help Falling in Love," his voice low and velvety, a pleasant sound that made even the hard-of-hearing residents lean forward. When he sang the chorus, a few ladies sighed out loud.

Admiration and envy mingled in Josh's thoughts. The guy looked so comfortable behind that guitar. Josh couldn't imagine that kind of ease.

Brett finished with a flourish and moved into "Hound Dog," hamming it up, swinging his hips, making the room laugh. Bill tapped the arm of his chair, keeping time.

Then Brett set the guitar aside and picked up the top of the Monopoly game on a nearby table.

"Well," he said, grinning, "since I've entertained y'all so well, I sure wouldn't mind a little help to get me on my way to Nashville. I'm gonna pass this box around. No pressure, but I'd appreciate it if you could donate whatever you can."

Josh stared. Most of the folks at Twin Oaks were on fixed incomes, and few could spare anything.

But Isabella—good-hearted Isabella—dipped her chin in a small nod, and Brett passed the makeshift collection box to Mrs. Ledbetter. She sniffed, muttered something about "kids these days," but pulled a dollar and a butterscotch from her purse and dropped them in. The lid moved from person to person as peer pressure worked its magic.

Some residents grumbled—Josh heard one old man call out, "Is he serious?"—but others smiled, charmed by the music and the novelty.

Through it all, Brett kept that easy grin fixed in place, his eyes bright and his shoulders loose. Josh stared at him, amazed at the man's nonchalance.

Bill shook his head. "Well, I'll be," the old man whispered. "That fella works a room even better than he sings."

Josh didn't envy Brett's boldness, but he did wonder how it would feel to move through the world unafraid.

The Monopoly lid made its way back to Brett. He peeked inside and released an exaggerated whistle.

"Much obliged," he said, giving the room a bow.

He received a patter of polite applause in response.

Josh found himself clapping even as he marveled at the guy's audacity. Maybe you had to be that brash to make it as a musician.

Brett slung his guitar over his shoulder and winked at Isabella before heading for the door.

When the man had gone, Bill leaned closer and nudged Josh's elbow. "Son," he said, "I don't know what that boy's after, but he sure knows how to ask for it."

Josh smiled, but his spirit stirred with a whisper he couldn't decipher. Something about that man—about the past few moments—made him uneasy, but why? The guy was a shameless huckster, but he wouldn't be sticking around. He was on his way to Nashville.

Bill reached for his cane. "Well, all this excitement has plumb wore me out. I'm going to go get my beauty sleep."

"Good to see you." Josh stood to shake the man's hand. "I need to take Hoss home."

"You do that. And mind how you go, son."

CHAPTER
THIRTEEN

Heather couldn't quite believe it—Brett returned from the retirement home with sixty dollars in his pocket. And a butterscotch.

He strutted around the picnic table like someone had knighted him for busking excellence, humming Elvis as he pulled bills out of his wallet and let them rain over Heather.

"Let's go," she said, tugging on his arm.

"Where?"

"To the grocery store!"

They ate like royalty that night—a rotisserie chicken from the Piggly Wiggly—hot and dripping down their fingers. A box of chocolate Little Debbies lay between them as they lounged in the van, along with a six-pack of beer Brett drank himself.

When they finished, the van smelled like grease, chocolate, and the lemon-scented wipes Heather insisted on buying. As the sun began to set, they went out and lay on the picnic table, listening to armadillos rustling the bushes and the gurgle of their full stomachs. She couldn't remember the last time she had seen Brett so relaxed.

The sun dipped low behind the pines, leaving the park awash in a soft Florida twilight—the humid air carrying the scent of someone grilling hamburgers.

"You must have been really good today," Heather said, nudging Brett's knee with hers. "Those folks must have loved you."

He grinned. "Yeah, old people go crazy for Elvis. My grandma used to sing those songs in her kitchen when she made cornbread."

"You found a winning formula," she said. "You could do this anywhere—Pensacola, Tallahassee, wherever we go. Find a retirement home, sing a few classics, charm the old folks, and make enough for a meal . . . or even a hotel."

He sat up, propping his hands on his hips, looking looser and more confident than he'd been in weeks. "Feels good to be appreciated, you know?"

And because the moment felt right—because his shoulders weren't tight and his eyes weren't searching for an escape route—she sat up and touched his wrist.

"Brett . . . I need to tell you something."

He froze for a second, then turned toward her. "What's up?"

Her pulse thudded. She had practiced this speech for days, rehearsed it every time he smiled.

"I'm pregnant."

Brett's smile faded. "I thought you might be," he said. "I'm not stupid."

So he had known.

He shifted on the table. "Is that really what you want? To have a baby?"

She swallowed as her hand drifted to her stomach. "I think I already *have* a baby," she said. "It's happening."

He looked away, his jaw tightening. "It doesn't have to."

Something familiar and cold slid through her veins. "We don't have to travel forever," she said, words tumbling out. She sketched a small, steady life where he worked, sang, and they stopped living in the van.

She waited for him to smile, to dream the dream with her.

He didn't.

Instead, he turned and looked at the ground beyond the picnic table. "So that's it, then. You get what you want no matter what."

Heather blinked, surprised by the venom in his tone. She tried again. "That's not what I'm saying."

"Feels like it."

"I thought we were in this together."

She wanted him to see that they should be a family. But when he refused to look at her—when his shoulders slumped and his fingers picked at the old paint on the table—she saw the truth without having to be told.

Brett had seen the signs and pulled away. His sharp quips, his indifference...

He did not want a baby in his life. He wanted to be free of houses and swing sets and a steady job.

Heather pulled her knees to her chest and studied the old two-story houses beyond the park, thinking about the peace and stability they embodied.

She would not lose Brett today.

But the unraveling had begun.

THE NEXT MORNING, Heather woke and breathed in a gulp of flat, stale air. She raked her fingers through her hair, trying to flatten the frizzy bits. She didn't have any decent shampoo—only a hotel sample she'd been rationing like liquid gold—and her head itched from days of wearing it in a ponytail.

She sat up, realizing that for the first time in a couple of weeks, she did not feel queasy. Her lower back hurt, but whose wouldn't after sleeping on two inches of foam?

At the front of the van, Brett was leaning toward the glove box, rummaging for something. Good. Time to leave Peculiar in the dust.

"Good mornin'," she called, reaching for the small bag that held her toothbrush and a few other toiletries. She brushed her teeth with a splash of bottled water, spit into a fast-food cup, then climbed into the passenger seat, hugging her knees while she waited for Brett to start the van.

He was hunched over the road atlas, his stubbled chin on his chest while his finger traced the blue line of I-10 like it was a route to Paradise. Last night's beer had left his breath sour and his eyes puffy, but he looked like a man determined to get to Nashville.

"You okay?" she asked.

Brett grunted, then turned to meet her gaze. "Fine. You?"

"Great. Ready to go."

"Me, too."

"Do we have enough money to fill the tank?"

"We have forty bucks. We'll see."

He turned back to the atlas, and Heather winced at a sudden cramp in her abdomen. If she weren't pregnant, she'd think that was a menstrual cramp, but maybe it was a result of stuffing herself the night before. She wrapped her arms around her middle and forced a smile.

"When we get gas," she said, trying to sound casual, "I

could use some money for toothpaste and shampoo. I can run inside and get it."

Brett's mouth pulled tight—one of those pinched expressions he got whenever she said the word *money*. But eventually he nodded.

"All right. We're outta here."

He turned the key. The engine coughed, sputtered, and caught with a rattling growl that vibrated the floorboards. Heather looked outside, silently saying farewell to Peculiar Park, then ate the last half of a Little Debbie she'd hidden in her toiletries bag. Would Brett have enough money to buy a muffin for breakfast? A biscuit? Even a yogurt. *Something.*

She didn't want to steal again. Not while she was—

"I'm glad we're headin' out," she said, forcing a smile. "I could use a decent bathroom. I'd like to wash my hair and—" she groaned—"honestly, I don't think that chicken agreed with me."

Brett ignored her comment as the van rattled out of the gravel lot, pebbles pinging off the wheel wells, then he exhaled through his nose. "I'm glad to see the last of this place."

Heather turned toward the window. Peculiar slid by them in soft, sun-faded streaks—the small shops with hand-painted signs, a barber pole that probably hadn't rotated in a decade, the thrift store where mannequins stared blankly through the dusty glass.

She pressed her palm to the window, feeling the warmth of the sun outside.

Peculiar wasn't much. But she felt a pang she hadn't expected.

Life had been quiet in Peculiar. Strange, but safe. People had waved. Kids had giggled at Brett's songs. And that sad-eyed man from the Victorian house ... Despite the death of his mother, he had a steady quality about him. A gentleness she didn't see every day.

She wasn't sure what it was about Peculiar . . . but she would miss the place.

Heather gaped when Brett handed her a twenty at the truck stop.

"Don't spend it all on shampoo," he said, clearly joking. "This ought to last you a while."

She smiled, realizing he must not have had a smaller bill, especially since it usually cost at least thirty dollars to fill the van.

Inside the store, she picked up a small tube of toothpaste and paused by the shelf of pastries. The doughnuts looked fresh, despite the plastic wrap. She added them to her shopping basket, then grabbed a lipstick—rosewood pink. She could use a little color on her lips and cheeks.

She set her basket on the counter. "Do y'all sell a good shampoo?"

The older woman behind the counter raised an eyebrow. "How do you define *good*?"

"Like, salon style?"

The woman chuckled. "Honey, all we have are the little travel bottles. Nothing fancy."

"Thanks—oh!" She grimaced as another pain stabbed at her midsection, this one worse than the others.

"You okay, hon?"

"Yeah. Just . . . something I ate."

Heather grabbed one of the shampoo bottles and paid for her items, glancing through the front window as she did. Brett was still at the pump, one foot propped on the van's bumper, his hair blowing in the breeze.

She turned back to the cashier. "Do I need a key for the restroom?"

The woman shook her head. "No, but lock the door. Not everyone remembers how to knock."

Heather took her bag and went to the back of the store, where she found the restrooms off a hallway. She went inside the ladies' and smiled in relief—it was spacious and clean. She washed her face with liquid soap and dried off with paper towels. She scrubbed under her arms. Because she'd left her hairbrush in the van, she finger-combed her hair.

A spit bath, Brett called it. The best they could do when they were on the road.

She moved toward the toilet.

Heather barely registered the next cramp until it crept down her spine, a low, twisting ache that made her fold forward on the toilet seat. She pressed a hand to her lower back, panting through the cramp. She'd felt miserable the last few days, but this was different. Deeper. Wrong.

When she looked down, the world upended and went dark.

On Friday, the twenty-second of December, Josh sat while Hoss chewed a bone in the corner.

Josh bowed his head over his bologna and mustard sandwich, elbows on the table, hands folded. Hoss paused mid-crunch and looked up, as if he knew what came next.

"Lord," Josh said, "thank You for this food. Thank You for this house, and for work, and for Hoss." His lips curved into a smile. "Thank You that the house doesn't feel so empty now."

He fell silent, letting the words settle, then murmured an amen and took a bite. The bread stuck to the roof of his mouth, so he washed it down with a sip of sweet tea, the ice long since melted. As he chewed, his gaze drifted to the other chair at the table.

Mama used to sit across from him with her coffee, blowing across the top of the mug, telling him about some verse she'd read, or some little miracle she'd witnessed in the grocery store. He could almost hear the clink of her spoon in her cup.

Hoss rose and padded closer, his nails clicking on the linoleum. The mastiff nudged his head against Josh's thigh, so Josh reached down and rubbed the thick skin around the dog's neck, his fingers sinking into dense, short fur.

"I'm all right," he said. "Just thinkin'."

The silence pressed in again. Even with Hoss for company, the house seemed to have more shadows than it used to. Josh took another bite of sandwich and chewed, listening to the refrigerator, a distant lawnmower, a mockingbird chattering in the oak outside. The sounds only made the emptiness louder.

He wiped his fingers on a napkin and looked at the worn Bible at the corner of the table, its black cover shiny at the edges, its pages crinkled from years of use. He usually read it first thing in the morning—"breakfast with the Lord," Mama called it—but feeding Hoss and establishing a new routine had thrown him off his old rhythms.

"Sorry I'm late, Lord," he said, a smile tugging at his mouth. "I know you're not a clock, but still."

He finished the last bite, balled up his napkin, and set it on his empty plate. Then he pulled the Bible toward him. He rested his hand on the cover, feeling the smooth leather under his palm, and bowed his head again.

"Lord," he prayed, "Mama always called this our marching orders. What do You want me to do today?"

He let the Bible fall open where it would. The thin pages fluttered and the book landed off-center, puffing up in the middle. Josh smoothed the thin paper, glanced at the top of the page, and let his gaze slide until a pair of verses rose up from the rest.

His finger traced the lines as he read aloud:
"Defend the poor and fatherless;
Do justice to the afflicted and needy.
Deliver the poor and needy;
Free them from the hand of the wicked."

The old, rolling cadence of the King James filled the little kitchen, wrapping around the hum of the refrigerator. He stopped, went back, and read it again, slower this time, tasting the words like another bite of bread.

"Defend the poor and fatherless..."

He sat back, Bible still open, and considered the verse. The *fatherless*. The word hit with a dull, familiar thud. He hadn't seen his own father since he was little, and all that remained was a blurry memory of a tall man with a loud voice and a hard hand.

Fatherless? He carried the word like a scar.

His mama had tried to fill the gap. She had signed him up for Little League, sitting in the bleachers with a big hat and a thermos of lemonade, cheering like he was the whole team. She tried to teach him how to throw a football, squinting against the Florida sun, laughing when he hit the mailbox instead of her hands. She worked at the school and still found time to read her Bible, drag Josh to church, and tell him God was a Father who would never walk out.

"You did good, Mama," he said. "You were the best mama I could have had."

Hoss released a chuff, as if agreeing, and rested his chin on Josh's knee. The weight was comforting.

"Defend the poor and fatherless," he repeated. "Do justice to the afflicted and needy."

He knew the poor; he saw them once in a while. Folks sleeping rough behind the grocery store, the tired woman at the laundromat counting out quarters, kids in the neighborhood running barefoot because shoes wore out too fast. He knew needy when he saw loneliness in their eyes.

"Lord," he said, fingers tightening around the Bible, "I hear You. I'll keep my eyes open. If there's somebody poor or fatherless crossing my path . . . if there's some needy person, someone who's afflicted . . . I'll help, if You'll show me how." He swallowed. "You know I'm not much with words. But I can fix things. I can mend what's broken, maybe. If I can help, use me."

Peace settled over him like a blanket laid across his shoulders.

"Okay," he murmured. "Marching orders received."

He closed the Bible, smoothing the pages with his thumb. Then he reached over and laid his hand on Hoss's big head.

"Lord," he added, a smile in his voice, "thank You for this dog. Bless him too. He's good company. Keeps me from rattling around like a loose screw."

Hoss thumped his tail against the floor.

"And if you do put somebody in my path . . . maybe that'd help give me purpose. If you send me someone to look after, I'll take care of them like Mama took care of me."

He pushed back his chair, gathered his plate and glass, rinsed them in the sink, and glanced out the back window. The slanted December light caught on the pile of scrap wood by the shed—old fence pickets, fallen branches from the oaks, a broken desk he had dragged home from the curb. To other folks, his collection looked like junk. To him, it was a pile of possibility.

"Come on, Hoss," he said. "Let's see what we can make today."

The mastiff lumbered to his feet, his joints popping, and followed as Josh slipped on his sneakers and opened the back door. Warm air and the scent of damp earth brushed his face. He paused on the threshold, that verse still echoing inside him.

Defend the poor and fatherless.

Do justice to the afflicted and needy.

Somewhere out there, somebody needed defending. Somebody needed a place, or a hand, or a lost soul needed to be found.

"All right, Lord." He stepped into the yard. "I'll keep watch, if You show me."

He headed toward the woodpile, the dog shadowing his steps, his heart open to a future he couldn't yet see.

CHAPTER
FOURTEEN

A voice floated toward Heather from a long, echoing tunnel.

"Honey? Are you all right in there?"

Heather blinked at the tile beneath her cheek. Tile—she was lying on the bathroom floor. Her head throbbed. How did she get on the floor?

"Honey? Do you need help?"

"No, I'm . . . sick." Her voice cracked. "I'll be out in a minute."

She pushed herself upright, the room swaying, her limbs weak and strangely distant from her body. She held onto the counter until the spinning settled. When she dared to look she saw what she already knew.

She'd had a miscarriage.

She drew a broken breath, fragile and trembling, then pressed her palm over her mouth to keep sound from escaping. No screaming. No falling apart. Not here. Not with strangers outside the door.

The moment she'd seen red she knew—her hope, that tiny flutter of possibility—was gone.

Why?

Maybe it was the hunger. The sleeplessness. Maybe it was nothing she could name at all.

A heaviness centered in her chest. She had already begun to love the baby and wanted Brett to love it, too. Wanted them to be a family, even if they were messy and poor.

Outside the door, impatient footsteps shuffled back and forth. She could hear a mother's gentle murmur, a child's soft whine.

Heather swallowed the lump in her throat, lifted her chin, and put on the bravest smile she could manage.

When she finally opened the restroom door, a woman and her daughter stood waiting—the little girl might have been four or five. Both looked at her with irritation. "So sorry," Heather whispered.

The cashier—the woman who had knocked—glanced at Heather's forehead. "Honey, you've got a bruise. You sure you're all right?"

Heather touched the tender spot and grimaced. She must have hit her head when she went down. "It's nothing," she said. "I'm fine."

She slipped away before her smile could collapse.

The air outside the market stank of diesel and gasoline. She stepped into the sunlight, blinking against the glare. Then her heart lurched.

The van—the old Westfalia—was no longer at pump three. No denim-clad figure waited outside the store. She saw no sign of Brett at all.

Just an empty space where he'd been.

Heather froze, her legs refusing to walk, but the world

around her kept moving—trucks rumbling past, the ding of the door opening behind her, music drifting from other vehicles—but none of it meant anything.

Brett had vanished.

CHAPTER
FIFTEEN

J osh blew a fine cloud of sawdust from the freshly carved block and ran his thumb over the edge. The grain was soft beneath his skin, warm from friction, and fragrant. Smooth, but not quite smooth enough. He'd take the sander to it before he started painting.

He studied the line of blocks on the porch railing, each one squared and solid in the afternoon light. He'd stripped the fallen log, cut it into chunks with the chain saw, then squared them with the table saw until they sat as neat as soldiers. He'd seen similar blocks at Retro Relics—cubes stained in muted pastels, their edges rubbed soft. Pretty enough, but too commercial—and fifty dollars a set. He could make something with more heart for half that price. Something that didn't feel store-bought.

He wiped each block with a damp rag, watching the dust darken and lift. He set the blocks in the sun to dry, then stretched his back. Three hours gone, and he hadn't even noticed. Easy to lose track of time when his hands were busy and his thoughts were quiet.

He needed a walk. Hoss probably did too.

"Come on, boy."

Hoss thumped his tail on the porch, then hauled himself to his feet.

"Let's go someplace different today," Josh said as they started down the steps. "You might as well learn your way around, in case you ever get lost."

The rhythm of their steps synced—man and dog moving together through the lazy Florida afternoon. A woodchopper droned a few streets away. Josh passed the post office and the Historical Society Museum.

They walked by the nursing home, where curtains stirred and an old woman raised her hand to wave through the wide window. Josh waved back.

God had been good, he realized, to spare his mama the pain of being taken from her home. She had been in good health until the day she had a stroke, so she didn't have to leave the house she loved.

He slowed as they reached the Old Florida Café. Hoss lifted his head, scenting the aromas of liver and onions. Two small tables sat out front, shaded by faded umbrellas. "Maybe we can eat here sometime," Josh told Hoss. "I'm sure they wouldn't mind, long as I pay for two dinners."

They passed Delectable Collectibles and the Bread Pit—both redolent of yeast and sugar—and Josh waved at Jackie when she smiled through the window of Retro Relics. She waved back, her bracelets flashing like sun off water.

He turned onto Tuscawilla, the road that marked the end of town and the beginning of the woods. The sky widened here, the tree frogs sang louder, and the air stilled. A few abandoned vehicles rusted beneath the scrub oaks, their sides streaked with graffiti and faded paint.

Without warning Hoss stiffened, his muscles bunching

under his coat. His tail went rigid as a line of fur rose along his spine.

"I'm with you," Josh said, halting. "This place is creepy."

He knelt to tighten a loose shoelace and caught the faint odor of stagnant water from the lake beyond the trees. One of his schoolmates had drowned in that lake, and the mere thought of that black water was enough to raise the hair at the back of Josh's neck.

He lay his hand on Hoss's head. "Whaddya say we head back?"

They crossed to the other side of the road, where sunlight shone bright on the pavement. Hoss kept his ears forward, scanning, on full alert. Josh's skin prickled as they walked. Nothing truly bad ever happened in Peculiar—or if it did, folks didn't talk about it. Still, he couldn't shake the feeling that they had walked past the dark edge of danger and it had taken their measure.

When they reached Main Street, Josh's uneasiness vanished. He was about to speak to Hoss when he spotted a man lying in the grass. A blanket of newspapers fluttered over the stranger's torso. Josh slowed, waiting to see the rise and fall of breath. Relief unwound in him when the man stirred.

He'd seen homeless men before. They came from the truck stop, where most of them had hitched rides with truckers. Sometimes, when they couldn't get another ride, they set off for Peculiar, probably hoping for a hot meal or a cheap hotel.

Hoss stepped closer, sniffing the man's face until the dog's touch roused the sleeper. "What the—" He sat up, startled, and squinted. Then his voice softened, shifting gears. "Hey, buddy." Spotting Josh, he fumbled beneath the newspaper and drew out a cardboard sign: *Out of work and hungry.*

"Hi." Josh didn't know what else to say. "You okay?"

The man waved the sign, as if Josh could miss it. "I'm as fine as frog hair."

Josh studied the man's sunburned skin, the gray in his beard, the desperation behind his bravado. He could have been anywhere from thirty to sixty, but without a doubt, he was desperate.

Josh reached into his pocket and pulled out a business card. "I don't carry my wallet when I walk," he said, "but this card's from my church. Go there and ask for Pastor Gary. He'll feed you, let you shower. If you need a safe place to sleep, I'm sure we can find someone with an extra room. No charge, and no strings."

The man took the card, then flipped it onto the grass. "Thanks for nothin'."

Josh's nerves tightened, but he maintained his even tone. "If I were you, I'd keep that."

"But you ain't me, are you?" The man scratched at his face. "I need cash, not cards and church."

"You said you were hungry," Josh said. "I told you where to get food. You want shelter, I'll take you to it. I'm tryin' to do right by you."

The man glanced at Hoss, whose tail hung as still as a question. "Forget it," he muttered, lying back down. "I can get what I need somewhere else."

Josh studied the man's grizzled face. Then he turned away, his thoughts as dark as the clouds gathering above the pines. He'd offered help, but some people didn't want help. At least he had made an effort...

As he and Hoss walked on, the air thickened with the smell of impending rain. Hoss brushed Josh's hand with a damp nose, as if to say *it's okay,* and Josh found himself grateful for the dog's quiet assurance.

If only people were as trusting.

Heather drew a breath and told herself not to panic. She had been in the restroom quite a while, so of course Brett had moved the van. Maybe he was in the men's room.

She circled the building, examining every parked vehicle. No camper van. The wide parking lot teemed with movement—big rigs roaring in and pulling out, brakes hissing like sighs, cars coming from the highway and heading out again. Parents herding kids into the snack shop; others having a meal in the diner.

Brett must have parked somewhere else.

She walked through the lot once. Then twice. Truckers whistled and made comments she didn't want to hear. She ignored them. Went back to the front of the snack shop, checked inside the diner. No van. No Brett.

Maybe he had to run an errand. But where? They didn't have cell phones, so he couldn't call. He could've asked the clerk to take a message, though.

She went inside and gave the cashier a smile. "Did anyone call for Heather?"

The woman frowned. "No, honey. You okay?"

"Yeah. Just misplaced my boyfriend."

Outside, she sat on a bench, tore open the doughnuts, and sipped from a bottle of water. She nibbled at her food, trying to look like someone waiting for a friend.

Maybe Brett left something at the park, so he had to go back to Peculiar. Maybe he wanted to surprise her with a present. Maybe...

But after an hour, the truth settled over her: He had driven away without her. On purpose.

That twenty dollars hadn't been for shampoo and toothpaste. It was meant for her survival. He'd said something about it lasting a while.

Her throat burned as she took another bite.

She should have seen it coming. He had stopped singing to her. Stopped looking at her like he was a lucky man. And when she told him about the baby, that sealed the deal.

She had been completely blind . . . about a lot of things.

Across the lot, a girl who looked about sixteen peered up into a truck driver's cab, smiling. A few minutes later, another girl tried the same thing. One got waved away; the other got invited inside.

The cashier came out as the sun dipped toward the trees on the horizon. "Is there anyone I can call for you, honey?"

Heather shook her head. "No, thanks. I'll be okay."

"You can't sleep here," the clerk said, her voice soft. "But I could call the Peculiar police chief. He'll take you to the jail, but at least you'll get a bed and a hot meal."

Heather shook her head again. "I'll move on."

The wind picked up as a gentle rain began to fall. She slung her bag over her shoulder and wandered back into the lot, watching as trucks came and went, headlights flicking on in the rain. Then she noticed a semi-trailer parked at the back of the property, unhitched, door swinging.

A girl stood in front of the door and used a step stool to climb in.

Heather hesitated, then jogged toward the trailer as rain began to fall in earnest. She was breathless by the time she pulled on the swinging door. "Hello?"

A young face—seventeen, maybe—appeared, framed in the glow of a security light. "You need something?"

"Yeah," Heather said, shivering. "I need to get out of the wet."

A pair of arms reached down and lifted her up.

CHAPTER
SIXTEEN

The rataplan on the metal roof finally stopped, but Heather remained soaked, her hair plastered to her neck. Inside, three girls sat around a burning candle, the air thick with the stink of cigarette smoke.

"You're soaked," one of them said. A brunette with hollow cheeks tossed Heather a thin towel.

"Thanks." She rubbed her face and hair. When she finished, she tucked her shivering hands into her sleeves.

"You're not a cop," another girl said, her eyes cold and assessing.

Heather shook her head. "I'm not anything."

She recognized them now—the truck stop girls she'd seen from a distance. The prettiest was brunette with red lipstick.

"Hungry?" The blonde held up a can of SpaghettiOs.

Heather shook her head. "No, thanks."

A movement from the back of the trailer caught her eye—a thin hand rising from behind a cardboard box. Heather flinched.

"That's Sarah," the blonde said, tilting her head toward the back. "She doesn't go out anymore."

Sarah lay on a pile of blankets, her belly round and taut beneath a sweatshirt that might have once been pink.

"Oh," Heather said. "I didn't see you there."

The girl smiled. "Hard to miss me these days."

The others introduced themselves—Jessica, Kayla, Amber.

Kayla, the blonde, cocked her head. "You run away?"

Heather snorted. "Boyfriend left me sitting on the curb."

"That's low."

Kayla drew on a cigarette, then flicked the ashes onto a blanket. "Why'd he leave?"

"Probably because I told him I was pregnant."

"You and Sarah should start a club."

"Whatcha gonna do?" Amber asked.

"I don't know. But the thing is—I'm not pregnant now. Not anymore."

Amber's eyes widened. "You need a doctor or something?"

Kayla grinned and reached into a box, coming up with a half-empty bottle of cheap whiskey. "How's this?"

Heather blinked. "Where'd you—"

"One of the truckers. Sometimes it helps to be tipsy."

Heather didn't want to understand, but she did.

Kayla took a swig and passed the bottle to Amber, who did the same. When the bottle came to Heather, she took it. The whiskey would warm her, wouldn't it? She'd stopped drinking beer, but now...

She raised the bottle and swallowed, wincing as the burn traveled down her throat.

She set the bottle on the floor and looked at Sarah. The girl had drifted off, one hand splayed across her belly.

"What's her story?" Heather whispered.

Amber smirked. "Whaddya think? She got pregnant, ran away, and wound up here. We look after her."

Heather couldn't stop looking at the rise and fall of Sarah's breathing. "When's the baby due?"

Nobody answered. Kayla took another drag of her cigarette, her grin fading.

Amber lifted her head. "Did you see the woman at the register?"

Heather nodded. "Yeah."

"That's Irene."

"That woman—Irene—doesn't she call the cops when she sees you in the parking lot?"

Amber took Kayla's cigarette. "It's not against the law to want to see the inside of a truck, is it?"

Heather blew out a breath, understanding more than she wanted to. And Brett had left her here . . . thinking she was pregnant with his baby.

Heather raised the bottle, then set it down before drinking. "Mind if I stay here tonight? I'll leave in the morning."

Kayla arched a brow. "Where you going?"

Heather twisted the cap onto the whiskey. "Back to Peculiar, I guess. Brett did well there, so he might come back."

Kayla released a weary laugh. "Whatever you say."

Heather wrapped herself in an old comforter, and laid down facing the wall. Behind her, the candlelight flickered. Sarah turned in her sleep, mumbling a word that sounded like *Mama*.

The thought of Sarah's baby released a flood of longing for her own child. She would never hold it, never know what sort of person he or she might have been.

Outside, the rain started again, a deafening thrum on the roof. The sound filled the trailer, masking the sound of her sobs.

By the time Heather woke the next morning, the rain had stopped. The air inside the trailer was still holding the ghost of the last cigarette. The three girls were gone, out doing whatever they had to do to keep themselves fed.

A low moan came from the back of the trailer.

"You okay, Sarah?"

The girl rolled and clutched her belly. Her face had gone white. "It hurts," she gasped. "Oh—oh, it hurts—"

Heather went over and knelt beside her. "Okay, okay, breathe. Maybe it's heartburn."

Sarah cried out again, louder this time.

This wasn't heartburn. Yesterday she had lost her baby, and Sarah was about to deliver hers.

Heather lifted her gaze to a God she wasn't sure existed. "Why are you doing this to me?"

She stood and hurried to the trailer door, then peered out. She searched for any sign of the other girls, but she saw no one.

She turned. "I'm gonna go look for—"

"Don't leave me! Please!" Pain and fear laced Sarah's words.

"I won't leave." Heather moved to the back of the trailer, pushed aside a stack of boxes, and sat by Sarah's side, then took the girl's hand. "I've seen movies."

"Movies?"

"Childbirth is natural, right? And I promise I won't leave you."

Like Brett left me.

For the next hour, Sarah writhed on the blankets, gasping, clutching Heather's hand hard enough to bruise. Heather tried to remember useful information from movies and high school health class, but her mind had emptied of everything but the rhythm of Sarah's cries.

Then the door swung open. Kayla climbed in, her eyes wide. "What the—she's having the baby?"

Heather nodded.

Kayla froze for a heartbeat. "We gotta call somebody. A doctor or—"

"No!" Sarah cried, her eyes wild. "No doctors. They'll take my baby."

Heather stared at her. "I don't think that's how it works."

But Sarah was shaking her head and sobbing. "You don't know. It happened to a friend of mine."

Heather pressed a damp towel to Sarah's forehead and tried to think. The air in the trailer was too close, too suffocating. The whiskey bottle beckoned.

"Okay," she said. "For now, we'll stay with you."

Kayla hesitated, then nodded, her lips trembling. Amber sat on the floor and clutched Sarah's other hand.

Outside, thunder rolled in, low and distant. Inside, Kayla lit candles. Heather sat on the floor, watching Sarah breathe, and waited for the next wave of pain.

THE SUN ROSE soft and gray, as if it didn't want to wake the world too quickly. Light spilled through the partly open door of the abandoned trailer, warming Heather's knees as she sat in the doorway and tried to breathe like a normal person again. Outside, the air smelled of diesel exhaust. Inside, it was heavy with the sour stink of sweat.

Behind her, Jessica, Kayla, and Amber lay scattered across the floor like dolls, wrapped in thin blankets, their breathing deep and exhausted.

She wiped her palms on her jeans and stood, her legs trembling with fatigue. Nearly a full day of helping Sarah deliver her baby. The memory felt like something that had happened to someone else.

Sarah lay where she'd collapsed after the last push, her back propped against a mound of old blankets. The newborn—tiny, pink, and impossibly fragile—was curled against her breast, rooting blindly, seeking, searching. Sarah slipped her pinky between the baby's questing lips.

A soft sound escaped Sarah's throat, half sob, half laugh.

Heather stood in the dim light, her heart tightening. She'd been sure the moment Sarah held her baby, something fierce would awaken in her. That was how it happened in movies.

Sarah looked up. Her eyes were red-rimmed. There was no awe in her face, only bone-deep weariness. Resignation sat on her like a second skin.

"I want you to do something for me," Sarah said, her voice rough.

Heather rubbed grit from her eyes. Her whole body hurt, but Sarah had to feel worse. "What do you need?"

Sarah dipped her chin toward the baby. "I want you to take her and give her to someone nice."

Heather frowned. "What?"

"I can't keep her." Sarah's voice cracked, but her gaze held. "She deserves more than a parking lot." She swallowed. "You said there's nice people in that town past the highway—"

"Peculiar?"

Sarah nodded. "Take her there. Give her to someone who'll be good to her. Someone you trust. Someone who has a door that locks."

Heather smiled at the tiny girl tucked in Sarah's arms. All night long, between contractions, Heather had talked—rambling to distract Sarah from pain. She'd described Peculiar like it was a storybook: old folks doing laps around the park and a little white church. She'd mentioned the young man she kept seeing in town—the one who looked gentle even from a distance.

She must've made it sound like a fairy tale.

"Sarah, you don't mean that," Heather said. "You're exhausted. You just had a baby. When you rest, you'll change your mind."

Sarah let out a short, bitter breath. "I won't. You don't know what my life's been like."

Heather drew a breath. "I could take her to the police station. They'd keep her safe."

"I don't want her *taken*," Sarah snapped, pain flashing in her eyes. "I want her *loved*."

Heather opened her mouth, then shut it. The words tangled. She didn't know anyone in Peculiar. Not in a way that counted.

But she kept thinking of that quiet young man with the uneven haircut and hunched shoulders. The one who smiled at the older folks like they mattered. The one whose giant mastiff looked at him like he'd hung the moon.

Maybe she was being foolish. Maybe she was guessing wrong.

"Are you certain?" Heather asked. "You don't want to sleep on this?"

Sarah shook her head. "Sleep ain't gonna get her diapers or clothes. I'm not changing my mind."

Heather's voice shook, but she made it steady. "Okay. If you're sure... I might know the right person."

Relief loosened Sarah's shoulders. "Good."

Heather gave mother and baby a moment, backing away as if privacy could still exist in a trailer. The part of her that believed in happy endings kept insisting Sarah would change her mind. At any minute she'd pull that baby close and say she'd had second thoughts.

But for now—

"First," Heather said, "you need to nurse her. Give her a good start."

Sarah released a weak laugh. "I can do that. I don't feel like doing much else."

"You made a beautiful baby," Heather said, and meant it.

She brushed a strand of hair from Sarah's forehead. For a moment they were just two girls—one barely old enough to vote, the other learning how fragile life could be.

Sarah gripped Heather's wrist. "When you take her, wrap her tight. It's cold, so don't leave until someone finds her."

Heather squeezed her hand. "I won't. I promise."

When Sarah's eyes finally fluttered shut, Heather found a blanket, piled it with others, and stretched out on the floor.

When she woke, the light had shifted—afternoon thinning toward evening. Her body still felt like it had been wrung out and hung up to dry. One thought threaded through her brain, stubborn as a burr: Sarah would change her mind. Of course she would.

CHAPTER
SEVENTEEN

Christmas Eve day arrived quiet, like a rabbit in tall grass.

Josh noticed it first in the light. The sun never fully rose—just hovered low, a pale pink smear across cloud. Cold had settled into the house during the night, a chill that seeped through window seams and settled in corners. He kept the thermostat set low out of habit. Mama used to say cold sharpened the spirit. He suspected she'd said it mostly because heat was expensive.

He went to church as usual, shook every hand extended to him, and enjoyed Pastor Gary's Christmas sermon. But aside from his neighbors' holiday decorations, he didn't feel much Christmas spirit.

Outside, his yard refused to acknowledge the holiday. Sawtooth palmettos crowded the fence line, their stiff fronds rattling whenever the breeze picked up. Live oaks hunched over the lot like sentinels, draped with Spanish moss that swished and swayed, gray against the sky. Philodendrons sprawled wherever they could, their glossy leaves darkened by the threat of rain. The weatherman had promised showers by nightfall. Cold rain. The dreary kind that made Christmas feel like a mistake on the calendar.

Josh sat on the old sofa, the one Mama had insisted on recovering years ago, long after the stuffing had given up its fight. The couch sighed when he shifted his weight, as if it, too, was tired of holding a single body when it had been built for company.

Across the room stood the Christmas tree.

It was smaller than the ones Mama used to choose, shorter and thinner, its branches uneven despite his best efforts. He'd set it up yesterday, thinking Hoss might enjoy it. He'd untangled the lights, remembering how Mama used to hum while she did it, tongue tucked against her teeth in concentration. Now the lights glowed in the gloom, but they didn't seem as bright as they once had. Maybe the room was swallowing light the way grief swallowed sound.

Hoss lay stretched at his feet, a massive presence against the sofa, his breath slow and even. The dog raised his head when Josh sighed, his brown eyes dark with concern, and after a moment he pushed himself upright. With deliberate care, Hoss placed his enormous head on Josh's knee, the weight of it solid and warm.

Josh rested his hand on the dog's broad skull, then slid his fingers down to the thick ruff at Hoss's neck. The connection helped.

"I know," he murmured, though he wasn't sure if he was talking to the dog or to himself. "Christmas is lonely without her."

The house creaked around them. A branch brushed the metal roof. Somewhere down the road, a truck passed, its tires humming over the wet pavement. The world went on, indifferent to the man sitting alone with a tree and a prayer he didn't know how to finish.

Josh closed his eyes.

"Lord," he whispered, the word barely leaving his mouth. He hadn't meant to pray out loud, but the quiet pressed in on him until something needed to break it. "I'm trying. I really am."

Hoss moved closer.

"I'm trying to learn how to live on my own." Josh drew a deep breath. Saying it made the truth heavier. "Mama said it would be easy but it isn't. She had a way of filling a room, even when she wasn't talking."

He thought of the kitchen table, where she used to sit with her Bible, glasses perched on the end of her nose. The sound of her moving around the house had been a language all its own. Now silence made the house feel like a foreign country.

"I know You know what it's like," he went on. "But You didn't live alone. You had Mary and Joseph. Friends. Disciples. People always around."

The lights on the tree flickered.

"I keep thinking maybe that's the way we're meant to be," he said. "Connected to people. I'm not... and I don't think I'm built for being by myself."

The confession hung in the silence.

His gaze drifted to the window, where the sky had darkened another shade. Rain would come soon. The yard would turn slick and muddy, the palmettos rattling harder, the dead leaves becoming a slick carpet.

This would be a bleak Christmas. Just him, Hoss, and a house that remembered far too much.

"How do I do this?" he asked, the question more breath than sound. "How do I live alone?"

He waited.

No answer came. No beam of light. No sudden peace. Only the steady presence of the dog beside him, the monotone hum of the refrigerator, and the muted glow of the lights.

Josh bent and rested his forehead against his knuckles.

"Okay," he said. "I'll keep trying."

Hoss nudged his knee, a small insistence, and Josh almost smiled.

Outside, the first drops of rain began to fall, pinging against the roof, each one counting down to a Christmas he didn't know how to celebrate.

AFTER CROSSING THE PARKING LOT, Heather pushed the truck-stop door open with her shoulder, balancing two paper cups of coffee against her chest. A bag with three sausage biscuits was tucked under her arm, bought with the last of Brett's money. Sarah needed food. All of them did.

Heather had taken her time in the store, wanting to give Sarah quiet with her baby. She'd washed her hair, scrubbed under her nails, finger combed her wet hair until she looked less like a drowned rat.

Outside, cold had moved in. Diesel fumes threaded the air, but the coffee warmed her palms and smelled like normal life.

She reached the trailer and paused at the rusted stepladder. The door hung partly open. The trailer was quiet. Too quiet.

She climbed inside, set the food down, and froze.

The blankets where the other girls had slept were empty now. Sarah's corner was empty too.

But the makeshift nest of blankets remained. And the baby —wrapped in the ratty sweater Heather had tied around her— was still there, asleep, lips pursing in soft suckling motions.

A bead of milk shone on her chin. Sarah had nursed her. So where was she?

"Sarah?" Heather called. Her voice sounded wrong in the cramped metal space—too loud, too scared. "Sarah?"

Nothing answered. Only the baby's soft breathing.

Heather set the coffee on an overturned box and leaned over the infant, checking her chest. The rise and fall of her breathing was so small it made Heather's throat tighten.

That was when she saw the folded scrap of paper tucked beneath the edge of a blanket.

Her fingers shook as she opened it.

Do what you said. Take her into town and leave her where she'll be loved.

And don't try to find me—I'm not coming back. —S.

Heather swallowed hard. The coffee turned to acid in her throat.

For a heartbeat she looked around, waiting for Sarah to step out, to laugh and say she'd only been testing Heather.

But the sweater Sarah had worn was gone. The purse was gone.

Sarah was gone.

Heather bolted to the doorway and looked out at the lot—idling semis, drivers moving like shadows, engines rumbling. Sarah could be in any cab already headed toward Georgia or deeper into Florida, away from this place and this life.

Heather had taken her time in the store, and Sarah had used it.

She turned back, heart pounding, and picked up the baby. The infant startled at the movement and released a thin whimper.

"It's okay," Heather whispered, pressing the baby to her chest. "I've got you."

She stood in the sour air and tried to think. A police station meant questions. Paperwork. A system that treated babies like cases.

And Sarah hadn't asked for safety. She'd asked for love.

Heather's stomach knotted. "All right," she whispered, as if the baby had a vote. "All right. Peculiar it is."

By the time Heather reached the "Welcome to Peculiar" sign, rain had begun to fall. Christmas lights blinked on as she passed. Plastic Santas grinned from porches. A Norfolk pine in the park glittered with oversized silver balls.

She'd known the holiday was coming, but was it close?

The Victorian house was easy to find. Heather turned in at the gate, followed the brick walkway, and lingered in the shadows, making sure no one was outside. Then she moved onto the porch, her knees shaking. She tightened the sweater around the baby, then lowered the infant to the welcome mat, tucking the oversized sweater snugly around her. The baby yawned, her breath a tiny puff in the cold air.

At least the porch would keep her dry.

Heather backed away, throat tight, and slipped behind the giant leaves of a sprawling philodendron.

She'd promised Sarah the baby would be found, and a newborn couldn't wait long in the cold.

Heather groped in the mulch until her fingers found a pinecone. She threw it against the door.

The dog's bark exploded in the quiet—deep and booming. Heather ducked lower as locks clicked and the door opened.

Josh Donnelly stepped out, long-faced and sad-eyed. The

mastiff stood behind him like a living wall. Josh looked out at the street, then down. Then he lifted the baby with both hands, as if she were sacred.

"Oh," he breathed, pulling her close. His voice broke. "Oh, sweetheart."

He kissed the baby's forehead, then carried her inside. The door clicked shut.

Heather stayed crouched in the wet leaves and watched the front room light come on. From where she crouched, she could hear the gentle timbre of Josh's voice from inside the house.

A single tear slid down her cheek. She would not have her baby . . . but Josh Donnelly would have Sarah's. That little girl would be treasured, for a while, at least.

Heather stood, shoulders stiff with cold and grief, and began the long walk back toward the truck stop.

Her arms were empty, and the cold rushed in to fill them.

But her heart—against all sense—felt fuller than it had in a long time.

Josh carried the baby inside his house, Hoss padding behind him, the dog's toenails clicking against the linoleum. Josh went straight to the kitchen—the warmest room in the house—and set the baby on the table between his Bible and the salt and pepper shakers.

His breath caught as he pulled the child from the grimy sweater. On his palms lay a baby so small he could have held her in just one hand—a pink, wrinkled creature with wisps of dark hair stuck to her head. Her tiny mouth opened in a silent O before the first sound came: a sharp, thin cry that sliced through the stillness.

Hoss whined at the sound.

Josh froze, his pulse pounding like a jackhammer. The baby trembled, her little fists jerking, her legs thrashing against the stiff sweater. She looked brand new—*too* new for Josh's comfort. Her skin was mottled, her belly button still marked by the dark stub of an umbilical cord.

Someone had given him a newborn.

"Oh, Lord," he whispered, glancing at the phone. "Should I call the police? Or 911?"

He waited, listening, and heard the inner voice he recognized at once.

Feed my lamb.

Josh exhaled in a rush. "Okay. But when I asked for someone to take care of, I was thinking of someone . . . a little bigger."

The baby's cries turned from weak whimpers to a furious, high-pitched wail that vibrated the window glass. "Okay, okay," Josh murmured, placing his hand on her tummy. "I hear you. You're right. This ain't right. Not supposed to find babies on the porch. Not at my house. Not ever."

After wrapping the baby again, he held her in one arm while he opened drawers with the other, metal clanging and wood scraping as he searched. What did babies need? His mind went blank for a moment, then steadied: Diapers. Bottles. Milk.

Anchored by those three words, he looked around for something—anything—soft. He found a clean dish towel near the sink, one his mama had embroidered. The cotton felt soft enough, so he laid it under the baby, folding it to make a crude pad. The tiny chest rose and fell in a fragile rhythm, her breaths so shallow he had to lean close to make sure they came.

He wrapped the makeshift diaper as best he could around her bottom, careful not to brush the cord stump. She was cold

—so chilled her skin felt waxy under his fingers. He scooped her up and hurried into the living room.

The air there was cooler, but his mama's crocheted afghan lay draped over the back of the couch. He spread it out, the thick yarn catching on his calloused fingers, and laid the baby in the center before folding the blanket around her. Then he went to the thermostat and pushed the heat to eighty degrees.

The afghan engulfed her, but the baby finally stopped shivering. Her whimpers softened to hiccups, then to faint squeaks.

Josh crouched beside her, staring, the enormity of his task chilled his spine. This baby couldn't be more than a day or two old. Whoever left her on his porch hadn't even bothered with a proper blanket.

He drew a shaky breath. "All right, sweetheart. You're safe now."

Then, like a match striking in his mind—milk. She needed milk.

"What am I gonna feed her?" He glanced at Hoss. The dog sat by the kitchen doorway, his brow furrowed. "Babies need milk, right? I got some, but—"

He blew out a long breath. He didn't know anyone who could nurse a baby, and he sure didn't have a baby bottle lying around. He could search the attic later, but this baby needed food *now*.

"Lord?" His voice cracked as he closed his eyes. "You sent this baby, so You're gonna have to help me out."

He poured milk into a small pot. The smell of warming milk rose into the air, sweet and soothing, filling the small kitchen.

Josh stirred, testing the temperature with his finger, then he scanned the counters. No bottles. No dropper. Nothing that looked remotely useful. He needed something—anything—that could act like a nipple.

Then he remembered. Years before, he and Mama had fed an abandoned kitten with a rubber glove.

It was worth a try.

He rummaged through drawers until he found a box of gloves, powdery and yellowed. He pulled one free, washed it with hot water, then funneled in the milk. He twisted the top shut and fastened it with a zip tie, then used the ice pick to prick a hole at the end of the index finger.

"Please work."

He applied gentle pressure, and saw a single drop glisten at the end of the finger.

He tested the milk on his wrist like he'd seen mothers do in movies, then went into the living room and cradled the baby in one arm. Her eyelids fluttered, lashes dark against her pink skin. She looked impossibly new and inherently breakable.

"I'm not very good at this," he told her. "But I'll do my best."

He guided the glove's fingertip toward her mouth. At first, she turned away, her mouth working uselessly, but when a drop touched her lips, she caught the glove. The suction was weak and her mouth trembled with effort. More milk went onto the baby's throat than in her mouth, but Josh smiled every time she swallowed. "That's it," he murmured. "That's my girl. You keep fighting."

Hoss lay beside the table, his head resting on his paws, his eyes steady.

"I know," Josh said. "Gotta keep her head up so she doesn't choke."

A painful half hour passed as Josh struggled to spot the small motion of swallowing. His hands steadied even as his heart hammered with anxiety.

Finally the baby's eyes closed and her lips stopped working. She fell asleep, her tiny body relaxing in the crook of his arm.

Josh stared at her in awe. She was perfect in every way—the delicate curl of her ear, the faint blue vein across her temple, the scents of milk and new life rising from her skin.

"Lord," he murmured. "I don't know what You're doing, but I know I'm in over my head."

If he'd been a swearing man, he would have sworn he heard the Lord chuckle.

He laid the baby on the sofa, surrounded her with pillows, then ran upstairs. In the spare room, he dumped the contents of a dresser drawer, spilling an old yo-yo, two Atari cartridges, a Transformer, and a G.I. Joe onto the floor. He lined the drawer with his high school sweater, added a tee shirt for softness, and carried it downstairs.

He transferred the tiny bundle to her new bed, unfolded the afghan, laid one of his tee shirts over her, then wrapped her in the afghan again. Her breathing had steadied, a faint flutter against his mama's handiwork.

"Right," he murmured to Hoss, who stood guard at the door. "We need a bottle. And clothes. And diapers."

He placed the drawer and its occupant near the clanking radiator, then leaned against the wall and exhaled a long breath.

Somewhere deep in his spirit, he heard it again—quiet and certain—like a whisper threading through his thoughts:

Feed my lamb.

CHAPTER
EIGHTEEN

While the baby slept and Hoss snored on the floor beside her, Josh stood at the top of the pull-down ladder and stared into the dark. The attic reeked of dust and cedar and age.

He squinted, searching for the pull-cord, and his fingers brushed a cobweb before he found the small bead on the end of the string. One tug, and a lonely bulb flickered to life, throwing a yellow glow over the stacked cardboard boxes that filled the attic from one end to the other.

He rubbed the back of his neck. "Lord, You sure don't make things easy."

His mother's handwriting glowed at him in faded red marker, careful and exact despite the years. Frugal to the bone, she had packed and labeled every scrap of their lives because "you never know when you're going to want these things."

He scanned the labeled boxes:

JOSH'S SCHOOL AWARDS.

JOSH'S YEARBOOKS.

JOSH'S CLOTHES, SZ 10–12.
JOSH'S CRAFT PROJECTS.
JOSH'S BABY CLOTHES.

His mama had saved things he didn't remember owning.

He crouched and pulled the last box out from beneath two others, the cardboard rasping against the floor. Dust motes rose in the light, swirling like tiny angels as he lifted the flaps.

Inside lay a jumble of blue cotton and yellow flannel, soft from years of washing. The faint scents of dryer sheets and time drifted upward as he sorted through the contents: sleepers decorated with trains and faded teddy bears, socks no bigger than his thumb, a bib that said *Daddy's Helper* in stitched blue letters.

"Guess that didn't pan out," he murmured.

He didn't care that most of the clothes were blue. The baby downstairs could wear the whole box if it kept her warm.

Some of the clothes were far too big, but the outfits grew smaller as he dug deeper—tiny shirts, tiny hats. At the very bottom, wrapped in tissue, he found a knit cap and a silver-plated rattle, nearly black with tarnish.

He picked up the rattle, rubbing his thumb across the engraved initials—J.D.—and for a moment, his vision blurred.

He cleared the lump in his throat and reached back into the box. A stack of white rectangles lay folded along one side. He unfolded one—it was soft, padded in the middle, and rectangular, edged with stitching. A cloth diaper, he realized. He held it up, wondering if fabric so old could still function. "We'll find out, I guess."

He hauled the box and its contents downstairs, each step creaking beneath his sneakers.

The kitchen still held the fragrance of heated milk. The baby slept in her makeshift crib, her lips puckering, one tiny fist moving beneath the tee shirt he'd used as a blanket. Hoss snored on the rug, his paws twitching.

Josh knelt beside the drawer. He pulled items from the box, inspecting each like a man studying treasures from a lost world—plastic baby bottles yellowed with age, a few glass bottles that were still clear, plastic rings meant to fasten rubber nipples that had long since disintegrated.

"No nipples," he muttered. "Figures."

He set the bottles aside, then unfolded thin blankets—worn but clean—and a hooded towel with a faded duck stitched in the corner. He ran his hand over the soft fabric, imagining how it would feel wrapped around that fragile little body.

What he *didn't* find were the things he needed most—disposable diapers, nipples, an instruction manual. He exhaled, frustration tightening his shoulders.

Through the kitchen window, he could see that the streetlights had come on. He guessed it was about half past seven—leaving just enough time to get to the grocery before it closed for Christmas Eve.

The thought of leaving the baby alone made his stomach twist. He couldn't risk it. Not with a newborn, and not with a dog who could accidentally upset her drawer.

Yet the idea of walking into the Piggly Wiggly with a baby in his arms was nearly as bad. The Powers that Be would take the baby from him. Later, he would call Chief Bowen, but not until the baby was warm, fed, and steady.

An image filled his head—a dour-faced social worker pulling the baby from his arms as she screamed.

No, he couldn't let that happen. Not when the Lord had sent her to him. Not when he had promised to defend the poor and fatherless.

Chewing his thumbnail, he paced between the table and

the stove, the floorboards groaning beneath his weight. Hoss raised his head, one ear cocked in question.

"I know, boy," Josh said. "I can't leave her. But I can't keep her if I can't take care of her, so I'm going to need some things."

He turned toward the stairs, his resolve hardening like stone.

"If God wants me to feed this little lamb," he said, "He's gonna have to show me how."

He climbed back to the attic, the house sighing around him as wind brushed against the eaves. Somewhere between the creaks and shadows, a spark of purpose flamed inside him—small, flickering, and stubborn.

DARKNESS DREW down fast in Florida, not with drama but with a hush, as if the world had decided to hold its breath. Tuscawilla Road unspooled ahead of Heather in a wet ribbon of asphalt as it reached for Highway 90. No streetlights lit the way in this bit of uncivilized territory, and only dirt, weeds, and wilderness lay between her and the truck stop.

Five miles had sounded manageable when she set out. Five miles was only ninety minutes at a steady pace.

She hadn't added exhaustion into that equation. Now her legs ached with a dull, trembling protest, and the skin at the back of her neck prickled with cold where sweat had dried under her hoodie.

She didn't see the hole.

One moment she was listening for the faint *shhhh* of cars on the highway ahead, and the next her foot plunged into darkness, twisting hard. Pain shot up her leg, sharp enough to steal the breath from her lungs. She cried out and staggered, windmilling, then went down on one knee in the wet dirt at the road's edge.

For a moment she sat there, hands braced on the ground, panting to catch her breath. The air smelled of wet earth and crushed grass. A car zoomed out of the darkness, its tires whispering over pavement, its headlights briefly highlighting the rain, then it faded to red lights in the distance.

The driver hadn't seen her. Or if he had, he didn't care.

Heather pushed herself up on one leg, her teeth clenched, and tried to put weight on her injured foot.

Fire ignited in her foot and traveled along her nerves.

"Dadgummit!" She tried again, stumping on her heel, stubbornness moving her forward half a step before her leg buckled. She hopped on her good leg, shaking, pain pounding in the steady rhythm of her heart.

Lying down wasn't an option—she knew that as surely as she knew her own name. Someone would spot her curled up by the road and see what they wanted to see. A passed-out addict. A drifter. A problem to be managed. Jail. Questions she didn't want to answer.

She lowered herself to her hands and knees and moved away from the pavement, lifting her injured foot, every movement sending little sparks of pain up her spine. The foliage thickened around her as shadows folded in on themselves. She found a Brazilian pepper bush by feel more than sight, its leaves stiff and waxy under her fingers. The smell was sharp and green when she brushed against it.

Good enough for camouflage and a bit of shelter, at least until morning.

She sank at its base as a sob escaped her. The ground was wet and cold, and the chill pebbled her skin. She tugged the cuffs of her jeans down and tucked them into her socks, fumbling with numb fingers, then pulled her hands into the sleeves of her hoodie until only the tips of her fingers showed.

She was in the woods, home to wildlife of all kinds. Snakes. Spiders. Coyotes, bobcats, and bears. Her skin prickled, every nerve alert. She hesitated, holding her breath, and listened.

Nothing but tree frogs, at least for now.

Maybe the ants had gone underground to wait out the cold. Maybe the spiders and snakes had done the same. Relief loosened the anxiety in her gut as she turned onto her side, knees drawn to her chest, her foot throbbing but bearable if she didn't move it.

Exhaustion swept over her like a riptide. The long walk. Sarah's labor and delivery. The feeling of the baby in her arms, made heavier by the weight of responsibility. Her body had been running on borrowed power, and now the debt was due.

As her breathing slowed, her thoughts drifted to the small, fragile bundle she'd left behind.

She'd kept her promise. The baby was safe in Josh Donnelly's arms, in that quiet house with the front porch and the humongous watchdog.

Josh Donnelly would look after her, Heather had no doubt. But she couldn't help but worry. What if someone saw him with the baby? What if someone decided they knew better? What if the baby was taken away and folded into the system that might never see her as more than another assignment?

Heather rolled onto her back, ignoring the tug of pain in her foot, and looked up through the branches of the Brazilian pepper. The stars were lost, blocked by the heavy clouds. Not even the full moon could penetrate the gray curtain.

Did anyone know where she was? Brett didn't. Her parents didn't. And friends? For Brett, she'd left them all behind. Only God, if He existed, could see her.

She hadn't prayed in years. Not since her prayers had begun to feel like letters returned unopened.

Still.

Her breath formed clouds as she stared upward, and the thought of Christmas rose unbidden. Jesus had been a baby once. Just like Sarah's child, He had been helpless and small and dependent on the kindness of others.

Yet He was carried. Fed. Protected because someone chose to protect Him.

The idea settled into her heart and rested there, warm and unexpected.

"Please," she whispered. "Please bless her and keep her safe." She paused, her throat tight. "And bless Josh Donnelly," she added, "for taking care of her. For doing the right thing."

The clouds didn't move. The night didn't answer, but the tightness in her heart eased.

Her eyelids grew heavy. The pain in her foot dulled to an ache. The ground molded itself around her as she settled onto the damp earth, becoming almost comfortable. Above her head, the Brazilian pepper's leaves stirred in the breath of the wind.

Wrapped in cold air, thin hope, and the distant promise of morning, Heather submitted and let the darkness carry her away.

FORTY-FIVE MINUTES LATER, Josh solved his problem.

In the spare room, where he'd slept ever since he outgrew the wallpaper in his childhood bedroom, he knelt on the floor and reached under the bed. Dust tickled his nose as his fingers brushed something smooth and cold. He pulled out his old red backpack, the one he'd carried through his high school years. It was stiff now, the vinyl edges cracked, the zipper sticky with age. But the body was strong and the straps sound. He rubbed his thumb over the initials he'd carved into the leather flap and sat back on his heels, his heart thumping.

He tested the buckles. They no longer latched, but that didn't matter. The baby would need air.

He found scissors in the kitchen drawer, sat by the window, and cut two holes near the bottom—wide enough for a baby's legs to slip through and hold her upright. The top flap would cover the opening and hold in the warmth.

He slipped the backpack over his shoulders, testing the straps, and studied his profile in the hall mirror. The backpack wasn't the strangest accessory he'd ever seen, but it did look odd. If he walked through the Piggly Wiggly with tiny legs dangling from it, someone would notice.

He turned toward the closet and pulled out his mother's gray raincoat. The thing was oversized, shapeless, and smelled faintly of mothballs. Perfect. The weather was damp enough that no one would question the raincoat hanging from his shoulders . . . and maybe they wouldn't notice the backpack hump.

If the Lord wanted him to feed this little lamb, this ridiculous getup would have to suffice, at least for now.

Before leaving the house, he fed the baby again. She stirred as he picked her up, her face scrunching, her tiny lips searching. He heated milk in a saucepan and tested it on his wrist. Rather than use the old glove, he grabbed the turkey baster instead.

The baster was a poor choice—it didn't drip, it squirted. She coughed, sputtered, and cried, his heart aching with every sound. He murmured apologies between breaths—soft and steady, the way his mama used to soothe him after bad dreams. "It's okay, baby. I've got you. Don't you worry now."

At last she sucked from the baster, weak but willing, and her tiny hands relaxed. Relief flooded him, so sharp it made his eyes sting. He burped her, waiting for the faintest sound, and smiled when she released the ghost of a burp against his shoulder.

He found a clean diaper in the attic box, and pinned it with safety pins from Mama's sewing kit. He dressed her in a sleeper so her little legs would be covered. When the baby was bundled tight in a blanket, he tucked her into the backpack, turning her head to the side so she could breathe. Remembering that babies had wobbly heads, he rolled another cloth diaper and positioned it around her neck to keep her head upright. Then he adjusted the straps and whispered, "You're safe now, little lamb."

He would walk to the grocery store. It wasn't far, the rain had let up, and walking was preferable to trying to drive with the baby on the passenger seat. Driving without a proper car seat was against the law, and Josh was not a law breaker.

At the door, Hoss looked up from his spot on the rug, his tail thumping. "I need you to stay here," Josh said. "Guard the castle for me, okay?"

The dog let out a low huff and dropped his chin to his paws. Josh gave him a nod and stepped out into the wind.

By the time Josh reached the Piggly Wiggly, the rain had returned—a cold drizzle. The hum of the fluorescent lights filled the quiet store, and he remembered it was Christmas Eve. He was lucky the store was still open.

He grabbed a buggy and headed straight to the baby aisle.

Rows of pastel packages stretched before him—tiny socks, pacifiers, rattles. He loaded his cart with disposable diapers, baby wipes, bottles, and a canister of formula favored by nine out of ten pediatricians.

Kelly Haviland was the only cashier on duty, and she was clearly eager to get home. "Merry Christmas," she said, reaching for his buggy. "You're my last customer for the night."

Josh set his items on the conveyor belt, and Kelly's brows—dark slashes drawn too high—shot higher when she saw what was in his buggy.

"My word, Josh," she said. "Since when have you needed baby bottles, diapers, and formula?"

He heard the false note in his voice before he spoke. "I, uh. I like to be prepared."

She threw her head back and laughed. "Well, I'd say you are! Could there be a girlfriend nobody knows about?"

Josh took out his wallet. "I don't want to hold you up. I think it's about to start raining again."

Kelly bagged his purchases and pointed to the diapers. "Store brand's cheaper," she said. "Get those next time. And have yourself a merry Christmas, okay?"

Josh murmured his thanks and took his bags before she could ask any more questions.

Josh's knees trembled as he pushed through the front door. Rainwater dripped from the brim of his hood and pooled on the linoleum. He closed the door and let the stillness of the house wrap around him. Behind the patter of rain on the metal roof, he could hear the baby's whimpering cry, like the sound of a bird calling from deep in the woods.

She had started fussing two blocks from home, a fretful little cry that never grew into a wail. He thanked God for that. The rainy weather helped—no one was sipping tea or enjoying the quiet of their front porch. No one hailed him, and no one commented on the hump beneath his raincoat.

Hoss hadn't moved from his post by the front door. When Josh entered, the mastiff sprang to his feet, tail wagging.

Josh peeled off his wet raincoat and laid it over a chair. His hands trembled as he slipped out of the backpack. The baby began to cry in earnest, her small face red and scrunched, her fists jerking. Josh set her on the couch's faded cushion.

"Watch her, Hoss."

The dog's ears pricked forward. He padded over, nose twitching, and sat beside the sofa, his brown eyes wide and solemn.

Josh hurried to the kitchen, where he tore into a grocery sack, unwrapped a plastic bottle, and washed it in hot water. The powdered formula looked like ground chalk. He measured with care, shook the bottle until it turned creamy white, then tested it on the inside of his wrist.

He went back to the sofa, scooped up the baby, and pressed the bottle to her lips. Her cry stuttered, then stopped as she latched onto the nipple. Her eyelids fluttered closed, her lashes trembling like moth wings. Tiny hands waved, slow and clumsy, and her legs kicked against his arm.

Something inside Josh gave way. A tremor of awe so sharp it hurt.

God had sent him a baby—*him*, who could barely manage his own life now that his mother was gone. Yet here he was, holding life itself, warm and breathing in the crook of his arm.

He marveled at her tiny strength, at the determined rhythm of her sucking. Beneath the amazement was another feeling—gratitude that they had survived their first few hours together.

As the baby drank, he let his gaze drift toward the rain-lashed window. Where had she come from?

Hoss had alerted him to the baby's arrival. But God didn't typically produce babies out of thin air, so this little one had come from *someplace* ... but where?

He remembered news stories—young women who had given birth and disappeared, too scared or too broken to face what had happened. Chief Goodman had mentioned the new state laws that allowed young women to leave unplanned babies at police departments, fire stations, or hospitals. So why had this baby been left at his house?

A tremor of fear shot through him. What if someone other than the mother had left the baby? What if she'd been taken from her family?

He balanced the bottle under his chin and reached for the remote. The TV clicked on, filling the room with light and chatter. News anchors smiled brightly, their voices crisp and jolly as they wished their viewers a merry Christmas.

But he heard no Amber Alerts. No mentions of a missing baby. Just celebrities, a stampede overseas, and commercials for cars, cereal, and toys.

Rain lashed the windows, a steady percussion against the glass. A gust of wind moaned under the eaves. Josh shuddered. If he and Hoss hadn't stayed home tonight—if they'd gone for another long walk—the baby could still be sitting on the porch. Alone. Chilled to the bone.

He looked down at the fragile being who had already faced so much. A wave of sorrow rose in him—sorrow for her, for the world, for everything that was broken. But God saw her. And God had called him.

Create yourself a family, his mama's voice whispered.

His eyes stung. Even now, his mother was encouraging him.

The baby's lips went slack. Josh wiped the dribble from her

chin with his shirt sleeve. She sighed, deep and contented, and he smiled. "Good girl."

He laid her against his shoulder, her tiny body feather-light but solid, and patted her back until he heard the softest burp. Then, careful not to wake her, he unwrapped the blanket. Her cloth diaper was soaked through. He winced as the cool air shivered her skin.

"Sorry, sweetheart."

He fumbled with one of the new disposable diapers, trying to make sense of the sticky tabs. When he was finished, the thing looked loose and crooked, but it would have to do. She didn't seem to mind.

He wrapped her in a clean blanket and carried her to the dresser drawer. He laid her inside and draped Mama's crocheted afghan over her, leaving only her pink nose and closed eyes visible.

The clock on the wall ticked in the hush. Nearly midnight. He hadn't eaten since breakfast.

He fed Hoss first—two scoops of kibble into the bowl, the familiar clink of the scoop oddly comforting—then made himself a peanut butter and jelly sandwich. The first bite stuck to the roof of his mouth. He drank a glass of milk to wash it down, all the while watching the baby's small chest rise and fall.

He didn't know much about babies. But he knew this: you fed them, you changed them, you held them close. You kept them safe. You loved them.

Caring for a baby wasn't so different from caring for a dog. They weren't the same, of course, not at all, but when he adopted Hoss, he had signed a paper promising to feed him, train him, and keep him well. Maybe God was asking him to do the same thing on a grander scale.

Thunder rolled across the sky, long and low. The house

trembled. Josh looked toward the window, where rain streaked the glass like melted silver. The baby would need a proper bed. Tomorrow, he'd check the attic for his old crib. If it wasn't there, maybe Jackie would have one at Retro Relics.

He yawned, his body sagging with the events of the day. His gaze drifted toward the bookshelf—rows of yellowed paperbacks and old hardcovers, some so old the spines had cracked. His mother had read them all.

Maybe one of them could teach him about what came next. How to feed and raise a lamb entrusted to his care.

CHAPTER NINETEEN

Josh winced when the rising sun shot a slanting ray through his bedroom window and pierced his eyelids like a blade. His skin was clammy, his shirt twisted against his back, and for a second he didn't know where he was. He shielded his eyes, blinked hard, and tried to remember what day it was.

Then a sharp, wet cry sliced through the morning stillness. It wasn't a bird or the squeak of the ceiling fan—a new, urgent sound now ruled his world.

He rolled over, groggy and stiff, and looked across the room. The baby was in her makeshift bed, her fists flailing against the afghan, her tiny face scrunched into a wail. Hoss lay beside her in a perfect down, every muscle taut with alertness, his gaze fixed on the infant. Had he been there all night?

Josh's brain served up blurry flashes of the night before—fumbling with a bottle at three a.m., the sticky formula on his hands, the rhythmic sound of rain against the roof. Hoss had been sprawled across the floor then, snoring so deeply Josh had envied him. But the dog was wide awake now, his body trembling, as if waiting for orders.

"Let's go," Josh murmured, his voice rough. His feet met the cool wood floor, and he reached for the book he'd found last night—*Braden O'Toole's Completely Revised Baby and Child Care*—its corners dog-eared from his Mama's use. He tucked it beside the baby in her drawer.

One of Dr. O'Toole's pet phrases still echoed in his head: *continuity in caregivers*. According to the expert, babies needed the same hands, the same faces, the same constant love, day after day. Last night, Josh had fallen asleep thinking about continuity until it spun into a dream.

In his dream, he'd walked into the police station and handed the baby to the chief, who passed her to a lady from the Department of Children and Families, who handed her to an older couple, who passed her to a younger one, on and on in an endless line. With each transfer, the baby grew smaller, quieter, fading like a guttering candle. When she was no bigger than a mouse in the palm of the last woman's hand, Josh had shouted, "Isn't it just better if I take care of her?"

He shook the image away as he made his way down the stairs, the drawer balanced in his arms.

In the kitchen, he set the drawer on the table and propped a couple of hardcover books under the back edge so the baby could watch him. Her cries softened, replaced by tiny hiccups and soft, shuddering breaths. Her eyes—shiny and liquid brown—seemed to follow his every motion.

Josh smiled, his heart doing a funny little skip. "You like watchin' me, huh? Don't worry. I'm fixin' your breakfast."

Hoss padded over, his nails clicking against the floor, and set his chin on the table's edge. The baby blinked at him. Josh laughed. "He won't hurt you," he promised. "He's just wonderin' which of you will get fed first."

He poured kibble into the dog's bowl, then moved to the stove where the pan of water had begun to bubble. The hiss of the burner and the baby's gentle gurgle mingled in a rhythm that, oddly enough, sounded like home.

When Josh lifted the little girl a few minutes later, her skin was soft and impossibly warm, her tiny fingers curling around the fabric of his T-shirt. She sucked at the bottle with fierce determination, making small snuffling sounds between swallows.

Josh studied her face—the faint down at her temples, the rose tint in her cheeks—and wondered how long she'd been hungry before he found her. If she'd been outside too long, she'd have been dangerously cold, but she hadn't been. Someone had kept her warm. Someone had cared.

And Hoss had barked, drawing Josh to the door. So Hoss had either heard the baby or a noise from the person who left her behind.

"The Lord is your keeper," he whispered, brushing a fingertip across the baby's brow. "The Lord is the shade at your right hand."

Her lashes fluttered as she drank, and Josh's chest tightened until it hurt. "I think I'll call you Maggie, after my mama. Margaret sounds too grown-up, but Maggie fits you."

He looked at the dog. "What do you think, Hoss?"

The dog released a low, approving woof.

The baby sighed, milk dripping from the corner of her mouth. Outside, morning light shimmered across the wet yard, highlighting the dewdrops on the foliage, reminding Josh of the silver ornaments on his Christmas tree.

Christmas—it had come, but not in the way he expected.

Josh smiled at the tiny miracle in his arms. "Maggie it is," he murmured. "Looks like the Lord and I have our hands full."

And for the first time since his mother's passing, a living warmth rose within him—not grief, not loneliness, but hope.

WHEN THE SUN had fully risen, Josh wrapped two grilled cheese sandwiches in tin foil, the butter warm enough to leave faint gold fingerprints on the shiny surface. He slid them into a grocery bag along with an apple and a banana. As an afterthought, he added a bottle of juice. If he came across the homeless man on his walk, this time he'd have more to offer than a card. It was the least he could do at Christmas.

He hesitated only once, his gaze drifting to the dresser drawer where the baby slept. Could he really take a newborn out so soon? He'd heard women at church say they kept their newborns home for at least a month, sometimes longer, to keep them from catching other people's germs.

But he wasn't planning to be around people. The baby would stay snug inside his backpack, wrapped in Mama's softest blanket, safe beneath his raincoat.

He slid the backpack straps over his shoulders, paused, and was almost certain he could feel the gentle rise of the baby's breathing against his spine—tiny, sure, and steady.

With the food in his pockets and the baby in her backpack, Josh opened the door. The morning air met him with the crisp scent of dew, pine needles, and the sweetness of chimney smoke—the perfume of small-town Christmas. Frost glazed the grass, glittering like crushed sugar.

He and Hoss followed their usual route, the dog's steady panting in rhythm with their steps. They passed the old oak that canopied Twin Oaks Drive, then the Piggly Wiggly, where an inflatable Santa bowed in the cold breeze. A few home residents were framed in the wide windows of the Foss Nursing Home, their aged faces like soft sepia portraits. Josh waved.

By the time they reached Main Street, the sun had melted the last of the frost. The wet sidewalk shimmered, and the air seemed empty without the yeasty scents from The Bread Pit and the Old Florida Café. Outside Delectable Collectibles, famous for its liver dog treats, Hoss stopped, his tail thumping as he sniffed the air.

"I know," Josh said, smiling as he tugged the leash. "But everything will be back to normal tomorrow. Today is a holiday."

Josh turned onto Tuscawilla Road, where the quiet was broken only by the croak of tree frogs.

The homeless man wasn't in his spot. They walked farther, past the dip where rain pooled after a storm. Josh caught a flash among the weeds—something white edged in brown. He stooped and picked up his church's business card, its edges soggy and torn. He brushed it off, smoothing it between his fingers.

"Guess we might as well go wish Chief Goodman a merry Christmas," he said. "He might be expectin' us to drop by—"

Hoss lunged. The leash jerked, nearly pulling Josh off balance. "Hoss!"

The mastiff turned, bucking and bounding, until he pulled his head free of his collar. And then, without so much as a grateful glance, the dog whirled and sprinted down the road, moving toward the highway.

Josh stood—mouth open, empty leash in hand. What had happened? Hoss had never been anything but gentle, docile, and obedient. Had he caught the scent of some animal? Had he seen a chance for freedom and leapt at it?

Josh took a deep breath, well-aware of the baby, small and precious, on his back. He couldn't go racing after Hoss, not with Maggie. He couldn't jostle her in the backpack, and he couldn't spend more than an hour looking for Hoss. Maggie would have to eat soon—every two to three hours, according to Dr. O'Toole's baby book.

"Lord, I need help."

He squinted down Tuscawilla. The narrow five-mile stretch ended at Highway 90, home to the truck stop and busy traffic. Hoss wouldn't stand a chance on that highway, and that realization convinced Josh to keep walking.

"He's not a fool," Josh said, speaking as much to Maggie as to himself. "He's a smart dog, and he should know not to go near a busy highway. And he's been happy with me. So he must have had a good reason to take off like that."

Josh walked nearly two miles, then heard a muffled woof. He picked up his pace and finally spotted Hoss near a wild Brazilian pepper.

"Hoss!" He rushed toward the dog, careful not to jostle the backpack. "What's got into you?"

He slipped the collar over Hoss's neck, then the mastiff dragged Josh toward the huge plant.

"Hoss!" Josh called, ducking as Hoss crawled through the branches. With every movement, the bush's red berries rained down on him. "What'd you smell, an armadillo? You can't eat a 'dillo, buddy. Don't even—"

A jolt went through him. A body lay half-hidden in the thicket—jeans streaked with mud, a gray hoodie covering most of the torso. The shoulder-length blonde hair was matted with leaves. Whoever it was looked small, crumpled, and dead.

"Lord, help me," Josh whispered.

Hoss whimpered, then belly-crawled through the foliage and lay next to the motionless figure. He raised his head, looked at Josh, and whimpered again.

"Who do you have there, buddy?"

The body moved, a hand rising to fall on Hoss's neck.

Josh crawled forward, breathing hard and making slow progress. "Hey," he finally said, extending a cautious hand. He leaned over the stranger and saw that the face—a feminine face—had only a pale touch of color, and no wonder. They'd had freezing rain last night, and this woman's clothes were soaked through.

"Lady? This isn't the best place for a nap."

The woman's eyelids fluttered, then her eyes opened—sharp, startled, and fierce. She pulled herself up, her breath coming in gasps. "Get away from me!"

"My dog found you, and it looks like you need help." Josh raised both hands, palms out. "I was checkin' to see if you're alive."

The woman hugged herself without looking at him, her teeth chattering. "I was walking last night, and hurt my foot. But I'm fine."

"You sure? You don't look—"

"I said I'm fine." She turned away, refusing to meet his gaze.

Josh pulled back, not wanting to crowd her. "I don't mean to bother you," he said. "But you've probably got hypothermia. Can I walk you into town?"

She shook her head. "You don't need to worry. I'm tough; I'll survive."

Josh hesitated, torn between wanting to help and needing to go.

"Well . . . I got a reason to hurry home. So if you don't want help, at least take this." He pulled the foil-wrapped sandwiches, fruit, and juice from his pockets and set them beside her.

For the first time, she looked at him . . . and froze. "It's you," she said.

Heather couldn't believe her eyes.

For a moment her mind refused to assemble the pieces. But the dog beside her was real, a warm furnace against her ribs, its coarse fur damp from dew and rain. Moments earlier she had wrapped herself around that living warmth without thinking, her fingers digging in, her cheek pressed to a shoulder that smelled of grass and life. Pain made her stupid. Cold made her brave in the worst way. She'd latched on to the first thing that offered survival.

Then she looked up and realized whose dog it was.

Josh Donnelly. Of course. Who else would be attached to a dog that looked like a walking couch? Her brain tried to rewind, to explain how he could have found her when she had been so careful to slip away unseen, but pain fogged the edges of her thoughts. When she first heard his voice, low and gentle, she had assumed he was a drifter or someone collecting cans.

Josh Donnelly was the last person she expected to see.

After the shock, her next thought was not about herself. What had he done with the baby?

A spike of panic cut through the dull throb in her foot. Had he left the baby alone? Taken her somewhere? Heather blew out a breath, suddenly aware of the wet denim clinging to her legs, the chill rising from the ground, and her utter helplessness.

Then he held out sandwiches.

She blinked at them. Of course. He probably carried granola bars in his pockets and spare blankets in his car. Still, his offer startled her.

"You always walk around with food for strangers?" she asked, her voice warbling like an old woman's. She hoped he wouldn't realize how desperately hungry she was.

"Sometimes." One corner of his mouth quirked. "If I think I might meet someone who's hungry."

The words loosened the tightness in her chest. The sandwiches, which smelled of butter and cheese, were mercy dropped from the sky.

Her pride barely put up a fight.

"I'll take those." She reached for them too fast, snatching both sandwiches and the juice bottle before he could change his mind or notice how her hands shook from cold and hunger.

"Are you sure you're all right?" he asked.

She stared at the foil, already tasting butter and bread. "I'm fine."

The lie was pure reflex. She couldn't remember the last time she'd answered that question with the truth.

"Okay." He hesitated, lingering in a way that tightened her nerves. "But if you change your mind, go into Peculiar and look for the community church. I'm a member there. Folks can help you."

Was he ever going to leave?

Every second he stayed increased her anxiety. The baby tugged at her thoughts like a hooked finger. Hurry, she wanted to say. Go home. Go check on her. Don't stand here worrying about me.

"Go on," she said, waving him off. "You said you had a reason to hurry home."

He studied her another minute, then backed out of the bush and pushed himself to his feet. The dog rose with a grunt and ambled back to his side.

"You take care, then," Josh said.

He turned and walked back toward town, the dog padding beside him.

Only when he had put a few yards between them did Heather breathe again.

She peeled back a corner of the foil and took a bite.

The flavor hit her like a benediction. Real cheddar cheese, melted and stringing, butter soaking through the bread until it slicked her fingers. She groaned. Heat spread through her throat as she chewed, and for a moment the pain and cold receded under the simple goodness of food.

She devoured both sandwiches, barely pausing between bites, then twisted the top of the juice bottle and gulped it until her stomach sloshed. Relief left her weak and shaky.

Okay. Fine. Eat. Drink. Now move.

She crawled out from beneath the sprawling bush, then braced herself, her hands pressing into the damp ground. She pushed herself up and stood erect, on both feet.

Pain detonated in her injured foot. A lightning bolt raced up her leg and snatched the breath from her lungs. She gasped and dropped back to the ground, her hands scrambling, heart hammering in her rib cage.

"Heather, you are a fool," she said, her voice rasping.

Her pride had lied to her, and why? She couldn't walk. She now knew it with cold, terrifying certainty. She couldn't even crawl without sobbing, and the truck stop might as well have been on the moon.

She lifted her head and looked down the road.

Josh and the dog were already a distance away, their silhouettes shrinking.

"Hey!" she shouted, panic shredding her voice as she dragged herself closer to the pavement. "Hey! Come back!"

Her voice was too weak and too small. It wouldn't reach him. Surely this was it, the moment where she faced the consequences of making the wrong choice—

Josh didn't turn. But the dog did.

Hoss stopped, his head swinging around, then he barked, a deep, authoritative sound that rumbled through the quiet.

Josh turned at once, and relief hit Heather so hard it almost stole her breath.

She raised both arms and waved, her pain and pride forgotten, moving her arms with every ounce of her remaining strength. When Josh began to walk toward her, his steps quickening, she sobbed, the sound spilling out on a rush of gratitude and relief.

BY THE TIME they reached the old Victorian, Heather's entire body throbbed. Every step had sent a bolt of fire from her foot to her thigh, and she had to lean on Josh Donnelly for balance.

She hated needing help from someone she didn't even know. She tried to keep her weight off him, but the pain in her foot was merciless.

He pushed the front door open with his shoulder, and warm air washed over her—stale, a bit musty, but comforting after a night of frigid cold.

"Have a seat," he said, nodding toward the couch.

Heather collapsed onto it. The cushions sagged under her, worn thin from use. Everything around her—the old rug, floral curtains, a boxy TV sitting on top of an even boxier television—looked like it had come from a 1975 time capsule. She breathed in dust and another unpleasant smell.

Maybe the smell was her. She hadn't had a proper bath in . . . she'd lost track of the days.

Josh disappeared into the kitchen, and within seconds, exhaustion weighted her limbs like a heavy quilt. Her eyelids drooped. She didn't want to fall asleep—not here, not like this—but her body didn't ask permission. It simply shut down.

CHAPTER TWENTY

After Josh returned to his kitchen, he stood for a moment, his breath still uneven, trying to understand what had happened.

He had promised to defend the poor and fatherless, to do justice to the afflicted and needy . . .

Now he had a giant dog, a woman on Mama's couch, and a baby in his dresser drawer.

And what would he do with the woman? A twisted ankle, maybe worse, had left her unable to walk. She wasn't much past girlhood, really—with tangled hair, torn jeans, and a face smudged with dirt and road dust.

She smelled of sweat and exhaustion . . . but when she looked up at him, her frightened eyes had tugged at a longing deep in his chest.

Now she slept on the couch, curled up like a little girl. One more fragile thing the Lord had dropped at his doorstep.

But the baby needed him now.

He pulled off the woman's muddy shoes and covered her with a blanket.

Then he shrugged the backpack from his shoulders. The sleeping baby stirred when he pulled her out, then she squealed in offended outrage. Holding her in one arm, he warmed a bottle, fed her, changed her diaper, and tucked her back into the dresser drawer. She blinked at him once, her eyes dark and solemn, then drifted into a soft, snuffling sleep.

Josh set the drawer by the radiator and sighed as relief settled into his bones.

The house felt different now, because the presence of a woman altered the air. Not a companion animal, not a helpless baby, but an adult: stubborn, bright, maybe a little crazy.

What had she been doing on Tuscawilla Road at Christmas? Nobody lived out that way except Darlene and Nolie Caldwell, and Darlene wasn't the type to welcome strangers.

He sank into the rocking chair across from the sofa and watched the young woman. Would she sleep through the night? After about twenty minutes, she stirred. A small sound —half-groan, half-sigh—escaped her, then her eyes fluttered open, wild at first, then wary.

Josh coughed to announce his presence. "Hey. You're in my house. You fell beside the road, remember?"

She pushed herself upright and blinked around the room. Her hair was a tangle of damp strands, her cheeks streaked with dirt. "Yeah. I remember."

"I'm Josh." He raised a brow. "And you are . . . ?"

She rubbed her eyes. "Heather."

"What can I get you?" he asked. "Besides dry clothes. You'll catch your death if you stay in those wet things."

She stiffened, her shoulders hunching. "I don't need anything from you. I need—" She bit her lip.

"What?"

Her chin quivered. "Everything, I guess."

He shook his head. "You look like you need a lot more than

a sandwich. You probably want a bath and a change of clothes. If you need a safe place to stay, you're welcome to bunk here for a while."

She looked away, her cheeks flushing. "I—my boyfriend left me at the truck stop. Took off and left me with twenty bucks." She bit her lip, as though the tears embarrassed her. "I don't know what to do."

"Do you want to call your family?"

She shook her head. "No."

He studied her again. Awake, she looked older—the wariness in her eyes spoke of experience. She wasn't a child. But at the moment, she was helpless.

"How old are you?" he asked.

That earned him a sharp look. "I'm not a kid," she shot back. "I'm twenty-two."

He lifted both hands in a placating gesture. "Just wanted to be sure. You're grown. So you can decide what you need."

Some of the tension melted from her shoulders.

He rose from the rocker and softened his voice. "I was about to fix something for lunch. If you're still hungry, I'll make enough for all of us."

"Us?" She glanced around. "Who else lives here?"

Josh drew a deep breath. He still had trouble thinking of the house as his alone.

"It's me," he said, "and Hoss, who you've met. And there's Maggie, who's a baby. But she keeps me pretty busy."

Heather hesitated, her throat working as she swallowed. "Okay," she said. "Thank you."

As Josh Donnelly rattled pans in the kitchen, Heather pushed herself up and bit back a groan. Every inch of her body felt bruised. She steadied herself on the arm of the couch, then reached for the drawer in the old end table.

She wasn't trying to steal, not really. She was trying to survive.

If she could find twenty bucks—even ten—she could hitch a ride back to the truck stop, meet up with the other girls, and figure out her next step. But she couldn't stay here. And she definitely couldn't let Josh Donnelly know what she'd done the night before. She didn't know Florida law, but she was pretty sure leaving a baby on someone's porch wasn't exactly encouraged.

But at least she knew the baby was safe. Josh Donnelly had lived up to his reputation.

The end table drawer held a pack of playing cards, some old pens, and a yellowed TV Guide. She lifted couch cushions—nothing but crumbs and a penny.

She slid down and checked the opposite end table—old sewing needles, a spool of thread.

Hoss raised his head and stared at her, but didn't growl. Apparently he didn't care if she looked around.

Supporting herself on pieces of furniture, she crossed the room and checked behind the curtains—nothing.

No cash. Nothing of value. Nothing helpful.

She peered into the kitchen and realized that Josh had disappeared. Curious, she took another step and spotted a set of back stairs, a common feature in houses of a certain age. Even the fridge was ancient—rounded corners, avocado green.

She shook her head. Josh Donnelly didn't decorate, he time-traveled.

She was about to open a kitchen drawer when Hoss's tail thumped the floor in a happy wag.

She spun too fast, pain ripping up her leg, and had to grab the counter to keep from falling.

Josh stood in the kitchen doorway, shy and solemn, the baby tucked into the crook of his arm. Her cheek rested against his shirt, her tiny mouth slack with sleep.

Heather froze, her heart slamming against her ribs.

But he didn't accuse her. And he didn't glance at the open drawers.

Instead, he looked down. "Shouldn't you try to stay off your foot?"

Her face flooded with heat. Shame rolled through her with such force she swayed against the counter.

"I—I was . . . trying to find something," she stammered.

"Money?"

Heather swallowed hard. "I need to go back. I can't stay here."

"You can't walk on that foot," he said, shifting the baby to his shoulder. "And it's Christmas."

She blinked. Despite the Christmas tree in front of the window, she'd completely forgotten what day it was. Holidays meant little unless you made something out of them, and Brett had never been big on holidays.

Josh nodded toward the living room. "Go sit. Let your foot rest while I feed this little one."

"Maggie, you said?"

"Yeah. I named her after my mother." His eyes filled, and in them Heather glimpsed pain to match her own.

Grimacing with each movement, she hopped back to the couch and lowered herself to the cushions. In the kitchen, the baby stirred, let out a tiny wail, and settled in Josh Donnelly's arms. Heather tried not to stare, but she couldn't help it. Only a few hours before, she had helped bring that little girl into the world.

But Josh couldn't know that.

"Do you like babies, Heather?"

The startling question ripped the scab off a fresh wound. She struggled to smile. "Who doesn't like babies?"

"Then will you hold Maggie while I fix her bottle? She's still half-asleep, but it's time for her to eat. Dr. O'Toole says so."

Heather smothered an almost hysterical laugh. "Doctor who?"

"He wrote the book my mama used to raise me. Since it worked for her, I figure his advice will work for Maggie, too."

Before she could protest, he lowered the baby into her arms. Heather shivered with an unexpected chill.

Josh must have seen the shiver. "Are you cold? If you want a bath, I put some clean clothes for you on Mama's bed. They're probably not your style, but they're dry."

"I can wait," she said, staring at the baby's delicate face. "Until you get the bottle ready."

Josh went into the kitchen.

Heather watched the baby, who blinked and tried to suck her own fingers. "That won't work," Heather whispered. "Silly girl."

But somehow, sitting in that faded living room with the gigantic dog and the baby she'd recently wrapped in a ratty old sweater, Heather didn't feel quite so alone.

CHAPTER
TWENTY-ONE

First thing the next morning, Josh called Dr. Carl Tompkins, who had been caring for the people of Peculiar as long as Josh could remember. Doc Tompkins was one of the few family physicians in the county who still made house calls—because, according to him, seeing patients in their natural surroundings helped his diagnoses. "For instance," he often said, "I never would have known that Kenny Foster's bronchitis was caused by allergies if I hadn't seen a dozen cats in the kitchen."

Josh figured Doc Tompkins would know exactly how to help the young woman who'd slept in his mother's bed. If Heather had only sprained an ankle, she could rest up and go on her way. But if her condition was more serious, Doc would know.

Doc took a quick step back when he found himself face to face with a gigantic dog, but Josh told the dog to sit, and Hoss obeyed. Josh invited the doctor into the kitchen and poured him a cup of coffee. As Doc sipped the fragrant brew, Josh asked if he could keep a secret.

Doc lowered his mug. "You got health problems, Josh?"

"Not exactly. But the thing is, I've got a couple of . . . um, guests, and I believe the Lord sent them to me. I'm planning to take care of them until He tells me to let them go."

The older man blinked. "Sounds like you've taken hostages."

Josh laughed. "I'll be right back."

When he returned, Doc's eyes nearly fell out of his head.

"This is Maggie," Josh said. "I need you to examine her and make sure I'm doing all the right things." Josh laid the baby on the living room sofa. "I'm following Dr. O'Toole's baby book as if it were the Bible, but I worry that I might have missed somethin'."

Doc followed him into the living room. "Josh, where did this baby come from?"

"The Lord sent her," Josh said, smiling. "On Christmas Eve she showed up on my doorstep, so I brought her inside and warmed her up. I thought about calling the police, but—" He shrugged. "That wasn't the right thing to do."

Doc Tompkins's hands trembled as he weighed the baby on the kitchen scale, checked the umbilical cord, and tested her reflexes. He remained somber throughout the examination, but relaxed when the baby smiled up at Josh. Josh brought out the canned formula, and Doc nodded.

"She looks good, Josh, but she's going to need her vaccinations. Do you know anything about where or how this baby was born?"

"Do I need to? She's here, and isn't that the important thing?"

Doc sighed. "The state's gonna have something to say about you keeping an abandoned baby. There are rules about vaccinations and custody and—"

"They'd put her in foster care, right? Well, why can't I be her foster person? I'm taking good care of her."

Doc raised his bushy brows and Josh could see thought working in his eyes.

"I tell you what," Doc finally said. "I shouldn't do this, but I'm going to keep your secret because nobody is working in the state offices during the last two weeks of December. I have the vaccines she needs out in my cooler, so I'll administer those before I go."

"And then?"

"I'll risk it for now, okay? But if I hear about a missing baby, I'll have to alert the authorities. Understood?"

Josh nodded and pulled the baby onto his lap. "Got it. Thanks, Doc."

Doc Tompkins stood. "If that's all—"

"It's not. I also need you to take a look at the woman upstairs."

The doctor sat back down. "You have a woman upstairs?"

"I found her, too."

"On your doorstep?"

Josh laughed. "No, on Tuscawilla Road. But she'd spent all night in the freezing rain, and I think she sprained her ankle. I put her upstairs in Mama's room."

"My, Josh, how you do surprise me."

As they climbed the staircase, Josh told Doc about how the woman's boyfriend had abandoned her at the truck stop. "Who would do that?" he asked. "At Christmas?"

"The world is full of people, Josh. And few of them are like you."

Josh knocked, a thin voice answered, and Josh opened the door. To his credit, Doc didn't speak when he first saw the thin woman with blonde hair and a worried face. Then he turned to Josh. "How long has she been here?"

"I found her yesterday."

Doc entered the room, introduced himself, and asked the young woman—who was wearing Mama's flannel pajamas—if he could examine her foot. She scowled, but slid her leg out from beneath the blanket.

Josh leaned against the wall as Doc held her foot and probed it until she yelped. Then he lowered the foot and sighed.

"Since there's no sign of swelling," he said, "I don't think this is a sprain. There are twenty-six different bones in the foot, and I'm pretty sure she has fractured the outer metatarsal. It will take about six weeks for that damage to heal."

"Does she need a cast?" Josh asked.

Doc shook his head. "She ought to do fine as long as she doesn't put weight on it. If you have a pair of crutches, you might want to dig those out. But the best and fastest way to heal—" he turned to Heather—"is for you to stay in bed or use crutches."

Heather's eyes widened. "You mean . . . I can't leave?"

"What I mean," Doc finished, "is if you want to regain the use of your foot, you won't even try for at least six weeks."

HEATHER WASN'T THRILLED about spending the next six weeks marooned in Josh's late mama's room, but when she woke with a fever after Doc Tompkins' visit, she barely had the strength to care. The walls around her wavered, the pale paint breathing in and out as if the house had taken ill along with her.

Her throat burned. Her skin felt tight and alien, too hot one moment, goose-pimpled the next. The quilt, neatly draped over her, weighed a thousand pounds. Even lifting her hand to her face took effort.

"Josh," she croaked, though the word barely made it past her lips.

She tried again. Louder this time, or at least she thought it was. The sound scraped her throat and sent a pulse of pain skittering up the back of her skull.

The door opened and he appeared in the hallway, a tall, narrow shadow in a flannel robe, his hair rumpled, his face creased with sleep and concern. Relief washed through her, swift and humiliating.

"Somethin' wrong?"

He crossed the room in long strides and bent over her, his hand hovering near her forehead before settling there. She felt the cool touch of his palm and flinched.

"You're burning up," he said.

She tried to shake her head. Tried to tell him not to fuss, not to call anyone, not to spend money on her. The words tangled in her mouth and dissolved into small, useless sounds.

He was already gone. When he returned, he brought aspirin and a glass of water that trembled in his hand. He helped her lift her head, held the cup to her lips. The water tasted like the inside of an old can, but she gulped it down, desperate for liquid.

"I'm calling Doc Tompkins," Josh said.

"No," she croaked, not sure if she was refusing the doctor or the kindness. But it didn't matter, he was already halfway out the door.

The doctor came again the next morning, his voice floating toward her through layers of heat and exhaustion. He took her temperature, peered down her throat, pressed cool fingers to her neck.

"A virus," Doc Tompkins said, his voice flat. "Antibiotics won't help."

Heather lay flat on her back, staring at wallpaper roses that seemed to unfurl before her eyes.

"The best thing you can do is keep her hydrated," the doctor continued. "Soup, fluids. And keep the baby out of this room. Wash your hands before picking her up."

"How'd she get it?" Josh asked. "From being cold and wet?"

"Being cold and wet can lower resistance," the doctor said. "But a bug that wouldn't bother you or me could be dangerous for a newborn—or someone as run-down as this young lady. So keep her comfortable and call me if you need me."

After that, Heather drifted in and out of awareness as they talked, their words pressing against her ears without quite settling into meaning. Virus. Baby. Contagious. The words slid off her like rain on glass.

Night came again, thick and suffocating. When her fever spiked, the world slipped its moorings.

She opened her eyes and found herself in a darkness deeper than any she had ever known. Not the comfortable dark of closed curtains or a moonless night, but utter blackness, as if every trace of light had been erased. Panic seized her lungs. She reached out and brushed fabric, soft and unfamiliar, not the crinkling plastic of the van mattress. That detail shocked her, grounding her for a brief second.

Then a thin, piercing cry split the silence and went straight through her, sharp as a needle. Her body reacted before her mind could form a coherent thought. Her arms prickled. An ache bloomed in her chest, a memory her body refused to forget.

A baby was crying. Her baby. Or maybe Sarah's.

She pressed her hands over her ears, her palms slick with sweat, but the noise grew louder, rising and falling, relentless.

The cry wasn't sound, it was accusation. It was everything she had lost and every guilt she carried.

"Please hush," she whimpered, though she didn't know who she was begging. God. Josh. The dark.

The room blurred. The cry dissolved into sobbing that sounded suspiciously like her own.

She opened her eyes and saw her mother, drunk, passed out on the couch. The woman who could not handle divorce, who refused to move forward. The woman who did not want any more trouble in her life, especially if it came from her daughter.

Heather slipped under again.

This time she was back in the trailer, the air thick and close, smelling of dust and sweat and gasoline. A single cheap candle burned on the floor, its flame guttering, throwing warped shadows against the walls. Heather sat cross-legged with the other girls, their faces pale in the flickering light.

Behind her, Sarah cried out.

Heather could hear her breathing, harsh and labored, could see the rise and fall of that rounded belly if she turned her head. She didn't want to. Looking meant remembering the baby. Looking meant the tearing-away that always followed.

"Push," one of the girls said, her voice too cheerful and bright. "You're almost there."

The girls laughed, encouraging, as if this event was beautiful and uncomplicated. As if love didn't always arrive stitched to loss.

What fools, Heather thought, and her bitterness surprised her with its force.

Then she heard the cry again. Sharper now. Closer.

She raised her head, her heart hammering, and the trailer dissolved into dark water and heat and pain. Tears leaked from the corners of her eyes and soaked into a pillow. She turned onto her side, her foot throbbing, and pulled the quilt over her head.

Somewhere in the house, a real baby cried. Or maybe it existed only in her heart.

Either way, the sound found her.

And this time, she didn't resist. She wept into the darkness, quiet and exhausted, mourning the babies she could not hold and the girl she had once been, finding that sleep was no refuge at all.

CHAPTER
TWENTY-TWO

Heather woke in a body that finally felt like her own. The fever had broken sometime in the night, leaving her wrung out and sore, her lungs thick with congestion that rattled when she took a deep breath. She rolled onto her side and coughed, a deep, tearing sound that made her foot ache.

But the heat was gone. No roaring in her ears. No hallucinations haunting her dreams.

She focused on the ceiling of Josh's mama's room, at the water stain shaped like Florida, and tried to gather her thoughts. She could think again . . . and she couldn't pretend anymore.

She sat up, inhaling the scent of something delicious drifting up from the kitchen. When the door opened and Josh stepped in with a bowl and spoon, she studied him through narrowed eyes.

He set the soup on the bedside table and turned toward her, his expression cautious, as if she were a skittish animal that might bolt.

"My fever's gone," she said before he could speak.

"Looks like it," he said, sliding his hands into his pockets. "You're breathing fire instead of radiating it."

She almost smiled. Almost. Then the moment passed and left her hollow again.

"I need to leave," she said.

The words sounded steadier than she felt. Her throat tightened, but she kept going before he could interrupt. "Not today. I know I can't. But soon, 'cause I've already been here too long."

He didn't move, just stood with his shoulders squared and his face calm. "Six days isn't so long."

"You shouldn't want me here," she added, because if she didn't say it, the thought might rot inside her.

"Why?"

She laughed, disbelieving. "Because no man in his right mind would."

"Why not?"

She clenched her fists in the sheets. How could he not know? How could anyone not know?

"Because I'm not worth it."

His spine went rigid, as if she'd struck him in the heart. For a minute he didn't speak and the silence grew heavy.

Then he said it: "You *are* worth it. Because God loves you and I care about you."

She flinched as heat flooded her face. For a terrible second, she thought she might shatter and prove him wrong in the ugliest way possible.

How dare he say such a thing. How dare he mean it.

"Don't," she snapped, her voice cracking. A string of cursing followed, loud and ugly, fueled by exhaustion and panic. She kept going until her chest burned and she had no more breath to shout with. She sat up, threw off the covers, and slid halfway off the bed, determined to leave.

But he was there.

He lifted her like she weighed nothing, as if she mattered. Panic surged and she slapped at his head and shoulders, the sound sharp and humiliating. "Put me down!"

He didn't.

He put her back in the bed and pulled the quilt over her, then set a box of tissues on the nightstand.

"There's a clean gown on the dresser." His voice was controlled, but she could hear strain beneath it. "I put crutches under the bed if you want to move around. You can take a bath whenever you like. You'll feel better once you're cleaned up."

She blew her runny nose and glared as he turned to go. "I was fine until I hurt my foot. And I didn't ask you to care about me."

"You didn't have to ask."

He took a step, then paused. "Since you're in no condition to walk out of here," he said, looking at her over his shoulder, "I guess you're stuck with me." He smiled. "I'm sorry if that's bad news, but my mama always said life is what you make it—once you decide to leave the pity party."

She scowled. "Not a great sales pitch, dude."

"I don't care." He smiled again, quick and stubborn. "'Cause I'm not sellin' anything. But the Lord led me to you, so I guess we'll be together a while."

He closed the door and left.

Heather listened to the quiet he left behind and looked at the soup cooling on the nightstand. Her chest ached for a reason that had nothing to do with congestion, and a thought crept in, unwanted and terrifying:

What if he was right?

With her fever gone, the quiet became unbearable.

Heather lay with her face to the wall, listening to the house breathe. The congestion still sat heavy in her lungs, and each breath whistled.

She heard Josh before she saw him. The soft tread on the stairs. The faint clink of china. The aroma reached her next, fragrant and impossible to ignore. Butter. Sugar. Real food. Her hands fisted in the pillowcase, bracing for impact.

He set the tray on the nightstand. "Seems to me," he said, "that if you wanted to, you could use this time to think about what you want to do with your life."

She kept her back to him. The wall felt safer than his eyes.

"You don't have to go back to wherever you came from," he went on. "I know—and I think you would agree—that you weren't in a good place."

A hot, defensive laugh burst out of her before she could stop it. She rolled enough to lift her head. "Oh, yeah? How could you possibly know anything about me?"

"I don't know much more than your name," he said. "But I'd like to learn."

That was the entire problem. Once he knew . . .

He sat in the wing chair near the door. She didn't look at him, but the room shifted when he settled in, attentive and patient in a way that made her antsy.

"You could start," he said, "by telling me where you came from."

The silence stretched. She counted the seconds, looked at the faint crack in the baseboard, and waited for him to give up and leave. He didn't.

Finally, she pushed herself upright. "Georgia," she said. "I'm from Georgia."

That much was safe.

"I was raised in what you'd probably call a nice Christian home," she continued, her voice flattening. "Church every Sunday. Bible verses in picture frames. But then my parents divorced and all that fell apart." She snorted. "Later, I dated a real nice boy. Everybody thought so."

"But he wasn't as nice as they thought."

She kept her gaze fixed on the dresser across the room. If she looked at Josh, she might see pity, and she wouldn't survive that. "When I got into trouble," she went on, "long after he dumped me, they took me to a clinic. And like that—" she snapped her fingers "—the problem was gone."

She didn't say *baby*. Didn't say she'd been screaming on the inside.

Josh groaned. "I'm sorry that happened to you," he said. "Truly. But God forgives—"

The words detonated.

"Like it was my fault?" Anger surged up, bright and sharp, a shield she knew how to wield. She turned so he could see her face. "They told me to say no, and I did. That's what kills me. I followed all the good girl rules. And I still ended up in that clinic."

She clasped her hands to hide the trembling.

"So when I met Brett and he asked me to go on the road with him, I said yes. Didn't have anything better to do." Her voice broke. "Going with him was the first thing I'd ever done that was truly my choice."

"Brett?"

"You probably saw him," she said. "Yellow camper van. We were basically an exhibit in your city park because we couldn't afford gas."

Understanding flickered across his face. "The guy with the guitar."

"Yeah." The word scraped her sore throat. "The guy who drove off and left me because I told him I was pregnant." Her chest burned. "And I was, when I told him. But then I wasn't." She laughed, brittle and sharp. "So he left for no reason. And I can't even tell him because he's gone."

She spread her hands. "So now my life's a wreck, and I'm stuck here—" She caught herself. Guilt rushed in, fast and unwelcome. She looked away, her cheeks heating.

"I know it's not your fault," she said. "And you've been decent. That's why—" She swallowed. "You shouldn't have to be stuck with me."

Josh didn't answer. She could see him thinking, weighing her words like they mattered.

Finally he spoke. "I'm glad you're here," he said. "And you can stay until you get better. No strings."

She flexed her jaw. She didn't trust that phrase. Strings always showed up later.

Josh went on, his tone hesitant. "I was thinking . . . I could use some help around here. I wondered if maybe the Lord had—"

"The Lord?" She barked a laugh. "No offense, but I'm not gonna be your maid."

"I don't need a maid."

She shot him a warning look. "I'm not gonna be your love slave, either. No matter how much you care."

"I *do* care," he said. "And I'm not gonna *make* you do anything. I thought maybe you'd like to earn some spending money. I carve nicknacks and toys for a living. You could paint them. Even here in this room."

She scoffed. "I don't paint. And what good is money if I can't get out of this house?" Her voice cracked again. "What I need is a way to contact Brett. I need to tell him there's no baby—"

"Maybe," Josh interrupted, "you've been needing the wrong things."

His words hung there, striking deeper than she expected.

She stared at her hands, and when she spoke again, her voice betrayed her. "You know . . . you might be right." She sniffed. "But once I can walk, I'm going to find him."

"God gave us free will," Josh said. "You can do anything you want."

She released an incredulous laugh. "That's a new one. The God I grew up with had a list of *don'ts*."

Josh didn't smile. "If you decide to stay awhile," he said, "I'll give you room, board, and a job. I've got plenty of paintbrushes."

Her gaze drifted to the tray on the nightstand. The French toast was golden. The eggs fluffy. A small glass pitcher glimmered in the light. "Is that maple syrup?"

"And real butter," he said. "Mama never liked the fake stuff."

The tightness in her shoulders loosened a fraction. The corner of her mouth twitched.

She didn't look at him when he stood to leave. Didn't say thank you. She waited until the door closed.

Then she reached for the fork.

CHAPTER
TWENTY-THREE

The next morning, Josh nearly lost the power of speech when he found Heather sitting on a freshly made bed. Her hair was clean, she wore her own clothes, and her face looked rounder than before. She looked downright pretty.

"Well." He set her tray on the nightstand. "You must be feeling better."

"Yep—and thanks for washing my clothes." She eyed the plate of bacon and eggs on the tray. "That for me?"

"Yeah, but if you want something else, I can get it."

"I don't care what it is, as long as it's not stale crackers." She snatched up a slice of bacon, then closed her eyes and sighed. "I never thought I'd be so happy to get a piece of bacon, but this tastes so good—"

"If you can say that about burnt bacon, you must be starving."

He turned to go, but hesitated in the doorway. "You look a lot better, you know."

She took another bite of bacon. "If that's your idea of a compliment, you should back up and try again."

He gave her an uncertain smile. "If you need other clothes, I can get some from the thrift store." He released an awkward laugh. "You're smaller than Mama, or you could wear hers."

She snorted. "Who cares what I look like? It's not like I'm going anywhere, at least not for five more weeks."

"Five weeks?"

"My foot should be healed by then, right? I can almost walk on it now. Sometimes I forget and take a step. It's still tender, but—"

"Don't push it," Josh said. "You might hurt it again."

"You're right, I don't want that. No sense in staying here any longer than I have to."

Josh wiped his hands on his jeans, realizing that he was now dealing with a different woman. "Now that you're feeling better, I was hoping you might be able to—"

"You want me to paint your stuff, right?"

"Just a minute," he said. "I'll be back."

AFTER FINISHING HER BREAKFAST, Heather watched the lace curtains breathe in and out with the howling of the wind. The old house creaked, settled. Somewhere, pipes grumbled in the walls. She sat absolutely still, every muscle poised.

If he came back with mending . . . or if he came back with a broom, a list, or a smile that said *you're well enough to be useful now*, she'd swing her legs out the window, drop to the ground, and limp her way back to the truck stop, pain or no pain.

But when Josh finally returned, it wasn't with thread or a list of chores. It was with the baby.

A soft, blue bundle squirmed in his arms, tiny fists

punching the air as if she were shadowboxing with the world. One hand caught Josh's stubbled chin. The other snagged his collar. Maggie's face was flushed and serious, her mouth making smacky little sounds.

Josh didn't look like a man performing a task. He looked besotted.

The softness on his face made Heather's heart hurt. The man was clearly in the grip of a goofy, helpless sort of love. The kind men didn't show unless they stopped checking themselves.

She had a feeling Josh Donnelly had never checked his reactions.

"Well," Heather said, because the silence was too loud, "let me guess. You want me to change a diaper."

Josh chuckled and sank into the wing chair, shifting Maggie so she faced Heather, her dark eyes alert and curious.

"You've already met Maggie," he said. "And if I'm going to make it to the grocery today, I need somebody to watch her. The Wiggly closes early on Sunday."

Heather stiffened.

"I'd rather not use my backpack," he went on, apologetic. "Which was never a great idea anyway. Hoss is good at watchin' her, but he can't exactly intervene if she starts to choke or somethin'."

The words hit her one after another, bouncing inside her skull. *Grocery. Watch her. Choking.*

Heather stared. "You want me to babysit."

Josh grinned. Full-on, open, and proud. "Isn't she the sweetest thing? I've been trying to keep her quiet so she wouldn't wake you, but she hardly ever cries. She's a good baby."

Heather blinked hard. He had heard her story. He sat there while she spoke the truth out loud.

Maybe he hadn't really listened. Maybe men never did.

"I'm not good with little ones," she said.

His smile faded. "What do you mean?"

"I mean," she said, her voice sharper than she intended, "I'll paint your carvings or scrub your floor or whatever, but I don't want to be your babysitter." She tilted her head, daring him. "Do I really have to spell it out?"

He shifted Maggie from one arm to the other, her cheek smearing drool across his sweater. "Maybe you should."

Her throat closed. "I've lost two babies," she said. The word *lost* felt too small. "Two."

She didn't mention the one she'd left on his porch. The drooly one with her head parked under Josh's chin.

Josh exhaled as if he were stepping back from a land mine. "Okay," he said. "I get it."

Heather sighed in relief. And guilt.

"But," he added, "I really do need to get to the grocery store. Tonight is New Year's Eve."

She huffed. "You got a big date or something?"

"It's a special time." He looked at Maggie, then back at Heather. "What if I put her down for her nap, and you listen in case she cries? She should sleep at least two hours. I won't be long. I promise."

Heather marveled at the earnestness in his face. The way he acted as if she was part of this small, strange household.

Her resistance softened. "Okay," she said. "But don't be long."

"I'll feed and change her before I go." He stood, turning toward the door.

"You really think of her as yours, don't you?" The question escaped before Heather could stop it.

Josh smiled at Maggie with an affection that hurt her heart. "Of course. The Lord knew I was lonely, so He sent Maggie."

Maggie responded by enthusiastically smearing drool on Josh's stubble.

Heather stared, stunned, as he headed down the stairs to heat the bottle.

He planned to keep her... as long as he could. The realization landed like a boulder settling into place.

She lay back on the bed and studied the ceiling. She had brought Sarah's baby to this house because Josh Donnelly was kind. Because he was steady. Because in the cold rain of that truck stop, she needed an answer and he had looked like one.

She hadn't thought past the handoff. Hadn't imagined mornings and bottles and grocery lists. Hadn't pictured a man accepting a baby and committing to it.

Josh Donnelly might be crazy. But as the house filled with the quiet sounds of his humming as he prepared the bottle, Heather realized something else—

For the first time since leaving Maggie on his porch, the thought of caring for a baby didn't feel like an absolute impossibility.

CHAPTER
TWENTY-FOUR

Heather swam up from sleep the way she had learned to over the years—carefully, and with suspicion.

Someone was saying her name.

"Heather," Josh whispered, his hand light but firm on her shoulder. "Hey. Wake up."

She groaned and rolled toward the wall, dragging the quilt with her. Her body still ached in dull, lingering ways that made no sense. "It's dark," she muttered.

"I know," he said. "But you need to come downstairs."

She opened one eye. The digital clock glowed—11:33 p.m.

"Absolutely not," she said. "I am horizontal for medical reasons."

He chuckled, then sobered. "I wouldn't ask if it wasn't important."

She sighed and pushed herself upright, gritting her teeth as the room came into focus. He was already reaching for her elbow, steady and patient, as if he knew exactly when to help and when not to.

"This feels like a trap," she said.

"It's more of a surprise," he said, smiling.

With his arm solid around her waist, he helped her down the stairs, one step at a time. The lighting was dim and cozy. The muted thump of music drifted from the living room, familiar in an end-of-year way.

When they reached the couch, he eased her onto the cushions.

"Okay," she said, lifting a brow. "What sort of weirdness is this?"

Instead of answering, he turned on a lamp.

Heather blinked.

On the television, Dick Clark's smiling face shared space with Mariah Carey and Ryan Seacrest as the familiar chaos of New Year's Rockin' Eve hummed in the background.

Near the TV, Maggie sat propped in an old-fashioned baby seat, yellowed vinyl cracked with age but scrubbed clean. Josh had tucked a blanket around her like a nest. Her eyes were wide and solemn, as if she understood this moment mattered. A tiny paper hat had been taped to her soft hair.

Beside her, on the rug, sat Hoss. Also wearing a cone-shaped hat.

Heather stared. "Oh no." She groaned. "I'm having a nightmare."

Josh beamed. "Found it in the attic. The baby seat, not the hats. Also a stroller. I figured once your foot is better, we can start taking walks."

We?

He put a paper hat on Heather's head before she could protest, then crowned himself. Hoss's hat slid over one ear, but he didn't seem to mind.

Against the wall, a TV tray had been filled with a feast. Steam curled from a bowl of crab dip. Cheeses gleamed under plastic wrap. Crackers lined the circle of a plate. Two stemmed glasses bubbled with gold liquid.

Heather's stomach growled.

"That looks—" she hesitated "—pretty good."

Josh brought the TV tray to the couch, then sat next to Heather.

She reached for a cracker, but Josh caught her wrist. "Wait."

She sighed.

"Every year, Mama and I did this." He drew a deep breath. "We'd talk about the darkest day of the year, then the brightest. Then we'd ask the Lord to make the new year everything He wants it to be."

Heather snorted. "You didn't ask for, I don't know... fewer dark days?"

He gave her a soft smile. "Why? That's when the light shines brightest."

His words landed in the room, quiet and steady. He nodded. "You go first."

She shook her head. "Nope."

Josh plunged ahead. "The darkest day for me," he said, his eyes filling, "was the day Mama died. Especially after I thought she was getting better."

Heather studied his hands. Still. Controlled.

"But the brightest moment," Josh continued, "was when I realized she's in the crowd of witnesses that watches what the Lord does down here. I want to make her proud. I want to do what she always said and fill this house..." His voice caught—"with life."

Heather's nerves tensed.

"Your turn," Josh said.

She smiled. "Maybe Hoss should go next."

Josh chuckled, but turned to the dog. "Hoss's darkest

moment was when the man who promised to love him left him at a shelter. And I'm pretty sure his brightest moment was when he saw me comin'."

Hoss thumped his tail.

"And we'll stay together," Josh added. "I'm not one to quit."

Then he looked at Heather, and she saw no place to hide. She blew out a breath. "I had a dark moment," she said, her voice thin, "when I realized I wasn't having a baby." She paused, her breath catching. "But the darkest was realizing that Brett had driven away without me."

Silence filled the living room, muting even Dick Clark and his party. Heather wiped her cheeks, angry at herself, and lifted her glass. "The brightest moment? Maybe that's now, because things can't get any darker. So my brightest moment has to be coming in the new year."

She drank, the bubbles tickling her nose, then erupted in a coughing fit. "That wasn't what I expected."

Josh sighed. "It isn't champagne."

"Sparkling cider?"

He nodded. "To 2007," he said, lifting his glass as well. "May the Lord bless us and keep us. May He make His face shine upon us—"

"And give us peace," Heather finished, pulling the words from some place deep in her bones.

In New York City, the ball fell and the crowd roared.

On Church Street in Peculiar, Heather held her glass and greeted the new year with a confidence she never expected.

Josh had only to look at his pantry to realize he needed to get back to work after the holidays. He and his mama had lived on her Social Security check and the small income he brought in from hand-carved crafts, but now he'd have to feed himself. He was willing to work harder and undertake bigger projects, but he had added responsibilities—a dog, a baby, and a guest. All three of them had hearty appetites.

Over the holidays, Jackie Leakey had left three messages on the answering machine—she wanted more carved blocks, but Josh hadn't had time to look for suitable wood. He needed to take a long walk around his property. If that didn't turn up anything, he would have to visit the dump or walk through town on trash collection day. In the past, he'd found an antique oak dresser, a three-foot log, and a princess headboard. All three were stored in the backyard shed, and once he figured out what they wanted to be, he'd make something of them.

Now though, he itched to carve toys for babies—something that wouldn't hurt their tender gums if they put it in their mouths. He'd have to find a wood that could stand repeated washing in hot water, like oak or mahogany. Maybe he could make a set of wooden keys on a ring—when she was older, Maggie would enjoy hearing them clack together. Or he could carve animals and put them on a rope: a dog, kitten, bird, and spider. Maybe a squirrel instead of a spider.

He smiled as another idea took hold—maybe he could carve a Noah's ark for the little girl. A hollowed-out log with a fitted lid, something he could fill with assorted pairs of animals. The project would take hours and he'd have to find the right kinds of wood, but what kid wouldn't love a toy like that? It would be the perfect gift for her first birthday.

But maybe he was getting ahead of himself. He shelved those thoughts and considered his pantry. On the first day of the new year, he was down to one can of soup, one loaf of bread in the freezer, and two cans of formula. The peanut butter jar held enough for one more sandwich, and the bologna had disappeared. Like it or not, he would have to return to the Wiggly.

Josh told Heather he had to go out, hoping she would offer to watch Maggie. When she didn't, he put Maggie in the stroller, told Hoss to guard the house, and set out. Maggie chewed her fist as the wind picked up and the stroller rolled through a cloud of leaves. Josh kept his head down, hoping no one would notice him.

Unfortunately, the grocery sat directly across from Twin Oaks. He did not want to face a dozen questions from the daily walkers, so he checked the covered driveway to make sure they weren't assembling.

He also looked for a patrol car. The deputy, Tony Kirkpatrick, patrolled Main Street every morning, and Tony liked to talk. If he spotted Josh with a baby stroller, he'd be drawn to investigate as surely as if Josh had been walking with a gorilla. Tony would not only press for details, he would spread the story until the entire town knew about Maggie, and that wouldn't be good.

Josh slumped in relief when he arrived at the grocery without having to face a blizzard of questions. When he realized he couldn't manage a stroller *and* a grocery cart, he reluctantly sat the baby in the cart. Since Maggie couldn't yet hold herself upright, Josh went to baked goods, picked up several bread loaves, and used them to support Maggie.

He wheeled through the canned goods aisle, tossing in baked beans, green beans, corn, and any soup that sounded nutritious. In the baby aisle, he picked up diapers, baby wipes, lotion, butt paste—his mama would have fainted at that name—and containers of formula. On a whim, he grabbed a few jars of baby applesauce and green beans. He wasn't sure when

Maggie would be able to eat mushy foods, but he'd consult Dr. O'Toole's book.

In the frozen food department, he selected a package of hamburger, some pizzas, and a couple of family-size Salisbury steak dinners. Remembering Heather's thin arms and legs, he added four boxes of butter-whipped mashed potatoes and three pumpkin pies. Along with whipped cream.

He zipped through the other aisles, chucking paper towels, toilet paper, deodorant, shampoo, toothpaste, and other personal items into the cart, then hurried to the check-out. He was taking out his credit card when Kelly Haviland asked the question he'd been dreading: "Josh Donnelly, where'd you get that baby? Is it yours?"

He blinked. "Um . . . who else would it belong to?"

"Well, I don't know! He's a cutie pie."

Josh looked at Maggie, clothed in faded blue baseball pajamas. "Um, thanks."

He paid for his groceries and hurried home.

CHAPTER
TWENTY-FIVE

On New Year's night, I stopped at the Wiggly for milk and ice cream—because a police chief cannot properly celebrate the arrival of a new year without both. I'd barely opened the freezer door when Kelly Haviland came running over to ask about Joshua Donnelly and the baby he'd been parading through the bread aisle like a civic announcement.

She didn't even bother with hello.

"Where do you think the baby came from, Chief Bowen?"

I paused with the freezer door open, cold air rolling over my boots, and wondered if she expected a full investigation. "This is the first I've heard of it, Kelly."

"Well, I thought you'd know," she said. "You always know."

That was mostly true. But this story had slipped past me like a cat burglar in socks. "How old was this baby?"

"He was wee little, Chief. Couldn't even sit up. Josh had him stuffed like a sack of flour between two loaves of bread."

That image lodged in my brain and refused to leave. "So not old."

Kelly shrugged. "I'm no expert, but I'd guess no older than a month."

I grabbed my ice cream and headed for the milk, my mind already starting to walk the perimeter of the situation.

Had some woman handed Josh Donnelly a baby and disappeared into the night? Had Josh—bless him—accepted the responsibility without knowing the full story? None of it fit the young man I knew, and all of it worried me.

I paid Kelly, told her to keep her ears open, and stepped out into the night with milk, ice cream, and a growing sense that something in Peculiar had shifted just enough to deserve my attention.

And Josh Donnelly, wherever he was, had some explaining to do.

Josh had come to a quiet, reverent conclusion: heat-and-serve Salisbury steak was the best-smelling meal on earth.

A few minutes after he pulled the paper tray from the oven, Heather appeared at the top of the stairs, moving cautiously, favoring her injured foot. She wore one of Mama's old housecoats, faded to a pale pink, the fabric soft from decades of washing. It hung on her, swallowing her thin frame, but the sight made Josh's eyes sting. Seeing someone else in his mama's clothes was unsettling. And oddly right.

Heather's lips were pressed together, but they curved upward when she inhaled the aroma coming from the kitchen. "What smells so good?"

She entered, one careful step at a time, her freshly shampooed hair loose around her shoulders. The kitchen light caught it, softening its darker strands, and for a moment Josh thought she looked like someone who belonged in his house.

"I woke up and thought I'd died and gone to heaven," she said. "As if I ever would."

"That could be arranged," Josh said, though the word *heaven* sat heavier in his thoughts than he let on. He gestured to the table. "Rest your foot."

She sank into a chair with a soft exhale, and Josh turned back to the stove. He speared a steak in the steaming tray and laid it on a plate, spooned buttery mashed potatoes beside it, and drowned the whole dish in gravy. The scent rose warm and comforting, reminding him of evenings when Mama had been too tired to cook but still wanted to make things special.

Heather leaned forward and inhaled. "I can't believe you're not feeding me more soup and another sandwich."

"To everything, there is a season."

That earned him a snort. She didn't say anything else while he fixed his own plate and sat across from her, but her hands trembled when they curled around her fork, which meant she was weaker than she wanted to admit.

"I'm glad you felt strong enough to come downstairs," he said, then, out of habit, he bowed his head. "For what we are about to receive, may the Lord make us truly grateful. Amen."

When he looked up, Heather's fork hovered halfway between her plate and mouth. "You think God hears your prayers?"

"I know He does."

She shook her head, dipping her fork into the gravy. "I can see why you'd think that. I mean, what horrible thing has ever happened to you?" Her gaze slid around the room. "Look at this place—the perfect little kitchen. The perfect little house. I'll bet your folks were perfect parents."

Josh cut into his steak, the knife heavy in his hand. "I don't know any perfect people."

"In a town like this?" She scoffed. "Ha! I'll bet your daddy took you to church every Sunday and taught you to play baseball and football and—"

"My father left us," Josh said. "I don't remember much about him."

Heather chewed in silence, then lowered her head. "Sorry. Sometimes I talk too much."

"It's fine. Mama and I were okay on our own."

"You didn't miss having a dad?"

Josh considered the question. Could you ache for someone you never really knew? "I had Mama. I had good neighbors. And I had Jesus."

"Sure you did," she said, not unkindly. "I know you were a mama's boy. I can see it in the way you keep her room."

"I loved her," he said. "And she hasn't been gone that long. One of these days I'll clean out her room, but not yet."

Heather glanced at the stove. "Is there more? I'm starving."

"I'll get it."

"No, let me. I'm trying to do things for myself."

She stood and hobbled over, leaning on the counter as she refilled her plate. "My foot's better," she said. "Now it only hurts if I try to walk normally. Soon I'll be walking good enough to get out of your hair."

Josh stopped eating. "Are you in a hurry to leave?"

She turned, her mouth spreading into a thin, determined smile. "Course I am. You've been crazy nice, but Brett left because of a misunderstanding. I need to find him and straighten things out."

Josh struggled to keep the incredulity out of his voice. "Find him how?"

She dropped back into her chair. "He was heading to Nashville. I could call some towns between here and there, ask around. Or find his parents to see if they've heard from him."

The food on Josh's plate lost its appeal. He set his fork down. "Sounds like a long shot. But if that's what you want—"

"Of course it is." Her eyes locked on his. "I wasn't myself when I got here. I don't remember what I said."

"Okay."

"Brett and I have been together almost three years. He needs me, and—" She shrugged, like the rest should be obvious.

"You love him."

"Of course." She hesitated. "Besides, you don't really want me around."

Josh leaned back and folded his arms. "How do you know what I want? I told you I could use your help. You don't have to go back to that life if you don't want to."

They stared at each other across a sudden ringing silence. "Yeah, I remember," she finally said. "I didn't think you meant it."

"I did."

"You gonna pay me? I got expenses."

"For what?" He laughed, then caught himself, hand over his mouth. This wasn't funny.

He lowered his voice. "I'm not rich, but I can make sure you have clothes, food, a roof while you sort things out. What else do you need?"

"Freedom," she said. "Brett and I went on the road because we didn't want to get stuck."

"You wouldn't be stuck. You could leave anytime."

"Even now?"

"You're not ready," he said. "You're not strong enough."

Her lips tightened. "Look, I'm grateful for what you've done. And for what you did for that baby. But I'm not your girlfriend."

Josh raised his hands and leaned back. "I never said I wanted that. I wouldn't take advantage of you."

Her brow rose. "You want me to paint."

"Yeah." He sighed. "And watch the baby sometimes. I can't get much work done otherwise."

She studied him a long moment. "If I stay, it's only until I find Brett. After that, you'll be on your own."

"Understood."

"And I want a lock on my door."

"Fine."

"And I want fifty dollars a week. Cash."

He smiled. "Okay. But I have conditions, too."

She folded her arms. "Let's hear 'em."

"I need you to be responsible with Maggie. I've heard about people who put babies in a corner and ignore them."

"If you don't trust me—"

"I want you to stay," he said. "But I need to know you'll be good for Maggie."

She drew a sharp breath, then abruptly nodded. "Okay, I'll help you while I'm here. But only if you serve this steak at least once a week."

"Only once?"

"Twice," she amended. "And pizza sometimes."

Josh smiled, relief loosening his shoulders.

She glanced toward the stove. "Your dog would love this gravy. I had a dog once, a shelter mutt. Best friend I ever had."

"What happened to him?"

She shrugged. "Life."

"There's more." Josh gestured to the stove. "And pumpkin pie in the fridge. With whipped cream."

Heather squealed, pushed herself up, and thumped across the floor.

Josh watched her go, his heart unsteady. Apparently she still loved the selfish guy who had abandoned her.

What would she do when the blinders fell off?

By late January, Heather was hobbling downstairs to watch Josh with the baby—anything was better than staring at the wallpaper in that pink bedroom. Every morning she put on clothes from the closet and dresser. The elastic-waist pants were far too short and hung on her narrow hips, but at least they were comfortable. The polyester shirts looked like floral tents, but she didn't care—and apparently Josh didn't care what she looked like. He spent more time watching Maggie than her, and when he did glance her way, his eyes held only an odd mix of curiosity and concern.

He never looked at her the way Brett had . . . like nearly all the men she met before she found herself in Peculiar.

And she couldn't help watching the baby, too. After all, her face was the first Maggie saw when she entered the world.

One afternoon Josh led Heather to the kitchen table, where he had set out paint brushes and a box of paint tubes. "I need to make some farm animals," he said. "If you really want to help, you could paint some of them for me."

She scoffed. "I told you, I'm not an artist."

"It's easy. I'll show you how to mix the colors."

He held up a painted wooden chicken the size of his hand, and though she was impressed, she tried not to be. The detailed chicken looked like a rainbow had exploded on its back. The beak was orange, the breast red and gold, the wing feathers black and red, and the tail feathers a glorious mix of gold, iridescent turquoise, and black. But the head! Josh had carved a crown of curving feathers and painted them in a brilliant mix of colors—gold, red, orange, black, blue, and white.

Next to the rainbow chicken stood an almost identical carving, unpainted.

Josh set a dinner plate on the table and grabbed a tube of yellow and another of red. "These are acrylics," he said, sitting next to her, "and they mix easily, but you have to be quick because they dry fast. Just squirt a few dabs of paint onto the plate and mix 'em until you get the shade you want. Then paint, but be sure to keep your brush wet so it won't dry out." He grabbed a Mason jar and filled it with water. "Clean your brushes in this jar."

She frowned at the intricately carved chicken. "I'm gonna mess it up."

"Nah." Josh wet a brush, swirled the yellow with red, then swiped the rooster's breast with a beautiful orange. "If you don't like the color, you can always paint over it. And don't worry—art is individual."

She threw him a sidelong glance. "You won't get mad if I ruin it?"

"I can't wait to see what you do with it."

She gulped. He was going to wish he'd never asked her to help. But she dipped the paint brush in the orange Josh had mixed and applied it to the carving. Sure, this was easy. But how was she supposed to manage all the other colors?

After an hour, she dropped her paintbrush into the Mason jar and stared at her chicken. It looked nothing like Josh's. If he wanted to sell these as a set, she had ruined his plan.

"You done?" Josh's voice floated in from the living room, where he'd been feeding the baby. Maggie rode his shoulder as he walked over to study Heather's work. "Good job," he said, his voice artificially bright. "Really good."

"Don't lie."

"I'm not lying."

"You are. The colors on yours are blended, but mine looks like a mess."

"So? Do you know how popular abstract art is?" He smiled at her. "Yours is different, but that's okay. That's what art is all about."

He placed her chicken on a shelf with his mother's teacups and crystal figurines. Clearly, that chicken wasn't heading to Retro Relics.

She frowned. "You can be honest—I stink at this. I'm not artistic."

"You are, you just never knew it. Now, want some hot cocoa?"

She stared at his back as he put the kettle on. The baby, still on his shoulder, gripped his tee shirt and grinned at Heather.

"By the way," Josh said, his voice light, "I picked up something for you at the grocery. Hair as pretty as yours deserves a new brush."

He bought her something? Heather looked away as tears stung her eyes. Brett never bought her anything personal; she always had to fend for herself. She tried to say thank you, but couldn't push the words over the lump in her throat.

For the first time in forever, an unexpected sprout of gratitude broke through the hardened surface of her heart . . . and the sensation terrified her.

CHAPTER
TWENTY-SIX

On a mild February afternoon, Josh scooped Maggie into his arms and pressed a kiss to her head. He breathed in the scent of baby shampoo as he tapped her back, listening for the little bubble of air that meant she was comfortable again.

The living room was a snug cocoon, late-afternoon light leaking through the lace curtains Mama had hung years ago. Outside, wind raked the palmettos around the porch, their stiff fronds rattling like paper fans. Somewhere down the street, a truck rumbled past and faded away. Inside, the steady tick of the wall clock counted out the moments.

Heather sat on the sofa, curled into one corner, an old magazine sagging open in her lap. The glossy pages caught a stray beam of light, but her gaze didn't follow the headlines or pictures. Her eyes, shiny with unshed tears, seemed fixed on some point beyond the living-room walls, as if she were staring through the pages, through the window, through the town of Peculiar itself.

Six weeks had passed, and her foot had healed. Nothing held her to Peculiar but the simple fact that she had no place else to go.

Was she thinking about Brett? Was she picturing some imaginary future that had never materialized? Or was she simply wishing she were anywhere but in this aging house with its crooked floorboards, dated furniture, and annoying owner?

Josh's heart pinched. He moved Maggie, careful not to jostle her, and wondered if he could do anything to ease the desolate look in Heather's eyes. A new magazine, one that wasn't curling at the corners? Or maybe she'd like a book from Mama's shelf, a romance novel that ended better than her story with Brett. Or flowers, maybe, in a jar on her nightstand. Fancy bubble bath that smelled of something more feminine than soap and shampoo.

Heather looked like a woman who hadn't been pampered in a long time. Maybe ever.

Maggie's burp erupted like a firecracker against his collarbone, sharp and unapologetic. Josh chuckled, lifting her from his shoulder to look into her face. Her brown eyes blinked up at him, her mouth working in sleepy confusion.

"That was a good one," he crowed. "Are you ready for tummy time? I hear it's important for babies. But let me get a clean blanket so you won't get dog hair all over your pjs."

Heather's head swung toward him, her focus slamming back to reality. "She has airplanes on her pajamas," she said, her tone brittle. "Couldn't you find something with hearts or flowers?"

Josh glanced at the little blue rockets on Maggie's sleeper. "I used what I found in the attic," he said. He smiled at the baby. "I don't think she cares, as long as she's warm."

He thought about asking Heather to hold the baby while he

went for the blanket, but his intuition nixed the idea. Heather had come downstairs more often in the last few days, and twice she had agreed to watch the baby while he went out to scout for wood. But she still held back, as if she didn't want to become attached to the little girl. She never reached for the baby first. Never lingered with Maggie, and rarely spoke to her. But she did stare at her, often with undisguised curiosity.

With Maggie on his shoulder, he climbed the stairs, understanding Heather's fear. She didn't want to attach. She was probably afraid of what she might feel when she left.

He couldn't blame her for that.

Despite her aloofness, Heather was helping. She painted in her own quirky style, bright strokes that rebelled against the bland colors of his kitchen walls. When he was home, Heather would call out if Maggie fussed or needed changing. He had seen her open the front door so Hoss could go outside, and sometimes she refilled the dog's water bowl without being asked. They were little efforts, but they added up. For a woman who'd arrived half-frozen and barely conscious, that was progress.

Josh headed down the short hallway to the baby's room. He plucked a clean flannel blanket from the stack and hurried back downstairs. He spread the blanket on the living room floor, smoothing the wrinkles so there'd be no bumps under Maggie's tiny limbs. Then he lowered her onto her belly, arranging her arms so her fists were tucked under her chest.

"There you go, little girl." He dropped to his knees and grinned when she raised her head and looked at him, her mouth curling in an expression that looked like a smile. Her eyes went wide, bright with effort and delight. "That's good, Maggie. Pretty soon you'll be crawling all over the place. We'll have to get a fence to keep you safe."

"A playpen," Heather said, her voice cool as she flipped a page. "They're called playpens."

"Good to know." Josh glanced at her tight mouth and decided against asking if she had a younger sibling. Something about her hunched shoulders said *not now*.

He tried another approach. "Any luck reaching Brett?"

Heather's jaw worked, then set. "Called his parents," she said. "They haven't heard from him in months. And they had never heard of me."

Josh winced. No wonder she was in a prickly mood.

He turned back to Maggie, giving Heather space. The baby kicked one leg and let out a squeal, delighted with the new angle of her own existence. Her fists opened and closed on the blanket, flexing like tiny starfish.

On the other side of the room, Hoss hauled his massive body from the rug and lumbered over. Ever watchful, he circled and sank at the blanket's edge, resting his huge head on his paws. Maggie stared at him as if Hoss were the most marvelous creature God had ever imagined.

Sitting cross-legged, Josh tucked his hands under his arms, letting the quiet settle. The ceiling fan hummed overhead, stirring the air. Somewhere in the kitchen, the refrigerator clicked on.

Now over a month old, Maggie was doing great.

On Christmas Eve, he hadn't been sure he could handle a baby, but Maggie was thriving. According to Dr. O'Toole's list of milestones, she was exactly where she ought to be.

Across from him, Heather wasn't even pretending to read anymore. Her gaze had fixed on Maggie and her expression had shifted into lines he couldn't decipher. He looked for tenderness, some softening in her eyes, but he saw a blend of wariness and anxiety, like a freezing person watching a fire they yearned to approach but didn't trust not to burn them.

Maggie kicked again, let out a delighted yelp, and Hoss's tail thumped in congratulation.

Josh closed his eyes, sending up a quiet prayer. *Lord, You know where she's been and what she's lost. I don't know how to fix any of that.*

He opened his eyes and watched Heather study the baby, the guarded look never leaving her face.

Would You teach her how to trust again?

HEATHER SAT ON THE SOFA, ignoring the magazine in her lap.

Josh Donnelly was kind. Gentle. She had clocked that much the first night she saw him. He noticed small things. He listened. He didn't crowd her or ask prying questions. On his best day, though, he was still as peculiar as this town.

With a baby in his arms, the man was downright ridiculous.

His voice slid all over the place, without warning, without embarrassment. One minute his baritone rattled the dishes in the kitchen cabinets; the next he was warbling in a sing-song falsetto, his pitch nearly as high as Maggie's cries. The contrast made Heather want to laugh and cringe at the same time. A grown man that size had no business singing like Minnie Mouse.

Yet the baby loved it.

Maggie might be sprawled on the floor, red-faced and furious, arms and legs windmilling like she was fighting an invisible foe. But the moment Josh opened his mouth, her crying stopped mid-note. Her eyes widened and searched until they found him, her mouth tipping upward into a smile.

Heather's chest hurt every time it happened.

When he returned to the living room with a bottle, steam

fogging the nipple, Heather shook her head. "Where'd you learn how to care for a kid? You don't seem like a guy with baby experience."

He released an easy, self-deprecating laugh and settled Maggie in his arms. "I didn't know the first thing when she arrived," he said. "But I found a baby care book and followed the directions. Anyone could have done it."

Heather shook her head, amazed. In bringing Sarah's baby to this house, she had trusted an instinct she didn't know she possessed.

She reached for another faded magazine, the paper stiff under her fingers. She flipped pages without reading. Josh could hint all he wanted, but she wasn't going to be sweet-talked into babysitting. Maggie was his responsibility, and he would look after her until the burden wore grooves into his life. Then he'd hand her over to the authorities and move on.

That was apparently what his father had done. What her father had done, too.

Her father had perfected the art of absence before he actually left. But when things got messy, when she needed comfort, he retreated to the safety of a new family. And then her mother wrote her off.

Josh was singing again.

He looked into Maggie's face while she drank, his expression softening in a way that made Heather's eyes sting. The baby's small fingers patted his hand, and the simple trust in that gesture squeezed Heather's heart.

She lowered her head and stared at a paint stain on her jeans. Josh was *too* perceptive. He noticed pauses. Glances. Silences. She didn't want him seeing her like this, didn't want him tracing a line from the ache in her heart to the secrets she had buried.

She ought to hide in that bedroom with its ruffled curtains and outdated wallpaper. But she was tired of being cooped up, tired of sleeping among someone else's memories.

She shifted her gaze to Hoss.

The massive dog snored in front of the fireplace, paws stretched out, chest rising and falling like a bellows. Josh was almost as devoted to the dog as to the baby, but dogs were supposed to be loyal. Whenever Josh had to run upstairs, he called, "Watch the baby," and Hoss parked himself beside Maggie like a sentry.

Heather thought she was hallucinating the first time she saw it.

Sighing, she folded her arms and looked around the room. Faded curtains to filter the light instead of blocking it. Sponge-painted walls in pale pastels. Flowering vines stenciled around doors and windows. Everything skirted, softened, homemade.

Her parents' house had never looked like this.

She had no idea where they lived now. Her mother was probably still in the ultra-modern condo. Her father had remarried, so he was living in a space curated by someone else's tastes.

Heather closed her eyes and let her head fall against the couch. Images of the past crowded her mind, then last night's dream returned to her in pieces: she'd been standing in the middle of a desolate intersection, wheat fields stretching endlessly in every direction. Four roads. No signs. East? West? North? South?

She turned in circles, searching for someone to tell her what to do. When no one came, she had collapsed, sobbing, and woke to the sound of Hoss scratching at her door because Josh was cooking breakfast.

She opened her eyes to the sight of Josh feeding the baby.

Maggie's sucking slowed as sleep claimed her. Josh's eyelids drooped, dark lashes resting against his cheeks. His rocking slowed. If she didn't interrupt, they would both fall asleep in that old chair...

"Josh?"

He startled, lifting his head. "Yeah?"

"Nothing." She gave him a small smile and pretended to read her magazine.

At least she was safe here. She would stay safe until she found Brett and said goodbye to Peculiar.

That morning she had looked in the mirror and barely recognized herself. Weeks of living on stale crackers and cake rolls had taken their toll before, but her eyes had regained their sparkle. Her face had softened. Her curves had returned.

She looked... almost pretty. And Brett would notice.

Her gaze drifted back to Josh and Maggie, both slumbering in perfect innocence. If not for his shaggy hair and worn clothes, Josh would be classically handsome. Strong jaw. Cleft chin. Straight teeth. When he looked at her, earnest hope enlivened his blue eyes.

He wanted the best for her. She knew that. But he had never wanted to escape. He had never needed to.

When Josh sank lower in the rocking chair, her breath caught. "Hey!" she called.

His eyes opened. "Yeah?"

"If you wanted to see if someone was busking in a town," she asked, "how would you go about it?"

He straightened. "I'd, uh, probably call the police department. If someone's loitering in a public place, the cops usually know."

"Thanks." She nodded toward the baby. "You should probably put her in her crib before you doze off and drop her."

"I'm not sleepy," he said, color touching his cheeks. "Just relaxed."

"Right. Then put the baby to bed so you can relax some more."

As he stood, careful and steady, the tug of war between staying and leaving tightened inside her chest.

CHAPTER
TWENTY-SEVEN

The cry that woke Josh sliced through his sleep, sharp and panicked, nothing like Maggie's usual soft complaints. This one scraped his nerves raw before his eyes were even open.

He was out of bed and down the hall in seconds.

He flipped the light switch and saw that Maggie's face was red, not the dusty pink of sleep but a blotchy, angry crimson. Her eyes, usually bright and curious in the morning, were squeezed shut, her mouth drawn tight as she screamed. When he gathered her into his arms, heat bled through the thin fuzz of her pajamas, startling him so badly he nearly choked on a breath.

Too hot.

Fear surged, fast and physical. His hands shook as he moved her to the other arm. Where was Dr. O'Toole's book? There, the one with the blue spine and the tidy lists. Should he look under *hot baby* or *baby wakes screaming*? He tried to think as he ruffled the pages with one hand, tried to slow his breathing, but fear crowded out everything.

No time for reading. He needed Doc Tompkins. Now.

"Shh," he murmured, though the sound came out ragged. He carried Maggie into the kitchen, the linoleum cold under his bare feet, the morning light too bright and cheery for the situation.

The answering service came on the line, responding to him with maddening calm. Dr. Tompkins was out of town. Fishing in Georgia.

Fishing? At a time like this?

Josh hung up, feeling as though a hand had closed around his throat. He turned and ran back upstairs, moving on instinct. The book was still in Maggie's room. He found the section on fever, but the words swam on the page as the baby's cries drilled into his skull.

"What's going on?"

Heather stood in the doorway, her hair rumpled, her face pinched with alarm. Her expression mirrored Maggie's in a way that made his stomach knot.

"She's burning up," he said, the words coming out harsh. "I don't know how to make her better. I don't know if I should give her formula, and I can't think with her screaming—"

Heather took the book without comment. He opened the window and paced in front of it, bouncing Maggie as cool night air brushed his shoulder. The baby's cries hitched and wailed, each one an accusation.

"Okay," Heather finally said. "This says fever can be caused by lots of things. First you need to take her temperature. As long as it's not dangerously high, you can give her water and clear liquids."

"What's dangerously high?"

"Anything over 107 means the child should be taken to the hospital asap. Otherwise, keep her comfortable. Light clothes. Fluids. Make sure she's wetting her diapers." She lowered the book. "Unless it's above that threshold, this isn't an emergency."

"It sure feels like one." He jerked his chin toward the hall bathroom. "There's an armpit thermometer in the medicine cabinet."

He half expected Heather to step aside so he could get it. Instead, she hurried down the hall.

Josh laid Maggie in the crib and unfastened the sleeper, the tiny teeth of the zipper loud in his ears. Her skin was even hotter under his palms. "It's okay," he whispered above his thundering pulse. "I know my fingers are cold. I'm sorry." He slid the thermometer into place and held it beneath her arm, praying without words.

When it beeped, he pulled it free and handed it to Heather. "Tell me. Please." He reached for a clean diaper, moving fast, needing to be useful.

"One hundred three point five," Heather said, her voice flat. "The book says ninety-nine is normal for an armpit reading. So her temp is high, but not dangerous."

"She feels like she's on fire."

"She's hotter than usual. But not an emergency."

His thoughts spiraled. What if the book was wrong? What if Maggie needed a hospital? He pictured the forms, the blank spaces where answers should be. Birthdate. Social Security number. He didn't have any of that information. He pictured hands reaching for her, procedures he didn't understand, doors closing. Police. Child services. Maggie taken away.

Gone.

"It's okay." Heather's hand rested on his arm, calm and grounding. "The book says no hospital. Cool water. Light clothes. You can handle that."

Josh turned back to Maggie, who was red-faced and trembling with sobs. "Father," he prayed, his voice tight. "Please. Tell me what to do."

Heather cleared her throat. "Watch her for the next twenty-four hours. If she's fine tomorrow, then this was nothing serious. But if she still has a fever, or if it goes up, you can take her in and let the experts handle it."

The word *expert* taunted him.

"You're new at this, Josh," Heather said. "And you're not really a dad."

The pain that flared in his chest surprised him. Was she right? Had he been pretending all this time? Fooling himself with lullabies and late-night prayers and thinking this was *easy*?

"How would you know whether I—"

Heather's mouth opened, then closed. For a heartbeat she looked stricken, as if she wished she could pull the words back inside herself.

"Clearly, I'm not mother material," she said. "Maybe you're not cut out to be a father. That's okay. She's young. You can still find her a home."

Find her a home?

The phrase rocked him like a blow. Before he could respond, Heather turned and left.

Josh scooped Maggie up and carried her downstairs, her cries softer now, worn thin. He gave Maggie a bottle of cool water and rocked her in the chair by the window, the rhythm steady and constant, as if he could rock the fear out of both of them.

"Lord," he murmured, pressing his cheek against Maggie's hair. "Maybe I don't know who I am to her or where she came from. Maybe I don't have experience. But You brought her to me, I know You did. And You told me to take care of her." His voice broke. "Please don't let me mess this up. Don't let me hurt her. Help me."

Eventually, Maggie's cries ebbed into small, hiccuping breaths. Her body softened against his, heavy with exhaustion. Josh remained where he was, afraid to move, promising himself he would keep rocking until she fell asleep.

HEATHER LAY on the bed and focused on the wallpaper, at the little flowers that had been sun-bleached into ghosts. She'd done it again—dressed her fear up as truth and flung it at the most convenient target.

Not cut out to be a father.

The words replayed with a dull, sick rhythm. She didn't even know where they'd come from, unless they'd sprung from the place inside her that didn't believe anything good could last.

How would she know what made a man a good father?

She shut her eyes and pressed her hand to her forehead, wishing she could wipe the sentence away.

She had warned him. Told him she didn't deserve help. Told him he could do better if what he wanted was a woman who stayed put and didn't bring problems in her pockets.

But Josh had looked at her like she was a person worth saving. Like she belonged in a house with clean counters and a baby's laugh.

He didn't really need her. He didn't need anyone. He had Maggie, and Maggie was the real thing—innocent and helpless and honest. Heather was a complication with a bad past and a tendency toward trouble.

He was probably downstairs right now, rocking the baby and regretting the day he ever walked down Tuscawilla Road.

A soft snuffling sounded at her door. Then a scratch—a deliberate scrape against the wood.

"Hoss?"

She swung her feet to the floor and opened the door. Sure enough, the mastiff sat there, tongue lolling, tail thumping. He looked up at her, panting, then turned and started down the stairs.

"What do you need, buddy?" she asked, even though she already knew. Dogs didn't fetch you unless something was wrong.

Hoss stopped at the bottom of the stairs to make sure she was following. Heather padded after him, barefoot, keeping to the edges of the steps so the wood wouldn't announce her presence. The air downstairs was cooler. Dimmer.

Then she saw them.

Josh lay stretched along the old sofa, his shoulders wedged against the worn arm, his long body folded into a shape that was never meant for sleep. Maggie lay lengthwise on his chest, small and utterly claimed, her knees tucked under her diaper. Her arms clung to his shirt, fingers splayed and trusting, as though she meant to hold him close even in sleep. Her flushed cheek was pressed into the soft cotton of his tee shirt, her mouth parted, the damp heat of fever still trapped in her tiny body.

Heather watched as they moved together—the steady lift and fall of Josh's breathing carrying the baby with him, as gentle as a tide beneath a boat.

And Josh—his eyes were shut, his head tipped at an angle that made Heather's neck ache in sympathy. His jaw was unshaven, the skin beneath his eyes shadowed. In sleep, he looked younger, almost boyish, like someone who had spent himself trying and finally ran out of strength.

Her heart constricted.

She stepped closer and laid her hand on his shoulder. The fabric of his shirt was still warm from Maggie's fever.

"Hey," she said, keeping her voice low so she wouldn't startle the baby. "Josh."

He didn't stir at first. She gave him a gentle shake.

His eyes opened, unfocused. He blinked once, twice, as if he'd been pulled from deep water. Then his eyes widened with panic, as if he expected Maggie to be gone.

"She's still here," Heather whispered. "But you both need to go back to bed."

Josh swallowed. "Yeah," he said, his voice rough. "Good idea."

He lowered a foot to the floor, but Heather kept her hand on his shoulder—not stopping him, but anchoring him long enough for her to do the thing she should have done earlier.

"I'm sorry," she said.

His eyes flicked to hers, wary. Anticipating the next blow.

She drew a breath and forced herself to meet his gaze. "I don't know a lot of good daddies," she said, the words tasting like confession. "But you're one of them."

For a second, he didn't move. Then his eyes filled, as if the tears had been waiting behind a dam and her words cracked it.

He looked away, embarrassed. He nodded, hard, as if the compliment had hurt.

Heather slid her hand from his shoulder. "Go on," she said, aiming for lightness and only managing gentle. "Put Maggie to bed and get some rest. I'll listen for her. If she cries, I'll be there."

Josh stood slowly, every movement deliberate. He held Maggie against his chest and took one step toward the stairs, then stopped. He reached back and caught Heather's hand for a squeeze, brief and grateful, as if he didn't know any other way to say *thank you*.

She curled her fingers around his without thinking.

Then he let her go and went upstairs, carrying Maggie like the most precious thing any man had ever been given.

Hoss sat at Heather's feet and leaned against her leg, heavy and steady.

Heather stared up the dark stairwell until Josh disappeared and the house began to breathe again.

The rest of Josh's day passed in a blur—snatched moments of sleep, pacing with Maggie, rocking her, and trying to cajole her into taking bottles of cold water. Heather sat on the couch, her knees drawn up as she flipped through O'Toole's baby book and read aloud about colds, ear infections, flu, roseola, and pneumonia. When Josh had to run upstairs for a fresh diaper, he instinctively handed Maggie to Heather. When he came back, Heather had Maggie on her knees and was whispering to her. Maggie was . . . asleep.

He'd been tempted to ask Heather to change the diaper, but he could see she wasn't ready for that. So he laid the still-sleeping Maggie between them and changed her, relieved to see that the baby was peeing as usual.

"Good to know," Heather said, chuckling. "I'll alert CNN."

Josh pressed his hand to the baby's forehead. "Much cooler. I think she's getting better."

"Maybe we can get some rest now."

Josh picked the baby up. "You wanna hold her?"

"Not now."

But she hadn't said *never*.

Josh took Maggie upstairs and put her back in the crib. When she didn't wake, he went down and told Heather that because fever meant infection and infection meant germs, he was going to scrub every inch of the house.

For most of the night, he sprayed and wiped and scrubbed and vacuumed and mopped any surface a tiny human might encounter. Heather lent a hand.

By the time the sun rose the next morning, Josh was exhausted and knew Heather had to be as well. Maggie was awake and hungry, her temperature back to normal.

Heather's mouth quirked in an exhausted smile. "What if I heat up some soup while you feed her?"

"I like chicken noodle."

Josh tried to nap with Maggie later that morning, but anxiety would not let him sleep. What if her fever had risen and he had to take her to the hospital? The risk of losing her was no longer an abstract possibility.

"I know You are in control," he whispered, staring at the ceiling above his bed. "I know if You have a better place for Maggie, I will need to let her go. But it won't be easy."

At lunchtime Josh went downstairs and fed Maggie, then submitted to an urge to go outside. With Hoss by his side and Maggie on his lap, he sat on the top porch step and stared past the yard, the gate, and the sidewalk that connected him to the people of Peculiar.

Rustling in a nearby oak drew his gaze upward, to where the clouds seemed determined to hide the sun.

It's time.

"All right, Lord."

He went back inside, set a sleepy Maggie in the baby carrier, and fell asleep on the couch, knowing that things were about to change.

CHAPTER
TWENTY-EIGHT

Two days after Maggie's fever scare, Heather came downstairs expecting toast or cereal and stopped short at the smell of homemade pancakes. Again, with real butter and heated syrup.

Josh stood at the stove, spatula in hand, looking triumphant. Heather ate and watched with quiet amusement as he scraped his leftovers into a bowl and set it on the floor for Hoss, who accepted the offering with enthusiastic tail wagging.

She was still smiling when Josh crossed his arms. "Looks like a good day for a walk."

Her smile faded. "You don't think it's too cool for the baby?"

"She's got fuzzy pajamas. And a blanket."

Heather shrugged. "She's your responsibility. Walk all you want."

"You want to leave in about twenty minutes?"

"Me?" The word slipped out before she could stop it.

He grinned like it was the most reasonable suggestion in

the world. "It's been seven weeks. Your foot should be completely healed by now."

"But I haven't—"

"We'll go slow," he interrupted, gentle but firm. "I don't want to overdo it on your first day out. But it'd be good for you to get outside, wouldn't it?"

Heather turned to the window. An early morning rain had rinsed the sky clean, and a pale blue canopy stretched wide and hopeful. Sunlight filtered through the live oaks, stirring the Spanish moss. She had planned to start calling police stations that morning, recite her story, and brace for whatever came next. But what would it hurt to go outside?

"Yeah. Okay. It does look like a pretty day."

Half an hour later, they were moving down Church Street. Hoss trotted ahead, his nails rasping against the concrete. Josh pushed the stroller, careful and steady, and Heather walked beside him, her hands tucked into Mama's soft cardigan. The air carried the scents of growing grass and sun-warmed bark.

Heather had insisted on choosing Maggie's outfit—a blue sleeper so faded it could pass for white, and a pink bow she taped to the baby's head. "If we're going out," she said, "at least let Maggie look like the beautiful girl she is."

Now she relaxed, breathing deeply of the fresh air and enjoying a chorus of birdsong. "I had almost forgotten how nice spring in Florida can be," she said, tipping her head back to take in the oak canopy overhead. "Feels like I've spent forever in your mama's room."

They paused when Grace Egan backed her Volvo out of the driveway next door. Grace leaned out her window, eyes bright with curiosity. "Josh! I haven't seen you in ages. You closed your kitchen curtains."

Her gaze flicked to Heather. Then the stroller. Then Hoss.

"Well," Grace said, smiling wider. "Looks like you've been busy."

Josh nodded. "Miss Grace, this is Heather. And this," he said, pointing proudly to the stroller, "is Maggie. You've probably met Hoss at the fence."

"I've met Heather, too." Grace adjusted her smile. "You may not remember, but you walked me home from Margaret's funeral. Nice to see you again, dear."

Heather blinked as the memory came rushing back. Grace had told her the story about Josh and the Little League game.

"Well." Grace checked her watch. "I'm off to brunch with a friend, but we'll catch up soon."

As Grace pulled away Josh turned to Heather, his eyes alive with question. "You were at Mama's funeral?"

Heather bit her lip. "Brett was singing in the park and I was bored. I saw the crowd at the church and walked over. But I didn't really know what was going on."

Josh resumed walking, his head lowered. "How long were you in town?"

Heather shrugged. "I don't know—a couple of weeks, maybe. We ran out of gas and had to earn enough to fill the van. It took a while." She forced a laugh. "Brett wasn't—isn't—as good a singer as he thinks he is."

Josh shook his head. "I can't believe I never saw you."

"I stayed in the van most of the time . . . I wasn't feeling like myself back then."

"That was when Mama had her stroke," Josh said, looking up at the trees. "Martians could have landed in that park and I wouldn't have noticed."

Silence fell between them, then Heather leaned toward him and lightened her voice. "You'll be the big news at that brunch."

He snorted. "Grace has been my neighbor forever. She knows all my stories, but her memory's startin' to slip."

"She doesn't know much about me," Heather said. "Does she know about Maggie?"

Josh shook his head. "Probably not. But I'll tell her the truth."

"And that is?"

"The Lord sent me a baby," he said, his blue eyes gleaming. "It's not complicated."

Heather almost laughed. The real story was knotted and ugly and heavy with possible consequences, but Josh seemed content with his simple version of events. She would let him keep it.

They walked past Twin Oaks, the Piggly Wiggly, and the brick nursing home where someone waved from a shaded bench. The rhythm of the walk soothed her, along with the quiet creak of the stroller wheels.

When they reached Retro Relics, Josh nodded toward the shop. "I need to pop in for a minute. You want to come?"

Heather sat on a bench. "Maggie and I will wait here. Take your time."

Josh went inside, the bell on the door announcing his approach. Heather rested her hand on the stroller handle as Hoss lay at her feet. She drank in the sights of the street, the passing clouds, and the baby's chubby face.

For the first time in over three years, she found herself longing for a similar place to call home.

JOSH TOOK his time on the walk, shortening his stride without making a show of it. Heather's gait was still careful as she pushed the stroller, and Josh didn't want to rush what felt like a small victory. The stroller wheels hummed over the pavement as Hoss ambled ahead, his leash loose in Josh's hand.

They turned off Main and headed back toward Twin Oaks, the sprawling complex nestled beneath two ancient live oaks whose branches arched together like clasped hands.

Heather slowed. "I hate hospitals," she said, her mouth tightening. "They're depressing."

Josh glanced up at the familiar building, the wide porch, the rocking chairs that were always occupied in the afternoons. "This isn't a hospital. It's assisted living. My best friend lives here."

"Is he old?"

Josh blinked. "Well . . . yeah. He used to be our police chief."

Heather stopped dead.

The stroller rolled a few inches farther before Josh caught it. He turned, puzzled, as Heather took a step back, color draining from her face.

"I don't want to go inside," she said. "I don't want your friend getting the wrong idea."

Josh frowned. "What wrong idea? You're sleepin' in Mama's room."

She shook her head, her eyes darting toward the building as if it might recognize her. "I'm tired, so I'll wait out here."

Josh searched her face, instinct telling him not to push when Heather's walls went up. "All right," he said, raising his hands. "But Chief Goodman would love to see the baby. Can you hold onto Hoss for me?"

"No problem." Heather took the leash and dropped onto a bench near the entrance. Her posture said no. Final.

Josh nudged Hoss toward her knee. The big dog settled instantly, leaning into her like a steady promise.

Inside, the air carried the scents of lavender and Lysol. The hum of voices echoed down the hall, laughter mixing with the clink of dishes.

Isabella spotted Josh from the reception desk and greeted him with a wide grin. "Well, look who just upgraded my day. Where have you been, Josh Donnelly? And what do you have there?"

Josh lifted Maggie from the stroller. Her eyes were open and calm, taking everything in. "This is Maggie."

Isabella's brows shot up. "Well, bless my soul. She's a little angel." She leaned toward the window, peering out. "That your girlfriend out there?"

"That's Heather," Josh said. "She's stayin' with us for a while."

Isabella's smile softened. "About time," she teased. "We were wonderin' if you planned to grow old alone. Where'd you meet her?"

Josh settled Maggie on his shoulder, one hand patting her back. "Hoss and I ran into her while we were out walking."

Isabella blinked. "I should walk more often." She crossed her arms. "Heather gonna come in and meet Chief Goodman?"

"Not today."

Josh waved Maggie's tiny hand at Isabella, then put her back in the stroller and pushed it toward the community room.

Chief Goodman sat near the wide garden window, sunlight striping the floor at his feet. A magazine rested in his lap, but he set it aside when he saw Josh approaching. He looked smaller than Josh remembered, and thinner, but his eyes were the same, sharp and assessing.

"Chief." Josh pushed the stroller closer. "I brought someone to meet you. This is Maggie."

For a heartbeat, Goodman's face remained stoic, then his eyes widened and his mouth softened. "You adopt a baby, Josh?"

Josh eased into the chair beside him. "Sort of. The Lord sent her to me."

"Did He, now." Goodman studied the baby, then looked at Josh, unreadable emotions flickering behind his gaze.

Nurse Shari hurried over, her hands clasped. "Josh? Is that you?" Her smile lit up the room. "I couldn't believe it when Isabella told me, but here you are with a real-live baby."

Josh grinned, pleasure expanding his chest. "Yes, ma'am."

"She's beautiful." Shari pointed toward the door. "Isabella said your lady friend is outside. Doesn't she want to come in?"

"Maybe later," Josh said. "She's recoverin' from an accident. I don't want to push her."

Shari nodded. "Well, this explains why we haven't seen much of you lately."

"Things have been busy," Josh said, rubbing the back of his neck. "In fact, I oughta get the baby home. It's almost feeding time."

"Well, don't be a stranger," Shari said. "We've missed you."

Josh stood. He was reaching for the stroller when Chief Goodman caught his wrist. His grip was weaker than it used to be, but still deliberate.

"Son," he said, his voice low, "I suspect there's a story behind this baby."

Josh reluctantly met his gaze. The former chief saw too much. Always had. "Yes, sir. And you'll hear it. Just not today."

Goodman released him, satisfied. "Take good care of her. And mind how you go, son."

Josh left the building with the baby tucked close, her weight warm and comforting against his chest. Outside, Heather sat exactly where he'd left her, Hoss leaning against her leg.

As Josh reached the bench, Heather looked up. Relief flickered across her face, then vanished. Josh noticed, but didn't ask why she'd stayed outside.

Yet the question followed them all the way home.

CHAPTER
TWENTY-NINE

As the current Peculiar police chief, I can confidently report that the news of Josh Donnelly's unexpected housemates spread faster than chickenpox and with twice the itch. Grace Egan let it slip at the Old Florida Restaurant as she leaned over her plate of fried mullet. By the time Jackie Leakey stepped out with her cup of sweet tea, she'd told Reverend Gary Walker, who nodded as if she'd handed him a prayer request involving national security.

On Sunday morning, while the ceiling fans pushed the humid air at Peculiar Community Church, Pastor Gary asked the congregation to pray for Josh Donnelly, "who apparently has unconventional houseguests." A few ladies in the second pew sucked in their breath at the same moment, creating a curious little choir of alarm.

Isabella the receptionist wasn't shy about adding her own fuel to the fire. By noon every staff member and most of the residents of Twin Oaks knew that Josh Donnelly was cohabitating with a young woman and a baby. Even Mr. Patel, whose hearing aids whistled like teakettles on the best of days, got the gist.

"Who's the woman?" he shouted at Isabella as the residents took their daily turn around the block, orthopedic shoes thumping on the sidewalk. "Is she from Peculiar?"

"Not likely," Isabella said, blowing a strand of hair off her forehead. "Everybody Josh's age has either married or left town. He said he met her while taking a walk."

"But Josh doesn't walk that far," Mr. Patel muttered. "So where's this woman from?"

No one knew, of course. But Peculiar is a fertile field for theories, and over the next week several stories sprouted from the rich compost of speculation.

Nurse Shari surmised that the woman and her baby had suffered a flat tire on the outskirts of town. Josh, out walking Hoss, had stopped to help. Shari said the woman had been smitten by his blue eyes and quirky charm. "I've seen the baby," she added, lowering her voice as if delivering medical testimony. "She looks nothing like Josh. So this relationship is still young, and that infant does not have Josh's DNA."

Employees of the Piggly Wiggly contributed their own hypothesis. "Josh has been buying diapers and baby formula since Christmas," Kelly Haviland told a cluster of women in her check-out line. The conveyor belt rolled beneath a loaf of bread and a bag of oranges as she continued, "And wouldn't you say that baby is about two months old?" A couple of the women nodded, their eyes bright with curiosity.

Kelly grinned. "If you saw the way Josh looks at that kid, you'd know how much he loves it. And who cares where they met? Josh is a family man now, and that's all we need to know." She sighed, a dreamy exhale that nearly drowned out the beep of the scanner. "I do love a good love story."

Over coffee—burnt, as usual—in my office one afternoon,

Pastor Gary told me that Josh had always been a God-fearing man, as righteous as his mama. "It doesn't sit right with me," he said, leaning in until I could smell the wintergreen on his breath, "for him to be sharing his home with a young woman. The Josh I baptized would never have relations before marriage, let alone live with a woman who wasn't his wife."

Then he dropped his voice, as if the file cabinets were listening. "I think she could be blackmailing our Josh. Maybe she's from a cult, telling him that the Lord wants that baby to be his. He's not the most sophisticated young man, so a con artist would find him easy prey. We haven't seen him at church since before Christmas, so she's had plenty of time to work on him."

I had been harboring similar suspicions, so it helped to know that someone else was thinking along the same line. "But why would anyone con Josh Donnelly?" I said. "He isn't wealthy or even ambitious. What's to be gained?"

"What Josh has," the pastor said, tapping the desk for emphasis, "is a big heart and a pure soul. Evil is attracted to innocence, you know."

I shrugged. Theology wasn't my jurisdiction. "Even so, what would she gain from blackmail?"

Gary thought a moment, then snapped his fingers. "Josh has a house. That place must be worth something."

I snorted, thinking of the ramshackle Victorian with its mildewed paint and the bougainvillea that had taken over the porch railings. "If I were a con in search of real estate, I'd work on the owners of the Beaufort Mansion, not Josh Donnelly."

We eventually agreed on one thing: if Margaret Donnelly were still alive, she'd be either heartbroken or furious about the whole affair.

By March, Peculiar had reached a verdict on Heather without ever asking her to testify. She felt it in the glances that skimmed her at the Piggly Wiggly and in the way conversations dropped when she walked past the post office.

People talked about her while stirring sugar into coffee and leaning against sun-heated pickup trucks. They talked about her and Josh and Maggie like the three of them were a story they owned.

Meanwhile, she woke every morning with the same knot in her chest. Another sunrise. Another page of phone numbers. Another stretch of calls to Georgia and Tennessee police stations that had neither seen nor heard of Brett Steelhawk.

Sorry, never heard of him.

Each one thinned her patience.

Josh never told her she should leave. Not once. He made her soup and sandwiches and folded the baby's laundry and pretended everything in the world was steady, but Heather could read a room. She saw that people looked at him with that tender, worried expression reserved for injured animals and unmarried pastors. Before she arrived, Josh Donnelly had been Peculiar's golden boy—sweet, faithful, and harmless. Now some folks studied him as if he were under a spell and too gullible to break it.

Not everyone thought that way, of course. The girl at the Piggly Wiggly told Heather she was thrilled that Josh's pot finally found a lid. It took Heather half an hour to grasp her meaning. When she did, she stood in the cereal aisle and wondered whether to laugh or throw a shoe.

One bright March afternoon—the kind of day when the sky looked freshly scrubbed and the heat stayed polite—Josh called from the bottom of the stairs.

"Heather, we're goin' for a walk. You comin'?"

Heather collapsed backward onto the bed. The comforter

sighed and released the clean smell of detergent. She looked at the long list of police stations on the nightstand. "Go without me."

"I'm not gonna do that. We'll wait."

"You'll wait a long time."

"Don't care. Might start singin', though."

Her jaw clenched.

She was about to refuse again when his voice traveled up the staircase, rolling out a hymn about a land fairer than day. His baritone swelled like the roar of a train she hadn't planned to stop for.

She buried her face in a pillow. The song tunneled through the stuffing. She tried humming something—anything—but his melody plowed over every tune she knew.

What was *wrong* with that man?

Heather shoved her feet into sandals, yanked the door open, and stalked past him. She barreled down the stairs, grabbed the stroller, and pushed it through the front door with such force that the breeze rattled the wind chimes.

"There's something about a good old hymn," Josh told Hoss while settling Maggie into the stroller. "Makes trouble want to pack its bags."

They had not walked ten minutes when they met the Twin Oaks parade. Walkers. Wheelchairs. Orthopedic sneakers. Volunteers in pastel shirts flitting in and out of the line like butterflies.

Every single person stopped to admire Maggie.

Nurses clucked. Retirees cooed. An especially sweet man, Jackson Fulbright, pressed a peppermint into Heather's palm, then rose on tiptoe to kiss her cheek. A woman patted Heather's arm with a squeeze that nearly sent her sprinting home.

But running back meant more singing. So she stayed.

She knew what people saw: a couple walking under spring sunshine with their baby. In Peculiar, that picture carried significance. Marital significance. No courthouse record needed, but definitely appreciated.

They were finishing the round of greetings when Chief Bill Goodman brought up the rear, his cane ticking, his eyes bright with mischief and kindness.

"Well now," he said. His smile saluted Heather first, then he turned it on Josh. "You are a man among men, Joshua. Didn't get a haircut and a pretty girl came anyway."

Josh scuffed his shoe, and the heat of his embarrassment reached Heather. She considered telling the old man the truth, but the look in Goodman's eyes stopped her.

"Heather," the old chief said, "think you could cut his hair tonight? Can't tell him and Hoss apart."

Josh flushed from neck to hairline.

"Yeah," Heather said. "I can cut hair."

Josh blinked. "You can?"

"Learned in another life."

"Well then." Goodman's grin sparkled. He clapped Josh's shoulder and gave Heather a small bow. "Thank you, young lady."

He moved on with the parade. Canes tapped. Walkers creaked.

Josh turned for home. "You don't have to cut my hair."

Heather opened her mouth—and a scream split the afternoon.

They spun. Nurse Shari knelt on the sidewalk beside a man sprawled on the concrete. The crowd pressed close.

"Watch the baby," Josh said, already running.

Heather's breath caught.

The man on the ground was Mr. Peppermint, Jackson Fulbright.

A MOST PECULIAR PROVIDENCE

Two middle school truants were sitting in front of my desk when Tony appeared, his knuckles white. Afternoon sun through the blinds striped the back wall like a jailhouse mural, dust motes drifting through the beams as if they'd been caught skipping class, too.

I gave the truants my sternest look, the one that had straightened many a small spine over the years. "Now you two run straight back to school, you hear? I'm going to tell your parents what you were doing while you were supposed to be in class. If I catch you climbing trees again, you'll be staying after school for a month. Would you like that?"

"No, sir."

"No, sir."

Their voices squeaked like rusty hinges.

"Good." I waved them toward the door. "I'll be calling the principal to make sure you check in."

The boys scrambled out, squeezing past Tony like rabbits who'd scented a bobcat.

Tony stepped inside, his face the color of skim milk. He lowered himself into the visitor's chair and tented his hands as if preparing to address a congregation. A crooked grin flickered across his face, the expression I've seen on men who are either about to confess or pass out.

"Chief—" His voice cracked like it hadn't fully committed to adulthood. "You ain't gonna believe what I just saw. I don't believe it myself, but I saw it. I've heard stories, you know, but I didn't believe them. People exaggerate."

A motorcycle backfired outside the station, rattling the windows.

"Tony, what are you talking about?"

Tony scooted closer. "I think Josh Donnelly might be a miracle worker."

I leaned back, my chair creaking as if it wanted to register its own opinion. "Why would you say that?"

"Because a few minutes ago I saw old Jackson Fulbright on the ground, his face as white as his hair. He was moaning that his arm was broken and the nurse was cryin' while she tried to get him up. He couldn't move without screaming bloody murder."

A ribbon of unease slid into my gut, but I kept my voice steady. "What happened?"

"Apparently he fell off the sidewalk."

"Is that even possible?"

"I don't know," Tony snapped, his voice a shade too loud. "But it happened. And the man's eighty if he's a day, so his bones are fragile."

"Okay, so he fell. Did you call the ambulance?"

"Didn't need to. Josh Donnelly was there."

"Josh called the ambulance?"

Tony gave me a look that accused me of deliberate obtuseness, then started again. "When I rolled up, Josh was kneeling next to the old man and praying. Then Josh opens his eyes and runs his hands over the old man, starting at his head, then he moves to the man's forearm and sorta pats him down."

I winced. "Josh isn't qualified to set a broken arm. My word, Fulbright must have been screaming."

"Nope, by then he wasn't makin' a sound. After Josh pats Fulbright down, he runs his hands over the man's shoulders and everything looks great—no weird angle to the arm, nothin'. Josh helps the old man to his feet and they grin at each other."

The radiator wheezed, as if the building itself had raised an eyebrow. Tony didn't smell like liquor, and his words, crazy as they were, weren't slurred. Still, a colony of doubts scuttled across the back of my mind.

"Was Fulbright on painkillers?" I asked.

Tony snorted. "The nurse hadn't given him anything. Josh steps back, Fulbright takes a few steps, puts his arm around the nurse, and starts dancing a two-step. The nurse is laughin', Josh is smilin', and all the old folks are chatterin' like sea gulls."

I shifted in my chair, which released a small wooden sigh. There had to be a logical explanation—shock, adrenaline, hysteria, something—but I couldn't find a string to pull. "Do you think the old man was faking?"

"Heck no. I think Josh healed him."

I took off my glasses and wiped the lenses, needing something to do besides frown. "The old man must have scared himself and tensed up. Josh prayed, Fulbright calmed down, and the witnesses filled in the rest. Happens all the time."

Tony's gaze drifted past me, as if replaying the scene frame by frame on the far wall.

"Whatever happened," I said, a touch more briskly than intended, "I'm glad the old man's okay. Now—don't you need to finish your patrol?"

"Right." Tony stopped staring at the wall, put his hat back on his head, and left, his boots creaking down the hallway.

Once he was gone, I frowned at his empty chair. Tony wasn't fanciful. He didn't drink on the job. He never exaggerated a report. And yet here we were, with stories already germinating in the Florida heat, primed to sprout into full-grown legends by sundown.

So what happened out there on the sidewalk?

I didn't believe in miracles. But I was fairly certain that by dinner time the town would be saying Josh raised Fulbright from the dead and fed the gawkers with five Twinkies and two peppermints.

CHAPTER
THIRTY

The chains of the porch swing groaned when Heather lowered herself onto it. Hoss settled beside the swing like a watchful lion, his breath huffing in slow, steady pulses. Josh unbuckled Maggie with calm hands that looked like they belonged on a farmer, not on someone who could do . . . whatever he'd done to Jackson Fulbright.

He opened the front door and glanced back at her, a question in his eyes. "Coming in?"

Heather shook her head. "I think I'll sit here with Hoss a while."

"Suit yourself. I need to fix Maggie's bottle."

The screen door slapped shut behind him, a homey sound that made her throat tighten. She would miss it.

She eased back and shut her eyes. The breeze smelled of damp soil and oak pollen, the golden dust that arrived with March and covered the porch, the swing, and every car in Peculiar. From the lot next door, Grace Egan sneezed, a loud *achoo* that startled a squirrel on the Donnelly porch railing.

Heather couldn't stop a smile. Everything around her

appeared beautifully ordinary, but this house, this situation, was anything but.

She tried to slow her breathing, but her thoughts kept spinning like laundry in a dryer. How could she be living with a man who could calm agony with nothing but a prayer and the touch of his hands? A man like that should not be living in Peculiar, Florida. He should be on Oprah. He should have a TED Talk. He should have handlers and book deals and people whispering in his ear about branding.

He shouldn't be living in a creaky Victorian house with faded curtains and a slobbering mastiff. And he shouldn't be living with a woman like her.

Her mind dragged her backward, to the funeral. Josh standing in front of the grave, his head bowed, his hands clasped. The neighbor leaning close, whispering that Josh might have raised a boy from the dead. Heather had dismissed the idea. People in small towns liked stories, and they liked them big. Nothing spread faster than gossip—except wildfire, and even that worked hard to keep up.

But today she had seen something that looked like a miracle. The old man's scream had ripped through her, sharp and helpless, and her own breath had stuttered, her fingers reaching for Maggie as if she could shield the baby from the sound.

Then Josh touched the man and everything went perfectly, impossibly back to normal.

Heather opened her eyes. The street blurred before her, the houses rippling in a thin veil of disbelief.

What she had witnessed was impossible. Because if Josh could do that, why hadn't he touched her foot when she'd been thumping around like a one-legged duck? Why hadn't he laid a hand on her fevered forehead and sent the sickness packing? Why hadn't he cured Maggie's frantic gasps and cries? He'd prayed, sure. He'd prayed hard. But he hadn't worked a miracle.

Maybe it didn't work that way. Maybe he couldn't call it up, like a trick. So she and Maggie suffered . . . a lot longer than the old man today.

She was losing her mind. Or Peculiar was. Maybe both.

The people of this town would go nuts over this. They'd spin today's scene until it gleamed like a polished river stone: *Josh Donnelly works miracle on sidewalk.* Most of them already believed that she, a rootless drifter, was Josh's girlfriend and Maggie's mother. They smiled at her in the check-out line, offered casseroles, assumed she belonged to the Donnelly house, tucked into Josh's orbit like some long-awaited blessing.

They didn't know she had stolen food from the Piggly Wiggly. They didn't know she'd taken a shirt and jeans from the thrift store because she couldn't bear the thought of wearing the same clothes one more day. They didn't know what she had been before Josh's house: a vagabond, a pickpocket, and Brett's shadow.

Life with Brett had taught her one thing above all: survive. Don't try to thrive. Don't trust. Don't stay.

She glanced toward the screen door, where Josh had vanished with the baby. The porch creaked as she lowered her foot, flexing the bones he hadn't healed. The fracture still ached occasionally. The skin was still tender. A reminder.

She didn't belong in this house. Didn't belong in this town. Didn't belong anywhere near a man people considered a saint even before Jackson Fulbright took a tumble on the sidewalk.

She had to leave before Peculiar figured out she wasn't worthy of Josh Donnelly. She could let folks have their romantic fantasy a little longer—after all, it provided her with tasty meals, clean sheets, and a roof that didn't leak . . . much.

But she wouldn't ruin Josh's life by staying. And she wouldn't let this place, with its Salisbury steaks and friendly greetings and improbable miracles, burrow under her skin.

She bent and ran her fingers through the ruff at Hoss's neck.

"Leave," she said aloud. Before the fantasy became a cage. Before Josh's kindness became another debt she couldn't repay. Before this town—and its resident saint—unwrapped her, layer by layer.

Before she forgot how to run.

WHILE MAGGIE NAPPED, Josh sat at the kitchen table with a length of oak balanced across his knees. Afternoon light slanted through the window above the sink, bright and golden, catching dust specks and turning them into tiny drifting lanterns. The soft rumble of Hoss's snoring came through the window, as did the creak of the porch swing where Heather sat. The house—his childhood home—brimmed with peace.

He turned the wood in his hand, his thumb brushing the rough bark, his knife gliding in slow, even strokes. He didn't yet know what the piece wanted to be. Sometimes wood revealed itself gradually, letting its shape bloom under the blade. Maybe a pen, or a comb for a woman's hair. He liked the idea of something simple, useful, and humble.

Or it could become sticks in a mobile over Maggie's crib. He could already imagine her wide eyes following the shapes he would carve for her: a dog, a cat, a star, maybe a crescent moon sanded as smooth as polished bone. If she loved it, he could make others. Retro Relics liked small, unique pieces. Things people picked up without thinking.

Heather entered the house without a word, her shoulders

tight, her face pale in a way that tugged at him. She glanced his way, then sat in the other kitchen chair. "How'd you learn to do that?" She folded her arms on the table. "Carving, I mean."

He smiled. "Chief Goodman gave me a pocketknife. When he saw that I liked whittling, he got me a nice carving set. I've been doin' it ever since."

She pulled one leg to her chest and wrapped her arms around it. "What kind of wood is that?"

"Oak."

"What will you do with it?"

"Not sure yet. But it'll come to me."

"This is pretty." She picked up a piece of cedar. "I like the stripes."

"It looks like a zebra," Josh said, smiling. "I had to get that on eBay, but I have a plan for it."

"And this?" She fingered a piece of spruce.

"That's white, so I was thinkin' that would make a nice dove. Or a polar bear."

She picked up a piece of ash. "And this?"

He looked up. "That's gray—so I was thinkin' wolf."

"Won't the paint cover all these pretty colors?"

He met her gaze. "Like a lot of things, good wood doesn't need paint. Its natural beauty shines through, the way it's meant to."

She laughed and looked away. "Now you're teasing me."

He shrugged. "Maybe."

She tilted her head, and he had a feeling she wanted to know about more than carving. "You're happy with your life, aren't you?"

His mouth quirked. "Sure. Why wouldn't I be?"

She shook her head, shrugging the question away. "Some people aren't."

"Some people," Josh said, "don't realize how blessed they are."

He didn't mean to point those words at her, but she gazed at him with a bewildered expression, then stood and went upstairs. She was probably worn out from the walk. Or maybe still rattled from Jackson Fulbright's screams. That sort of sound sank into a person and stayed a while.

He looked up a few minutes later when he heard the sound of thuds above him—Heather, moving stuff around. The bedsprings groaned, then fell quiet. He paused, listening, his knife still. After another moment of silence, he figured she had fallen asleep. Good. Rest was good medicine.

Once he had peeled the bark away, he set the stick aside and pulled a frozen lasagna from the freezer. He squinted at the directions. Two hours? Mercy. But Heather said she loved Italian food, and lasagna was the most Italian meal he could think of. It had stretched his food budget—he would need to be disciplined with groceries this week—but the cost didn't bother him. Heather was worth it.

As he unwrapped the lasagna, he tried to imagine how she felt when her boyfriend abandoned her. Though he had glimpsed the guy's van at the park, he'd been too consumed with caring for Mama to notice people coming and going. Still, he prayed for the man—not always kindly, but sincerely—because anyone who left someone like Heather had to be dealing with some kind of brokenness.

What sort of man would walk away from her?

Heather, with her sharp eyes and sharper instincts. Courage tucked beneath wariness. Mama would've called it spunk. Josh thought of the way Heather laughed on her good days—bright, ringing, like a glass bell. She didn't laugh much anymore, and she had barely smiled today. But glimpses of her humor assured him she wasn't beyond hope. She was healing, even if she couldn't see it.

Who had convinced her she didn't deserve happiness? The question stuck in his ribs, pressing like a bruise.

Sighing, he set the oven and slid the lasagna in. Soup and sandwiches would've been quicker, but he had a responsibility. Feed my sheep, the Lord said. Sometimes feeding meant late dinners. Or supermarket lasagna. Or offering a safe place for someone trying to rebuild a life.

He went upstairs to check on Maggie and found her awake, her brown eyes blinking in the dim light. Her tiny fists fluttered when she saw him, and his heart lightened. He changed her diaper with practiced efficiency, then carried her downstairs while the house filled with the slow-building aroma of tomato and melted cheese.

After finishing her bottle, Maggie pushed up on her little forearms, straining to lift her chest like a determined turtle. Every few seconds she lunged for Hoss's whiskers. The dog endured this with saintlike patience, turning his head away whenever her grasping fingers got too close.

"You're gettin' strong," Josh said, leaning toward her. Her eyes sparkled, her lips dribbled spit bubbles. She had changed so much. She babbled now—endless gurgles and coos. No words yet, but the music of her voice softened every rough edge in him. She studied him when he spoke, her eyes locking on with startling attentiveness. She was sleeping through the night most nights, and she smiled whenever Josh called her name.

Heather insisted the smile came from gas, but Josh knew better. Maggie only smiled at the people she trusted.

"What a smart girl." He scooped her up after ten minutes, her tiny body warm against his shoulder. She let out a soft yawn that scrunched her entire face. He rubbed her back. "Are you ready for a cat nap?"

He carried her upstairs, laid her in the crib, and pulled the blanket up around her legs. On his way back down, he paused outside Heather's door. Silence.

He released a breath and headed downstairs, wondering how he could help someone who didn't believe she was worth the effort.

THE SHADOWS outside Heather's window had cooled to dusky blue by the time Josh called up the stairs and said dinner was ready.

Her stomach growled in response, but she hesitated. She should answer that she wasn't hungry or needed to rest. She didn't need to have yet another meal at his expense.

Yet the aroma drifting up the staircase—garlicky, warm, and cheesy—wrapped around her like a hand prodding her forward. Josh had clearly outdone himself. She didn't want to hurt his feelings, and she couldn't ignore a practical truth: she didn't know where her next meal would come from. It might not come for hours or days, and she needed the calories. She would need strength to leave.

She drew a breath, braced herself, and went downstairs.

Josh was pulling a lasagna from the oven when she reached the kitchen. Steam rose from the pan in slow, fragrant curls. Her heart twisted. "Oh my," she said, unable to hide her surprise. "That smells unbelievable."

"Mama used to cook these." He set the pan on the counter. "I'm not sure if warming it up qualifies as cooking, but they sure are good."

Heather blinked. She didn't know much about Josh's

mother, but the woman must have been a saint to raise a man like this.

She cleared her throat. "Are we celebrating a special occasion? Your birthday, maybe?"

His cheeks reddened. "Nothing special. But you said you liked Italian and I thought you might want something different."

"Well, thank you." She forced a bright note into her voice. She would not hurt him, not now. "You want me to serve? I think there's a big spoon in the drawer behind you."

"Sure, if you want to."

She dished generous helpings onto their plates while Josh set out a bowl of salad and two bottles of dressing. "So you'll have a choice."

Choice. The word pricked her like a needle. Did she have a choice? Not really.

She'd spent days calling police stations, but no one had seen Brett. If she was going to find him, she'd have to go to Nashville and look for him waiting tables or bagging groceries.

Staying here would only be taking advantage of Josh's hospitality. And he knew she was Brett's girl, though lately she'd noticed a certain look in his eyes . . . a look she didn't want to encourage.

She picked up her fork, but Josh bowed his head. Heather froze as his voice folded through her.

"Heavenly Father, thank you for lasagna. Thank you for taking care of little Maggie and for making Heather well. Bless each of us to do Your will. In Jesus' name we pray, Amen."

His prayer hit her heart like taps from a tiny hammer. She swallowed hard. "Looks good," she muttered. "Thank you."

"You're welcome."

They ate in silence. Heather chewed mechanically, trying to

force food around the boulder in her throat. Every bite tasted delicious—a wonderful last supper.

He'd be hurt when he found the empty room, but he wouldn't hurt forever and he wouldn't be alone for long. Peculiar people would swarm him with casseroles and sympathy, and by next week some would be trying to set him up with nieces or coworkers.

Soon she would be nothing more than a footnote. A story people told at potlucks.

And Maggie ... she reached for her glass and swallowed a gulp of sweet tea. She would miss that little girl. She wouldn't see Maggie's first steps or teach her how to eat a Cheerio, but at least she had been able to bring that baby into the world.

Her throat closed, tight as a fist. She couldn't breathe. Panic rippled through her until she slammed her hand against the table, begging her body to function.

Josh shot up so fast his chair skittered backward. "You okay? Are you choking?"

She thrust her hand out in warning as her throat unlocked. "I'm okay," she rasped. "I—couldn't swallow for a minute."

He lowered himself back into his chair, concern shining in his eyes. "Can I make you somethin' else? Chicken soup?"

"No." She forced a smile. "Don't worry about me."

They had barely resumed eating when Maggie started to cry. Josh lowered his fork. "Time for another feedin'. Be back in a minute."

His footsteps clunked on the stairs, the sound tightening the knot in her throat. Memories of the past few weeks rose in her mind, memories she would soon have to bury.

She had to move forward. She had to leave this house and find Brett. Break out of this comfortable cocoon and fly free.

A tear slid over her cheeks as she tried to swallow another bite. What she was about to do wasn't fair. Josh deserved the moon, not a runaway with a suitcase full of bad decisions. He had chosen to bring her here—foolish, generous man—but that didn't mean she belonged. If he knew half her truth, he wouldn't want her shadowing his life.

So she had to go. Tonight.

She swiped the wetness from her face and forced herself into motion. Bite. Chew. Swallow. Drink. Repeat.

The stairs creaked; Josh descended with Maggie in his arms, both smiling like they'd been painted with sunlight. "Look who's up and ready for her bottle." He handed Maggie to Heather before she could object. "I can do this faster with two hands."

Maggie's small, chunky body landed in Heather's arms before she could refuse. She set the baby on the table's edge and held her there, struck again by those bright, trusting eyes. "Look at you," she whispered. "Clueless, aren't you?"

Josh glanced over his shoulder. "What's that?"

"Nothing." She pressed a kiss to Maggie's forehead. "You're gonna have a great life, kid, but it sure won't be predictable."

A moment later, Josh brought the warm bottle. "You want to do the honors, or eat while the lasagna's hot?"

She couldn't feed the baby, not when she was planning to walk away. "She's all yours."

He sat, feeding Maggie with easy tenderness, letting his own dinner grow cold. That struck her more than anything—his willingness to put others first. Even her. Especially her.

She set her fork down. "Josh—" She hesitated. "I hate to ask, but I don't have any money and I need to get a few things at the grocery."

"No problem. I can zip Maggie into a sleeper and we can all go together."

"You don't need to come. I'll be okay."

"But you shouldn't walk alone in the dark."

"We're in Peculiar. Nothing's going to happen to me."

He frowned. "You could trip on the sidewalk or—"

"Josh, I want to go by myself, okay?" She ducked her head, softening her voice. "I need to get girl things."

"Oh." His cheeks reddened again. "Okay. Well, how much do I owe you for painting?"

"A hundred dollars. It's been two weeks since you last paid me."

His brow wrinkled. "Do you need that much now?"

"Yeah. I need shoes too. My sandals are falling apart. I can't wear your mama's shoes."

"Let me see what I have." He shifted Maggie and reached for his wallet. "Would you mind picking up another carton of formula?"

If she refused, he'd know something was off. "Sure."

He pulled out his cash—every last bill—and set it on the table.

Heather stared at it. Stared at him. "You sure you can spare this much?"

"I'll be fine. The Lord always takes care of me."

She snorted before she could stop herself.

"What's so funny?"

She speared a piece of pasta. "You are. Sometimes you talk like an old man."

"Maybe I talk like a believer."

"Is that what it is?" She laughed—a thin, fragile sound, but genuine. "If you say so. In any case, you're funny. But sometimes—like when you warm up lasagna—you could give Prince Charming a run for his money."

He blushed again, but his smile eased the knot inside her. Good. She wanted him relaxed. When she walked out, she wanted him to have at least one happy memory of her.

Walking away would hurt, but staying would destroy them both. And she wouldn't let that happen.

CHAPTER
THIRTY-ONE

Heather pretended to watch TV until five p.m., when Josh always took Maggie up and read her a story before bed. If he thought she'd left for the Piggly Wiggly, he wouldn't be alarmed to come downstairs and find her gone.

When Josh finally took Maggie up, Heather counted to fifty while listening for the creak of the steps in case he'd forgotten something.

Only then did she open the coat closet.

The old red purse, packed with her things, sat on the floor, its strap stiff with age, the leather smelling of dust and old perfume. She hoisted it and paused, the weight reminding her that this action was irrevocable. This was not a plan she could abandon once set in motion.

She closed the closet door and set the purse on the sofa.

The sweater she wore was too big, so she pushed the sleeves up and checked the purse one last time. Her clothes, folded tight. A towel rolled thin. The hairbrush tucked into a side pocket. She slipped her fingers around it, grounding herself in the solid feel of the handle.

Hair as pretty as yours...

Josh's words landed again, uninvited. She'd been startled when he said it, in the way an unexpected sound makes your heart leap before your mind catches up. She had laughed it off, but the words followed her, clinging like burrs. Yet *pretty* was not a word you planned your life around. It was not protection. It was not a future. Still, Josh's gift had warmed the heart she tried to keep numb.

Brett had driven away with her brush in the van, and Josh must have thought her hair looked a mess. So he had bought her a brush, a simple act of kindness Brett would never have considered.

She zipped the purse and looked around. Fortunately, Hoss had gone upstairs with Josh, so he wouldn't bark when she went out the door.

"I'm going to the Wiggly," she called. "And I might do some shopping after."

She thought Josh replied, but couldn't hear him over her pounding heartbeat.

She picked up the purse and opened the front door. The spring air slipped in, sharp and alive, smelling of damp earth and pine needles. She stepped onto the porch and pulled the door closed, then rested her forehead against the door frame. The solid, patient house stayed quiet. How old was this place? It would be here in the morning, but she wouldn't.

She hurried down the walkway, and the iron gate creaked as she pushed it open. She winced, then looked back at the window in Maggie's room. The curtain did not stir. Hoss did not bark. The neighbors did not call out as she turned and began to walk.

The live oaks were spaced far enough apart that she moved

in and out of their shadows, her sandals slapping against the pavement. The soles bent with each step, as thin as promises. She adjusted her grip on the purse strap and set a pace she could maintain for hours if necessary. Walking, she understood. You put one foot down, then the other. You didn't think about what you were leaving, you just moved forward.

The wind picked up as she left the neighborhood, whipping through the oaks and generating a shower of last year's leaves. The breeze cut through her sweater, raising gooseflesh along her arms. She tucked her chin and kept going, counting her steps, watching the edge of the road.

Cars passed occasionally, their headlights sweeping over her and then vanishing. She did not wave. She did not want to attract attention.

Her thoughts kept circling back to Nashville, the name glowing like a neon sign on a dark road. Brett had talked about the city as if it owed him success. She pictured him there, guitar slung over his back, smiling his easy smile. Maybe he would be happy to see her. Maybe relieved. Maybe both. She did not need anything from him but a welcome.

She passed the Piggly Wiggly without slowing, the store brightly lit, its lot filled with cars. She passed the thrift store and the city park, and a few minutes later she passed the city limit.

The farther she walked, the more the afternoon opened around her. Frogs croaked in the ditches. A bird called, sharp and sudden, making her jump.

She moved the purse to her other shoulder and felt the hairbrush against her hip. She did not take it for sentimental reasons. She needed a brush, that was all. But she knew she would keep it long after every other Peculiar memory had faded.

The road sloped upward, and she welcomed the ache when

her calves began to burn. Pain meant she was moving forward. It kept her from thinking about the softness of a bundled baby and the way Josh had looked at her that afternoon, his eyes open and unguarded, as if trust were not a gamble.

Trust was dangerous. Hope even more so.

By the time she reached the deserted stretch that led to the highway, the wind had grown cold. She unrolled the sleeves of her sweater and quickened her step. Five miles. She could do five miles. When Brett's van broke down, as it frequently did, she had walked longer distances to find help.

Ahead, Tuscawilla road disappeared into darkness, but she walked it anyway, her sandals slapping against the pavement, the purse thumping at her side. Whatever waited for her at the truck stop, whether it was a ride or temporary shelter, at least it would not look like home.

When Heather didn't come home by seven, Josh told himself not to worry. When the clock struck eight and she still hadn't returned, he sat on the porch with Maggie in his arms, hoping to catch sight of her.

At twelve minutes to nine, with Maggie on the sofa, he dialed the Piggly Wiggly. The receiver was slick in his hand, his palm damp despite the cool breeze drifting through the house. The ceiling fan clicked with each rotation, a sound he usually found comforting. Tonight it grated.

Leo Wilkerson answered on the third ring, his voice flat and tired.

"Heather said she was going shopping there," Josh said, trying to sound calm. "Did you see her, by chance? Blonde hair, shoulder length, about five-six? She was wearing an orange sweater and dark pants, and she was going to buy formula."

"Sorry, Josh," the manager said, papers rustling in the background. "We had a bunch of customers tonight. I haven't had a minute to look around."

"That's okay." Josh forced a smile, though Leo couldn't see him. "I'm sure you've been busy. She probably went to the Seven-Eleven instead. I'll check there."

Leo hung up and Josh stood listening to the dial tone. He didn't really think Heather would get baby formula at the Seven-Eleven, but she was unpredictable. She might have decided they sold flip-flops. Or hot food. Or maybe she just wanted time away from the house.

He called, but the clerk at the Seven-Eleven hadn't seen her.

Josh thanked him and set the phone down, aligning it with the edge of the table as if order might keep panic at bay. But the gesture did little to conquer the cold sense of dread uncoiling in his belly.

He closed his eyes and leaned against the wall. Mama would know what to say right now—she always did. He could almost hear her voice, firm and affectionate all at once.

A leopard can't change its spots, Joshua.

The phrase landed with a dull ache. Mama had been kind, but she was also practical. She believed in helping people, but not in letting their troubles climb into your lap and make themselves at home.

But after a moment she would have taken his hand and softened her voice. *A girl like that has to change how she thinks, son. She'll have to do that for herself.*

When ten o'clock came and went, the silence thickened, pooling in corners. Josh stayed inside with Maggie, though every nerve in his body urged him to do something, anything. He sat on the couch, his eyes fixed on the television, not really seeing the flickering images. He half expected to hear a breaking news alert, a reporter standing in the dark while flashing lights painted the trees.

Nobody needed four hours to shop at the Piggly Wiggly.

The truth pressed on him, heavy and undeniable, but his mind refused to shape it into words. Something had happened. Trouble always seemed to know exactly where to find her.

A quieter, more insistent voice suggested she might have run, but Josh rejected that idea. Heather wouldn't do that. She knew he locked the door at ten. She knew he needed help with Maggie. She wouldn't leave without saying something. She couldn't.

He began pacing, the worn floorboards creaking under his steps. He moved from the couch to the window and back again, glancing at Maggie every few minutes, reassured by her gurgles and grunts. The television droned on, an anchor laughed at some trivial quip, and Josh felt an irrational surge of anger at the glibness of it all.

Peculiar wasn't dangerous. Trouble usually came from outside, drifted through, and moved on. But Heather never explained how she'd ended up by the side of the road that first night, and his imagination filled in the gaps with vivid, unwanted detail. A stranger stopping too long at the truck stop. A ride that went wrong. A sudden decision to bolt, run, and hide.

Maybe she'd been running from Brett, the man she was determined to find.

He scrubbed a hand through his hair, tugging at it hard enough to hurt. His thoughts stacked up, one leading inexorably to the next, until guilt joined dread in a messy knot of regret.

If he hadn't taken Maggie and Hoss for a walk on Christmas Day. If he'd never gone down Tuscawilla Road. If he hadn't adopted Hoss, hadn't been tired and lonely and desperate to please his mother...

Each choice lined up, a path of stepping stones he could trace with terrible clarity.

"Mama," he said, his voice too loud in the empty room. He turned his gaze toward the rocking chair, toward the place he still wanted her to be. "You were right. People need to be protected from the world, not get involved in it."

The words echoed in the empty house, and even as he spoke, he knew they weren't true. He had heard the Lord's voice. He had obeyed. He had done exactly what he was supposed to do.

"Then why did You lead me to her?"

He sank onto the couch, his elbows on his knees, his hands dangling uselessly between them. His eyes drifted to a cobweb in the corner of the ceiling, its strands catching the light as the fan stirred the air. It floated lazily, indifferent to his turmoil.

"I could have handled the baby on my own," he whispered. "I could've hired a babysitter. I didn't need Heather, but I feel responsible for her." His voice broke. "I feel..." He gulped, the admission burning all the way down. "*Deep concern* for her."

The words startled him. He tested them, turned them over in his mind. He had never felt this kind of concern for a young woman, so he had no reference point. But he always ached when someone was hurting. He had been concerned for Mama and carried her grief as if it were his own. He had been concerned for Jackson Fulbright, had felt despair and helplessness when the man was writhing on the ground. He was fiercely concerned for Maggie, and often surprised by the intensity of his feelings.

His concern for Heather had doubtless bubbled up from the same deep well. Feelings that were protective. Tender. Painful.

He went to the window and gripped the frame as he looked out over the yard. Shadows moved beneath the oaks, Spanish moss swayed, and the philodendron leaves looked like giant silver hearts in the light of the full moon.

Would it be bright enough for Heather to walk home?

"I tried my best," he said, leaning on the windowsill. "I tried to feed Your lamb, and I failed." His voice thickened. "I can't help wanting her to come back. So please, Lord, either move her out of my heart or bring her home because I can't stand not knowing that she's okay."

He stood in the silence, waiting. He closed his eyes, bracing for silence or rebuke.

Instead, the Voice responded with a calm command:

Seek my lamb.

HEATHER SAT up as daylight crept along the door, a thin blade of pale gold slicing the gloom. The air inside the trailer was stale and heavy, breathed far too many times. Her body ached from the strain of the five-mile walk and the pain of saying goodbye.

She was lying on a metal floor scattered with cigarette butts, candy wrappers, crushed cups, and crusted blankets stiff with old sweat. Nearby, Jessica and Kayla slept on separate heaps of bedding, their bodies curled inward, their knees drawn up in the chilly air. Piles of discarded clothes served as pillows, denim and sequins and frayed cotton jumbled together. Heather saw no sign of Amber or Sarah.

For a moment, she sat in the stillness, listening.

Outside, semi engines growled and downshifted, the long exhale of trucks rolling off the highway. Somewhere a backup alarm beeped, sharp and insistent. A gull cried overhead, too far inland, its voice thin and lonely. The world had moved on since she left, but this place had not changed.

She pushed herself up, her palms pressing into the gritty floor. Her muscles protested, especially her foot, which sent a dull ache up her leg. The walk from Peculiar replayed itself in fragments: the long ribbon of road, the ache in her bones, the relief of seeing the trailer's rectangular silhouette at the edge of the parking lot. It wasn't shelter, exactly, but it wasn't asphalt either. Last night, it had looked like grace.

Now it felt like consequence.

She dragged a hand through her hair. It was tangled and stiff, and probably smelled of smoke and sweat.

Josh's kitchen flashed into her mind. The clean counters. The hum of the avocado refrigerator. The steaming, absurd goodness of a premade lasagna. Maggie's breath, milky and sweet. Hoss's tail thumping against the cabinet.

She squeezed her eyes shut and forced the images away.

"You're up early."

She turned at the sound of Jessica's voice. The girl was leaning against the wall, her back curved, her shoulders slumped. Her eyes were open but dull, as though she hadn't rested.

"We wondered if you'd be back," Jessica said. "I figured you would. But you were gone a while."

"Yeah." Heather folded her legs beneath her, wincing as her foot complained. "I took the baby into town, like Sarah wanted. Broke my foot on the way back." She hesitated. "But this guy found me."

Jessica's brows rose, sharp and skeptical. "A guy? He held you captive all this time?"

"I wasn't a captive." Heather smiled. "He was a good guy. Too nice, really." She crossed her arms. "He's the one I trusted with the baby."

The words lay like a stone between them.

Against her will, memories of Josh filled her head: his earnest face bent over Maggie, his voice rising in that ridiculous falsetto, praising the baby for lifting her head, for blinking, for existing. The way he clapped like she'd won an Olympic medal when she first rolled over. The way Hoss lay nearby, his eyes half-closed but alert, both guardian and witness.

Of all the people in the world, she'd chosen the right man to care for Sarah's baby.

Heather rubbed her eyes, wishing memory worked like a light switch. What had Josh done when she didn't come home? He would have waited. Counted minutes. Made excuses for her absence until the excuses ran out. Maybe he called the police. Maybe he bundled Maggie into the stroller and hurried to the Piggly Wiggly, scanning the sidewalk for a flash of blonde hair. Maybe he'd taken Hoss, foolishly hoping the dog could track her.

But Hoss tracked food, not flight risks.

Jessica pulled cigarettes and a lighter from her jacket pocket and tapped one free of the pack. She held it out. Heather shook her head.

"I'm trying to save money," Jessica said, lighting up. She brought the cigarette to her lips and inhaled as if the smoke were oxygen. "This time of year's busy. Lots of college guys heading to Daytona. Gotta be careful, though. The old woman who owns the place calls the law if she sees me."

Heather frowned, thinking of the Peculiar deputy who'd shown up when Jackson Fulbright fell. Vigilant wasn't the word. The Peculiar police were starved for action.

"Don't the cops ever check here?" she asked. "The station's not that far."

"Ju-ris-dic-tion," Jessica said. "Truck stop lady has to call the highway patrol, and they're usually busy with the interstate." She exhaled smoke, then studied Heather through it. "Why'd you come back? Planning to work with us?"

"I need a ride," Heather said, hugging her knees. "Brett went to Nashville, and I'm going to find him." She forced herself to keep going. "He left because I was pregnant. And now I'm not."

Jessica tapped ash onto the floor. "Then it was good to see you. Take care."

Heather's gaze drifted to Kayla, still asleep, her face slack with youth and exhaustion. She was too young to look so old.

What was going to happen to these girls? She had Brett, however flimsy that lifeline might be. These girls had nothing but the next truck, the next man, the next morning.

Heather blew out a breath. "Hey, have you thought about where you're gonna end up?"

Jessica drew on her cigarette, then let a ribbon of smoke escape her nostrils. "Probably the same place as you."

Heather shook her head. "I've got Brett," she said, resting her chin on her arms. "But this guy I met in Peculiar might help you. He bought me a hairbrush. Made lasagna because he knew I liked it. Let me sleep in his mama's room and never once tried to mess with me."

Jessica flicked ash away. "Really?" She leaned closer. "Does he know you're here?"

The question landed like a dropped plate.

Heather bit her lip. Josh would never think to look for her here. He probably couldn't even imagine a place like this. He was probably still scanning sidewalks and grocery aisles, praying into the quiet.

She lowered her head onto her folded arms and closed her eyes.

She didn't deserve better than these girls. She had stolen

and lied and pretended her way through the last three years. All those months with Brett had etched something permanent into her bones. *Drifter* didn't describe her life; it defined it.

She lifted her head. "There's nothing good here," she said, her voice sharp. "This life will use you up."

"And you got somethin' better?" Jessica shot back. "What makes you think you're better off than me?"

"Nothing," Heather said. "Only difference is I've got a man who loves me."

"Girl, I have one of those every night."

Kayla stirred, blinking sleep from her eyes. "Hey," she said, smiling in recognition. "You came back."

"Just for the night," Heather said. "I'm heading to Nashville."

Kayla shrugged. "Okay."

"But before I go—" Heather grabbed her purse, grateful that it contained more than clothes and the hairbrush. "I'm hungry, and I want a big breakfast. And I want you guys to order whatever you want."

Kayla stared. "Really?"

"Yeah." Heather forced a smile. "Come on. Make yourself presentable, and let's go eat."

She might not be able to give these girls a new life, but thanks to Josh, she could at least give them breakfast.

CHAPTER
THIRTY-TWO

March in Peculiar is when the wind forgets its manners and the rain comes in sideways, like it's trying to read over your shoulder. By the time Josh Donnelly called me, my knee was humming its usual complaint, which meant a front was rolling in hard from the Gulf.

"Chief," Tony said, "Josh Donnelly's on line two."

I picked up the phone and stared out the window, where the flag was snapping itself half to death. "Put him through," I said. I figured he was calling about some minor problem. Josh was the sort of man who worried out loud and apologized for it later.

"Morning, Chief," he said. His voice sounded like it had been out in the weather without a coat.

"Well," I said, settling back in my chair, "if it isn't Peculiar's most dependable citizen. What can I do for you, Josh?"

"I was wondering," Josh said, "if you or your deputy have seen Heather today. She didn't come home last night."

Outside, rain rattled against the glass like handfuls of gravel.

"Lose her, did you?" I smiled at my own joke.

Josh didn't laugh. That's when I knew this call was going to take a while.

He told me she'd gone to the grocery and hadn't come back. No note. No slammed door. Just absence, which is the sort of thing that creeps up like a bad cold. He spoke in plain sentences, but underneath I could hear the strain, like a rope pulled tight enough to start fraying.

"Did you two argue?" I asked.

"No, sir."

"Anything seem off before she left?"

He hesitated. "Not really. Heather had moods. I understood if she wanted to go. I told her she could anytime. But I don't understand why she wouldn't say goodbye. Maggie and I have been waiting and—"

"Hold up," I said, straightening. "The baby's still with you?"

"Yes, sir."

I leaned forward, elbows on the desk, watching rainwater snake its way down the windowpane. I'd seen all sorts of departures in my career. Folks leave towns, leave marriages, leave jobs with a box of desk junk and a promise to call.

But a woman leaving her baby behind? That gave me pause.

"Did she pack?" I asked. "Suitcase? Backpack?"

"She didn't have much to start with," Josh said. "The only thing missing is Mama's big red purse. I only know that because I saw it sitting on her bed yesterday."

That earned a snort from me. I remembered his mother's purse well. If civilization ended overnight, she could have survived three days on what she kept in there.

"Any money missing?" I asked. "Valuables?"

"I paid her for some work she'd done. Other than a few clothes, I don't think she took anything."

Only a bag. Cash. No baby.

I rubbed my temple as thunder rolled somewhere south of town. "Josh, I'm going to say something you won't like. It sounds like Heather may have gone back to wherever she came from. I can't explain why she'd leave her baby, but—"

"She had a boyfriend," Josh interrupted. "He left around Christmas."

"Well," I said, letting the word stretch. "Do you think she went back to him?"

The line filled with static and the distant rush of wind. Then Josh spoke again, steadier than I expected.

"She doesn't have a car. To catch a bus, she'd have to get to Marianna."

"If she hitched a ride," I said, "she could be anywhere by now."

"Even Nashville," Josh said, calm as a man reciting facts he's already accepted. He took a breath. "I know she thought I was strange. She teased me some, but I never called her names. Never embarrassed her. I tried to give her time. Dignity."

I closed my eyes. I didn't know Heather Thomas, but I knew enough about people to recognize a story that didn't make sense.

"All right," I said. "I'll take the report. But if she chose to leave, there may not be much we can do. You did right by her, but sometimes right isn't enough. Now, about the baby—"

"I'm taking care of her," Josh said, firm as a courthouse step.

I sighed and wrote Heather's name on my pad, the ink bleeding slightly in the humidity. "Let's give it three days," I said. "After that, we'll have to talk options. And Josh—"

"Yeah?"

"Let me share something my mama told me once—if you love someone, sometimes you have to let them go."

I felt a bit silly, dispensing advice like some kind of Dear Abby, but Josh thanked me and said good-bye.

When I hung up, the rain was drumming the roof like impatient fingers. I figured Heather Thomas didn't want to be found, and women like that usually succeed.

What I didn't count on was Josh Donnelly, praying into the wind and walking the wet roads of Peculiar like a man who'd misplaced something precious.

Josh said Heather hadn't taken anything valuable.

I didn't argue. But I'd heard enough to know that she'd walked off with more than Josh realized.

JOSH TOLD Hoss to guard the house, an order the dog accepted with a solemn huff and a deliberate sprawl across the front door rug. Maggie gurgled as if she approved of the arrangement. Josh put her on his shoulder, then grabbed the car seat he'd bought at the thrift store, its faded straps smelling of disinfectant.

Just before easing into the driver's seat, he stopped. The wind rattled the palmettos, and heavy clouds threatened more rain—as if someone was trying to talk him out of this.

"Am I doin' the right thing, Lord?"

Seek My lamb.

The words came with the quiet certainty he had learned to trust. Not thunder. Not command. Just truth settling into place.

Reassured, Josh strapped the car seat into the sedan and buckled Maggie in, tugging on each strap the way the manual described. In the rearview mirror, she thumped the padded safety bar as if this adventure was all for her benefit. He smiled, though his chest still ached.

He didn't regret calling the police. Chief Bowen had given him an idea and some advice, and Josh intended to follow both.

First he drove a slow loop through Peculiar, just in case. Past the Piggly Wiggly, where the flag snapped in the wind. Down residential streets slick with rain, lawns littered with pine needles and last week's fallen camellia petals. He scanned sidewalks and bus stops, porches and parking lots.

No Heather.

At the edge of town, he turned onto Tuscawilla Road and headed toward Big Al's Truck Stop, his windshield wipers thumping like a nervous heart.

Heather may have gone back to wherever she came from.

He was hoping she had, and that she'd stayed put. She hadn't loved her home, wherever that was. The only place she had mentioned more than once was Big Al's.

Despite the weather, the truck stop churned with life. Spring breakers spilled out of cars in flip-flops and hoodies, laughing as rain slicked their hair. Families trudged in from the parking lot with sleepy kids. Semis idled in long rows, their engines grumbling like enormous, patient beasts.

The chief was right. If Heather wanted a ride, she could be anywhere by now.

But the Lord had been insistent.

Josh parked, tucked Maggie's blanket closer around her chin, and pulled her from the car seat. The smells of coffee, fryer grease, and donuts greeted him when he entered the convenience store. He moved down each aisle, searching faces, jackets, looking for blonde hair.

No sign of Heather.

At the counter, the cashier smiled at Maggie. "Cute baby. How old?"

"Three months," Josh said. The words felt strange and right at the same time.

He hovered near the hallway to the women's restroom, his heart lifting when the door opened. A dark-haired woman emerged. Not Heather.

He checked the pump area, the row of semis, even the narrow spaces between trailers where rain pooled and cigarette butts floated in shallow puddles.

Finally, he pushed open the door to the restaurant.

The noise hit him first—the cheerful clatter of dishes and silverware. Laughter. Plates sliding across tabletops. The aromas of bacon, syrup, and strong coffee wrapped around him.

"How many?" a waitress called out, already reaching for menus.

"Uh," Josh said, aware of Maggie on his arm and how damp his jacket felt. "Just coffee to go."

"Counter's fine, hon," she said. "Be right with you."

He walked toward the counter, resting a steadying hand on Maggie's shoulder, and let his eyes sweep the room. A booth of noisy college kids, their eyes half-closed from sleep deprivation. Couples leaning close over plates of eggs. Families with crayons and coloring placemats, kids dragging syrupy fingers across the table.

"Excuse me," a waitress said, squeezing past with three loaded plates.

Josh followed the plates without meaning to. Pancakes stacked high, eggs glossy with butter, bacon curled and crisp.

The waitress set them down in a shadowed corner booth. Two dark-haired girls. One blonde.

Josh's pulse kicked. Heather.

For a moment, he couldn't move. She looked tired. But she was there, a fork in her hand, her shoulders hunched like someone guarding what little energy she had left.

She looked up when he reached the table. Her lips parted, surprise flashing across her face.

"Heather." He let out the breath he'd been holding all morning. "Thank God."

She blinked. "Josh?"

"Heather," he said, his words steady because he'd practiced them all morning. "If you love someone, sometimes you have to let them go."

One of the dark-haired girls giggled. The other leaned back and said, "Is this the guy?"

Heather didn't look at them; her eyes stayed on Josh. "What are you doing here?"

He swallowed as Maggie squirmed in his arms. "If you want to go to Nashville, I'll take you. If you want to find Brett, I'll help you." His voice lowered. "But come home where you'll be safe. We miss you."

The table went quiet. Even the restaurant noise seemed to fade.

Heather bit her lower lip. Josh studied the debate on her face, the war between pride and weariness, between running and resting.

She glanced at the girls and sighed. "I told you he was nice."

She reached into her purse, pulled out a few bills, and set them on the table. "This should cover breakfast and anything else you want." Then, softer, "You girls be careful."

She stood.

Josh stepped back to give her room, his heart pounding so hard he was certain everyone within fifty yards could hear it. When she walked past him, he turned with her.

Outside, the rain had eased to a fine mist, but the wind was still tugging at everything that wasn't nailed down. Heather stopped beyond the awning and looked at Maggie. Her shoulders sagged, the fight draining out of her.

"Okay," she said. "I'm gonna trust you to keep your word."

Josh nodded, afraid to say anything that might undo her decision. He opened the car door, settling Maggie inside before walking around to open the passenger door for Heather.

She was already in the car.

And for the first time since she'd left, the ache in Josh's chest eased.

AS JOSH DROVE BACK to Peculiar, Heather turned and looked at the baby in the car seat.

"Hey there, Mags."

The baby turned toward her, and then it happened—not gas. Not reflex. A full, deliberate smile.

Heather's heart clenched. The baby had smiled at her.

After having come from the trailer, the smile was especially meaningful. An inadvertent acknowledgement of how far they'd come together.

Coming back to Josh's house felt like crossing a threshold Heather hadn't realized she'd memorized. The front door shut behind her with a familiar, reassuring sound, and for a moment she stood in the foyer, breathing in the house. Coffee. Clean laundry. Dog. A faint undercurrent of old wood and pine cleaner. The smells of a place where people *stayed*.

Hoss barreled toward her, his paws thumping the floor, tail working so hard the rest of him had to sway along. She laughed before she could stop herself. Hoss pressed his massive head against her thigh, demanding attention, granting forgiveness, and acknowledging her existence all at once. She sank her fingers into the loose skin at his neck and squeezed, grounding herself in his joy.

Even Josh's mother's room looked different. The bedspread still bore the old roses, but the colors seemed steadier and more vibrant, as if the house had taken a spa day while she was gone. As if it had been waiting.

She dropped the huge red purse on the bed and unpacked in efficient movements. Shirt. Jeans. Socks.

Then she took out the hairbrush and set it in the center of the dresser. It was proof she belonged here, at least for now.

When she finished unpacking, the purse sagged in on itself, as if relieved to go back to Mama's closet.

Downstairs, Josh sat at the kitchen table with Maggie in his arms, the bottle tipped into her mouth. Exhaustion had settled into the lines around his eyes. Had he not slept?

Heather slid into the chair across from him and pressed her palms to the table, the surface cool beneath her skin.

"I know what I did was bad," she said. "Leaving without saying anything."

Josh didn't contradict her. He raised one eyebrow and glanced at Maggie, as if she had been hurt, too.

"I hate good-byes," Heather went on, words spilling onto the table. "They feel like traps. So I leave. It's easier."

"Easier... for you," Josh said.

Heather blew out a breath. Fair point. She'd left exactly like Brett had.

Josh eased the bottle from Maggie's mouth. Her eyes were already closed, lashes resting against her cheeks, her mouth still making small, hopeful motions. Heather studied his hands. Careful. Practiced. The hands of someone who'd learned how to hold on without squeezing too hard.

"It wasn't easy for me," he said, his voice rasping. "I was

worried sick. Afraid you'd hurt yourself, or someone had hurt you." The words landed and stayed.

Heather shook her head. "I'm sorry." Her apology sounded thin, and she knew it was too little, too late. "And thank you for coming. I was thinking I'd hitch a ride to Nashville." She shook her head. "Which was probably not the best idea."

"No," Josh agreed.

She tilted her head, studying him. "You said you'd help me find Brett."

"I will." He set the bottle on the table. "I figured out a way."

Hope flared before she could stop it. "How?"

"Chief Bowen." Josh moved Maggie to his shoulder and began to pat her back. "You wouldn't happen to know Brett's license plate number, would you?"

Heather shook her head. "Kansas plates, though. That's where he's from."

"And his full name?"

"Brett Steelhawk."

Josh arched his brows.

Her face heated. "I know it sounds made up, but that's his legal name."

"All right," Josh said. No smile. No skepticism. Just acceptance.

Maggie released a tiny burp and settled, her body slack with sleep. Josh stood and held her out to Heather.

"You put Maggie to bed," Josh said. "I'll call the chief. They can run a search on the vehicle."

Heather took Maggie. "It's that simple?"

"I don't know," Josh said. "But it works on TV."

Heather held Maggie close as she headed up the stairs. Hope frightened her. But this time, it had arrived with real things: a kitchen table, a sleeping baby, and a man who was already reaching for the phone.

CHAPTER
THIRTY-THREE

I was surprised to see Josh Donnelly's name pop up on the phone again. Josh didn't call people without a reason.

"Josh," I said, leaning back in my chair. "Any news on your girl?"

"She's home," he said, relief riding shotgun in his voice. "Everything's okay."

"Well, I'll be." I glanced out the window at the parking lot I'd been staring at for nearly twenty years. "That's good to hear. I had a hunch things would settle down."

I heard a hesitation, the kind that signals more trouble ahead.

"I need a favor, Chief," Josh said. "I don't know how this stuff works, but—"

"What's up?" I swiveled my chair and woke up my tablet. Police reflex. You hear a tone like that, you start taking notes.

"Heather's boyfriend, Brett Steelhawk. She needs to find him."

I propped my chin on my free hand and let the pieces click

into place. Young woman runs away with a man who promises the moon and delivers a parking lot. Now she's under pressure, with a baby. He takes off, leaving her with no resources. No support. She runs when reality catches up. It usually does.

At least she'd found a safe harbor with Josh Donnelly.

"All right," I said. "Where does she think he is?"

"He could be anywhere," Josh answered. "When he left Peculiar, he talked about heading to Nashville. I don't know if he made it that far."

Of course. Every man with a guitar and a dream eventually points his compass toward Tennessee.

"Okay." I scribbled on the tablet. "Let's start with the basics. Year and make of the vehicle?"

Josh covered the phone, muffled voices murmured in the background. Probably Heather.

A moment later Josh came back. "1988 VW Westfalia. Yellow. Kansas plates. She doesn't know the plate number."

"Yellow," I repeated, typing. "That helps. Hard to miss a rolling banana." I paused. "Full legal name?"

"Brett Steelhawk," Josh said. "For real."

I snorted before I could stop myself. "Of course it is."

Josh didn't laugh. He was taking this seriously, and that told me plenty.

"All right." I straightened in my chair. "Here's the thing. We need a reason to go looking. Vehicle stolen? Outstanding warrants? Something that fits in a box."

More murmuring. When Josh finally came back, his voice had changed. "Is it against the law to abandon your girlfriend?"

"Not quite," I said, thinking of the baby, "but it's close."

I entered *unlawful desertion of a child* as the charge and sent the information down the line. A few keystrokes, a few databases, a quiet ripple moving outward. Sometimes that's all police work is. You toss a stone into the water, watch the expanding rings, and wait to see what floats back.

"Okay, Josh," I said. "I'll put this out. No promises. Might take a while."

"That's fine," he said. I couldn't tell if he sounded relieved or was bracing for disappointment. "Thanks, Chief. I owe you."

As our chilly March shrugged itself into a sunny April, I started seeing the same tableau whenever I cruised past Josh Donnelly's place: Josh on the steps with a block of wood braced between his knees, knife flashing in small, patient strokes. Heather on the porch swing feeding the baby, her posture saying she might be ready to bolt if the wind shifted. And Hoss, planted front and center, chest out, eyes tracking traffic like a guard who'd been promised extra rations.

Now that I knew more about Heather Thomas, I paid closer attention. Occupational hazard. You don't spend decades in law enforcement without learning how to watch without staring. Josh was probably watching too, but his interest ran on a different frequency. Mine was about risk assessment. His was about whether anyone needed a sandwich or a blanket.

Jackie Leakey owned Retro Relics, which meant she knew everything that happened in Peculiar three business days before the rest of us.

"Josh's work is better than ever," she told me, dragging me toward the counter like I was a captive jury. She pointed to a nativity scene carved from oak. "Look at Joseph. Tell me that's not a self-portrait. And Mary. Don't she look like Heather?"

I squinted at the figures. All I saw was wood and skill and a man who knew how to leave space where it mattered. "I don't see the resemblance."

Jackie looked disappointed. I had the feeling she'd run that theory past every customer who came through the door, hoping someone would validate it. Not that she was accusing Heather of divine motherhood, mind.

I was pretty sure that baby belonged to the Elvis wannabe, but I kept my lip zipped.

"I find it strange," Jackie said. "One day I've got a single man livin' next to me, and the next day there's a family. Somethin's off. Then again, who's ever been able to explain Josh Donnelly?"

Tamera Parker, at the Coif It Up salon, added her own expert testimony. One of her clients, who apparently had a Ph.D. and a lot of opinions, said Josh was "probably somewhere on the spectrum." Tamera shrugged and said, "He's different, but he's okay. And different plus okay usually means people don't know what to do with you."

The speculation didn't amount to much in my book. Heather was polite and Josh had never so much as jaywalked. If a good man found happiness helping a confused young mother and her baby, I wasn't about to write them a citation.

But not everyone agreed.

The longer Heather stayed, the more some folks became convinced that they'd been personally wronged by her presence.

"His mama would rise out of her grave if she knew Josh was livin' with a woman without benefit of marriage," one woman informed me, arms crossed like she was guarding a moral perimeter. "Margaret Donnelly was a church-goer."

"So is Josh," I said. "And Grace Egan says Heather sleeps in Margaret's bedroom, not Josh's. Grace has a direct sightline into the house, so if anyone knows, it's her."

The woman's brows snapped together. "And that baby? Where do you suppose it came from?"

"If the baby isn't breaking the law, I'm not concerned. So Heather had a child before she met Josh. Happens all the time. Josh doesn't seem to mind caring for another man's kid. He's clearly attached."

"Still—" the woman shook her head—"the church council will have to meet if he brings that woman into the House of God."

I raised my hands and beat a tactical retreat. I've been in shoot-outs that were less risky than church council meetings. In a gunfight, at least, you know where the bullets are coming from.

BECAUSE HE HADN'T HEARD anything from Chief Bowen, on the first Sunday in May Josh decided he would go to church. Not because it would be easy, but because he wanted his life to get back to some semblance of normal.

The waiting for news about Brett weighed on him. Each day that passed without word was a promise suspended in midair, and Josh didn't like not keeping his word. He had promised to find Brett, and he intended to do that, even if the road led straight out of Peculiar and took Heather with it.

Sunday he stood in the vestibule with Maggie in his arms. At four months old, she was no longer content to be merely transported through the world, but craned her neck, her fists opening and closing, her fingers holding tight to his shirt. She made a few low, bubbling sounds, and he bent his head toward her.

"I know," he murmured. "A lot to look at."

Heather walked into the sanctuary with him, one hand

clinging to the strap of the diaper bag, the other clenched at her side. He could sense her anxiety in the quick rhythm of her breathing. He heard it in the huff she released when the opening hymn swelled and the minister of music raised his arms... and froze.

The man's face slackened and his arms hung in the air as if they had forgotten how to move. The piano stopped. A few voices stumbled on, then the room turned and every pair of eyes found them.

Heat rushed into Josh's face, but he didn't look down. He'd lived too long being observed and labeled. So he smiled and gave a small, ordinary wave, as if he and Heather were nothing more than a couple of late arrivals.

Beside him, Heather chuffed a breath that sounded suspiciously like a laugh. Maggie chose that moment to squeal, a bright sound that cut through the tension like birdsong. Someone near the front laughed. Someone else dropped a hymnal.

Then the minister of music recovered, and the song staggered forward.

Josh guided Heather into the back pew and stood next to the aisle, holding Maggie tight against his shoulder. He wanted to stand under the pressure of their collective gaze. Didn't want anyone to think he was sneaking in under the cover of worship. He met eyes as they turned toward him. Some people flushed. Some stiffened. A few nodded, cautious but polite.

Heather slid into the pew and folded her hands in her lap. Her new skirt rustled and she muttered under her breath, but he couldn't make out the words. Maybe she was counting in an attempt to cool her temper.

Maggie reached for the colored light pouring through the stained-glass window and gripped empty air. She babbled, a string of soft consonants, and Josh's throat constricted. The little girl trusted him completely. He prayed he wouldn't let her down.

Pastor Gary was working through a series in John. That week, they landed at the well.

Josh listened closely, not because the message was new, but because it seemed pointed. When the pastor mentioned that the woman had had five husbands and was living with a man she wasn't married to, Heather's chin rose and her mouth pressed into a thin line. But when Pastor Gary quoted Jesus, her shoulders relaxed.

After the benediction, Josh slipped out of the pew and extended his hand, silently urging Heather to hurry. He could feel people surging toward them as curiosity sharpened its elbows.

Pastor Gary beat them to the back. "Josh, always good to see you," he said, clasping Josh's hand. "And who do you have with you this morning?"

As if he didn't know.

Josh patted Maggie's back. She had gone still, her eyes now heavy-lidded, her thumb wedged into her mouth. "This is Maggie," he said. "And this is Heather Thomas. She's stayin' with us for a while."

Heather took the pastor's hand.

"Glad to meet you," Pastor Gary said.

Heather dipped her chin in a curt nod. "Thanks."

As they hurried into the parking lot, tension drained from Josh's shoulders. Heather let out a long breath, a sound between relief and exhaustion.

"Well," she said, adjusting the diaper bag on her shoulder. "That went better than I thought."

Josh smiled, though his thoughts wandered as he looked

through the parking lot. No yellow van, and he looked for it everywhere. Not a single vehicle he didn't recognize.

He'd heard nothing from Chief Bowen. No report on Brett or where he might be. At this rate Heather might end up staying forever, but he had made a promise. Until he fulfilled it, he would keep her safe . . . and keep a short leash on his heart.

CHAPTER
THIRTY-FOUR

I didn't attend the church council meeting. Even though those meetings can get unruly, Peculiar Community Church was a long way from needing a cop to maintain the peace.

But on Monday, Vernon Williams, Peculiar's mortician and the church's head deacon, gave me a blow-by-blow over his morning coffee.

According to Vernon, two hours after Sunday services ended, he called an emergency meeting in Pastor Gary's office. Emergency church meetings usually involve theology or potato salad. Theology was the main dish at this one, served up with a side of concern.

That afternoon, Vernon had leaned forward in his chair and cleared his throat the way men do when they believe righteousness is about to stream from their lips.

"I've always admired young Donnelly," Vernon told the group. "But I don't see how he can continue to fellowship in this church while living with that young woman. The Word clearly says we have to make sure things are set right."

Several heads bobbed. One man leaned back until his chair complained.

"That's right," someone added. "We've got to think about the example we're setting. The morals of society have slipped enough already. The church needs to hold the line."

Pastor Gary, seated behind his desk, waited for the rumblings to settle.

"Of course we're called to obey Scripture," he said. "But how do we know Josh and Heather are living in sin?"

"That woman has a baby," another man shot back. "And we never saw hide nor hair of her before Christmas, so the child can't be Joshua's."

Nora Meens, who has never been accused of subtlety, nodded briskly. "Margaret Donnelly would be horrified. We should count it a mercy that she doesn't know."

At that point, young Stephanie Corbett spoke up. "Hold on," she said. "The Lord does work in mysterious ways."

"Which is why we ought to follow Scripture," Pastor Gary said, reaching for his Bible. "Paul wrote that if another believer is overcome by sin, those who are godly should help restore him." He looked around the circle. "Do any of you have evidence that Joshua Donnelly has been overcome by sin?"

According to Vernon, silence settled over the room like dust.

Finally, a woman raised her hand. "I saw her once, and the V-neck she was wearing left nothing to the imagination. A Christian woman should dress modestly."

"I saw that, too," Stephanie said. "And I recognized that V-neck—it was Margaret Donnelly's. Maybe Heather wore it because she didn't have anything else to wear."

Pastor Gary didn't even blink. "Do we know Heather's a Christian? If she doesn't claim to follow Christ, why should we hold her to the biblical standard?"

Vernon cleared his throat. "We know he's living with her. And the Bible tells us to avoid even the appearance of evil."

"But what's the evil?" Pastor Gary asked. "If Josh were renting out rooms and Heather rented one, would that be a problem?"

No one answered.

"Have any of you spoken to Josh," the pastor continued, "or have you only spoken *about* him?" He paused. "The Episcopal rector in Marianna lives with his housekeeper and no one questions him. Why is Josh Donnelly under suspicion while the rector is beyond reproach?"

Nora chimed in again. "Maybe we worry about Josh because he's young. And, well . . . you know how young men are. They have a weakness."

Pastor Gary raised an eyebrow. "What weakness is that, Nora?"

She smiled. "Raging hormones!"

The room erupted. Laughter bounced off the walls, and even Pastor Gary cracked a smile.

When the noise died down, the pastor leaned forward. "If Josh was indulging his sinful nature, I doubt he'd be attending church. If I were doing something I shouldn't, I can think of a dozen things I'd rather do on a Sunday morning than sit in a pew."

Vernon chuckled. "Fair enough," he said. "So maybe we should wait and see."

"Josh has always been quiet, so we actually don't know much about him," Pastor Gary said. "So let's get to know him, and Heather, too. Until then, let's pray for them and be ready to offer our help when they need it."

The meeting had ended without torches or pitchforks. Over coffee, Vernon assured me there would be no inquisition, though a few members might invite Josh and Heather to lunch under the banner of Christian fellowship.

"And if they keep coming to church," Vernon said, stirring his coffee, "we've decided we'll thank God and keep praying. World's lost enough as it is. We could all use some help from our friends."

For the first time in a long time, Peculiar managed to surprise me.

I WAS HALFWAY into my coat, already anticipating the comforts of a quiet supper and a recliner that knew my shape, when the phone rang. The old rotary on my desk sounded louder after hours, like it resented being woken from a nap.

Tony had already clocked out, so I turned back and picked up the receiver. "Chief Bowen."

"Horace? Is that you?"

The voice carried a twang I hadn't heard in years, and with it came a sudden memory of sweat-soaked academy uniforms and laps we were far too old to be running.

"Jake Williams," I said. "Well, I'll be. You still breathing up there in Ozark?"

"Most days," he said. "Though I swear this job's gonna finish me off before the cholesterol does."

We chewed the fat for a minute, traded updates on knees that no longer liked stairs and women who kept threatening to replace salt with good intentions. As we talked, I leaned against the desk and listened to the hum of the fluorescent lights overhead. The building always felt lonelier after five, like it exhaled once the place emptied out.

Jake cleared his throat, the way cops do when playtime's over.

"Hey, got a bulletin about a vehicle you're searchin' for. It's here. Been here a couple weeks. You need us to arrest this Brett Steelhawk?"

I moved back to my chair, the springs squealing under my weight. Even the furniture knew this wasn't good news.

"You found him?"

"Yep. Been buskin' in the park nearly every day. Guitar, bad Elvis impressions, the whole nine yards. Sleeps in the van, apparently. Hasn't been much trouble, but we've been keeping an eye on him."

I closed my eyes for a second. In my mind, I could see him clear as day: skinny, restless, chasing applause like it might finally stick to him.

"Thanks, Jake," I said. "Just keep an eye on the guy. I'll pass the news on to the interested party."

"Abandonment, huh?" Jake said. "Let me guess. Deadbeat dad. You want us to bring him in?"

I pictured Heather Thomas's face as I'd last seen it. Guarded. Tired. Hope hanging by a thread so thin you'd miss it if you blinked. I thought of that baby too.

"No," I said. "Let me see what the mother wants to do. I'll let you know."

Jake weighed my response, probably wondering why I didn't want him to lock up the no-good bum. For a minute we listened to the faint crackle of distance between two cops who knew better than to expect happy endings.

"Fair enough," Jake finally said. "For what it's worth, Horace, he doesn't look like much."

I almost smiled. "They never do."

After we hung up, I sat a moment longer, the receiver still warm in my hand. Outside, the sun had dropped low enough to stain the schoolhouse brick a tired orange. Somewhere down the street, a car door slammed, laughter floated, and life went on.

Brett Steelhawk, located at last. Not in Nashville, but barely over the state line. Not on a stage. Just another man with a guitar and a van, singing to strangers who didn't know what he'd left behind.

I set the phone back in its cradle, picked up my coat, and this time I didn't hesitate. Tomorrow, I'd have a conversation that could change a few lives. Tonight, all I could do was lock the door and carry the knowledge home with me.

Funny thing about answers. They never arrive when you're ready, and they never come without consequences.

When Heather brought Maggie back inside, one look at Josh's face told her something was wrong.

Out on the porch swing, everything had felt free and easy. The swing creaked in a lazy rhythm, Maggie's socked feet kicked at a strip of morning sunlight, and the breeze carried the clean smells of pine and laundry soap. Josh sat in his rocker and whittled at a block, slowly turning it into something amazing.

Heather had let herself believe that this gentle interlude might last a while. Then Josh went in to answer the phone.

Now the house felt cool, as if a door had been left open and a chilling fog had drifted inside.

"Everything okay?" Heather asked, shifting Maggie on her hip as she paused in the foyer.

"Go ahead and take Maggie up for her nap," Josh said. His voice was calm, but his face had a careful, tight look. "We can talk when you come back down."

She carried Maggie upstairs, her thoughts churning with every step. Josh didn't have family emergencies. His parents were gone, his bills were paid, and the fridge was filled with food. So what could have upset him?

Heather kissed Maggie's forehead and laid her in the crib with her favorite stuffed lamb, watching her eyelids flutter closed, her rib cage rising and falling. The sight made Heather's throat ache. Babies believed the world would take care of them.

Was she hoping for the same thing?

When she went downstairs, Josh was sitting at the kitchen table, his elbow braced, his chin resting in his palm. He wasn't looking at her, but staring out the window.

She slid into the chair across from him, the vinyl cool under her legs. "What's wrong?"

He turned and offered a stiff smile. "The chief found Brett in Alabama."

The words landed, then echoed. *Found Brett.*

Heather forgot how to breathe. Her hands flew to her head, fingers digging into her hair because she needed something to grip. "What? Are you sure it's *my* Brett?"

"Brett Steelhawk is in Ozark," Josh went on, his voice steady. "About an hour north of here."

She snatched a breath. Ozark. Alabama. Not Nashville, but close enough to drive to. Almost close enough to touch.

"Oh my goodness," she said. "I had about given up hope."

And she had. Nearly two months had passed since Josh called the Chief, two months with no word of Brett at all. She had told herself that hope was childish and dangerous. But her hope didn't disappear. It went underground.

"They found him," Josh said again. "And I promised I'd take you to him. So whenever you're ready, I'll drive you there."

She resisted the urge to pinch herself. Nashville had always felt like a fantasy, a place too big and too far away to believe in. But Ozark... she could believe Brett made it to Ozark.

Josh's eyes were clear and steady, and his face left no room for doubt. He meant it. "Do you want to go today?"

"Could we?" The words escaped before fear could catch them. "Yes!"

He nodded. "Chief Bowen said Brett's been busking there for a couple weeks. No telling when he'll move on." One corner of his mouth dipped. "Unless he's run out of gas again."

A laugh burst out of her, sharp and half-hysterical. She stood so fast her chair scraped the floor, then she went around the table and kissed the top of Josh's head, his hair soft beneath her lips, smelling of soap and sunshine.

"You really are too good to be true, Josh Donnelly," she said, her voice clotting with gratitude. "Let me get my stuff. If we leave now, we can find him before dinner."

"Yeah," he said. "And Maggie and I can get home before dark."

Something in his tone tugged at her, a hollowness that didn't belong in a moment this bright. But the image of Brett waiting somewhere up the road, alive and well, overwhelmed everything else.

"I'll be down in twenty minutes," she said, turning for the stairs.

Josh stood in the doorway of his old bedroom, listening.

Across the hall, Heather was moving around in his mama's room, quick and purposeful, the way she got when her mind leapt ahead of herself. Drawers opening. A cupboard closing.

The faint scrape of a chair leg. Each sound landed in him like a dropped coin, small and sharp.

He crossed to his old room and gripped the baby bed. Maggie lay there blinking up at him, her fists loosening from their sleepy curl. Five months old and sturdy now, thighs round as loaves, her belly round and solid beneath his palm.

"All right, Little Bit," he murmured. His voice came out calm, which surprised him. "I hate to wake you up, but you can sleep in the car."

He unsnapped the tabs of her sleeper. She cooed, the sound she made when she woke up happy. He'd learned her sounds the way some men learned engines or crops or card tricks. This one meant hungry. That one meant tired. The shrill one meant she needed him right now.

He worked with care, habit smoothing the edges of his thoughts. Undo the diaper. Fold it back. Wipe. The ordinary motions gave his mind room to wander, which might have been a mistake.

He tried, against his will, to imagine the house without Heather.

No humming drifting down the stairs in the morning. No laughter bursting out of nowhere, bright and sudden as a struck match. No moods, either, the silences that meant he'd said the wrong thing or not said enough. He hadn't known how much noise she made just by existing in the same house with him.

The house would go back to the way it had been when she left for two days. Too neat. Too still. Every clock loud. Every shadow stretching too far across the floor.

He swallowed.

When Mama was alive, he never thought of the house as empty. It had been full of Mama's footsteps. Her voice calling him for supper. The rhythm of two lives fitting together without effort. He hadn't noticed the fullness then, any more than he noticed the air.

But once she was gone, he felt the vacuum.

Heather changed the house again. Not the same way Mama had because Heather was louder. Messier. Human in a different register.

But the air was already thinning.

How could men like Brett appreciate women like her?

The thought came unbidden, sharp with a bitterness he didn't like but couldn't deny. Brett, with his egotism and his ambition and his way of bending the world so it revolved around him. Brett, who took and took and still walked away, chasing his dream the way a dog chases its shadow.

Josh fastened a clean diaper, his fingers suddenly clumsy. He blinked hard, staring at the little green ducks marching across the tabs until they swam back into focus.

"Sorry," he said, though Maggie hadn't fussed. She kicked once, pleased with his attention, and released a small, breathy sound that might have been a laugh.

He picked her up and held her against his breastbone. Her weight grounded him. Her cheek warmed his neck as her head slipped beneath his jaw, and he wanted her to stay there forever.

"We're going to have to get used to things being different," he told her. "That's all."

Maggie's hand found his shirt collar and gripped it, trusting and unquestioning.

The chief's voice echoed in his memory: *If you love something, sometimes you have to let it go.*

Even if it breaks your heart.

Josh closed his eyes and breathed Maggie in, this child who had rearranged his life in ways he never expected. Heather had done the same thing.

He heard her race down the stairs, then she called up to him. "Hey, Josh! Ready to go?" She laughed, and the sound sliced clean through him.

He held Maggie a little tighter and stood in the small, quiet room, memorizing the way the house felt in that moment, knowing he had already begun to grieve.

CHAPTER
THIRTY-FIVE

Josh drove with both hands on the wheel, the way a man should when faced with a serious responsibility.

Maggie rode in the back, strapped into the car seat, her head tipped to one side, eyes heavy with sleep. Heather sat up front, turned halfway toward him, talking as if the words themselves might carry her to Ozark, Alabama.

"I was working the counter at the gas station," Heather said, smiling at the windshield. "That's where I met him. He came in carrying that guitar case like it was an extension of his arm. Asked if we sold strings. I said no, but I knew where he could get some." She laughed. "He said I looked like someone who knew things."

Trusting his instinct, Josh nodded in all the right places.

"He was so smart," she went on. "Not book smart exactly, but he saw the world differently. Didn't want to be tied down. Hated the idea of a clock telling him where to be." She glanced at Josh, her eyes bright. "You know what I mean, right? Being free."

Josh knew what she meant. He also knew what had happened since that first meeting.

The road unwound beneath them, flat and familiar, pine trees blurring into green walls. Heather talked about sleeping in the van under stars so bright they looked close enough to touch. About waking up wherever they happened to land. About music and long conversations and how Brett always had a plan for the future, just not one that involved addresses or schedules.

Josh listened for the spaces between her sentences.

She didn't mention the nights she'd gone to bed hungry. Or the days she'd counted the change in her palm and pretended it was enough. She didn't say anything about rain leaking through the van's roof or the way cold crept in because the window didn't fully close. She talked about freedom like it was a feast, but Josh heard the clink of an empty plate underneath.

"He couldn't stand being ordinary," Heather said. "Always said the world didn't deserve him yet."

Josh gritted his teeth.

They passed through Marianna, storefronts slipping by, then took the detour around Dothan. The land opened up, wide and patient, fields resting under a pale sky. Maggie stirred and made a small sound, and Josh glanced in the rearview mirror, reassured when she settled again.

"He hated it when anyone tried to tell him what to do," Heather continued. "Said people were jealous. That they couldn't stand anyone who shined too bright."

Josh thought about gravity. About how stars pulled everything into their orbit, not because they meant to, but because that was their nature. And how nothing else was allowed to shine around them.

They passed Midland City, the sign flashing like a mile

marker counting down to the inevitable. Heather leaned back in her seat, quieter now.

"He's going to be so surprised," she said. "Thrilled, even. I mean, the last time he saw me, I was pregnant." Her laugh faltered. "He probably thinks I'm as big as a barn now."

Her voice caught, and Josh felt it like a blow to the throat.

She rarely mentioned the miscarriage, but the grief of it still shadowed her. He could hear it, rising up without permission, dragging the past into the present. He kept his eyes on the road because if he looked at her, he might say words he couldn't take back.

Ozark appeared without warning, the town unfolding around them. Josh slowed as they passed the police station, its brick façade solid and unremarkable.

"We should stop there first," he said. "Let them know we're—"

"No," Heather said. "Let's find the park 'cause that's where he'll be. Please. I want to surprise him."

Josh hesitated, then sighed. He wouldn't stand in the way of her hope.

They turned toward the city park, then Heather squealed. "Oh! Josh—look!"

The yellow camper van sat under a stand of trees like a misplaced toy, its paint dulled by sun and miles. A few feet away, Brett Steelhawk perched on a picnic table, his head bent over his guitar. His fingers moved automatically, strumming for no one. No crowd. No applause. Just music drifting into the air and disappearing.

Heather made a small, joyful squeak and clutched Josh's arm. "That's him. And he's playing the song he wrote for me!"

Josh pulled over, barely getting the car into park before she flung the door open.

"He'll be so happy," she said, her hair catching the light as she stepped onto the damp grass.

Josh got out, his attention split between Heather and Maggie. Maggie was fine in her car seat, and Heather was running toward Brett as if she could outrun the last six months.

Then the camper door opened.

A blonde woman stepped out, stretching like she'd just awakened from a nap. She walked toward Brett with easy familiarity, slid her fingers into his hair, and bent to kiss him.

Brett stopped singing and pulled the woman closer.

Heather slowed. Then stopped.

She crumpled, looking as though someone had reached inside her and cut the strings holding her body upright. She stood on the grass for a moment, watching Brett caress another woman...

Then she turned and walked back to Josh's car.

Josh cut across her path and opened her car door. She climbed in and buried her face in her hands.

He ran around to the driver's side, got in, and looked at her.

"Please," she said, lifting her head but not meeting his gaze. "Get me out of here."

He didn't argue. He started the engine and pulled out of the parking lot. In his rearview mirror, the yellow van shrank until it was nothing more than a blur of color among the trees.

Heather didn't say another word.

The drive home stretched long and silent, the road unspooling beneath them again. Maggie slept, unaware that a dream had ended in heartbreak.

Josh listened to the silence beside him, far heavier than Heather's chatter. He kept driving, taking them home, not understanding how a man could be handed something holy and treat it like it was nothing.

Heather closed Mama's bedroom door with care. The latch clicked, and the house fell quiet behind it. She leaned back against the wood, breathing through her nose because her throat had tightened.

The room smelled of clean cotton and lavender soap. The bedspread lay smooth, pale pink tucked tight at the corners, roses faded but stubborn. Everything looked tended. Lived in by a woman who had not spent her nights listening for danger.

Heather sat on the edge of the bed. The mattress dipped beneath her, solid and steady.

Since Christmas, she had buried two dreams.

The baby she'd wanted.

And the man she thought wanted her.

The truth settled deep. Brett hadn't loved her. He loved what she did for him—the listening, the believing, the way she made life easier.

"I'm a fool."

The word broke her open. She bent forward, forehead to her knees, and wept. For the baby. For the months spent building a future that was never meant to be. For the bright story she had carried into this house and dropped at Josh's feet.

Downstairs, the house made quiet sounds. Wood settling. A faint clink in the kitchen. Hoss crossing the floor. Life moving on.

She waited for Josh to call her name. He didn't. The silence felt like permission.

She lay back and stared at the ceiling until the room went dark.

When she woke again, the light had shifted. She stayed under the blanket.

A knock came at the door. Gentle.

"Heather? I'm setting a tray out here. You don't have to answer."

His footsteps faded down the hall.

Food. The thought brought a rush of guilt. She turned her face toward the window and shut her eyes.

The next time she woke, morning had come. Coffee drifted up the stairs. A chair scraped below. Maggie made small sounds between bites. Josh spoke to her in that silly voice he used at breakfast.

Heather sat up. Had he known about Brett? He hadn't looked surprised in the car. Had he realized the truth long before she did?

If he had, he kept it to himself. He opened her door. He drove her home. He never said a word to shame her.

Gratitude rose, sharp and hard to hold.

She swung her legs off the bed and crossed to the door.

A breakfast tray waited on the floor. French toast. Eggs. Bacon. Orange juice sweating in the glass.

She crouched and lifted it, her arms trembling.

In the kitchen, Maggie brightened when she saw her. Hoss thumped his tail from the living room, his leash tied short. She shot Josh a questioning look.

"It was the only way to save your breakfast," Josh said, holding a bottle.

Heather set the tray down and freed the dog. "Sorry, buddy."

She walked over and touched Maggie's cheek. The baby grinned.

"Josh."

He looked up.

"Thank you."

He nodded.

"Not just for this. For everything."

He stayed quiet, giving her space.

"What happened in Ozark was humiliating," she said. "And I brought all of it here. Into your house."

"I didn't know what we'd find," he said. "I was afraid for you."

She swallowed. "You didn't say I should have known better."

"I don't think you deserved that."

Her throat closed. "I don't know how to be where people are kind."

The corner of his mouth lifted. "Hungry is a good place to start."

She laughed through tears and covered her face. His hand squeezed her shoulder.

"You can eat," he said. "You can cry. You can stay upstairs another day. I'll still leave a tray."

She nodded and picked up her fork.

Later, after more sleep, she went downstairs again. Evening light filled the living room. Maggie played with a ring of carved toys. Josh stood by the window.

"I may need to stay longer than I planned," she said.

"That's okay."

He reached for her hand, but she pulled back.

"You deserve someone better," she said. "I knew Brett was wrong for me, and I stayed anyway."

"I'm not perfect," he said. "But I care about you. You're welcome here... for as long as you want to stay."

Her resolve gave way. She stepped into his arms and held on. He folded her close, careful and steady.

She cried into his shoulder until the tears eased.

At last she leaned back, her hands still clutching his shirt.

"Hey," she said. "Where do you think Maggie came from?"

"The Lord sent her to me."

"Beyond that, Josh." She drew a breath. "You deserve the truth about Maggie."

Josh sat, the couch springs sighing beneath his weight. Maggie rested in his lap, her bottom tucked into the crook of his arm, one socked foot pressed against his stomach.

Heather stood in the middle of the living room, her hands clasped, shoulders still curved with grief. Then she sat on the edge of the rocker across from him.

"When Brett left me, I found shelter with some girls at the truck stop. There was an empty trailer. Not safe, but dry and mostly warm." She paused. "I knew I couldn't live like they were living. Not even to survive."

Her gaze flicked to Maggie and away.

"One of them was very pregnant. Sarah," she said, a faint smile touching her mouth. "When the others went out, she went into labor. I was the only one there."

Josh's breath caught. He pictured the cramped trailer, the smell of fear and sweat, the urgency.

"You delivered Maggie?"

"I didn't have much choice. I talked Sarah through it. To keep her mind off the pain, I told her about Peculiar. And about you."

He blinked. "What?"

She glanced down. "I'd been watching you. You seemed kind. The neighbors liked you." Her cheeks colored. "You're sorta handsome, in your own way."

Heat burned Josh's ears. He focused on Maggie, who had begun to gnaw on his sleeve.

"After the baby was born, Sarah held her. Nursed her. We cleaned her up with a rag and some water." Heather swallowed. "She said she wanted her child to grow up somewhere safe. A place with decent people. Peculiar sounded like that. So did you."

Silence filled the room. Hoss lifted his head and watched Heather.

"Sarah told me to leave the baby at your house. I argued. She was hungry, so I went out to find food. When I came back, she was gone. But she left the baby. And a note."

Josh shifted Maggie against his shoulder, his arms aching with the need to hold her closer.

"What was I supposed to do?" Heather said. "We didn't have formula or clothes, not even a real blanket. And it was cold in that trailer. So I walked to Peculiar and put her on your porch. I didn't realize it was Christmas Eve. But I knew you'd help her."

Josh released a long breath as the pieces settled into place. "And on the way back, you fell and broke your foot."

She nodded.

"And you were out in the rain all night."

"I guess so."

He looked down at the worn pattern in the rug, at the place where his mother's coffee table used to sit. His eyes burned, but he didn't blink.

"Now you know," Heather said. "That's all of it. I don't even know Sarah's last name."

Josh lowered his gaze to Maggie—to the tiny fist knotted in his shirt, the steady rise and fall of her chest against his palm.

The story didn't break him. It answered the question he hadn't known how to ask.

She hadn't been dropped into his life by accident or cruelty. She had been carried. Through fear. Through cold. Through a girl who had almost nothing left to give.

Josh swallowed and lifted his head. "I'm sorry you went through that," he said. "It must have been hard. But I'm grateful too . . . because the Lord used all of it to bring us together."

HEATHER SURPRISED JOSH the next day.

He had eased Maggie into her crib, rocking her until her breathing deepened and her fists uncurled. Then he placed her favorite lamb toy by her side. The stuffed lamb held the soft smell of her, and its ear was permanently bent from her grip. Josh lingered a moment, listening to the steady sounds of her breathing, then he turned toward the stairs.

Heather was waiting at the bottom.

She held a towel over one arm and a pair of scissors in her hand, the metal catching the light. Her mouth was set in her tight-lipped smile, the one that meant she'd made a decision and was daring the world to argue.

"Come on," she said. "The old man asked me to cut your hair, and I promised I'd do it."

Josh blinked. Her scissors snipped the air, a small, intimate sound that made his shoulders tense before he realized why. Haircuts belonged to barbers and strangers who asked about the weather while they studied the shape of your head. Not to kitchens. Not to women standing this close.

He followed her anyway.

In the kitchen, she pulled out a chair and pressed her hands to the back of it. "Sit."

"Yes, ma'am," he said, the words automatic, though his pulse rate had increased.

She draped the towel around his shoulders, her fingers brushing the back of his neck. He inhaled, caught off guard by the scent of her skin. What was that, soap? Something clean. Something floral. Her nearness, her quiet competence, felt intensely personal.

"Where did you learn to do this?" he asked, watching her from the corner of his eye.

"Stop it." She gave his shoulder a light slap. "Like I told the old man, I learned out of necessity. Brett and I never had money for salons. But he knew he could do better if he looked good, so I learned."

Josh absorbed that news in the same place he stored other uncomfortable truths. Always Brett, hovering like a bad smell you couldn't quite chase away.

"Tilt your chin down."

He obeyed. The comb touched his neck, cool and precise. The scissors followed, snipping with soft authority. Strands of hair slid onto the towel, light and dry, reminding him of how much time had passed since anyone tended to him like this.

"Speaking of the old man," Heather said, working at his nape, "you two seem close."

Josh nodded, then winced when the scissors paused. "Sorry."

"You've gotta sit still."

"I've known Chief Goodman for years," he said. "I used to think he was sweet on Mama. He'd stop by every week to check on her."

"And your dad didn't mind?"

The familiar hollow opened, small but deep. "He was long gone. I don't remember much about him. Not anything good, anyway."

Heather dropped the comb into a glass of water. She picked up the scissors again and cut more slowly. "Nice of him to come around so often. I wouldn't expect that from a cop."

"He was retired by then. Had time." Josh closed his eyes as she worked, feeling himself relax. "Took me to ball games. Museums. Stuff Mama didn't have time to do."

Snip. Snip.

Hair kept falling, and with it came a strange sense of shedding, as if pieces of the old, solitary Josh were sliding away with it.

"Can I have a mirror?" he asked.

"Only when I'm done."

He sighed, then ventured a question. "Mind if I ask you something?"

"Depends."

"When I found you at the truck stop . . . were you planning to come back?"

The scissors paused, then resumed. "Yes."

"Back to Peculiar," he said, "or to me and Maggie?"

"Does it matter?"

Ouch. "If you'd rather be somewhere else," he said, "that's okay."

Snip. Snip. Snip. "Can you think of anyone else in Peculiar who'd have me?"

He remembered the way people looked at her. Curious. Cautious. Measuring. "I hear Tamera Parker's lookin' for a hair cutter at the beauty parlor."

"Stylist," Heather said. "And it's a salon."

He smiled. "Workin' there might be more fun than paintin' my carvings."

"You have to go to beauty school for that," she said. "Not for me. Besides, I'm gettin' pretty good at painting your stuff. Mixed a gorgeous color the other day. Forgot how I did it, though."

He laughed. "You used it on the little hippo. Kind of iridescent."

"Yeah. Now sit still. I'm almost done." She hesitated. "Can I ask you something serious?"

"'Course."

"How'd you fix the old man after he fell?"

Josh blew out a breath. "I didn't do anything. The Lord did."

"But you put your hands on him. And then you—"

"I prayed," Josh said. "I did what I thought I was supposed to do."

She slapped his shoulder again, firmer this time. "Face front. I can't finish if you keep movin'."

Josh complied, though his thoughts lingered on her resistance, on the way faith made people uneasy when it brushed their wounds. But she would come around. God had brought her to Peculiar for a reason.

The scissors made the final snips. Heather stepped back, surveying her work with a critical eye. "All right," she said. "Now you can look."

Josh reached for the mirror, his heart thudding, aware that

this had been more than a haircut. It was an exchange of trust. It was an expression of gratitude. It was the quiet, risky business of letting someone else tend to your needs.

Their eyes met in the mirror, and something unspoken settled between them, a promise neither of them was ready to name.

CHAPTER
THIRTY-SIX

Over the next couple of months, folks from Peculiar Community Church kept their promise to look in on Josh and Heather. I expected quick peeks through the windows and a few pointed questions dressed up as concern, but what I saw was supervision.

Casseroles appeared on the Donnelly porch like manna. Someone scraped and painted the rails that had been peeling since Watergate. Babysitters rotated through so Josh and Heather could go out to eat without packing half the house into a diaper bag. If there was a merit badge for Organized Kindness, the church ladies earned it.

The babysitter brigade reported back, of course. Separate bedrooms, they said. No funny business.

This seemed to settle everyone's nerves. Peculiar relaxed, satisfied that propriety had been preserved, and the tide of goodwill flowed even stronger. Nothing reassures a small town like moral order and a steaming casserole dish.

Josh and Heather looked a bit bewildered by all the attention, but Heather—who had carried herself like someone bracing for a blow—began to soften. She smiled more. Tight-lipped, mostly, like she was testing the idea that happiness might stick if she didn't admit to it.

She did her part, too. Leo Wilkerson told me that one day Heather came into the grocery without Josh and held out two hundred dollars. "Here," she told him, "this should cover the stuff I took from this store when I was here with Brett."

Leo squinted at her. "Doin' this to clear your conscience?"

"Maybe." Heather bit her lip. "Mostly, I'm doing it for Josh. I don't want anybody criticizin' him."

Leo was gobsmacked. He had to deal with shoplifters on occasion, but he had never had the opposite occur. When he hesitated, Heather thrust the money into his hands and said she'd earned that money painting toys for Josh Donnelly. "And she had the paint on her hands to prove it," Leo added.

By midsummer, Josh, Heather, and little Maggie were seen as a matched set. They showed up everywhere, and were frequent visitors at the retirement home. Bill Goodman soaked up their visits like sunshine. He held Maggie as if she were a fragile treasure, which was saying something, given that the kid had a grip like a dock cleat and a set of lungs that could wake the dead.

Maggie had grown, too. At seven months, she could sit up, hold her own bottle, and scoot across the floor with alarming speed. Every time I ran into Josh, he gave me a progress report.

"She grabs her toes now," he told me once, eyes shining.

Another time: "She belly laughs when Hoss sneezes."

Once I pulled over because I saw Josh talking with Jackson Fulbright and figured I ought to check on the old coot. Instead, I got a full briefing on Maggie.

"Mags talks now," Josh said, beaming like it was Christmas morning.

Fulbright leaned on his cane. "What does she say?"

Josh didn't blink. "Ba ba ba. It's amazing."

Jackson and I exchanged a look and managed to keep straight faces. Neither of us wanted to dampen Josh's joy, though neither of us was entirely sure what to call his role. Father? Guardian? Or something in between?

We weren't the only ones keeping an eye on things.

One afternoon, patrons of the Coif It Up salon nearly slid out of their styling chairs when Heather walked in like she belonged there.

"She came right in," Tamera Parker later told everyone within earshot in the school pickup line. "We'd been talkin' *about* her for months, and all at once I was talkin' *to* her. Nearly dropped my scissors."

Kelly Haviland stuck her head out her window. "What'd she want?"

"A haircut. What else?" Tamera said. "I chopped off all those split ends and talked her into going shorter. If I had curls like that, I'd never let my hair grow so long and heavy."

Kelly's mouth fell open. "She's curly-headed?"

"You never noticed those little wisps at her neckline?" Tamera said. "She didn't say why she kept it long, but people have a right to make stupid decisions. Anyway, she told me she's feelin' better than she has in a long time. And I told her—couldn't help myself—that she's lookin' better. She's filled out, she's smiling, and she's not slouching anymore."

From a Toyota, another woman called, "Where's she from?"

The white-bearded crossing guard chimed in. "How'd she meet Josh? I'd like to meet a woman like that."

Tamera wagged a finger at all of them. "She didn't volunteer, and I didn't ask. In my chair, folks tell you what they want to tell you. No sense pryin' and losin' a customer." She grinned.

"But give me time. People relax, and then they talk. All I know is, I like her. I hope she comes back. Next time, I'm fixin' those eyebrows."

My deputy, Tony Kirkpatrick, had been in that pickup line and replayed the whole conversation back at the station.

"Poor Heather," he finished. "But at least we know she's not stayin' with Josh because he's rich."

I looked up from my paperwork. "What do you mean?"

He scoffed. "She's a pretty woman. Could probably have any guy she wants. Josh Donnelly's not rich, so she must actually like him."

Tony said it like he was honestly surprised.

Everyone in Peculiar had a theory about where Heather came from and why she stayed with Josh. Most of the theories were tidy, comfortable explanations, the kind that let you sleep at night.

None of them landed anywhere near the truth.

JOSH COULDN'T HELP NOTICING that Heather seemed more comfortable with Maggie now that Brett was finally out of the picture. The change wasn't dramatic, but steady, like a knot loosening. She began to get up early, often padding downstairs while the house was still half-asleep. More than once he wandered into the kitchen to find her already seated at the table, Maggie propped in her highchair, baby cereal cooling in a shallow bowl.

As morning light slanted through the windows, Heather would lean in close, patient and focused, coaxing each spoonful where it needed to go. For someone who claimed no experience with babies, she had a natural rhythm. Scoop.

Offer. Wait. Swipe the excess neatly from Maggie's chin with the curve of the spoon.

"You're pretty good at that," Josh said one Saturday morning.

"I like feeding her." Heather scooped again. "This is girl-bonding time."

"Girl-bonding?" Josh made a face as he filled Hoss's bowl. "Whatever you say. Thanks for starting the coffee."

Heather made a ridiculous face that sent Maggie into a fit of snorting, breathless laughter. "Good girl. She really likes this oatmeal. I mixed applesauce into it."

Josh grunted. "I wouldn't have thought of that."

"Seems like babies ought to get extra fruit," Heather went on, "since they're busy growing."

Later, over refilled mugs and the quiet satisfaction of a morning going right, Josh suggested they drive out and look for craft shows. "Maybe Gainesville. I'm always looking for new ideas."

"I've got a better one," Heather said. "We should wallpaper Maggie's room."

Josh blinked. "Yeah, I guess we could. But wouldn't you rather go someplace? I haven't driven much lately, but I think there's plenty of gas—"

"The wallpaper in her room is for boys," Heather said, cutting in. "Bad enough you started her out in blue blankets and airplane pajamas. But that wallpaper's faded, it's ugly, and you don't even like it. So let's get rid of it."

Josh wrapped his fingers around his mug. The memory of that room rose up uninvited, sharp and foreboding. He hadn't slept in that room in years. Hadn't sat in the old chair. Hadn't stood too close to those walls.

"I tell you what," he said. "You tear the paper down, and I'll go to the hardware store. What kind of paper do you want? Pink flowers? Daisies?"

She laughed. "Maybe you should take the paper down while I shop. You might pick something crazy."

"Or," he said, grasping for a compromise, "you could rip it down while I ask Jackie if we can borrow her wallpaper tray. Then we pick the new stuff together."

Heather's brow furrowed. "I've never met anyone who was so determined to avoid old wallpaper. If you're worried about offending your mama, I promise she won't mind."

"It's not Mama." Josh shook his head. "It's the dust. I'll be sneezing all day."

"Wallpaper isn't dusty." Heather's eyes narrowed. "You pull up a corner and it comes right off."

He set his mug down. "Okay, I'm going to be honest." He clasped his hands. "Yeah, dust makes me sneeze. But that wallpaper gives me the creeps."

Her mouth fell open. "You're freaked out by *wallpaper*?"

"That wallpaper, yeah." He nodded. "I've had nightmares about those little red trucks. They chase me. And when they catch me, bad stuff happens." He hesitated, then lowered his voice. "I haven't slept in that room since I was a kid."

"You're afraid," she said, her voice wobbling between disbelief and amusement, "of little red trucks?"

"They have eyes."

"Those are headlights."

"They look like eyes. And the grill looks like a big mouth with teeth." He folded his arms. "Doesn't anything scare you?"

Heather shrugged. "Spiders, maybe."

"All right. Say your bedroom was wallpapered with spiders, floor to ceiling. Could you sleep in there?"

She sighed, the humor draining out of her expression as

understanding took its place. "Okay. I get it." She stood and pulled Maggie to her shoulder. "I'll take down the terrifying red truck wallpaper. You do whatever you need to do. Then we'll go to the hardware store together."

Josh let out a breath he hadn't realized he'd been holding. The house settled back into its familiar sounds, and for a moment, that was enough.

HEATHER WAS RIGHT, Josh realized. Maggie deserved a room that belonged to her, not to a boy who'd grown up years before.

The new wallpaper softened the space immediately. Tiny birdhouses decorated the walls in gentle pastels, little birds perched between flowers that looked as if they might sway if you stared too long. The room looked lighter and breezier, as though it had exhaled after holding its breath for decades.

"I like it," Josh said that evening, leaning in the doorway while Heather put Maggie in her crib. "And we did a pretty good job. Nobody's going to notice that crooked seam by the window."

"We make a good team," Heather said. She bent to kiss Maggie's head, lingering there a second longer than usual. When she straightened, her voice softened to a careful tone. "I've been thinking."

Josh stiffened, alerted to the undercurrent in her voice.

"At first I thought you didn't want to get rid of the old wallpaper because you didn't want to change anything your mama had done," she said. "But then something else struck me—maybe you're afraid to do things like this because you're afraid of losing Maggie."

The words slid straight through his ribs and into his heart.

For a moment, the room seemed too small. Too close. His

pulse thudded in his ears, loud and uneven, and he fought the urge to step backward, as if distance might dull the sting.

Heather squeezed his forearm, her grip strong and solid. "I know you must have thought about what might happen if—"

"Nothing's going to happen." Josh shook his head as if that motion alone could eliminate the possibility. "The Lord sent her. Everything that happened between you and that young woman—it was meant to be."

"I know." Heather moved closer. "But you need to stop saying that out loud. People wouldn't understand." Her gaze held his. "Right now, everyone in town thinks Maggie is my daughter. We need to let them go on believin' that. We need to let that be our story so we don't lose her. So people don't ask questions."

Josh blinked at the new wallpaper, which had begun to grow fuzzy. "But that's not the truth."

"I know you don't lie," she said. "So don't. Just keep the truth to yourself. Let it stay between us." A small smile touched her mouth. "Because we really do make a good team."

She rose on tiptoe and kissed his cheek. The contact was brief, but it left heat behind, a lingering pressure that made it hard for Josh to breathe. Then she crossed the hall and closed her bedroom door.

The click sounded final.

Josh sagged against the baby crib, the significance of her words sinking into his bones. Again, Heather was right. They would be safer if he kept quiet. What did it matter, anyway? They had come this far together. Somehow, by God's grace, they were becoming something that looked an awful lot like a family.

He leaned over the crib and kissed Maggie's forehead. She stirred, grabbed her stuffed lamb by the ear, and rolled onto her side.

As he straightened, his gaze drifted around the room.

The old wooden dresser now painted white. The bookcase padded and repurposed into a changing table. The rocking horse, waiting for its future as Maggie's favorite toy.

Then he saw the wooden chair.

It sat in the corner of the room, exactly where Heather had dragged it while cleaning. Same shape. Same dull finish. Same tilt in the front legs that made it lean slightly forward. An odor rose from the woven seat—old sweat and something sour—and for a second he was six again.

Fear slid down Josh's spine. His hands tingled. His jaw tightened so hard his teeth ached. The room seemed to narrow, the birdhouses on the walls wavered, the cheerful little birds shrieked a warning—

Run.

Before he could stop himself, Josh crossed the room in three strides and lifted the lower window sash. Warm summer air rushed in, damp against his skin. He grabbed the chair, his fingers slipping on the worn wood, and heaved it through the opening.

The crash echoed on the driveway below. Wood splintered. Something snapped in two.

Josh stood there, chest heaving, the metallic taste of blood on his tongue. Cold sweat prickled along his jaw. He dragged in a shaking breath, then another.

That thing did not belong in Maggie's room.

"Josh?" Heather burst through the doorway, her eyes wide. "What was that?"

"I —" He snatched a breath. "That old chair wasn't safe. I tossed it out."

"Out the *window*?"

He shrugged, forcing his shoulders to loosen. "Belongs in the trash. I'll pick up the pieces later."

"I was going to paint that chair," she said. "It looked sturdy enough to me."

Josh shook his head, the answer rising from a place he didn't fully understand. "No. That thing was rotten to the core."

CHAPTER
THIRTY-SEVEN

July slipped into August. Our humidity gauges parked at ninety-nine percent and the sidewalks could sear a steak. Everyone in Peculiar, even proper church ladies, took to wearing sleeveless shirts, shorts, and sandals. The postal workers and my deputy wore short pants to work, but I maintained my dignity and my long pants by remaining indoors as much as possible. When I had to go out, I cruised the streets in my air-conditioned patrol car, looking for trouble and hoping I wouldn't find any.

One night, near the end of my shift, I spotted Josh and Heather on their front porch, she in a rocker, Josh sprawled on the steps, leaning back on his elbows.

The object of their attention was little Maggie, who stood in the middle of the brick walkway leading to the house. I rolled by, about to wave, but through the fence rails I saw Maggie take a step . . . and realized what I'd seen.

I hadn't talked to the couple in over a week, so I nosed the patrol car into their driveway and plastered a smile on my face

—didn't want them to think my visit was anything but a cordial hi-and-how-are-ya.

Josh grinned when I pulled up, but Heather's smile faded—call it a lawman's instinct, but I had the feeling she wanted to run into the house. She didn't, though, so maybe I was imagining things.

I leaned against the hood of the car and crossed my arms. "Did my eyes deceive me, or did I just see that baby walk?"

Josh's grin broadened, and Heather gave me a small smile. "She's been walking a couple of days," Heather said. "If you call two steps and a dive *walking*."

"At eight months," Josh added. "Doc Tompkins says it's early."

"Early?" I said. "At eight months I was still trying to master drool."

I glanced at Maggie and sure enough, she was back on all fours. "She must be smart," I said. "So which of you is responsible for all that intelligence?"

Heather and Josh shot each other a glance, and too late I realized I'd put them in an awkward position. Everybody knew Maggie was Heather's baby, but for all I knew Josh had been plunking the kid down in front of Baby Einstein.

"I don't know," Josh finally said. "I wasn't a super baby, not by any means."

Heather picked up a magazine as if she wanted to read. I shrugged the matter away and chatted with Josh about his carving for a few minutes. I was about to say goodnight when Josh's monster of a dog came around the corner.

"Hoss, where've you been?" Josh called. "I hope you haven't been digging again. We're tired of mopping up muddy footprints."

The dog trotted toward Josh with what looked like a small log in his mouth.

"It's a bone." I blinked and stepped closer. "That's too big to be from a coon or possum."

Josh whistled to bring the beast into the yellow cone of porch light. "Whatcha got there, Hoss?"

I approached with caution—I had developed an innate distrust of other people's pets—as Josh took from the dog a bone as long as a man's thigh.

I stared, tongue tied. "Josh," I finally said, ghost spiders scooting up the back of my neck, "I think you and I should go see where your dog's been digging."

"As long as it's not in Miss Jackie's gladiolus bed," Josh said.

He grabbed a flashlight and led me around to the back of the house. He shone the light all around Jackie Leakey's flower beds, then under palmetto bushes and in every clearing until I pointed to the shed, where a sagging door hung on rusty hinges. A gust of wind blew the door open, and Josh pointed his flashlight inside. Muddy dog prints on the old wooden floor led to a mound of dirt beyond.

"What in tarnation?" Josh knelt and aimed the light at a gaping hole toward the back. "Maybe an animal got under here and Hoss smelled it. He's never been much of a digger before."

I tugged at a piece of the rotten flooring. When it broke off, I lifted my gaze to the roof. "Look there—you've had a leak. Over time, the floor's rotted. That's how the dog was able to break through." I studied Josh. "When's the last time you were out here?"

He shrugged. "I don't know—months ago, I guess. I keep all my tools in the garage."

After I removed another rotten board, Josh's light revealed a deeper hole—undoubtedly the work of Hoss's huge paws—and something white shining in the mud. I grabbed a garden spade and cleared dirt from around the object.

Then I stared, stunned by sheer disbelief at what I saw.

"Josh," I finally said. "I hate to tell you this, but I need to get a forensic team out here right away."

"Wh—what?"

"I'm no expert, but I'm pretty sure that's a human pelvic bone."

THE NEXT MORNING, Josh put Maggie on the floor and handed her a bottle, then went back to gazing out the kitchen window. Deputy Tony, the medical examiner, and two technicians from the county had been at work for hours. Their flood lights had shone through the shed door and lit his bedroom all night, making it nearly impossible to sleep.

No one told him what was going on, but that might be a good thing.

Heather was cooking bacon and scrambled eggs. Judging from her puffy eyes, she hadn't slept much either.

"Sorry about not goin' to church this mornin'," Josh said. "But with all the craziness goin' on—"

"You don't think there's an actual skeleton out there, do you?"

Josh shrugged. "Beats me. Mama told me the house was built in 1906. My parents bought it a couple of years after they were married. I remember learnin' this area was old—older than folks like to admit. Natives lived here long before any of us."

"So this house could have been built on a burial ground or something?"

"I wouldn't be surprised." Josh leaned forward to peer out the window. "Will you keep an eye on Maggie? I wanna go check things out."

"Hurry back," Heather said. "This is creepier than spiders on wallpaper."

Josh found Tony and the medical examiner standing outside the shed, the morning air thick with heat and the sour tang of disturbed earth. Cicadas screamed from the trees as if they were trying to drown out the men's voices.

Two men in white jumpsuits emerged from the shed, their boots caked with coffee-colored mud. A third man followed, a camera hanging from his neck, his expression preoccupied, as if he were already cataloging the images.

Josh wiped his palms on his jeans and gestured to the shed. "Can I take a look?" he asked, surprised his voice didn't crack.

The medical examiner glanced at him, his eyes assessing, then nodded. "Just don't touch anything."

The air inside the shed was cooler and smelled of wet soil and decay. At the back, the wooden planks of the floor had been pulled up and stacked against one wall like discarded ribs. Plastic sheeting lay crumpled in a corner, smeared and dull.

The earth had been opened up in a deep, rectangular wound. Fresh dirt rose in uneven mounds around it.

As Tony followed, Josh stepped closer, his boots sinking. His stomach clenched as his eyes adjusted, and then he saw what had caused so much commotion.

A skeleton.

Pale. Complete except for the leg bone Hoss had unearthed, the rest arranged as if someone had laid the body out with care. The skull tilted to one side, the teeth yellowed but intact, fixed in a grin that looked less like a smile than a challenge.

"Oh, my." Josh gulped, the sound loud in his own ears. "Think it's a native of these parts?"

Tony stared into the pit, his jaw tight. "Medical examiner figures this man—he's assuming it's a man, based on size—has been in the ground several years, but probably not more than twenty."

Josh studied the bones, baffled. That didn't make sense.

"There's something else," Tony said, pointing.

Josh followed his finger. At first all he saw was dirt clinging to a dark object, then the shape resolved. A rubber sole. Worn smooth. A faint logo still visible.

A sneaker.

A cold knot formed in Josh's stomach. Native Americans didn't wear tennis shoes.

But twenty years couldn't be right. He'd lived in this house twenty-six years, and he remembered almost every season of it. Surely further testing would reveal a mistake. A miscalculation. Something.

Tony crossed his arms. "When did your father leave, Josh?"

The question hit him sideways. "What?"

Tony's voice softened. "How long has your father been gone?"

Josh frowned, his thoughts scrambling. "Um. I was six. He walked out one night and never came back."

"You saw him leave?" Tony asked. "Or is that what your mother told you?"

A chill slid into Josh's gut and spread outward. His ears rang. "You can't think Mama—" He stopped, the words tangling. His mother's face rose in his mind. Tired. Gentle. Loving.

A technician stepped into the shed with a large vinyl bag, the zipper already half-open. The sight of it made Josh's stomach clench.

Tony leaned closer, lowering his voice. "Josh, it's not my job to decide what happened here; I'm just helping these folks gather evidence. But they're going to want a DNA sample from you." He nodded toward the door. "I can do that now, if you'll come with me to my vehicle."

Josh blinked, trying to process the words. "You . . . you carry DNA stuff in your car?"

Tony managed a faint smile, though his eyes remained serious. "Don't worry. This probably has nothing to do with you."

Josh nodded, though the grinning skull still burned his peripheral vision. *Probably.* Probably meant everything was fine.

But the word echoed as he followed Tony back into the sunlight.

SLEEP CAME that night in broken pieces and ugly colors.

Josh's dreams flashed red and blue, lights spinning without sound, then his mama's face rose out of the darkness, twisted with a grief so sharp it hurt to look at her. Somewhere a woman screamed. The sound drilled straight into his head, and he bolted upright, heart hammering.

"Heather!"

He was on his feet before his mind caught up, crossing the hall in four long strides and yanking her door open, braced for violence, for blood, for an enemy he could fight.

But the room was still.

Heather lay curled on her side, one hand tucked beneath her cheek, her breathing slow and even. Moonlight spilled across the quilt and traced the familiar line of her shoulder. She didn't stir.

Josh stood there, his chest heaving, shame washing over his fear. He eased the door shut and went back to his room.

He didn't sleep again.

He lay on his side and stared at the walls, studying the faint shadows cast by streetlights, listening to the house settle and creak. Every sound felt significant, as if the house were sending a message he couldn't translate.

When the clock finally crept toward five, he swung his legs out of bed and stood, grateful to hear movement from Maggie's room. Her small, delighted noises cut through his thoughts like sunlight through fog.

"Well," he murmured as he took her from the crib, "I'm glad one of us is awake and cheerful."

She kicked happily as he changed her diaper, grabbing at his fingers, unconcerned with skeletons or sheds or questions that had no answers. He snapped her onesie and kissed her soft hair. "Let's get you some breakfast and watch the sun come up."

Hoss followed them into the kitchen. Josh filled the dog's bowl while Maggie sat in her highchair, painstakingly pinching Cheerios between her fingers and bringing them to her mouth as if each one were a small triumph.

When her bottle was ready, Josh carried her out to the front porch. Dawn hovered below the horizon, the sky pale and waiting. The summer air was already thick and damp, clinging to his skin.

"Well, Hoss," Josh drawled, "you had to go and dig up trouble, didn't you?"

The dog thumped his tail, unapologetic.

The screen door creaked behind him. Heather stepped out in his mama's robe, her hair loose, her face drawn.

"You couldn't sleep either?" she asked.

He shook his head. "Bet you didn't know you were stayin'

with a guy who's got skeletons in his closet." He tilted his head toward the yard. "Or at least under his shed."

She studied him, her expression sober. "If that was meant to be a joke—"

"I don't blame you for not laughin'."

She dropped into the wicker rocker, the old chair sighing under her weight. "I don't know what you're feeling," she said, "but I know you. And I know you're not to blame for whatever happened out back."

"Because I was too young," he said.

"No." She leaned forward. "They could tell us that man was buried last week, and I'd still know you had nothing to do with it."

Josh stared past the railing, his gaze unfocused. "I'm afraid," he said. Saying it aloud felt like admitting weakness, but he couldn't deny the fear coiled inside him. "I'm afraid they're gonna say it's my father. And then they're gonna look at Mama."

Heather's brow furrowed, so he rushed on. "She's a Christian woman," he said. "And there's no way on earth she would've had the strength to bury someone under the shed."

"Not even years ago?"

"Not even," he said, certain.

The sun broke free of the horizon, spilling gold across the yard. Trees erupted with birdsong, whistles and trills and sharp cries filling the air though Josh couldn't see a single bird. Life announced itself, loud and insistent.

His eyes burned. He blinked hard.

He couldn't see God's hand, either. But that didn't mean it wasn't there.

"Don't worry," Heather whispered. "The truth will come out. It always does."

"Does it?"

The question hung between them, unanswered. If that man under the shed *was* his father, then his mama—his good, gentle mama—had lied to him most of his life.

Josh tightened his hold on Maggie as she finished her bottle, the warmth of her body anchoring him while the restless past stirred beneath the ground.

Friday morning, when I pulled up to the Donnelly place with the medical examiner riding shotgun, Josh was on the front porch with the baby in his lap. Folks say stress ages a man, but I'd never seen it happen so fast. Josh looked like he'd aged a decade in the last forty-eight hours.

The dog noticed us before Josh did. Hoss rose, all muscle and suspicion, and let out a growl that vibrated the porch boards.

Great. I bring bad news and get eaten for breakfast.

I stepped out slow and pointed at the dog. "He looks like he wants to bite me."

"Don't look him in the eye," Josh said, like this was advice he'd given before. "Just look away and act friendly."

I waved Dr. Dan Lorenzo over. "You remember the medical examiner from yesterday."

Josh stood, shifted the baby to his other arm, and came down to shake Lorenzo's hand. The doctor's smile looked like it had been glued on in the car.

"Sorry to trouble you on a fine morning like this," Lorenzo said.

Josh nodded without speaking. That was my first clue this was going to be worse than I'd feared.

I cleared my throat. "Josh," I said, "there's no easy way to say this."

His eyes flicked to mine, sharp and alert despite his exhaustion.

"The remains we found are those of your father."

The words hung there, heavy and unmannered.

Josh blinked fast, like he was trying to reset the world. He pushed the baby higher on his shoulder, his hand splayed protectively across her back.

"That's not possible," he said, lifting his chin. "My dad left. Mama always said he walked out. Did you check the DNA?"

Lorenzo shook his head. "No need. The records at Dr. Kohlberg's dental practice were a perfect match."

Josh's knees buckled enough to notice. He dropped onto a porch step, his eyes unfocused, and for one alarming second I thought he might drop the baby.

"Mama couldn't have done it," he said, fast and fierce. "She was tiny. Even in her prime she could barely lift a suitcase. And she wasn't violent. Ever."

I'd heard that tone before. The voice of a man building a wall as fast as he could.

Josh looked at Lorenzo. "Can you tell what killed him?"

"Hard to be definitive," Lorenzo said. "But the compound fracture in the skull suggests something circular. A hammer would be the most logical possibility, especially given the location."

Josh's head snapped up, relief flaring so bright it hurt to watch. "The only tool Mama ever used was a screwdriver. So maybe he got jumped. She said he drank. Maybe he got into a fight, or someone followed him home—"

I cut him off with an uplifted hand. "We're not going to solve this with guesswork," I said. "We'll have to open an investigation."

The word landed hard. It always does.

I pulled out my notebook. Not because I needed it, but because silence can get dangerous if you let it stretch too long.

"Did your father have any relatives we can contact?" I asked. "Brothers or sisters?"

"Not that I know of," Josh said. "Why?"

"He might've reached out after he left. Told someone he was coming and never showed." I jotted a meaningless note. "We'll also talk to the neighbors. Grace Egan and Jackie Leakey lived next door even back then, right?"

"Yes, sir." Josh leaned back, which creaked the porch step like it was protesting the conversation. "They had husbands then. Kids."

I scribbled some more, mostly for show. Sometimes a pen moving across paper is the only thing holding a moment together.

"That's all I need for now," I said, snapping the notebook shut. "I'll be in touch."

Josh nodded, but his eyes were fixed on something beyond me, beyond the yard, beyond the shed. I figured the past had finally stood up and introduced itself.

As I walked back to the car, Hoss lay down again, content that we were leaving. The baby gurgled, unaware that she'd become the thing that kept Josh from going to pieces.

Behind me, a young man was learning that the past doesn't stay buried just because someone wanted it to.

CHAPTER
THIRTY-EIGHT

I had just settled into my chair and opened the first folder of a new week when the courier envelope landed on my desk. The medical examiner's report.

It wasn't thick. That alone told me most of what I needed to know.

I slid the pages free and started reading. *Remains identified as George Donnelly. Dental records from 1985 matched.*

No surprise there.

Cause of death: *Homicide.* How? Blunt force trauma. *A compound fracture to the occipital region of the skull. Likely instantaneous.* The ME also noted a linear fracture of the temporal bone, but that wouldn't have been life-threatening.

Time of death? *Acidic soil speeds bone degradation, so it is impossible to pinpoint exact year with any degree of accuracy. However, due to changes in bone chemistry over time, including the loss of collagen and soil mineral infiltration, we estimate that the body was buried between 1986 and 1996.*

The estimate on time of death sat in the middle of the page

like a bad joke. Ten years? Ten years is a lifetime in a small town. Ten years is the difference between a boy and a man.

I kept reading. Estimated age at death: *After studying the surface morphology of the pubic symphysis, we can estimate with reasonable accuracy that the deceased was in his early thirties at the time of death.*

Now we were getting somewhere. George Donnelly might have a birth certificate at city hall . . . if not, the county clerk would have a copy of his marriage license. Simple math might tell us what we needed to know.

I leaned back and stared at the ceiling fan, which clicked like it was counting down to a deadline. Josh Donnelly had been shaken when we brought the news about his dad—trouble was, I couldn't be sure what had shaken him. The news itself, or the fact that the ground behind his house had finally coughed up what it had been holding all these years. A man can look exactly the same whether he's stunned by a truth he never knew or by a secret he's been living beside. And right then, I didn't know which kind of look I'd seen.

I was still chewing on the ME's report when Tony came in, hands on his belt. "What'd the ME have to say?"

I filled him in. Tony digested the details, then grabbed a sheet of paper from my desk.

"A timeline," he said, pulling up a chair. "This here's 1986." He drew a dot on the left side of the page. "That's when George Donnelly allegedly left Peculiar. Josh was six years old."

Tony slid his finger to the right. "This dot's 1996. The far end of the ME's estimate."

I glanced down. Straight line. Clean dots. Simple enough to make complicated things look polite.

"In 1996—" Tony arched a brow—"Josh Donnelly would've been sixteen." He punched that date. "Plenty old enough to swing a hammer at the daddy he hated for running out on him and his mama. And a sixteen-year-old plus his mother? More than capable of burying a body."

The ceiling fan kept clicking, unconcerned with other people's lives.

I shook my head. "The ME's report says the deceased was probably in his early thirties at time of death. That favors the earlier date."

"Those things are educated guesses," Tony said. "And we don't know how old George was when he went missing."

I rubbed my chin. "Josh doesn't strike me as the type to commit murder."

Tony snorted. "Don't you remember sixteen? Hormones racing, sense packed up and gone. I've read case files where kids killed for less than a sideways look."

"I've never seen Josh lose his temper," I said. "Not once."

Tony leaned forward. "Let's say George wanders back into town around '95 or '96. Maybe he wants forgiveness. Maybe money. Maybe a divorce. And maybe he's drunk."

Tony's eyes narrowed. "Margaret resists. George gets mean. You telling me Josh Donnelly wouldn't step in? A boy that devoted to his mama?"

His theory had shape . . . and I didn't like it.

"Possible," I said. "But *possible* can't convict anybody. We don't have sightings, reports, nothing. As far as the town knows, George Donnelly left in '86 and never came back."

Tony smiled. "Which is why we should start a proper investigation. Interviews. Gas stations. Motels. See if anybody remembers George coming back to visit his wife and son."

He stood, energized. "You might wanna talk to Bill Goodman. He and Josh are close."

I nodded, remembering the envelope locked in my gun drawer. "I will."

When Tony left to work the school crossing, I looked again at his neat little line. Two dots. A straight path. And a lifetime of fear and silence in between.

We had work to do, but I wasn't looking forward to it. I've been a cop long enough to know this: when you pull on the past, it doesn't come back gentle.

It comes back hungry.

As always, Twin Oaks smelled of boiled vegetables and furniture polish, a combination that could make a man contemplate his own mortality before lunchtime. Tony and I signed in at the front desk under the watchful eye of a Ficus that had given up on life, then took the elevator and followed the muffled sound of a baseball game down the hall.

Bill Goodman's door was cracked open. Inside, the television hummed with crowd noise and optimism, the announcer's voice rising and falling like he still believed every inning mattered. Bill sat in his recliner, long legs stretched out in front of him, one hand on his cane, the other resting on his thigh. He was eighty-five, tall as a fence post, but his eyes were sharp and alert. He noticed us the second we stepped in.

"Chief Bowen," he said, nodding. "And Tony. Come on in, and excuse me if I don't get up. The Rays are ahead, which means they'll probably find a way to lose."

"Do you mind if I turn this off?" I gestured to the TV. "We need to talk."

Bill's mouth kept smiling, but not his eyes. "Suit yourself."

I crossed the room and clicked off the TV. The sudden quiet rang in my ears, like shutting a door on summertime.

"How you doin', Bill?" I asked.

"Still vertical," he said. "Still breathing. Can't complain too much."

We stood for a moment, Tony and I, with sunlight slanting through the blinds. The place was neat in that careful way that comes from having fewer things and too much time to arrange them. A couple of framed photos sat on the dresser. Franci and Bill in uniform, back when his hair was thick and black. Bill holding a fish that looked suspiciously smaller than the grin on his face.

"Have a seat," he said, gesturing to the sofa next to the wall. "Make yourselves at home."

We talked shop for a few minutes. Safe topics. Familiar ground. Then I cleared my throat.

"I suppose you've heard about what we found in Donnelly's backyard."

Bill frowned. "Backyard? I heard it was the shed."

I felt the tiniest hitch of surprise. "You're right. Who'd you hear that from?"

"Jackie Leakey," he said, without hesitation. "She was all in a tizzy. Which is pretty much her natural state."

That tracked. Jackie knew more about Peculiar than the census bureau, and she shared information like it had an expiration date.

I studied Bill a moment. "You've known Josh a long time, haven't you?"

"Years," he said. "Ever since the boy's father left."

He shifted in his chair. "I felt sorry for Josh. Nice kid. No father around, and Margaret doing her best but carrying the whole load alone. So I started taking him fishing. Took him to a few minor league games. Tried to teach him how to throw a ball."

He shrugged. "Josh wasn't much for athletics. More an

artist type, which meant he got bullied on occasion. But he tried. Tried hard."

A muscle tightened in my back. Everybody in Peculiar knew that boy. Quiet, earnest, trying his best to do right in a world that didn't always make it easy.

Tony edged forward. "Were you ever sweet on Margaret Donnelly?"

I lifted a brow, eager to hear his answer. I was 99 percent certain Margaret was his unrequited love, but I had no proof. And no confession.

Bill snorted. "Everyone was sweet on Margaret. She was a nice lady." His expression sobered. "But no, even as a widower, I couldn't think of her in that way. As far as I knew, she had a husband. One who might come back."

Tony and I exchanged a glance, then Tony cleared his throat. "*Did* George come back?"

Bill shook his head. "Not that I ever heard. I'm sure Josh would have mentioned it if he had."

He looked straight at me then, his eyes steady as a sightline. "As you might have noticed, that young man is practically incapable of telling a lie."

"Nobody tells the truth *all* the time."

"Josh does," Bill said. "It's smart to tell the truth as often as we are able, right?"

"It is."

Goodman looked toward the window and smiled. "Bottom line? Josh Donnelly is unique. I'd do anything for that young man."

We stood, thanked him for his time, and shook his hand. His grip was still firm, as if he hadn't quite let go of the job even though he had turned in his badge.

Out in the hallway, the odor of boiled vegetables followed

us like a bad memory. Tony didn't say anything until we reached the elevator. Then he exhaled. "Well."

"Yeah," I said. "Exactly."

The doors slid shut, and as we descended, I found myself thinking about truth. How some people manipulate it with ease, while others trip up because they don't know how to hide it.

I was beginning to believe Josh Donnelly didn't know how to hide anything

And that, I suspected, was going to matter.

Tony and I found Jackie Leakey's place just west of the Donnelly home, a narrow little house with a lawn like a putting green. Seashell wind chimes clicked and clacked in the breeze. Somewhere inside, a radio broadcast an old hymn I couldn't quite place, the kind of tune that stays with you long after the words leave.

Jackie answered on the second knock.

She was small and spare, the kind of woman whose bones seemed to protrude from her flesh. Her hair was silver and pulled back in a clip. Her eyes were sharp, alive, and assessing, as if she'd been rehearsing this conversation for years.

"Well," she said, taking us in with a sharp look. "It's about time."

Tony gave me a sideways glance.

We stepped inside, my nose picking up the scents of lemon oil, dust, and the tang of a cat litter box. Three portable fans were stationed in the living room—one aimed at the sofa, one at a recliner, one at nothing in particular.

She motioned us to the sofa and perched on the edge of the recliner. Folded her hands and looked straight at me.

"You want to know about that night."

No sense in rehearsing the obvious, so I nodded. "1986. You called in a domestic disturbance."

Her throat worked. "I'd heard it before," she said. Her voice dropped, the words turning brittle. "But never that bad. I always figured Margaret would tell me if there was serious trouble in her house, and she never said a word. But that night—"

Jackie stopped. Looked at the floor. "That night was different."

The room seemed to lean closer.

"What did you hear?" Tony asked.

"Yelling. Screaming. The kind that comes from deep inside." She pressed her hand to her breastbone. "Not anger. Terror."

I'd heard that sound. Every lawman had.

"I called the station," she said. "Bill came quick and went into the house. Things got quiet. After that, I went to bed and turned on my fans. All of them." She gestured around the room. "I have box fans upstairs, and they block out the noise. I didn't want to hear anything else."

I looked at the fans again. Tools of surviving more than the heat.

"Did you see George Donnelly after that night?" I asked.

"No." She shook her head. "He left town."

"How do you know?"

"Margaret told me." Her chin lifted. "Margaret was a good Christian woman. She had no reason to lie."

The words hung between us, delicate and doomed.

Tony cleared his throat. "People lie for all kinds of reasons."

Jackie's eyes flicked at him, then back to me. "I can't imagine why Margaret would, unless it was to protect someone. Maybe her son. Someone she loved." She nodded. "Or maybe herself."

Jackie's gaze lowered. When she looked up again, moisture shone in her eyes.

"I care about that boy," she said. "I watched Josh grow up. He deserved better than the father he got. So that's why I called."

That one hit the bullseye.

We sat a moment more, the heaviness of old choices pressing on the furniture, the walls, the whole careful house.

When we stood to leave, Jackie walked us to the door. She hesitated, then touched my sleeve.

"Chief," she said. "Whatever Margaret did . . . she did out of love."

I nodded. That was one truth I couldn't dispute.

Outside, the afternoon sun felt too bright for what we'd just heard.

Tony exhaled. "The Donnelly house has been keeping secrets longer than we've been wearing a badge."

I glanced back at Jackie's porch, where the shell chimes clacked in the heat.

"Yeah," I said. "Now we learn what those secrets are gonna cost."

Tony and I wiped our feet on the mat Margaret Donnelly probably bought before Josh was born, then stepped into Josh's living room. The Donnelly house always felt smaller once you stepped inside, as if it held its breath while waiting for you to leave. The house was cooler than I expected, and smelled of baby powder and warm dog.

Heather sat on the sofa with the baby, Maggie wearing a

little sundress and a diaper on account of the heat. The window AC unit was blowing full blast and barely making a dent.

Josh remained by the door, wavering between staying on his feet or inviting us to sit for a chat. "Chief," he said, smiling like always. "Deputy."

"Josh," I said. "Heather. Maggie." I nodded at the baby, who regarded me with the same suspicion I got from most citizens under the age of one.

We exchanged the usual pleasantries. Weather. Baby sleeping? How hard it was to get Maggie to keep her socks on.

When Josh didn't ask us to sit, I jerked my chin toward the front porch. "Josh, you mind stepping outside with us a second?"

He nodded as if he'd been expecting it, and followed me through the front door. He stood in front of me and Tony, his hands folded, posture straight, eyes attentive.

"Josh," I said, keeping my tone light, "what can you tell me about the last time you saw your father?"

I watched his face, hoping for a flash of insight. A memory anchored to a grade or a year. Middle school. Late elementary. Something I could hang a date on.

Instead, he shook his head. "I don't really remember him."

"Not at all? How old were you when he left?"

Josh frowned. "I was in first grade, I think."

That'd be six. Not ten. Not twelve. I filed that answer away.

"We just came from seeing Bill Goodman," I said. "He said to tell you hello."

Josh's face brightened, genuine affection lighting his eyes. "How is he?"

"Still watching baseball. Still convinced the Rays are going to break his heart."

Josh chuckled. "I need to go see him. Things have been hectic around here."

"Sounds like he means a lot to you."

"He does," Josh said. "For years we did things together. Fishing. Baseball games. He was like a father, but he didn't punish me or anything. He was just there. Always ready to listen or help."

The word *punish* landed with a soft but unmistakable thud. I kept my expression neutral. "Did your mom punish you?"

Josh chuckled. "Mama believed in restitution. When I called Alyce Jones a freckle face, Mama made me apologize and pay her a compliment." His smile softened. "I told her she had nice teeth, but I'm not sure she appreciated it."

When Tony chuckled, I gave him a sharp look. I couldn't have him getting so lost in Josh's stories that he forgot to investigate.

Josh crossed his arms. "Once when I was really little, I took a piece of candy from a shelf at the grocery. Mama not only made me spit it out, she made me mop the floor until I earned the quarter to reimburse the store."

I could picture it. Margaret Donnelly, calm as a church pew, turning a small crime into a lifelong lesson. No raised voice. No belt. Just consequence and correction.

"Sounds like she did a good job," I said.

"I reckon."

We stood on the porch a moment longer. When Josh didn't volunteer anything else, I thanked him for his time. He nodded like he'd been honored by the request.

Once Josh went back into the house, Tony walked with me down the porch steps. "Well," he said.

"Yeah," I said again. It was becoming a habit.

Six years old. No memory of his father. Another man who

was "just there," never a punisher. A mother who taught instead of hurt.

Margaret had made the best of a bad situation. And Josh was the result.

As we got into the car, I glanced at the house one more time. It looked the same as always. Neat. Modest. But relaxed now that we had gone.

Josh Donnelly might remember more than he realized. And if he did, it would come out the only way he knew how.

Truthfully.

CHAPTER THIRTY-NINE

After a night filled with troubling dreams, Josh sat at the kitchen table and stared at his untouched cereal bowl.

"Not hungry?" Heather asked.

He shook his head. "I can't—I can't stop thinking about yesterday. About the chief's questions."

"How much do you remember about your dad?" Heather asked.

They sat at the kitchen table with the morning light slanting in, the air scented with butter and fried potatoes. Maggie banged the tray of her highchair while Heather reloaded her spoon. "Surely you have some memories."

Josh's stomach twisted so hard it stole his breath. Had he picked up a virus? His gut twisted again, hot and sudden, as if something sour had spilled inside him.

"Josh?" Heather said. "Are you listening?"

"I might've caught a bug," he said, forcing his words through a suddenly tight throat.

She leaned across the table and pressed the back of her hand to his forehead. "You do feel warm."

The room wobbled. Josh shoved his bowl aside, then folded his arms on the table and let his head drop onto them. He hadn't sat like this since he was a kid, cheek against the table, pretending the world could be held at bay if he stayed still long enough.

What had happened to his father?

The question crept in sideways, unwelcome. Josh tried to think of his dad as a person, but his mind slid off the image like rain off tin. Mama never talked about him. When Josh had asked, she always answered the same way, pinching his cheek and smiling. *He was half as sweet as you and one-quarter as good-lookin'.*

That was it. That was all.

A bead of sweat traced a slow, icy path down the hollow of Josh's back. He searched harder, pressing into memory like a tongue probing a sore tooth.

What came back wasn't a face, but a voice. Gravelly. Low. Followed by the metallic chink of a belt buckle. A sense of air tightening in the room—

His stomach lurched.

Josh groaned and swallowed hard, forcing the nausea back down. "I think the heat is gettin' to me."

"Josh!" Heather was on her feet, her hand sliding to the back of his neck, firm and cool. "You should go lie down."

"Just—let me sit a minute," he said. "I'm dizzy."

He didn't move. He couldn't. The kitchen sounds swelled until he could hear the metallic whir of the refrigerator's motor. The clock ticked like a hammer striking stone. Pipes hummed inside the walls. The floorboard beneath Maggie's highchair squeaked, sharp and accusing.

Then the edges of the room blurred. The light smeared. And everything went black.

When he opened his eyes again, Heather stood by his side. Her eyes focused on his face as she gripped his arm. "Better or worse?"

"Better," he said, blinking. "I think. Whatever that was . . . it's passed."

"You scared me," she said. "I didn't know what to do."

Josh nodded, propping his head on his hand.

Heather went back to her chair and the world returned to a manageable size. Maggie released a happy snort as Heather gave her another spoonful of cereal.

He watched Maggie eat, her movements delicate and purposeful, as if each bite was crucial to her well-being.

Without warning, she grinned, thrust out her arms, and leaned toward Josh.

"Whoa!" Josh lunged and caught her. "You're gonna hit the ground, baby girl."

He put Maggie down, and the baby crawled across the floor, racing toward her favorite lamb toy with the focus of a bloodhound.

Heather looked at Josh. "What're you thinkin' about?"

He exhaled. "The chief should know Mama's innocent. She could never hurt anybody."

His gaze drifted to the counter, where his cereal sat untouched, the flakes soggy. The sight turned his stomach again.

"I'm sorry," he said. "But I'm not hungry."

"You've got nothing to be sorry for," Heather whispered.

Josh stood, steadying himself with a hand on the chair back. He meant to go upstairs, to sit with his Bible and let it anchor him. But before he could take a step, through the window he saw the police chief's car turning into the driveway.

Apparently the past wasn't finished with him.

The minute he opened the door Josh knew he would hear bad news.

Chief Bowen stood on the porch, but he wasn't alone. A woman stood beside him, her posture rigid, a hard-sided folio tucked under her arm like a weapon. His mind flashed a warning before he could shape it into thought.

He cleared his throat, buying himself a second to think. "We weren't expectin' to see you today, Chief."

"I know," Bowen replied. "But we need to talk."

Josh stepped aside. Heather came in from the kitchen with Maggie on her hip, and the sight of their guests made her flinch. "If y'all don't mind," she said, her voice low and careful, "I think I'll take Maggie upstairs and give her a bath."

Josh nodded, wanting to rewind the moment, send Heather and Maggie up the stairs, and keep them ignorant of the danger at the door.

"Can you wait?" the chief asked, addressing Heather. "You need to hear this too."

She froze, then lowered herself onto the couch and set Maggie on the floor. The color drained from her face, leaving her pale.

"Heather, Josh," the chief said, "this is Marlene DuBois. She works for the county, Department of Children and Families."

Josh nodded because politeness had been drilled into him since childhood. Heather didn't move. Her gaze traveled over the woman's sensible shoes, the pulled-back hair, the practiced calm that looked more dangerous than anger.

"Josh," the chief continued, pausing to clear his throat, "I was talking to Grace Egan about your father. One thing led to another, and she mentioned meeting Heather at your mama's funeral. That was December, right?"

Behind him, Heather groaned.

"What surprised me," the chief went on, "is that even with Grace's failing memory, she clearly remembered Heather . . . and remarked on how thin she was." One of the chief's brows rose. "Oddly enough, it never occurred to Grace that Heather shouldn't have been thin in December."

Josh's blood raced in a surge of panic. He didn't like where this was going.

"By my reckoning," the chief said, "if Heather is Maggie's mother, in December she should've been close to giving birth."

Josh's gaze dropped to Maggie. She was holding her stuffed lamb with both hands, mouthing its nose, as content as sunlight. The room seemed to shrink around her.

"I checked with Doc Tompkins," the chief said. "He said he examined Heather and a newborn the day after Christmas. Heather had a fractured bone in her foot, but she showed no signs of having recently given birth."

Silence swelled in the room, so thick Josh could barely breathe.

"So I need the truth," the chief said. "Is this baby biologically related to either of you?"

Josh's heart hammered. He tried to push past the question. "What . . . what do you mean?"

Bowen sighed. "Son, are you the biological father of this baby?"

Josh dropped his gaze. The words lodged in his throat before he forced them free. "No, sir."

The woman beside the chief shifted, but the chief turned to Heather. "Miss Thomas, are you the biological mother?"

Heather looked at Josh, and he read the wordless promise in her eyes. She would lie for him. For Maggie. For all of them.

He shook his head.

Heather lifted her chin. "What does biology matter? Josh is the only daddy Maggie's ever known. She loves him."

"I stopped believing in the stork years ago," the chief said, his voice gentle. "So where'd you get this baby?"

Josh folded his arms, bracing himself. "I found Maggie on my front porch. That's the truth."

"That's difficult to accept without documentation," the woman said, her nostrils flaring.

The chief shot her a look sharp enough to make Josh flinch. "If this young man says he found her on his porch, he did."

Maggie chose that moment to haul herself upright by climbing up Josh's pants. She grinned, proud and triumphant, as if she had scaled a mountain.

"When you found her," the chief continued, "why didn't you call us? Or take her to the hospital?"

Josh drew a steadying breath. "I was more worried about savin' her life. She was cold and hungry. It was Christmas Eve. I figured maybe the Lord had arranged things."

"Newborns need appropriate nutrition," the woman said. "What did you feed her?"

"Warm milk," Josh said, heat creeping into his face. "Then formula the next day. I'm not stupid."

"You did right by her, Josh," the chief said. "But you should've called us."

Josh lowered his gaze. "I prayed, then I did what I had to do. If I hadn't brought her in, she'd have died out there. I've taken good care of her."

"He has," Heather said, her eyes blazing. "Maggie is fed, clean, and loved. He's with her all the time."

The woman's gaze slid to Heather. "And you are . . . his partner?"

Heather hesitated. "I'm not sure that's your business."

"Oh, it is," the woman said. "Like Josh, you are living with a baby who is not yours."

Josh nodded at Heather, who flexed her jaw. "We're friends."

"Friends who cohabitate."

"Friends who live in different rooms," Heather shot back. "Our relationship is none of your concern."

Before the woman could answer, the chief stepped forward. "Here's the problem, Josh. Legally, Maggie is a ward of the state. Abandoned children go into foster care while we look for their parents. It's the law."

Something inside Josh snapped. He pulled Maggie into his arms. "No. She stays with me."

"It doesn't work that way," the woman said, reaching for her folio. "Failure to report an abandoned child is a felony and—"

"That's enough," the chief barked.

"But—"

"Marlene? Outside. Now."

The woman huffed and went outside, the door slamming hard enough to rattle the windows.

Bowen turned back, his face lined with concern. "I know you love this little girl. But the law's the law. The baby has to go into foster care."

Josh's legs turned to rubber as he wrapped both arms around Maggie. "I can't let you take her."

"I know you don't want to," the chief said. "But I need you to cooperate."

Heather clutched Josh's arm, her fingers digging into flesh.

Fear and respect for the law smothered Josh's defiance, leaving him with the hollow ache of defeat.

"I'll wait outside," the chief said. "When you're ready, bring Maggie out. Can you do that?"

Josh's voice barely worked. "I . . . I need to change her diaper. She hasn't worn her new dress. And she can't sleep without her little lamb."

The chief nodded, his eyes shining. "Put whatever she needs into a bag. I'll make sure it goes with her."

"Okay." The word felt like betrayal.

The door closed behind the chief, leaving Josh standing in the quiet, Maggie's heartbeat pressed against his own. He buried his face in her hair and breathed her in, memorizing her scent, her hands, the way she trusted him completely.

Lord, he prayed silently, *don't let them take your lamb.*

I SLID into the driver's seat and shut the door with a soft thump. Marlene climbed in beside me, purse and leather notebook stacked on her lap.

The late-morning heat had soaked into the car. The vinyl seat stuck to the back of my trousers. Down the block a lawn edger whined with the grim determination of a man who refused to admit it was too hot to be workin' with the sun set on broil.

I adjusted the rearview mirror—mostly for something to do.

"Well," I said. "How do you think that went?"

Marlene let out a long breath. "These things rarely go well, Chief. The girl's angry. He's defensive. We'll be lucky if we get outta here without a scene."

I studied the Donnelly house. Neat as a Sunday bulletin, if a little worn. Curtains drawn. Walkway swept just enough to pass inspection.

"Josh doesn't have a violent bone in his body."

Marlene arched an eyebrow. "We'll see."

That was Marlene. She'd seen too much to be impressed by tidy houses or polite young men. If optimism were a muscle, hers had been overworked, sprained, and medically retired.

I nodded toward the east. "So. How're things over in Marianna?"

She laughed—no humor attached. "Fine, if you don't mind—"

Her phone rang, and the look that crossed her face when she saw the caller ID was anything but amiable. She gave me an apologetic look and answered the call. "Marlene DuBois."

I leaned back and turned on the AC. No sense in us baking while we waited for Josh.

"I know," Marlene said, frustration in her voice. "But the placement is only temporary. It won't hurt the kid to be in temporary care for only—" She looked at me again and rolled her eyes while someone filled her ear.

"Okay," she finally said. "Do what you have to do, Mr. Henry. You're the man with the lawyer."

She dropped her phone back into her purse and stared straight ahead.

"Trouble in paradise?" I asked.

She snorted. "Trouble with Mr. Henry. He has a thing about consistency of care. The man would move a mountain if it meant he could keep a child with the same caregivers. And he'd do it in an hour—the man has connections."

I adjusted the air vent so she could feel the AC. "I'm not familiar with the name."

"Lincoln Henry." She shook her head. "Head of the State Guardian Ad Litem office. Stubborn little man in baggy clothes, and untouchable. He's the governor's uncle or cousin or something. All I know is he's a pain in my derriere."

Uh-oh. I leaned back and rested my arm on the door. That tone meant misery had unpacked and was planning a long stay.

"Why does he wear baggy clothes?" I asked.

"How should I know?" Marlene flapped her hands. "I think he lost a lot of weight and is too cheap to buy a new suit. But whenever I hear him swishing outside my office, I want to hide under my desk."

I chuckled, entertained by the image.

"A few months ago," she said, wagging her finger at me, "I had a special-needs baby all set for a foster placement. Kid was in the hospital, waiting for the doctor to come in the next morning, but Lincoln Henry swished in, waved an emergency custody order in front of the nurses, and took the kid out in the middle of the night."

"Without the doctor's permission?"

"Henry had a signed statement—had the doctor send an email."

I chuckled. "I gotta say—sounds like this guy gets things done."

"As long as it's done *his* way," Marlene said. "He's a loose cannon, and no one can stop him because he's got lawyers and the governor on his side."

I snorted. Politics—the only profession where bad decisions come with benefits.

We sat for a moment, engine ticking, the AC working overtime. Then I circled back. "So the kid—he was okay?"

She hesitated, just a beat. "Yeah. The foster family got out of bed, got him settled, and he's doing well."

"So the outcome didn't bother you."

"Henry's *methods* bother me." She folded her arms. "The

system works, but you have to give it time. People have days off. Hospitals and courts have schedules."

"So he bucks the system."

"All the time," she said. "If he thinks he can find a better home, next thing I know the kid's got a lawyer and Lincoln has an emergency transfer order. All my work goes right out the window."

"I get it," I said. "The head of the FDLE is appointed by the governor, too. But Peculiar's so small they don't bother us much."

I tapped a rhythm on the steering wheel. Ba da boom.

"You know," I said, changing the subject, "that baby girl in there? She's in a good home. You saw her. Healthy. Happy. Josh is solid. And Heather's trying—"

"They're not licensed foster parents," Marlene snapped. "Josh Donnelly might be a certified saint, but we cannot let people play finders keepers with babies."

"But do you have to take that baby today?"

"If you saw me rob a bank, would you wait and arrest me tomorrow?"

She checked her watch, the clink of her bracelet too loud in the silence. "I thought he'd bring her right out."

"So did I."

That put a crease in my forehead. Josh Donnelly wasn't the type to stall. If he said he'd do a thing, he did it. On time. With his shirt tucked in.

I looked at the front door again, that old cop itch tweaking the muscles between my shoulder blades.

Beside me, Marlene stared straight ahead. For a second her hand tightened around her notebook, knuckles whitening, then she loosened her grip . . . as if she'd caught herself doing something she wasn't supposed to do.

I made a mental note.

People like Marlene didn't show their hearts often. When they did, it was usually by accident.

And accidents, in my line of work, couldn't be ignored.

THROUGH THE WINDOW in Maggie's room, Josh studied the patrol car in the driveway. Heat shimmered above the hood, warping the outlines of the chief and the social worker as they sat inside. Even from a distance he could read them. The chief's shoulders were hunched, hands locked on the steering wheel as if it were the only solid thing left in the world. The woman beside him sat stiff and straight, her jaw working, her irritation practically fogging the glass.

Heather's fingers dug into Josh's arm.

"You can't let them take her," she said. Her voice shook like a wire pulled too tight. "You can't. Tell me you won't."

Josh drew a breath that burned all the way down. "But it's the law," he said, and the words tasted like sandpaper.

"Yeah, right." Heather laughed, sharp and bitter. "You hand Maggie over and they might put her someplace where babies lie in cribs all day. How's she gonna like that?"

She wiped her palms on her shorts, then pressed her knuckles to her stomach as if she could hold the panic in.

"No tummy time. No playtime. Nobody talking to her or singing to her. No walks. No cuddling with a dog." Her voice sped up, as if she were racing a memory. "And when she's older they'll stick her in a house with too many kids, where she'll learn how to fight. And how to disappear."

Maggie moved against Josh's shirt, warm and alive, her fingers clutching the fabric as if she knew what was at stake.

"And when she runs away," Heather said, her voice breaking, "and she will, she'll end up at a truck stop with girls who call themselves Tiffany and Starlight and Delicious. She won't finish school. She won't go to church. And she'll never meet a man who really knows how to love her—"

Heather stopped short, her breath hitching. Tears spilled down her cheeks, unchecked.

Josh's heart twisted so hard it hurt to breathe. Heather's words hadn't sprung from imagination or exaggeration. They came from *memories* carried like scar tissue beneath her skin.

He looked down at Maggie, at the soft strands of her hair. How could he place her on a road Heather had walked barefoot and bleeding?

Determination settled in him, heavy and immovable.

"Okay," he said, his voice low. "Take Mags to your room. Lock the door. Sing to her and keep her happy. Then put her down for a nap. That'll buy us a few hours."

Heather stared at him, startled, then pulled Maggie into her arms. "And then what? What are you going to do?"

Josh straightened. "I'm gonna tell them they're not taking her today. Not without a judge."

"I'm not sure it works that way," Heather said, turning toward the hallway.

"I'm not either," he admitted. His pulse roared in his ears, but his resolve held. "But they're gonna have to go through me to get to her."

Heather looked back at him.

"God sent her to me," Josh said. "To us. And until He tells me somethin' different, Maggie's stayin' right here."

Heather nodded, then disappeared into her bedroom. Josh stood alone in Maggie's room, the tiny wallpaper birds watching him, the patrol car waiting outside.

For the first time in his life, he figured obeying the law was the wrong thing to do.

CHAPTER
FORTY

I've seen men come unglued over money, women, liquor, football, and once, memorably, a missing lawn gnome. But I don't believe I've ever witnessed a human combust the way Josh Donnelly did that August afternoon.

When I stepped out of his house, I honestly believed he'd follow me within a minute or two, red-eyed and miserable but obedient, Maggie tucked into his secondhand carrier like a surrender flag. Josh was a rule-keeper by nature. Order made him feel safe. Right and wrong had always come with clear fences.

Ten minutes passed. Fifteen.

The house stayed quiet, then the front door flew open and Josh came barreling down the steps empty-handed, Hoss right behind him, his nails skittering on the old brick walkway. Josh's ears were red, his jaw set so tight I thought he might crack a molar, and if anger had a smell it would have been rolling off him like ozone before a lightning strike.

Only one thing could've lit that fuse: fear for Heather and Maggie.

"You're not comin' in here again!" he shouted, voice raw, jogging toward me like a man who'd already made peace with whatever came next. "Not without a judge or the Almighty Himself."

I got out of the car and planted my boots on the Donnelly walkway. "Josh," I said, calm as a man could be with two hundred pounds of dog eyeing his kneecaps, "you promised to make this easy."

"It's not easy," he shot back. "And takin' a baby from the only people who ever loved her shouldn't be easy for you. So you go make your calls, sir. But you're not takin' Maggie today."

He said *sir* like it hurt.

I took a deep breath, the kind you exhale while you're reminding yourself that you're here to keep things from getting worse. "Josh," I said, "trust me. You do not want to make trouble for yourself."

He lowered his head, dipped his shoulder, and rushed me —two steps, then a hard pivot—

Marlene gasped. I raised my hands, thinking I'd grab Josh's shoulders, talk him down, remind him of the years I'd known him and the casseroles his mama brought to my house when my wife passed.

That's why I never saw the fist.

Josh clipped my jaw hard enough to rattle my teeth and knock every clever phrase clean out of my head. My hand twitched toward my gun on instinct alone, muscle memory from hours of training and a thousand what-ifs. But this was Josh Donnelly. He didn't have cruelty in him. What he had was love gone feral.

Righteous anger is a dangerous thing. You can't reason with it. You can only meet it with a cause equally righteous, and right then all I had was the law. Cold. Unyielding. Unromantic law.

Before he could swing again, I caught his arm and twisted him around. I was halfway to cuffing him when I remembered something that had slipped my mind.

The dog.

Hoss hit my thighs like a freight train with fur. I went down hard and slid across brick, the breath blasting out of me in an undignified grunt. Hoss stood over me, his chest heaving, breath hot and wet on my face, a growl vibrating low enough to rearrange my insides.

Slobber dripped onto my cheek.

I did not move.

I did not look him in the eye.

Ever so slowly, I drew my gun and pointed it at the dog's chest, every nerve in my body screaming that this was the worst day of my career. I kept the muzzle low, finger straight along the frame—praying bluff would beat blood.

"Josh," I called, steady as I could manage with a canine death sentence inches from my face. "I don't want to shoot your dog. But I will if you don't call him off."

Josh's anger dissolved. I heard the break in his voice, the way grief rushed in behind it. "Hoss," he pleaded. "Hoss, come here, boy. Come on."

Hoss hesitated, then stepped back and trotted to Josh's side, pressing his massive body against his legs like an apology.

I sat up, checked Marlene, holstered my gun, and got to my feet. My hands shook, though I'd have died before admitting it out loud.

"Turn around," I said, and snapped the cuffs on Donnelly's wrists. "Doggone it, Josh. Why'd you make me do that?"

"Because this ain't right," he said, voice breaking. "And you know it."

"The law says I have to take her," I reminded him. "I thought you understood."

I walked him to the squad car and settled him in the backseat beside Marlene's baby carrier—sitting there like the universe had a sense of humor and no conscience. Hoss barked himself hoarse behind us, the sound scraping my nerves.

I slid into the driver's seat and called it in. "Donnelly house," I told Tony. "Now."

My deputy arrived within minutes, took one look at Josh, and blinked. "What for?"

"Battery on a law enforcement officer," I said. "If he gives you trouble, add resisting arrest."

Tony stared like I'd told him the sun had fallen. "Didn't think he was the type."

"Neither did I," I said. "And speak gently, or the dog will file a complaint."

I put Josh in Tony's car, sent them off, and turned back to the house.

I could've pushed my way in and let the paperwork argue later. But Heather hadn't threatened anybody, and I didn't have a warrant—only a mandate and a mess.

I rang the bell. Knocked. Nothing.

I motioned Marlene over. "You're a witness," I told her. "We're goin' in, but don't take charge."

She squared her shoulders. "Not my first rodeo, Chief."

We stepped inside, inhaling the scents of baby powder and old wood. When we reached the stairs, the sound of sobbing went straight through me. If one of my kids was crying like that, I'd burn down the state capitol to make things right.

I knocked on the only closed door. "Heather," I said, my voice low. "Josh is at the station, and I don't want to take you too. Let us take Maggie where she can be protected. That's the best thing you can do."

Silence.

"I care about you," I added, because it was true. "I promise Maggie will be safe."

The door opened.

Heather placed Maggie in my arms like she was handing me something she could not afford to lose. The baby was asleep, mouth slack, lashes resting on her cheeks, unaware of what adults had just decided.

Heather thrust a grocery bag at Marlene. "You'd better make sure she's okay." Then she looked at me. "Tell Josh I'm sorry."

"You're doing the right thing," I said. "That counts for something."

"Really?" she said. "I hope you're right."

So did I. Taking Maggie felt like taking a pulse from a living heart.

Then Heather closed the door, and I carried Maggie out into the sunny afternoon, wishing that in situations like this the law had more room for mercy.

By late afternoon my bones felt like they'd been run through a cement mixer, and a steady ache sat between my shoulder blades. I'd packed three days' work into one, but the clock over the booking desk remained stubborn. According to it, I still had hours to go.

And a prisoner.

The Peculiar Police Department is not exactly Alcatraz. We have two cells. When both are occupied, we call it a crime wave and order pizza. The place smelled like disinfectant and damp wool, with an undertone of desperation.

I was heading down the hall to check on Josh when my phone rang.

"Chief Bowen."

"Chief, it's Marlene. I wanted to thank you for facilitating the pickup this morning."

I leaned a hip against the counter, tracing the dark grooves in the linoleum left by forty years of pacing. That pickup had been rough, no two ways about it. But Marlene hadn't been the one standing in front of a young man who looked like a sinkhole had opened up right in front of him.

"All in a day's work," I said. "Is the baby all right?"

"She's with a foster family in Marianna. Placement went by the book."

I followed the hallway with my eyes. Toward the cells. Toward the small, ordinary rooms where we keep people while the world decides what to do with them.

"Good," I said. "That's good."

She hesitated—a silence that pretended to be nothing but was, in fact, important. Cops develop an ear for it.

"And Josh?" she asked, as careful as a woman crossing thin ice. "How is he taking all this?"

There it was. "About as well as you'd expect," I said. "He's still here."

Another hesitation. Longer.

"Right," Marlene said. "Of course he is." She cleared her throat. "Listen, Chief... I don't know how things work over in Peculiar, but if any families in your town ever express interest in fostering, or, you know, longer-term arrangements, I could send you some brochures. There's also a website. Application info. Orientation classes."

I almost smiled.

That was Marlene—enforcing the law with one hand and leaving the door cracked with the other. She'd never say the word *adopt*, not over an official line, not in broad daylight. But I knew exactly what she was offering.

"Actually, Marlene," I said, "I'm glad you called. I talked to Josh. Solved the question of where that baby came from."

"Really?"

"A runaway," I said, "gave birth in an abandoned trailer at the truck stop. Then the mother disappeared—left a note and told Heather she wanted the baby taken to Josh Donnelly's house."

A soft gasp floated over the line. "Why on earth would she—"

"Apparently Heather had been watching Josh and decided he was a good man." I paused. "In her world, good men are rarer than a childhood that doesn't leave bruises."

Marlene went quiet. "I don't know the young man personally," she said at last, "but—"

"He *is* a good man," I said before policy could lace up its boots. "And I sent my deputy back to the truck stop. The girls are gone. Trailer's locked. Whatever was happening out there is done. Odds of this repeating are slim."

"A young woman can always take her baby to the hospital," Marlene said. Her voice had gone husky. "Or a fire station."

"Sure," I said, "if she has transportation. If she has someone to tell her where to go. If she isn't alone and scared and having a baby in the dark."

Silence again. Not official silence. Human silence.

"Thank you for telling me," she said. "And . . . thank you again for this morning, Chief."

"Any time."

We hung up. I slid the phone into my pocket.

Tony was watching from the desk, curiosity written all over his face, but I wasn't ready to explain the chain of human decisions that had dropped a baby in Josh Donnelly's arms.

So I stood in silence a moment longer, listening to the building breathe—vents rattling, the ancient copier wheezing—thinking about laws and systems and how they're built to be one-size-fits-all, but sometimes the heart sneaks in.

Order is a comforting thing, but it's fragile. And when it cracks, strange, even miraculous things have a way of slipping through.

Josh was in the left cell, sitting on his cot with his shoulders slumped, staring at the iron bars like they had personally betrayed him. He looked the way men look when something precious has been lost and there's no arguing it back.

I propped my forearms on the bars and addressed him in my friendliest voice. "You know, most folks apologize after they punch the chief."

He didn't look at me.

Truth was, I'd been hoping for an apology. Not because I needed it, but because it would give me something to tell the prosecutor—evidence of remorse. A reason for the judge to go easy and sentence Josh to a hundred hours of community service.

When he finally glanced up, whatever flicker of hope had been in his face had guttered out. I could see the picture in his head: Maggie in some unfamiliar place, clutching that bunny and crying herself hoarse.

He turned away, silent as a shut Bible.

Okay, then. So much for the easy ending.

I straightened and cleared my throat. "I can't let you go," I said, though I suspected he already knew that. "Even if I wanted to."

That earned me nothing but an audible sigh.

I couldn't blame him. Not for the punch or the silence. If someone had tried to take one of my daughters, there wouldn't have been enough handcuffs in Jackson County to keep me polite.

But the law doesn't bend for sympathy. It stands resolute, arms crossed, daring you to argue. Judges get the gray areas. Cops get the paperwork.

And speaking of paperwork...

I went back to my desk, which was lit by a flickering fluorescent tube and buried under forms from the Department of Children and Families. Their packets always smelled of toner and despair.

I filled in boxes, checked codes, and tried not to think about Maggie and her little lamb.

After all, I had a murder on my hands, too.

George Donnelly hadn't buried his own body under his shed. That much I'd bet my pension on.

I studied his old mug shot on the computer. George looked like half the men in Peculiar: square jaw, tired eyes, a mouth that suggested regret came easy on Sunday mornings. Everyone I'd spoken to said the same thing: Ex-military. Decent husband. Tough father. Drank too much and prayed about it afterward. By all accounts, George Donnelly paid his taxes, loved his wife and kid, and stayed put.

Until he didn't.

Records showed no calls from 1423 Church Street. Ever. No domestic disputes, no noise complaints, not even a loose dog report. That alone made the place stand out. Perfect silence is louder than trouble.

The only blip was January 10, 1986, at 1930 hours. Chief Bill Goodman had responded to a call from Jackie Leakey at the house next door. No incident report attached, which meant it could have been anything from a prowler to a raccoon with ambitions.

January nights fall fast. By six-thirty the dark settles in and imaginations start freelancing. People call the police for shadows, but Jackie had called because of screaming. Because it was worse than usual.

What happened that night? Did George Donnelly leave, or did his wife kill him?

If he did leave, did he come back to a struggling wife and an angry teenager?

I searched statewide databases for Donnellys, but none of them listed George. No digital footprints matched his name, no distant cousins raised their hands.

But in 1986, few people had digital footprints. Facebook hadn't been invented.

By the time I made my final prisoner check, night had engulfed the station. The hum of the lights was louder and the silence made my footsteps sound like accusations.

Josh lay stretched out on the cot, eyes closed and hands folded on his ribcage like a man rehearsing for worse things. I couldn't tell if he was asleep.

"Josh," I said, keeping my voice official. "We go to Marianna in the morning for your arraignment. I can call Heather and ask her to bring you a suit."

The words hung there, as heavy as the bars.

"Okay," he said.

"I'll be here for the night shift," I added. "Need anything?"

Any other man might've cursed me, demanded a lawyer, or asked for a cigarette we couldn't allow.

"No, thank you," Josh said. "Good night, Chief."

I stayed for a minute, listening to the hum of the lights, wishing I could fix more than the law allowed.

CHAPTER
FORTY-ONE

Josh sat on the narrow cot and whispered the words that had steadied him since childhood, the ones his mother used to murmur when storms rattled the windows or worry crept too close.

"No evil shall befall you, nor shall any plague come near your dwelling. For He shall give His angels charge over you, to keep you in all your ways."

The cot creaked when he shifted. He opened his eyes and studied the ceiling, tracing a crack that ran like a fault line from corner to corner. The Lord had told him to care for Maggie and Heather. He was sure of it. *Feed my lamb. Seek my lamb.* He had done what was asked, hadn't he? So why did it feel like he'd abandoned the two people he loved most?

Josh's pulse jumped when keys jangled and the cellblock door creaked. A minute later Tony Kirkpatrick appeared, his shadow stretching across the concrete.

"You okay, Josh?"

Josh nodded because it was easier than answering. Tony lingered a second, then left.

Josh focused on the round clock on the wall, where the hands refused to budge. The silence filled with the hum of overhead lights and the distant ring of a phone. Then the keys rattled again and Tony showed Heather into the hallway.

She carried Josh's only suit draped over her arm, along with a dress shirt on one of Mama's wooden hangers. The sight of her made his throat ache. Only then did it strike him—she would walk back into that house alone tonight. And he knew how unbearable an empty house could be.

"I'm so sorry, Josh," she said, the tremor in her voice cutting deeper than jail ever could.

Tony hung the clothes on a hook, then locked the door behind him. "Ten minutes," he called over his shoulder. "Then you'll need to head out, miss."

Heather pushed her hair back with shaking fingers and leaned forward, positioning her face between the bars. Her eyes brimmed. "I couldn't stop him from taking Maggie. I tried, but I was afraid he'd arrest me for interfering."

Josh brushed her cheek with his fingertips. "I understand," he said, though it hurt. "The law's the law."

"But it isn't right. There's no reason they couldn't let you keep Maggie while they do their paperwork." She pulled back and covered her mouth.

Josh knew that gesture. He ached to pull her into his arms, to let her cry against his shoulder the way she had before.

"You can't blame yourself," he said. "You got the worst part of this. I know you didn't want to be reminded of babies, but—"

"Don't," she said, a sob tearing loose. "Please don't. I can't talk about that."

She sank to the floor and clutched the bars like they were the only thing holding her upright. Josh slid down until they were eye to eye through the iron.

"It doesn't matter what they say," he told her, his voice soft but certain. "No matter what that woman says, we're a family, official or not. We care about each other." He tried to smile. "Even Hoss knows that much."

Heather released a broken laugh. "Shut up," she said, swiping at her face. "There's something I need to tell you, but I don't know how."

She crossed her legs and scooted closer, but the words didn't come. Her shoulders shook, thin and fragile, and guilt washed over him. His outburst had left her alone. Heather wasn't weak, but she must have been terrified to see him taken away.

"It's okay," he said. "You don't have to explain anything."

"Yes, I do." She drew a shaky breath. "There's a reason I didn't want Maggie going into foster care. After my parents divorced, I ran away from my mom's house. When the cops tried to take me home, Mom said I was too much trouble. My dad didn't want me either—didn't want to cause trouble with his new wife." Her voice thinned. "So I went into the system. And when I turned eighteen . . . that's when I started hanging out with guys like Brett."

Josh listened, his hands curling around the bars, the cold sinking into his bones. She'd been abandoned, just like Maggie. Just like he'd felt after Mama died. No wonder she'd fought so hard for that baby.

"I'm not the kind of woman you should have in your house," she finished. "If I stay, I'll be used as proof that you're unfit . . . and I don't want that life for Maggie."

The kind of woman he should have in his house? He had only one answer, and he didn't dare say it aloud.

"My family's far from perfect," Josh said, managing a wry chuckle. "I don't know how my dad ended up buried in the backyard, and maybe I don't want to." He slid his fingers through the bars. "But you can't look backward, Heather. All that matters is what we do now."

Tony's footsteps approached and the door opened. "Time's up."

Heather stood. "Goodbye, Josh. I'd go to your arraignment, but maybe it's best if I don't."

"I'm sorry," Josh said. "I'm so sorry."

"For what?"

"For everything. But mostly for putting you through this."

Her brow furrowed, and when she spoke again her voice sounded resigned. "Goodbye, Josh Donnelly. Have a good life."

Something cold slid up his spine and took his breath. "Wait." He stood and reached through the bars, desperate to catch her hand. "You don't have to leave the house. Stay. Please."

She held his gaze until Tony cleared his throat. Then she turned and walked away.

Josh watched her go, his hand extended through the bars like he could pull her back by sheer will. The hallway swallowed her up, and the truth arrived with painful clarity: he wanted a lifetime with her—one life, shared, under that roof, through whatever came.

And the worst part was this: if she stayed, tonight and maybe many nights after, she would sit alone in that house because he had failed to keep her safe.

He couldn't blame her if she decided to go.

HEATHER STEPPED out of the police station into a summer night that felt too large for her heart.

The full moon hung low and bright, washing Peculiar in pale silver. Streetlights glowed along Main Street. Somewhere in the dark, tree frogs tuned their throats and sang, a steady, pulsing sound that rose and fell like breath.

She turned toward Church Street.

Each step carried her farther from Josh—from the iron bars, from the way he had looked at her—not accusing, not frightened, but concerned, as if she were the one who needed comfort.

Josh didn't need a woman like her.

The thought arrived whole and heavy. She let it walk beside her beneath the live oaks, Spanish moss stirring in the night breeze. She wasn't like him. Not even close.

Josh was good in a way that felt almost out of place in the world. His goodness wasn't showy or strategic. It didn't reach for approval. It simply existed—quiet, steady, unembarrassed. People underestimated him because of it.

He had been good for her.

Heather slowed as she passed the closed storefronts, their dark windows reflecting the moon. The house on Church Street came to her in pieces—not as a building, but as a series of small, ordinary mercies.

She remembered holding her breath while painting tiny wooden toys, forcing herself to move slowly, to be careful with something that mattered. She remembered listening for Maggie in the night, learning the difference between cries of hunger and fear, between fussing and real distress. She remembered the weight of the baby's fingers curled around her thumb, as if Maggie needed her to stay anchored.

And she remembered Josh trusting her—with Maggie, with Hoss, with himself—without testing. That realization settled over her like the warm night air.

He trusted her.

He wasn't someone who wanted to rescue her. Not someone who offered escape or a wild ride or the electric rush of chaos. Freedom without a foundation was only motion pretending to be life.

Josh had given her a place, a rhythm, a reason to wake up that didn't involve running or chasing something that would vanish the moment she caught it. He had given her stability, solid ground beneath her feet, and she was grateful for it.

The moon lit the familiar lines of the house as she approached—the sagging steps, the worn rail, the rocker Josh rarely used because it creaked. She opened the front door and Hoss burst past her, nails clicking across the porch boards, tail sweeping the air.

"Sorry," she said. "Go do your business."

He bounded into the yard and vanished into shadow with a snort and a huff. Heather returned to the porch and stopped.

Something rested on the table near the front door, covered with a cloth. A folded card lay beneath it. She picked it up and moved to read it under the porch light.

Heather—I heard the awful news. Josh asked me to hold this as a surprise for Maggie, but now . . . maybe you should have it. —Jackie

Her chest constricted as she lifted the cloth.

For a moment she could only stare. A thick, two-foot section of log had been split lengthwise, the bark stripped away, the surface polished to a soft glow. An arched lid, carved and varnished, rested on top. She lifted it with careful hands.

Inside lay pairs of animals, dozens of them—spruce, ash, cedar, rosewood. Horses with flowing manes. Dogs with cocked heads. Cats caught mid-stretch. Birds with unfurled wings. Lions and polar bears. A kangaroo with a joey in her pouch, so delicate it made her breath catch.

Every piece was smooth, gentle, sized for a child's palm, with no sharp edge anywhere.

Josh lived in every inch of the carvings—his patience, his

quiet joy in the work, his stubborn hope. Hours of his life, given to a baby who might never remember him.

Heather pressed her fingers to her mouth. A broken sob tore free, sharp and exposed in the quiet night.

Love looked like a man sitting alone on his porch, carving animal after animal for a child, doing the small, unseen work no one would ever applaud.

Josh had given her goodness. The kind that made her want to be better.

He had given her a home. A purpose. A version of herself she could live with.

A realization struck her, clean and unarguable—she loved him.

She set the lid back in place and sank onto the porch swing.

Before last Christmas, her life had led nowhere. Brett's world had been all motion and no direction. He loved what she did for him—how she listened, how she sacrificed, how she reshaped herself to suit him.

She had thought she wanted freedom. Now she understood that what she needed was a place to land.

What she needed, what she yearned for, was a steady flame that would keep her warm through long, cold nights. The kind she could build a life around.

Josh was that flame.

A weight pressed against her knee, and she looked down. Hoss stood beside her, his great head lowered, eyes steady and luminous in the moonlight. She slid her fingers into the thick fur at his neck, remembering how Josh sat when she trimmed his hair, how completely he trusted her.

"Who would feed you if I left?" she said, her voice breaking.

Hoss blinked.

She let out a small, cracked laugh and wiped her face. "Don't worry, boy. I'm not going anywhere."

The words settled something inside her.

Leaving would mean walking away from the first man who had ever made her feel like she was enough and the first place that had ever felt like home.

She wasn't a frightened girl anymore.

Josh hadn't changed her by asking. He had changed her by demonstrating what goodness looked like, what steadiness felt like, and what love did when it kept showing up.

She looked at the house, at the table, at the quiet evidence of a good man's love. Walking away would not be noble. It would be fear wearing the mask of sacrifice.

And he needed help.

Tomorrow morning, she would start with the one person who might know how to untangle this, the one person who would listen.

Heather rose from the swing, her legs steady beneath her, and took Hoss inside to wait for morning.

Josh sat on the edge of the narrow cot, his hands on his thighs because he didn't know what else to do with them. He breathed in the scents of old wool, Lysol, and loneliness.

He had never prayed in a place like this. He had never risked as much as this.

He breathed for a minute, then confessed. "I don't know what I'm doing."

The words felt thin. He swallowed and tried again.

"I don't know how to be everything Maggie needs." He pressed his hands together, as if he could hold the pieces in place. "But I know I can't let her go. I don't think I was built for that."

His throat tightened. "If You want to keep her in my life, I'll take the risk. I won't give up. I won't walk away from the fight. But I need You to show me where to put my feet."

He bowed his head, the metal frame of the cot cold through his jeans.

"I'm not askin' for easy. I'm askin' for enough."

After his words died away, he sat in the quiet, the sounds of the station closing around him, his heartbeat loud in his ears.

Somewhere in the building, a door opened and closed.

He didn't know how long he sat there, but the fear loosened. And into the emptiness came a certainty he could not explain:

I will supply all you need.

CHAPTER
FORTY-TWO

I was at my desk pretending to do paperwork when the night settled around the station. The kind of quiet that doesn't mean nothing's happening, just that whatever's coming hasn't introduced itself yet.

The clock over the booking desk clicked past ten. Tony's radio hissed. I'd opened the door to the cell block so I could hear Josh if he needed anything, but he wasn't moving. Hadn't been for a while.

I told myself that was a good sign. Sometimes when a man stops pacing, it means he's found a place to stand.

I'd just started another form when someone knocked at the front door. Not hard. Not dramatic. But the knock of a man who expected to be answered.

Tony let him in, they exchanged a few words, then came down the hall toward my office.

I looked up.

A man with a full head of white hair stood behind Tony with a brown folder in one hand and a bundle in the other. The bundle wiggled and sneezed.

He nodded at me. "I'm looking for Joshua Donnelly."

I raised a brow. "And you are?"

"Lincoln Henry, of the State Guardian ad Litem office."

The name landed before the rest of him did.

Henry.

Marlene's Henry. The man who, according to her, couldn't walk into a room without knocking over three carefully stacked plans in the name of saving a child.

"Donnelly is in cell one," I said. "What's this about?"

Henry shifted the bundle on his hip and glanced at the folder, the corner of his mouth twisting. "I've got paperwork. Emergency placement, with a signed order from a judge. I also have a letter from the governor, if you need it."

That got my attention.

I took the folder from him. My eyes skimmed what I could while he kept talking—names, dates, signatures. Everything where it was supposed to be. Everything impossible.

"Her name's Maggie," he added. "Maggie Doe."

I didn't ask why he'd come in the middle of the night or why he'd brought a baby to a jail. Some questions could wait.

"Come on back," I said.

Josh was sitting on the edge of the cot when I led Lincoln Henry into the cellblock.

"Josh," I said, unlocking the cell door, "you've got company."

Maggie's eyes locked onto Josh the instant the light caught his face, and her mouth split into a gummy grin. She began to babble, soft syllables tumbling over each other, her arms pumping as if she would swim to him through mid-air.

Josh didn't move at first. He stared, as if the room was spinning and he was waiting for it to stop.

"Mags?"

She squealed and reached harder, then he pulled her into his arms.

"I think, Mr. Donnelly," Lincoln said, "you should consider a permanent arrangement."

Josh didn't answer—he was too busy smiling at Maggie.

I cleared my throat. "You're the fellow Marlene says shows up after the plans are made."

Henry's mouth curved. "Children have a way of changing the plans."

Lincoln and I gave Josh and Maggie a minute. That's the part the handbook never mentions: when to step away.

Outside the cell block, Lincoln gave me a smile and a firm handshake.

"All in a good day's work," he said.

I nodded. "If that's what it looks like when you ruin a plan, you're welcome back anytime."

He chuckled, already turning away. "Carry on, Chief," he said, waving over his shoulder. "Keep doing good work."

When I went back to the cell, Josh was sitting on the edge of the cot with Maggie tucked inside his arms. He didn't speak. He didn't rock her. He just held her and breathed.

Maggie made a soft, humming sound and sneezed again.

"Josh," I said.

He looked up, careful not to jostle her.

"I think we'll move you to another room. Get you someplace more comfortable. Tony went to get some formula."

He nodded. "Yes, sir."

That *sir* nearly undid me.

I set him up in the file room, the one with the old couch, battered filing cabinets, and the box fan that only worked if you threatened it. I brought a light blanket from the trunk of my car and laid it across his knees, over Maggie's feet.

He thanked me like I'd given him the moon.

The building had gone still. The lights were low. The radio crackled and fell silent again.

I went back to my desk, reviewed the paperwork twice, and listened.

Maggie cried once. Josh murmured something I couldn't hear. The crying stopped.

Near one in the morning I heard the couch creak. Josh was awake. I could feel it.

I walked down the hall.

Josh looked up at me. Maggie's fist was tangled in the front of his shirt. Her sleeping face was pink and relaxed and entirely unbothered by the fact that she was in a police station.

"She's breathing funny," he said.

I leaned in. Watched her chest rise and fall. "She's fine, Josh. Maybe a little chilled by the fan, but I'll turn it off."

He nodded, absorbing my words like scripture.

"She's really here," he said.

"Yes, son. She is." I hesitated. "Do you know why?"

He smiled. "Because I prayed." Then he pressed a kiss to the top of her head and closed his eyes.

I sighed, then went back to my desk.

Somewhere between the ticking clock and crackling radio, I understood something I hadn't known before: The world doesn't always announce its miracles.

Sometimes it places them in your arms and waits to see what you'll do.

As soon as the sun was well and truly up, I made the coffee and went back to my office, the baby's laughter tinkling in the background. I pawed through the mess on my desk until I found Marlene DuBois's number, scrawled on a Post-it stuck to the side of my monitor like a warning label I had chosen to ignore.

I dialed.

It rang longer than it should have. When she answered, her voice came out thick and gravelly, the sound of a woman yanked out of sleep and none too pleased about it.

"H'lo?"

"Marlene. Horace Bowen, Peculiar PD. I know it's early, but I can't help wondering how you managed to get little Maggie delivered to a police station."

"Why . . . what?"

"Maggie—the baby we picked up yesterday. She's here."

More silence. Then—"Have you been drinking, Chief?"

"No, ma'am."

"Because I don't find this funny. Especially not at this hour."

"Good, because I'm not joking. You didn't know about the move?"

"Why would I?"

"That's what I'm trying to find out."

"You must be mistaken," Marlene said. "Last time I saw her, she was with a licensed foster family in Marianna."

"She's not there now," I said. "If you—"

She hung up.

No goodbye. No explanation. Just a hard click.

I sat a moment, tapping my fingernails on the desk, staring at the phone like it might confess if I applied enough pressure.

The radio crackled. The soda machine clunked. Somewhere down the hall, the baby giggled.

I checked the paperwork again. The Honorable Sam Clarkson, a judge from the Jackson County court, had approved the emergency pickup order. Lincoln Henry, guardian ad litem for Maggie Doe, had transferred the child from a foster home in Marianna and placed her in the custody of Joshua Donnelly, who just happened to be sitting in the Peculiar city jail.

I flinched when the phone rang.

"Marlene."

"I called the foster family. You're correct, but you can't say I didn't warn you."

"About Lincoln Henry, right?"

"Yep."

I sat up straighter. "Met him last night, along with a pile of paperwork."

Marlene sighed. "Apparently he learned about Maggie's case yesterday afternoon. He engaged a pro bono lawyer to represent her and secured an emergency order before the judge went home. Then he personally transported the child to Peculiar. Enough details for you?"

"Not quite." I massaged my temple. "How'd he know Josh was in jail?"

"Considering Peculiar, he could have asked almost anyone."

"Granted—but how did he hear about Maggie's case? Of the hundreds of kids involved with DCF—"

"The man has ears in every courthouse in the state. Apparently he heard the story and is convinced the charges against Donnelly will be dismissed at the arraignment. After all, there were extenuating circumstances."

I closed my eyes. Yes, there were, but if today's judge woke up in a bad mood, Josh could find himself looking at a second-

or third-degree felony. But Marlene would know that. What she didn't know was that Josh was on our list of potential suspects for his father's murder.

"So," I said. "I have a baby in my jail and a man scheduled for arraignment in a couple of hours. What happens next?"

"Well, I suppose you will go to court and—"

"Here's what I'm doing," I interrupted. "Maggie and Josh are technically in my custody, so I'm bringing them both to Marianna. I'll meet you at the courthouse."

"I am no longer responsible for that child. Josh Donnelly is."

"Josh Donnelly," I said, "happens to be a person of interest in a murder case. So we'll need someone to watch the baby while we're in court. If things don't go well for Josh today, you'll need to find another placement for that little girl."

I ended the call before she had a chance to catch her breath, then stood and stretched the kink from my neck.

Before I could go to Marianna, I had to speak to Josh. Because against all odds, a baby had been delivered to a place where babies are generally not allowed.

And I had a sinking suspicion that the simplest part of my day was behind me.

I DRAGGED a chair into the file room and planted it in front of Josh, then lowered myself into it. The metal legs screeched against the concrete, a sound that usually rattled nerves.

Josh didn't even flinch.

He was lying on the couch, but he looked at me, nodded to the baby curled on his chest, and pressed a finger to his lips. "Sorry for not sittin' up, but I finally got her to sleep," he whispered. "By the way, do y'all keep baby food around here?"

I raised a brow and let it stay aloft. "Josh, we need to talk about this morning. We need to leave for court in less than an hour, and what happens there is going to matter a whole lot more than how Maggie got here."

He studied my face, and I could see the change register. The easy calm retreated, replaced by something watchful.

"The way Maggie arrived here last night," I went on, "was highly irregular. But it isn't likely to decide your future."

Josh sat up, eased Maggie onto the couch with slow care, and tucked the blanket around her. Then he leaned forward, elbows on his knees, hands laced.

"So tell me this," I said. "Did you call Lincoln Henry for help?"

Josh's eyes widened. "Who?"

"The man who brought Maggie."

Josh grinned. "I never knew the man's name. But I met him."

"What do you mean, you met him?"

Josh shrugged. "At the hospital, I helped him pick up some papers. But that night I was only thinking about Mama."

I stroked my chin, trying to put the odd puzzle pieces into a frame—and trying not to think about other pieces, like the photos on my office wall and a shallow grave in damp Florida soil.

"So maybe you told Heather about him, and she called the Guardian ad Litem office."

Josh looked at me like I'd just grown an extra head. "What? No! I've never heard of whatever office you're talking about."

I rubbed my jaw. "Then can you explain how Lincoln Henry was able to get a pickup order for Maggie? When I need something from the county court, I have to wait days, sometimes weeks."

Josh shook his head. "All I know is I prayed."

I followed his gaze to the floor.

I saw the same grocery bag I'd seen at his house the day before. Diapers. The little dress Heather had picked out. Maggie's stuffed lamb, one ear still bent.

I inhaled slowly and congratulated myself for not banging my head against the cinderblock wall.

I'd heard a lot on the job. People said God healed them, saved their marriages, helped them find lost keys. This, however, was new ground.

But none of that would matter if the judge ruled against Josh. And if the judge didn't, other questions waited in the wings.

I glanced at the baby, then my watch. Forty-five minutes.

"I've got a few things to handle," I said. "While I'm gone, get dressed. And you'd better pray that the judge sympathizes with your situation, because this morning could decide the rest of your life."

His eyes darkened. "If he finds me guilty?"

"A third degree will get you up to five years in prison," I said. "Judges and prosecutors don't approve of people who commit battery on officers of the law."

CHAPTER
FORTY-THREE

As Josh dressed for his trip to Marianna, I retreated to my office. Paperwork lay in drifts across every flat surface, the accumulated snow of other people's bad days.

I was pulling up the paperwork for Josh's arrest when a soft shuffle distracted me. Tony stood in the doorway, cup of coffee in hand.

"Morning, Chief. How'd it go last night?"

"Fine, once the baby settled. I even managed to get a little shut-eye."

"Ready for court?"

"Yeah—though I don't know what to make of Donnelly's chances."

Tony didn't smile. "That baby might be the least of his problems." He nodded toward my office wall.

Crime scene photographs stared back at us. Black-and-white shots of the exhumation site. Dirt-stained bones. Evidence markers standing in the soil like little white tombstones. Tony refused to take them down until the case was closed.

I had a strong feeling the family judge wouldn't have signed that pickup order if he'd known Josh Donnelly could be implicated in a murder case.

"We still got a murder," Tony said. "Two suspects right here in Peculiar."

I shook my head. "We don't have any evidence."

"You still think Donnelly can't be violent?" Tony asked. "No matter what happens today, we gotta find out if George Donnelly came back after '86."

I thought about what I'd seen last night—Josh's smile, Maggie nestled against his chest, his face lit up like he'd been given the world.

I wanted to hand Josh his coat and tell him to take his baby home. But until George Donnelly's murder was solved, I couldn't trust him with a child.

And I couldn't trust myself to look the other way.

CHAPTER
FORTY-FOUR

By the time I walked Josh and Maggie out to my vehicle, news of Maggie's return had already made the rounds. That part was unavoidable. We had to locate a safety seat for Maggie, and Peculiar isn't a town where a discreet inquiry about borrowing a car seat goes unnoticed. We don't usually load babies into the back of police vehicles, but the rulebook had been thin on guidance, so we improvised.

Tony held Maggie while I cuffed Josh and guided him into the back seat. Then I took the baby from my deputy and fastened her into the borrowed safety seat, tightening the straps with the care usually reserved for explosives. Maggie slept through the whole thing, quiet and cozy, blissfully unaware that she'd become the town's latest miracle.

By the time I shut the back door, a small crowd had gathered. The crowd swelled when the ambulatory residents of Twin Oaks altered their walking route, drawn by the rumor that Josh Donnelly was about to leave town under police escort. Among them was Bill Goodman.

Old Bill stood apart, one arm folded across his chest, the

other raised as he pressed a finger to his lips. It wasn't a gesture for silence so much as for restraint, the kind he'd spent a lifetime practicing. His gaze followed our movements with calm precision.

I wish I could say I didn't care what the former chief thought of my work. But even after twenty years wearing the badge, I couldn't shake the feeling that he was measuring me against an invisible standard... and finding me wanting.

I focused on the task at hand and tried to ignore the murmurs drifting toward me like gnats.

"Why does Chief Bowen have Maggie in the back of his car?"

"I heard they took her to Marianna."

"Josh Donnelly in handcuffs? I never thought I'd see the day."

I got behind the wheel, started the engine, and eased the car toward the highway, resisting the urge to duck.

As I turned onto Tuscawilla Road, Bill Goodman separated himself from the walkers and stepped closer to the sidewalk. He straightened enough to aim that laser stare at me, the same one he'd worn when I was green and reckless and convinced rules were suggestions.

The force of it followed me onto the highway.

I sank lower in my seat. I hadn't wanted to arrest Joshua Donnelly. But when a man strikes a police officer, you don't get to pretend the law took the day off.

The ride passed mostly in silence. I focused on the road. Josh stared out the window. Maggie slept, her breath soft and steady, her chest rising and falling like a quiet tide against the shore.

We were several minutes outside Marianna when the radio crackled.

"Chief, you there?"

"Go ahead," I said.

"Got a call from old Chief Goodman. He's on his way to Marianna."

I glanced at the rearview mirror. Josh hadn't looked at Goodman when we pulled out, but I knew they were close. Goodman was probably coming to offer moral support.

For Josh. Not me.

"Tell Goodman there's no need," I said. "I've got it covered."

"Too late, Chief. I think he's already talked Heather into drivin' him up. Over."

I set the radio down and signaled for the exit ramp.

On one hand, Goodman's presence might not be a problem. He'd been off the force for twenty years. On the other hand, the people of Peculiar would almost certainly interpret his presence as proof that I'd mishandled Josh's case and needed his supervision to make things right.

The closer I got to the courthouse, the less sure I was about what right meant anymore.

"Almost there, Josh." I checked the mirror. He nodded, then reached—awkwardly—to brush a strand of hair off Maggie's forehead. Not an easy maneuver in handcuffs.

"I'll be glad to get this over and done," he said. "Maggie's comin' in with us, right?"

I shrugged. "I don't see another option. Marlene Dubois will join us as soon as she can, and I expect she'll take custody of Maggie right away."

Josh didn't answer. But in the mirror, I saw his jaw tighten.

JOSH'S CASE had been assigned to Judge Robert Peterson, a man I'd encountered often enough to know he disliked surprises, rambling explanations, and humanity in general. Peterson favored punctuality, brevity, and the efficient crushing of hope.

Because of the overnight chaos, I hadn't yet spoken to the prosecutor or the court-appointed defense attorney, responsibilities that gnawed at me as we pulled into the courthouse parking lot. If this were only a battery charge, I'd already be rehearsing how to suggest we all pretend it never happened. But the open murder investigation sat in my chest like a stone.

What if Josh had killed his father?

I had no evidence. No witnesses. Just bones, questions, and a medical examiner who still needed time to come up with an approximate date of death. If Josh was guilty, dropping the charge would look like negligence. If he was innocent, keeping it could ruin his life.

Yet we were at the courthouse because of the battery, a misdemeanor if you punch a civilian. But battery upon a law enforcement officer can earn you up to five years in prison.

Five years—for hitting a man who was about to take away the child you loved.

The law was the law, but the law had never met Josh Donnelly.

I'd spent my career believing in evidence, fingerprints, and motive. But evidence didn't usually go to court wrapped in a blanket and carrying a bent-eared lamb. And children weren't typically returned to their families only hours after being removed by DCF.

We must have looked like an odd trio as we entered the building. Josh walked beside me in his suit and handcuffs, shoulders squared, eyes calm. I wore my uniform and carried Maggie, who had discovered my hat and was gnawing on the brim like a determined beaver.

The air inside the courthouse carried the faint odor of cleaning solution with coffee and human worry stitched through it. Our footsteps echoed in the lobby, drawing glances from clerks, bailiffs, and a woman who clutched her purse like we might all be contagious.

We met Josh's court-appointed attorney near the courtroom doors. Fletcher Pettinato looked about twelve years old. His gaze went straight to Maggie. One eyebrow climbed.

"Are you allowed to bring a baby into the courtroom?"

"An officer from DCF is on her way," I said. "Any minute now."

He hesitated. "Still, I'd advise finding someone else to hold the child. We don't want to distract the judge."

Judge Peterson didn't like distractions like babies, coughing, whispering, and blinking too slowly.

I scanned the lobby for a friendly face and found none. "I'll handle Maggie," I said. "Did you get my report?"

"I skimmed it," he said. "Charge is battery on a law enforcement officer?"

"Yes."

"First offense?"

"Yes."

"Aggravated? Weapon involved?"

I glanced at Josh. Tall, thin, built like a scrub pine. "No weapon. Just his fist."

"Okay." Pettinato nodded. "What's our best explanation?"

"They were going to take Maggie," Josh said. "And God sent her to me."

Pettinato looked like he'd bitten into a lemon. "I'm sorry—what?"

"Josh," I interrupted, "we should stick to the facts in there."

"Okay," the lawyer said. "Who's Maggie?"

Josh raised his cuffed hands and pointed. "She is."

The lawyer blinked. "And who was going to take her?"

"The children and families people."

"Why?"

"I don't know," Josh said. "She wasn't in any danger."

Pettinato turned and gave me a *can-you-help-me-out* look.

I sighed. "DCF took the child after Josh punched me. But now she's back."

"Why?"

"Long story," I said. "But we're not here to argue custody. We're here about the battery charge. Let's keep things clean."

My name echoed down the hallway.

"Chief Bowen!" Marlene Dubois came speed-walking toward us, her shoes squeaking with urgency. "I have things to discuss with you."

"Perfect timing," I muttered.

I turned to Pettinato. "She'll hold the baby. You just tell the judge that Josh acted out of distress. He believed he was losing a child he'd spent months caring for. In a moment of passion, he struck me."

The lawyer looked between us, his expression sour but resigned. He needed experience. Josh needed mercy.

"Come on," he said. "We could be called any moment."

I handed Maggie to Marlene. Maggie refused to surrender my hat, so Marlene peeled it from the baby's grip and handed it back to me, damp and misshapen.

"Let her keep it," I said. "Please wait here. We'll talk when this is over."

Marlene sighed and sat on a bench, clutching Maggie like an answer she wasn't sure she wanted.

As the courtroom doors loomed ahead, I squared my shoulders and prayed that Judge Peterson wouldn't require a blood sacrifice to start his day.

CHAPTER
FORTY-FIVE

Pettinato guided Josh toward the defense table, and I slid into the bench behind the low wooden partition—close enough to feel implicated, far enough to pretend neutrality. The bench had been smoothed by generations of nervous backsides and creaked like it knew secrets.

Across the aisle, Marcia Bonaventure, Jackson County prosecutor, rifled through her file with the controlled irritation of someone handed a live grenade without the pin. Given that I'd filed my report barely an hour earlier, I doubted she'd made it past the header.

She scanned a page, then looked up to study Josh.

I could have saved her the effort. Josh Donnelly was exactly what he appeared to be: tall, thin, awkward, and utterly out of place in criminal court. His face was open, even hopeful—as if he still believed people would be reasonable.

He caught Marcia staring and smiled.

She startled and looked away, a blush climbing her cheeks. Not every day a defendant disarmed a prosecutor with nothing but good manners.

When she noticed me, she crossed the aisle, professionalism snapping back into place.

"Good to see you again, Chief Bowen. But I have to ask—why are you sitting over here? Looks like you're rooting for the defendant."

"You know Peculiar," I said. "We're one big happy family. Dysfunctional, but loyal."

Her gaze flicked back to Josh. "What can you tell me about him?"

"There's a lot about Josh Donnelly I can't explain. But I like him."

"Even though he attacked you?"

"He had his reasons."

Her head tilted. "Anything else I should know before this gets interesting?"

I hesitated, then decided honesty was cheaper in the long run. "We recently found his father's body buried under a shed. The ME puts the death somewhere between ten and twenty years ago."

"That's a wide window."

"We're waiting on more tests."

"Suspects?"

"Two or three, depending on the timeline. One is the wife—deceased. One is Josh."

"Number three?"

"A long shot."

"Any evidence tying Josh to it?"

"No."

"But you're still investigating."

"Yes."

"So you don't want me to let him walk."

I exhaled. "I don't know what I want. But he punched me while trying to defend a baby, and frankly, I don't blame him for that. If, as a teenager, he needed to defend his mother, he might have killed his father. But he's not acting like someone with blood on his hands."

"Does anyone?" she asked. "Or is he just confident he won't be convicted?"

"Your guess is as good as mine. But his record's cleaner than spring water. If he's innocent of the murder, I'd drop the battery charge today."

She studied me a moment longer, then nodded. "Thank you."

The bailiff stepped forward.

"Case number two-nine-three-four-seven-seven-nine-three. State of Florida versus Joshua Donnelly."

Judge Peterson leaned toward the microphone, peering at the paperwork as if it had personally offended him.

"Mr. Pettinato, do you waive the reading of charges?"

"We do, Your Honor."

"Ms. Bonaventure?"

"Your Honor, the defendant is charged with battery upon a law enforcement officer during the lawful execution of his duties."

Judge Peterson fixed Josh with a practiced stare. "Battery on a law enforcement officer is a third-degree felony in this state. How do you plead?"

"No contest, Your Honor," Pettinato said. "The incident occurred while the officer attempted to remove a child from my client's care. Mr. Donnelly was under extreme duress."

"Noted. Ms. Bonaventure, bail?"

Before she could answer, a stentorian voice rose from the back of the courtroom.

"Your Honor, may I address the court?"

Every head turned.

Bill Goodman made his way down the aisle, Heather

Thomas at his side, both of them looking like they had wandered into the wrong building and decided to stay.

"Sir," Judge Peterson said, "this is an arraignment, not a community forum."

"With respect," Goodman said, "I have information that will save the state considerable time and expense—and prevent an injustice."

"This is highly irregular," Peterson said.

"I know, Your Honor. But my information bears on why Josh reacted the way he did. That's why I'm begging the court's permission to speak."

The judge's eyes flicked to counsel, then nodded. "You may proceed. But not another word until you've been sworn in."

Goodman drew himself upright as the court bailiff hurried forward with a Bible. After the oath had been administered, Goodman rested both hands on his cane. "I am William Goodman. For twenty years, I served as police chief in Peculiar. At twenty-two hundred hours on January tenth, 1986, I received a call from a resident reporting a woman's scream..."

The courtroom fell into a stillness that felt like held breath.

Goodman went on, relating the story of how he'd gone into the Donnellys' shed and found George beating his wife. Bill intervened, and in the scuffle, George got his weapon. But before he could fire, Margaret struck her husband with a hammer.

"At that point, Your Honor, I escorted Mrs. Donnelly into the house. Her eye was swelling and her arms were badly bruised. I went outside to check on George Donnelly, who was deceased."

The old chief pulled a handkerchief from his coat and wiped his face. "I was an officer of the law, sworn to uphold it. I knew the penalties for not reporting a death, but I was six months away from retirement and I'd spent at least ten years quietly admiring Margaret Donnelly's courage. So I decided it would do no good for her to suffer public humiliation. She acted not only to save herself, but her young son and a police officer. Concealing the Donnelly death was not my finest hour, but it is one I do not regret."

When he finished, the judge remained motionless, one hand resting against his face, eyes unreadable beneath the lights.

"I fail to see," Judge Peterson said at last, "what this confession has to do with the matter before this court."

"It bears directly on the defendant's character and circumstances," Goodman said. "And on whether he deserves leniency."

In the resulting silence, Heather stepped forward. "I'm the reason Josh hit Chief Bowen. He was trying to do right by Maggie. I talked him into fighting for her."

Sighing, Judge Peterson surveyed the room. "Anyone else care to confess to a felony this morning?"

Goodman gestured toward me. "Your Honor, now that Chief Bowen knows Joshua Donnelly had nothing to do with his father's death, I believe he and the prosecutor will be willing to withdraw the charge."

I rose. "Yes, Your Honor, that is true."

Marcia stood as well. "The state will not proceed."

Judge Peterson picked up his gavel, his gaze steady, solemn, and a shade bemused. "The State's motion to *nolle prosequi* is granted." The sound of the gavel cracked through the room like the closing of a door.

Then Peterson looked at me. "But your work is far from finished, Chief Bowen."

I met his gaze and nodded—because I knew he was right, and because in Peculiar, the truth never arrives without leaving a mess behind.

Josh sat motionless on the hard wooden bench, his hands folded, head bowed as if in prayer. When old Bill Goodman began to speak, Josh closed his eyes.

Bill spoke of years long past, of a night when fear filled a small house, of a woman who made an impossible choice. Josh did not hear every word, but the meaning found him anyway.

His mama killed his father. Not in rage. Not in hatred. She had done it to save Bill Goodman. She had done it to save *him*.

The truth surged without warning, swift and merciless. Pain followed, with a suffocating dread that pressed against his throat until he had to swallow to breathe.

He had buried this. All of it.

He had done what children do when the truth is too huge to hold. He had let his mama cover it by telling him his father had gone away. Gone for reasons that did not involve blood or terror or violence in the dark.

An image rose unbidden. The narrow space of his bedroom. His daddy's belt, taken from its hook and folded in a hand that knew exactly what it was doing.

No wonder he had hated that chair—the one his father claimed every evening like a throne. The place where discipline was decided and delivered. The place where silence was law, and any undisciplined laughter or cry was met with punishment.

Be small. Be quiet. Be good.

When he looked up again, the courtroom appeared too bright. His hands trembled in his lap.

Lord, he prayed, the words rough and urgent, *don't ever let me be that cruel to anyone. Give me the courage to not be that man.*

Chief Bowen said something. So did the judge.

Someone said Josh's name. Then another voice joined in,

and another. Words floated toward him like harmless birds. *Congratulations. Good man.*

He opened his eyes.

Faces turned his way, smiling. Nods of approval. A hand clapped his shoulder. Someone squeezed his arm. The moment demanded a response, so he smiled. He nodded. He accepted congratulations as if nothing inside him had cracked open.

Then he folded the memories back into the place where he had stored them for years. For now.

THE VOLUME INCREASED in the lobby, as if the building itself had exhaled once the hearing ended. Voices echoed off polished floors. Shoes clicked. A vending machine hummed somewhere nearby.

As Bill Goodman rested on a bench in the hallway, Josh stood with Heather, Fletcher Pettinato, and Chief Bowen, trying to remember how to exist in a world where people smiled and spoke as if nothing out of the ordinary had happened.

Marlene Dubois stood a few feet away, Maggie balanced on her hip.

Josh felt . . . hollow. Like a house after a storm, the walls still standing but everything inside jolted, drawers pulled open, things that had been put away for years knocked loose.

He heard Pettinato say, "I've never seen an arraignment like that," followed by, "Most unusual."

"He's an unusual guy," Chief Bowen replied, his tone downright cheerful.

Josh knew they were talking about him, but he couldn't quite bring himself to join the conversation. His mind was still crowded with Bill Goodman's voice. The courtroom's hush. The truth rising like a tidal wave.

Then Maggie spotted him.

Her small arms lifted, her mouth burbling with sound, her fingers opening and closing as if she knew exactly where she belonged.

Before he even realized he'd moved, he took her and she settled against his breastbone as if she'd been waiting to be held. She patted his jaw, babbling happily, and Josh's shoulders loosened for the first time since Bill Goodman had begun to speak.

Chief Bowen was talking now, asking questions about Florida law. Family law.

Josh heard without listening, the words drifting past like leaves on water, until one phrase caught and held.

"If relatives can't be found," the lawyer said, "the party who found the child can apply to adopt."

Josh's breath hitched. Lincoln Henry had mentioned adoption, but at the time Josh had other matters on his mind.

He hadn't dared imagine this. Not really. He had prayed, but his prayers had been small and careful, shaped more like pleas than hope.

Lord, help me do right by her.
Lord, don't let her be harmed.
Lord, I'll give her back if You ask.

But this?

He looked down at Maggie, who had discovered the texture of his jacket button and was gnawing on it with fierce devotion.

A year, the lawyer was saying. Home studies. Waiting periods. Judges. Paperwork.

Time.

Time was something Josh could give.

Chief Bowen's voice cut in again, confident and calm, talking about emergency custody, about how keeping Maggie in the only home she knew was the best option.

The words struck Josh with quiet force. Not pride, but responsibility and calling. Hope unfurled in his heart, as cautious as a leaf testing sunlight after a long winter.

"We can wait for an appointment." Chief Bowen looked at him. "We have time to kill, don't we?"

Josh nodded, the answer rising from a place deeper than logic. "You bet," he said. "Just as soon as we feed this girl and change her diaper."

Marlene held out a diaper like a white flag. Heather took it while Pettinato consulted his phone.

A judge. Sixth floor. Right now.

Decisions were made. Movement followed.

Marlene declined to join them, her responsibilities pulling her back to other children, other needs. As she walked away, she glanced over her shoulder, curiosity shining in her eyes.

Josh barely noticed.

He was focused on the reality of Maggie in his arms. On the surprising steadiness of his hands. On the quiet, unmistakable sense that a door had opened to let light through.

Lord, he prayed as the elevator doors parted, *is this our answer?*

Maggie responded by patting his cheek and offering a gummy grin.

Josh stepped forward, hope cradled in his arms, and followed the others toward whatever came next.

CHAPTER
FORTY-SIX

Judge Lorna Nelson studied them for a long moment.

Heather felt that look like a head-to-toe x-ray. Not unkind, but assessing. The sort of look that burned through excuses and peered straight into intention.

"This should be interesting," the judge said at last, arching one brow. "Who wants to begin?"

Heather shifted Maggie, grateful that Josh had handed her the baby before they entered the judge's chambers. Holding Maggie gave her something to do, and kept her focused.

Because they'd filled him in, Pettinato laid out their story in careful, orderly sentences. Dates. Events. Words like *abandoned* and *custody* floated through the room, tidy and bloodless, nothing like the way their experiences had actually felt.

"So," the judge said, "Joshua Donnelly and Heather Thomas, you have cared for this child how long?"

"Since Christmas," Josh said without hesitation. "We're her family."

Heather's brow shot up. He said *we*.

"And you are willing," the judge continued, "to share

everything you know about this baby with DCF so they can conduct a thorough search for relatives?"

"Yes," Heather said, her voice steady.

The judge studied them again, and Heather realized she wasn't shaking. She had been afraid for so long that fear felt like second nature. But sitting in the wood-paneled room with Maggie on her lap and Josh's knee against her own, fear loosened its grip.

"Very well," Judge Nelson said. "I will grant a custody order under the following conditions."

Heather listened as the judge outlined them. Foster licensing. Background checks. Home studies. CPR instruction.

Each requirement landed like a weight and a promise.

She and Josh nodded. Yes, we'll do that. Yes, we can learn. Yes, we'll wait.

Heather had waited her entire life for things she never received. But she would wait for this.

"You will receive a small stipend," the judge said, "but you must demonstrate that you are able to financially support your family without it."

Family. The word sounded like music.

Heather smiled at Maggie, who blinked up at her with complete trust, then turned toward Josh's voice.

An emotion swelled in Heather's heart, a feeling dangerously close to joy.

"You must attend orientation and thirty hours of training," the judge continued. "And you must be willing to wait up to a year before the adoption can be finalized."

A year? Heather could wait five years if it meant Maggie stayed where she belonged.

"Do we have to be married?" Heather asked, the question escaping before she thought.

When Josh's eyes widened, she resisted the urge to apologize.

The judge smiled. "Marriage is not a legal requirement," she said, "but being in a committed legal relationship might make the process easier for you."

Heather nodded. Committed—that, she could be. And legal, if that's what Josh wanted.

As the judge finished and papers were gathered and signed and chairs scraped the floor, Heather held Maggie a little closer.

When Josh found her on that rainy, miserable Christmas Day, she had thought her life was ending.

But that day had been a beginning.

I STOOD in the courthouse lobby feeling the kind of satisfaction that comes when the law behaves itself and nobody makes you regret believing in it. My mood was polished enough to match the marble under my shoes. A cleaning crew had used lemon oil on the wood benches, so the whole place smelled of lemons, old money, and good intentions.

Josh stood a few yards away with Heather and Maggie, his arm looped protectively around both of them. Maggie had one fist tangled in his tie while the other waved at the world like she'd just been elected mayor.

Temporary custody. Not permanent. Not yet.

But close enough to make a grown man believe in miracles.

Marlene DuBois waited near the window, her leather folio tucked under her arm, posture straight, eyes scanning the room the way only people from DCF ever do—looking for danger and hope in the same breath.

I drifted over. "Marlene."

She glanced at me. "Chief."

"I know."

She blinked. "Know what?"

"You called Lincoln Henry."

Her eyebrows arched with professional innocence. "Did I?"

"You told him keeping Maggie with Josh was in that child's best interest. That was all it took. You knew exactly what he'd do."

Marlene gave me a look of manufactured offense. "Are you accusing me of working against my own department? My own case?"

"Maybe," I said. "I can't see any other option. No one else had the knowledge or the authority. And having him float the idea of adoption? That kept Josh from giving up."

She snorted, waved the whole notion away, then smiled at the courtroom's polished doors. "Mr. Donnelly was never going to give up," she said. "Not in my lifetime. I could see he'd do anything to keep that baby. Even deck a friendly police chief."

I studied her face. There it was, in her eyes. A twinkle of light behind the armor.

"Ms. DuBois," I said, "you're all right."

She rolled her eyes, squared her shoulders, and put the bureaucrat back in place.

"Call me if you need me," she said, switching her leather folio to the other arm. "But don't ever accuse me of breaking the rules."

She walked off, her heels clicking against the marble, folio tucked tight.

I watched her go, my heart lighter than it had been in months.

Across the lobby, Josh laughed as Maggie tried to eat his brochures. I smiled and went to join them.

The courthouse doors shut behind them with a solid sound Josh felt more than heard. That was it, then—he and Heather and Maggie were free to go home.

He settled into the driver's seat and started the engine. The old sedan coughed once, then caught, its familiar rattle grounding him in a way the judge's words hadn't. Temporary custody. Home study. Training. Adoption, if all went well. The phrases floated through his mind like butterflies, fragile and miraculous.

Heather opened the back door and buckled Maggie into the borrowed baby seat. Maggie accepted the indignity with solemn patience, then discovered one of her socks and tried to eat it.

Bill Goodman eased in beside Maggie, dropping his cane to the floor. The car filled with the leather-and-mint smell of Bill's after shave.

Heather slid into the front passenger seat, and Josh pulled onto the road that led to Peculiar.

He drove without speaking. Both hands stayed fixed on the wheel, his knuckles pale, his eyes steady on the narrow strip of asphalt ahead. Relief should have made him lighter, but it had cracked open a vault.

Heather noticed. "You okay?"

Josh nodded, because it was easier than explaining the way the courtroom had pulled memories out of him. "I'm . . . thinkin'."

"Well," Bill said, "you've earned the right to do that."

Josh almost smiled.

The road unwound in familiar greens and browns, pine trees standing like sentinels who'd seen worse days than this.

The tires hummed. Maggie gurgled, the baby seat creaking with each gentle bump.

After a mile or two, Heather turned toward him, as much as the seat belt would allow. "Can I ask you something?"

"Yes, ma'am."

She snorted. "You're out of trouble. You can stop talkin' like you're twelve."

He laughed.

"Have you remembered more about your daddy?" she asked.

The question slipped in sideways, careful and considerate.

"I didn't think I did," Josh went on. His fingers tightened on the wheel. "But what I heard in court . . . explains some things."

Heather waited.

"Why I tiptoe around the house," he said. "Why I don't like shoutin', not even outside. Why loud noises make my heart race." He paused. "And why Mama didn't keep pictures of Daddy in the house."

Maggie kicked, creaking the baby seat.

From the back, Bill cleared his throat. "Your father wasn't all bad, Josh."

Josh glanced in the rearview mirror.

"But he was a mean drunk," Bill added. "When the army discharged him, he tried to run his home like a drill sergeant."

The words settled into Josh like truth finally given a name. Not memories, but rules he had followed without knowing who'd written them.

"And I am so sorry," Bill said. "If I'd known what was goin' on back then, I'd have arrested him."

"How could you know?" Josh said. "Mama wouldn't have reported him. She was trying to survive."

"And she did," Bill said. "She had to survive for you."

Blinking, Josh kept his eyes on the road until the sting of tears passed. A mailbox slid by. Then another. Peculiar lay beyond the next turn.

Heather slid her hand toward him, and Josh took it without looking. Her grip was warm and steady, holding a promise born of recognition. Two people who had learned to live small were learning to live brave.

Maggie sighed in her seat, a breath away from sleep.

Josh drove on, carrying the truth of his past without letting it steer him, the afternoon light gilding the trees as the *Welcome to Peculiar* sign came into view.

For the first time he could remember, he wasn't anxious about traveling the road ahead.

Because he wouldn't be traveling it alone.

CHAPTER
FORTY-SEVEN

The next morning, on the Donnelly porch where the bougainvillea had begun its yearly attempt to engulf the railing, Josh proposed.

The proposal went about the way you'd expect. He tried to get down on one knee before remembering he was holding a squirming baby in one arm and a bottle in the other. For a moment it looked like he might attempt the maneuver anyway, but Heather caught his elbow in time, laughing and crying so hard she startled Maggie.

"You don't have to do this," she whispered, stepping closer.

"I know," Josh said. "But I want to be your husband, your friend, the one you turn to at the end of the day. I want to hold you when you cry, laugh when you rejoice, and pray with you when you don't know what else to do. Say you'll marry me, Heather, and make me the happiest man in Peculiar."

That last part mattered. In Peculiar, happiness gets noticed.

They married in November, on a Sunday afternoon so

golden it looked like God had set a lantern in the sky and turned up the wick. Peculiar came out in force.

The choir sang "Come Thou Fount," and Heather cried so hard she made the alto section lose their place. No one complained. Grace Egan dabbed her eyes with a handkerchief she pretended was for allergies.

Maggie toddled down the aisle in a white dress sewn by hand, each step a small victory. Jackie Leakey scooped her up while Josh spoke his vows in that steady way of his, promises about love and protection and choosing Heather every day—especially on the hard ones.

Then Heather spoke, her voice trembling but sure, words spilling out about gratitude, joy, and the God she'd learned to trust, the One who met her when she had nothing and led her home.

I stood in the back, where a police chief belongs when he's off duty, thinking about the crooked paths life favors. How a girl abandoned at a truck stop and a boy raised to tiptoe through his house could become the makings of the finest family Peculiar had ever known. How a baby left on a cold doorstep could become a Peculiar miracle.

It was around then that the other part of the story finally caught up.

IN CASE YOU'RE WONDERING, I couldn't exactly let Bill Goodman confess to being an accessory to murder and then wander off into the sunset.

Tony and I opened a full investigation. In time, the state charged Bill with unlawful disposal of a body and concealing a crime.

The trial came a few months later. Bill was nearly eighty-six.

The prosecutor laid out the evidence: the recovered remains of George Donnelly, and Bill's own confession, read aloud in a flat, court-reporter voice that never wavered.

Bill didn't look at the jury. Didn't look at the judge. He kept his eyes fixed on the far wall, as if listening to something only he could hear. When the reading ended, he exhaled once and sat taller.

The jury took little time.

Goodman was found guilty. He lost his certification and much of what remained of his pension, and he was sentenced to five years in a minimum-security facility.

When they led him away, he didn't look at me. He looked toward the gallery, where Josh sat. In that glance I saw, clear as daylight, a man paying his debt... and willing to pay it again if it meant the boy could finally live free of it.

Peculiar didn't hide how it felt. Folks understood that Bill had broken the law, and that a price had to be paid. But they also knew how rare an honorable man is. Before long, the town council renamed the park on Church Street: Bill Goodman Park.

Prison didn't diminish Bill; it redirected him.

Every Thursday morning he led the men in hymn singing. Most afternoons he played chess. And whenever they could, Josh and Heather came—the girls, the dog, and more light than a place like that usually allowed.

I went as often as my schedule permitted, not out of duty, but because I still wasn't done learning from him.

On my most recent visit, I signed in and waited in the community room while Bill finished a game of ping pong. He won—not theatrically, but clean—and a few of the men clapped. He set the paddle down like a man hanging up his badge.

I walked over and shook his hand. "How you gettin' on?"

He looked around at the bolted tables, the painted cinderblock, the men who called this place home, and gave me that crooked smile of his.

"As you can see," he said, "not much has changed for me." He squeezed my hand once, then let go. "There's the law, Bowen... and then there's what's right."

And I realized he would have walked back into that shed all over again.

These days, if you drive past the Donnelly house at dusk, you don't see polite light, you see *lived-in* light.

You hear Maggie laughing as Hoss submits to dress-up with the patience of a long-suffering saint. You hear little May squealing while Josh counts too loudly in the overgrown yard. And you see Heather on the porch swing, one hand resting where her heart used to ache, watching the life she once believed impossible unfold in front of her.

One evening, after my rounds, I eased the cruiser down Church Street the way I do when the day sits heavy on the badge.

The Donnelly house glowed—porch light burning, windows open, voices drifting out to the sidewalk. Josh's laugh carried all the way to the street. A baby cried. Heather soothed her without hurry, then went back to her painting.

I parked across the street and lingered longer than I needed to, watching the light spill across the yard, thinking how strange and gentle the world can be when God leaves a door open.

Then Hoss spotted me and barked at the cruiser, like he knew I should be off the clock.

I figured that was as good a dismissal as any.

Acknowledgments

No writer works alone, and I certainly didn't write this one by myself. Jerry Jenkins edited an early draft, and my agent, Danielle Egan Miller, offered wise counsel when the story was still finding its feet.

For a while, this book lived in a drawer, waiting patiently while I tried to figure out what it wanted to be. When I finally returned to it in the fall of 2025, the answer came the way answers often do—once I cleared my desk and opened my mind. I had spent time in the fictional city of Peculiar before, in *Five Miles South of Peculiar*, and it felt like exactly the right place for Josh's story to unfold. Writing during the Christmas season added the reverence—and a bit of wonder—needed for Josh's first encounter with Maggie.

I love these characters, and I'm deeply grateful to everyone who came alongside to help bring them to life. Thank you—from me, and from the good people of Peculiar.

FOR BOOK CLUBS

A Most Peculiar Providence explores what happens when ordinary people are confronted with extraordinary responsibility.

When a newborn child arrives in the most unlikely of places, the residents of the small town of Peculiar are drawn into a web of choices involving law, faith, loyalty, and love. At its heart, this novel asks what it truly means to protect what matters most, even when the future is uncertain.

Discussion Questions

1. Josh repeatedly chooses what is right over what is easy. Where do you see this most clearly in the story, and what do you think that choice ultimately costs him?

2. Maggie arrives almost like an interruption . . . or a miracle. How does her presence change the lives of the people around her? Do you view her arrival as coincidence, Providence, or something in between?

3. Heather begins the novel carrying fear, shame, and

uncertainty. How does her self-image evolve by the end of the story?

4. Chief Bowen and Marlene represent two different approaches to justice. How do their perspectives complement each other? Where do you think the line lies between following the law and doing what is right?

5. The town of Peculiar functions almost like a character. How does the setting influence the events and the people who live there? Could this story have been set in a large city?

6. Several characters wrestle with loneliness and loss. How does the novel suggest that love often arrives when it is least expected?

7. Marlene's hidden compassion becomes essential to the story's outcome. What does her character reveal about the tension between professional duty and personal conviction?

8. The courtroom scenes bring faith, law, and human judgment together. How did these moments affect your understanding of justice?

9. Josh loves Maggie without any guarantee of permanence. What does the story suggest about loving fully when the future is uncertain?

10. The title centers on the idea of *providence*, the protective care of God. Looking back over the story, where do you see evidence of unseen guidance at work?

11. Where in your own life have you seen hope arrive in unexpected ways?

12. Josh hears the voice of God—not audibly, but as an inner voice he recognizes as the voice of the Spirit. Have you ever heard that voice? How do you know it comes from God and not your own desires?

JOSH'S RECIPES

Hoss's Favorite Dog Treats

Take **one pound of liver.** Try not to think too hard about where it came from—Hoss certainly won't.

Crack **one egg** into the blender with the liver. You could throw in the shell, because Hoss would consider that a bonus, but you don't have to. We're civilized people.

Liquify the whole business until it looks like something only a devoted dog could love. Try not to make eye contact with it.

Pour the mix into a bowl. Add one cup of flour and one cup of cornmeal, and stir until it becomes a thick, obedient paste. If you're doing this right, Hoss will already be sitting at your feet, pretending he has been patient his entire life.

Grease a baking sheet with edges—or give it a quick spray of Pam, a miracle of modern living. Spread the mixture out evenly, the way you'd tuck a blanket over a sleeping baby.

Slide the baking sheet into a preheated 400-degree oven and bake for about 15 minutes. While it cooks, you can wash the blender, talk to Hoss, or explain to Heather why your kitchen smells like you've made a deeply questionable life choice.

When it comes out, let it cool, then break it into bite-size pieces and freeze them.

Pull them out as needed—especially for training, bribery, or apologizing to Hoss after you've been gone too long. With these treats, any dog will sit, stay, lie down, fetch, and probably balance a spoon on his nose just to make you happy.

And if someone shakes their head at you while you're doing all this? Just tell them it's for love. They'll understand.

Josh's Bologna Sandwiches

Take **two slices of bread** and lay them on the counter.

Put a **couple slices of bologna** on one piece. If it folds over itself, that's fine—things don't have to be perfect to be good.

Add **mustard**, but not too much. You want flavor, not a sermon.

If you feel like giving the bologna a little more dignity, you can fry it until it sizzles. Listen to it. When it sounds cheerful, it's ready.

Set the second slice of bread on top and press downlike you're settling something precious into place.

Eat slowly and savor.

Josh's Grilled Cheese Sandwiches

Take **two slices of bread** and **butter** one side of each. If the butter is cold, give it a moment—it's doing its best.

Lay **cheddar cheese** between the unbuttered sides. Don't be stingy. Life is hard enough.

Heat your skillet over low to medium heat. Not too hot—we're making comfort, not smoke.

Set the sandwich in the pan and let it cook until the bread

turns a gentle gold. If you're nervous, just breathe. The bread will tell you when it's ready.

Flip and cook the other side until the cheese melts into something warm and forgiving.

Cut it diagonally. It feels kinder that way.

Mama's "Homemade" Lasagna

Drive to the Piggly Wiggly. Try not to look like you're on a mission, even if you are.

Pick up **one Stouffer's lasagna**. Hold it like it contains all your good intentions.

Preheat the oven to 400°F (204°C) and stand there for a minute, feeling generous.

Set the tray on a baking sheet so it doesn't make a mess. Mama would approve.

If it's frozen, bake for 1 hour and 45 minutes. If thawed, bake about an hour. You can use this time to wash a few dishes, talk to Hoss, or think about how much your family loves lasagna.

Take the lid off during the last 15 minutes so the top gets that golden, bubbly crust that makes people happy.

Pull it out of the oven and let it rest—even food deserves a minute.

Serve it with care. If anyone asks, just say, "Mama taught me how to do this."

SNEAK PEEK: FIVE MILES SOUTH OF PECULIAR

Chapter One

Residents of Jackson County, Florida, held their breath the morning of July 3, 1968, when old man Caldwell took to his bed complaining of a monstrous headache. As the clock struck two, he sat up, sneezed, wheezed, and lay back down, expiring before his head hit the pillow. The doc pronounced him at 2:03, then placed a call to the county seat. Someone in the county clerk's office reportedly clicked a stopwatch and set it in the safe. County officials and city planners nodded to each other with greedy smiles, knowing that Charles Caldwell's precious estate, known to all as Sycamores, would officially become county property at 2:03 p.m. on July 3, 2018. As to what purpose the property would serve, no one dared offer an opinion. But they could spend the next fifty years dreaming...

    Darlene Caldwell Young, who was only six when her grandpa died, would later take quiet pride in the fact that her family home was not built on the sweat of slaves or the commerce of cotton, but on the courage, cunning, and risk necessary to garner a fortune during Prohibition. Though a current visitor to Sycamores would find alcohol only in bottles of vanilla, rum, and peppermint extract, Darlene considered her grandfather a genius. He not only managed to shelter Sycamores from taxes, but the charitable gift annuity he devised also provided a monthly income for any immediate Caldwell descendant residing on the property.

That income allowed life at Sycamores to continue as it always had, with a sedate and stately elegance. "Chase" Caldwell's progeny were more than willing to let the rest of the world rush and worry and gobble meals behind a steering wheel. At Sycamores, and in Peculiar, the nearest town, life was meant to be savored.

Ready to take a load off her feet one Friday morning, Darlene sank into a rocker on her front porch. She pulled a tattered Japanese fan from her apron pocket and snapped it open, then frantically thrashed at the hot air. The porch lay in deep shade, but beyond it simmered a sun-spangled garden where roses nodded their heavy heads and sunflowers followed the blazing torch in the sky. Next to the sunflowers, Nolie was staking the top-heavy gladiolus while her dogs, Lucy and Ricky, romped across the grass edging the mile-long driveway.

Darlene frowned. The grass looked to be ankle-deep, but ever since Daddy's accident Nolie didn't like to ride the tractor mower. Darlene would cut the lawn herself, but in this heat, she'd have to do it either before sunup or after sundown, and she didn't want to risk running over a possum or armadillo in the vague half-light.

"Lawn needs mowin'," she called, trusting that Nolie could hear her above the barking dogs. "Do you think we could get Henry to find somebody to come out and take care of it?"

Nolie looked up, her eyes shadowed by the wide brim of her straw hat. "Didn't we just cut it?"

"Been nearly two weeks." Darlene fanned herself again. "Those dogs are gonna be itchin' if the grass gets too long. We won't be able to keep the fleas off 'em, and I'm not gonna put up with another infestation in the house."

Nolie turned, the hot breeze ruffling her long pullover apron as she watched her pets play. "You'd better call Henry, then." She picked up her gardening basket. "Ask if he can find someone regular."

"Only till the heat passes. Might as well save some money and do it myself once the weather cools off."

Nolie waved in silent agreement as she followed the dogs and walked toward the driveway.

Inhaling the sweet scent of the honeysuckle vines, Darlene propped her hand on her chin and watched her baby sister. Oh, to be young and carefree again. Though Nolie had recently celebrated her fortieth birthday, her face was still unlined and her figure trim. Come to think of it, Nolie was still a child in many ways. Not surprising, considering she'd never been married, never raised children, and never been widowed. Darlene had borne the stress of all three, and wore the resulting laugh lines and worry ridges on her face.

She straightened as an unfamiliar vehicle slowed on the highway and turned onto the property. A red pickup rattled over the gravel drive, its bed covered with a bright blue tarp and bulging like a gypsy's wagon. Nolie slowed as the truck drew closer, then the driver stopped and leaned over to lower his passenger window.

A chill climbed the chinks of Darlene's spine as she stood and walked to the edge of the porch. This was how every TV crime show began—a suspicious vehicle pulled up beside an innocent woman while the driver asked about a missing puppy or for directions to the police station. But this road led to Sycamores and nowhere else, so the stranger had either made a wrong turn or he was fixin' to kidnap one of the Caldwell women.

Darlene clenched her teeth. "Don't be a dumbbell, Nolie. Don't you get in that truck."

As if she'd heard and *wanted* to rebel, Nolie stepped over the shallow drainage ditch at the side of the drive and walked toward the vehicle. Without even a moment's hesitation she reached for the door handle and hopped into the cab.

Honestly! That girl had no awareness of danger, no understanding of propriety, and absolutely no common sense. Darlene had spent many a sleepless night worrying about what would happen if Nolie met a dangerous killer who summoned her into his car—well, now she knew. Nolie would not only get in, she'd invite the maniac home for supper.

Even Darlene's children had never been that trusting.

She stood in hypnotized horror. If that truck started kickin' up dust in a sudden u-turn, she was calling the sheriff and raising holy heck—

But the pickup continued rumbling toward the house, its giant tires making soft popping sounds as it rolled over the gravel. Darlene pressed her lips together, then stepped inside the foyer, where Daddy's shotgun leaned against the marble windowsill.

The stranger in the truck might not have evil intentions, but when two single women lived only a short distance from the state hospital for the criminally insane, Darlene would rather be safe than sorry.

Nolie pushed at the brim of her hat to better see the man who'd identified himself as Erik Payne. He was certainly spruced up for a hot day in May—the middle-aged man wore a white shirt, a red tie, and dark blue trousers with a crease so sharp it might have been top-stitched. He looked like a politician on parade, but what kind of man deliberately chose to hang a tie around his neck in this heat? Then again, he said he was from Chattahoochee, and everyone knew that place was home to the Florida State Mental Hospital.

She pursed her lips, dreading what Darlene would say about her getting into this man's pickup. Darly would take one look at him and figure he was either a recovering mental patient, an escaped criminal, or, given his red, white, and blue attire, a desperate politician.

Nolie tilted her head. "You say you're from Chattahoochee?"

He kept his gaze on the driveway as the truck rolled forward. "Yes, ma'am. Before I lost my job I was pastor of the First Community Church there. You ever hear of it?"

She shook her head. "I don't get over that way much." She shifted her gaze from his clean-shaven face to his hands. Smooth and pale, with clean and evenly trimmed nails, they looked like a preacher's hands.

"So." The reverend cleared his throat as he applied the brakes and stopped a few feet from the front sidewalk. "Should I be nervous about talking to your sister?"

"Why would you be?"

"Didn't you notice? The woman's carrying a shotgun."

Nolie laughed. "She won't hurt you. But she sees herself as bein' in charge of the house, so she tends to be a little overprotective. She's the one to talk to if you're lookin' for work." She gripped the door handle and grinned. "And you're in luck—I happen to know she's looking for someone to mow the lawn and all like that. Since she started having hot flashes, Darlene can't take the heat."

A wave of crimson brightened the preacher's face as he shut off the engine and pocketed his keys. "Alrighty, then. I guess I'm as ready to meet her as I'll ever be."

"Her name's Darlene Young. Come on with me, and I'll introduce you."

Nolie slid out of the truck and stopped to pat Lucy's and Ricky's heads—the anxious dogs had followed the pickup after Nolie hopped in. After seeing that she was okay, they positioned themselves like armed guards between the preacher and their mistress.

Erik lifted both hands. "Do those lions bite?"

"They're Leonbergers, and they've never bitten anyone—yet." Nolie stepped toward Erik, then looked at the dogs and touched the stranger's arm. "It's okay, baby dogs. This man is a friend."

The dogs' stiff tails relaxed to swing back and forth in happy arcs. "They're beautiful," Erik said, following Nolie as she led the way up the sidewalk. "I've never heard of that breed."

"Not many people have," Nolie answered, pleased by his interest. "They're a lot more common in Europe than over here. I had these two flown over from Germany when they were pups."

Giving the preacher another reassuring smile, Nolie turned toward the porch—and stifled a groan. Darlene stood between the center columns at the top of the stairs, holding the shotgun as if she meant business. "Darly—" Nolie gave her a warning look—"you can put the gun away."

Her sister eyed the stranger with a steely gaze. "I don't know this fellow."

"That's only because you've never met him. Darlene, I'd

like you to meet Reverend Erik Payne. Reverend Payne, this is my sister Darlene Young."

The minister took a hesitant step forward, his hand extended. "Mrs. Young. I'm pleased to meet you."

Darlene lowered the gun and shook his hand without smiling. "What brings you all the way out here, Reverend Payne? We don't need any more Bibles—we already have one for every room and a twenty-pounder on the coffee table."

"Please, call me Erik. And I'm not selling anything." He pulled a folded handkerchief from his pocket and wiped perspiration from his forehead. "Since you asked, ma'am, I was pastoring a church in Chattahoochee until those folks decided the time had come for me to move on. With the employment situation being what it is, one of the deacons gave me your name—he said you and your sister might be willing to take in a stray. I'm not looking for a handout, mind you, but a job and a place to live for a short while. I had to leave the parsonage, so I've been staying in a cheap hotel off the highway while I look for work."

Nolie tugged on Darlene's apron. "You were just sayin' we need a man to mow the lawn. And wouldn't it be nice to have someone replace that old siding on the guesthouse? He could do that and a lot of other chores around here. I know you have a long list of things that need fixin'."

Darlene glanced back at the old house behind her. Nolie knew her sister was thinking about the shutters that needed painting, the mud dauber nests needing to be knocked down, and the guesthouse that could use a facelift . . .

"That's just part of owning an old house. No matter where I sit, I find myself lookin' at somethin' that needs doin'." Darlene shifted her gaze back to the minister. "Before we can commence, Reverend Payne, I have to ask somethin' and I'd appreciate an honest answer. Why did that congregation ask you to leave?"

The minister blinked. "I beg your pardon?"

"Did they catch you stealing from the offering plate? Or were you spending too much time counseling somebody's wife?"

Nolie lowered her gaze, afraid the minister would see the blush she could feel burning her face. Darly had never been one to mince words, but why did she have to be so blunt with a man of the cloth?

The reverend's mouth twisted as he loosened the knot of his tie. "Nothing like that, ma'am. I—well, I was five years married when I took the church. My wife supported me all the time I was going to school and seminary, but once we went to Chattahoochee and actually got into the work of the ministry, she decided she didn't like being a pastor's wife. She didn't like living in a parsonage, she didn't like going to parishioners' baby showers, and she didn't like sharing me with a hundred other people. So a year ago she picked up and left, and after six months she divorced me. The church was good enough to allow us some time in case God wanted to restore our marriage, but when that didn't happen, the church decided that a divorced man couldn't be a good example to the flock. They asked me to leave, so here I am. And that's probably a whole lot more than you wanted to hear."

Nolie studied her sister, but she'd never been good at guessing Darlene's thoughts. Anything could be going on behind that implacable expression.

The preacher dabbed at his forehead again, then shoved his handkerchief back into his pocket. "That's God's truth, ma'am, you can call and ask anyone in Chattahoochee."

Darlene leaned the shotgun against a porch column, then

folded her arms. "What could you actually do for us, Reverend Payne?"

He glanced at Nolie as a half smile crossed his face. "Honestly, ladies, I haven't done much manual labor lately. But as a kid I did some painting, lawn mowing, and gardening. You tell me what needs to be done, and if I don't know how to do it, I'll go to the hardware store and find somebody who can teach me."

Darlene looked away a moment, then nodded. "In return for your help we'll give you use of the guesthouse and supper every day. But how long do you think you'd be stayin'?"

He took a deep breath and scratched his chin. "I don't rightly know about that. I *do* know I've been called to the ministry, so as soon as I'm settled, I'm going to start sending out resumes. God called me to preach and teach, so that's what I intend to do . . . just as soon as the Lord opens a door."

Nolie smiled. "So we'd be waitin' on God with you."

"That's the gist of it, yes ma'am. Would that be acceptable?"

"Hold on a minute." Darlene narrowed her gaze. "The man who sent you to Sycamores—he got a name?"

"Yes—Beverage Simmons."

A smile finally broke through Darlene's inflexible mask. "All right, then. I know Beverage, and I know he wouldn't have sent you to us if you couldn't be trusted." She nodded at Nolie. "I s'pose we can work something out. You agree, Magnolia?"

Nolie stared in pleased surprise, then grinned. "I don't see why not."

The minister practically melted in relief. "Thank you, ma'am. Thank you, *ladies*."

Nolie smiled, glorying in the moment. She'd been holding her breath, hoping Darlene would see that the good and Christian thing to do would be to help this man regain his footing.

He had a look in his brown eyes, the same look she saw when one of her dogs got hurt, and she couldn't bear to see any living creature in pain.

Like Momma always said, far too many people were quick to dish out advice when what a hurting person really needed was a helping hand.

"I say, 'Welcome to Sycamores.'" She grinned as the dogs picked up on her excitement and began to bark. "Come on. I'll walk you over to the guesthouse. It's not fancy and it needs some work, but it'll keep you cool at night and dry in the rain."

"No matter what it looks like," the reverend said, following her, "it'll serve as an answer to prayer until it's time for me to move on."

In her doctor's Manhattan office, Carlene Caldwell looked out at the downtown skyline and couldn't resist a sense of foreboding. Where was her young doctor, and why did he have to keep her waiting? She eyed the thick folder on the man's desk. Why did one simple procedure require so much paperwork?

She folded her hands in her lap and wished she hadn't given up smoking. If ever a situation called for a cigarette, this one did.

"Are you okay?" Martin asked.

"I'm fine." She tried not to look at her agent, who sat next to her and jiggled his crossed leg more energetically than usual. "By the way, I want you to know how grateful I am that you were willing to come down here with me. I've been dreading this appointment for weeks, so it's nice to have someone along. You know, for moral support and all like that."

"You must be anxious—your Southern speech patterns are showing." Martin laughed, but his laughter had an edge that did little to comfort her. "I'm always happy to help you, Carlene. It's the least I could do after all our time together." His brow furrowed. "How many years has it been?"

She turned, grateful for the change of subject. "Let's see—I got my first part in '84, and signed with you right after. So that's—what?"

"Twenty-eight years. You never have been any good at math."

"That's why I trust you to keep my accounts straight." She smiled at him. "We've lasted longer than a lot of marriages."

"Including yours . . . and all three of mine."

Carlene glanced at her watch, then sighed and crossed her legs, struggling to get comfortable in the utilitarian chair. "Good thing *we* never married."

"Good thing I never asked. I knew you had better taste."

She looked over her shoulder at the closed door. "What could be keeping that doctor?"

Martin's eyes softened. "Are you worried about what he might say?"

"No—well, yes. I keep hoping for good news, but common sense tells me something's not right. My *throat* tells me something's not right. I don't even talk like I used to; this rasp in my voice is driving me crazy—"

"Some people might find it sexy."

"Those people know nothing about how the human voice makes music."

Martin fell silent, then he reached across the space between them and squeezed Carlene's arm. "I'm sorry you're in this spot."

She choked on a desperate laugh. "If I'd known losing my voice for six months was even a possibility, I would never have had the surgery."

"Didn't they warn you about all the things that could go wrong?"

"Of course, and I signed the stupid consent form. But nobody ever expects that any of those things will actually happen."

Martin shifted in his chair, then cleared his throat. "By the way, how's your understudy doing? Are the producers happy with her?"

Carlene shrugged. "I think so. But almost anyone could play Golde. It's not what I'd call a demanding role."

"Any thought about what you might like to do next?"

"That will depend on what I learn today, won't it?"

The door behind them finally blew open, revealing a young doctor who wore a wrinkled brow and a concerned expression. He walked around the two guest chairs, then paused to shake Carlene's hand. "Thank you for coming in, Ms. Caldwell."

Carlene introduced Martin, who stood to shake the doctor's hand. She leaned forward. "I hope we can skip any other formalities, Dr. Weston. I have to know—is my throat going to get better, or will I spend the rest of my life sounding like I have laryngitis?"

The doctor twisted his mouth and perched on the edge of his desk. "You sound fine to me."

"I don't think I sound fine. I want the voice I had before the surgery."

"You haven't noticed any improvement since I last saw you?"

"None."

"Your upper register is still affected?"

"My upper register is *gone*. I used to have a five-octave range; now I can barely manage two."

"I'm sorry to hear that." The doctor rubbed his palm along the seam of his trousers, then released a rapid volley of words: "The reason I asked you to wait for the result of the latest scan is because I was hoping the scar tissue would recede. But apparently the thyroid cartilage has elongated and reinforced the loosening of your vocal cords. I was hoping you'd be better after several months of recuperation, but sometimes, due to factors beyond our control, our purposes are thwarted and our goal is not achieved. You are able to speak, and that may be the best result we can hope for."

Carlene blinked, her mind reeling in the verbal onslaught. Finally she grasped one word: "You thought I'd be *better*? Doctor, I can't simply be *better*. I have to be *exceptional*. I have to be able to sing like I used to. I was hoping to sing *better* than before."

The doctor's expression remained locked in neutral. "I'm sorry the results of your surgery were not what we expected."

Carlene struggled to swallow as her scarred throat tightened. *Not what he expected?* Why didn't he call this what it was—a *disaster, catastrophe, calamity,* and *tragedy?*

"Martin, I can't—" She closed her eyes as the office walls swirled and swayed. Martin barked a command, then a strong arm supported her shoulders and he held her upright.

A moment later, she opened her eyes to find that the room's walls and ceiling had resumed their proper places. She fixed her gaze on the doctor's white lab coat, now only a few inches away.

Martin took her hand. "Are you all right, Carlene? Would you like to go home? I could call a cab—"

"So that's it?" She lifted her chin and looked at the doctor, who was moving back to the chair behind his desk. "My voice is ruined." The sounds rasped as she forced the words over her wounded vocal cords.

The doctor's mouth changed just enough to bristle the

fashionable stubble on his cheeks. "I'm so sorry the results were not . . . optimal."

"You've already said that." She blinked, then focused on Martin. "I think I'm ready for that cab now."

Martin helped her up as the doctor stammered. "If—if there's anything I can do—"

"You can explain everything to my lawyer," she said, walking toward the door, "when you tell him how you destroyed my life."

Carlene let her head fall to the back of the seat as Martin slid in beside her and gave the cab driver her address.

"No." She shook her head. "I'm not going home. I ought to be at the theater."

"Whatever for? Your understudy has the part covered."

"I've been helping out backstage. I don't want everyone thinking I'm some kind of invalid, and as long as I'm getting paid . . ."

Martin stared at her, then waved in surrender. "The Forty-sixth Street Theater, then," he told the driver. "And Sixth Avenue after that."

She crossed her arms. "Thanks for humoring me."

"I don't understand why you're doing this to yourself. You ought to go home; you need time to consider your options."

"What options? I'd say the doctor was pretty definite about my prognosis."

"I think you should get a second opinion. What does this young guy know? After all, he botched the surgery—"

"And I'll let my lawyer take care of that. I'm not going to confront a hotshot medical expert about his substandard surgical skills."

"So you're going to sue?"

"If I have a case, I'd be foolish not to. Isn't that why surgeons carry malpractice insurance?"

"Fine. But while your lawyer's pursuing justice, you and I need to talk about your future. Just because your voice isn't what it used to be doesn't mean you're ready to be put out to pasture. You're a fine dramatic actress, and I'm not giving up on you."

"I'm almost fifty, Martin—too old to be a leading lady."

"No one has to know how old you are. You look great, and that's all anyone cares about."

She snorted. "I look like a spit-polished used car. People can tell my odometer's been set back, they just can't tell how far."

Martin ignored her quip. "We could find a play with a great supporting role. Look at all the actresses who have played Broadway well into their eighties—"

"That's a pretty short list. And actresses, even great ones, are a dime a dozen in New York. I wouldn't make the cut. Any success I might have achieved has come because I could sing."

"That's not true."

"It *is* true, though you're sweet to try to convince me otherwise. But you're right about needing time to think. Maybe I should go home."

Martin tapped the Plexiglas window between the back seat and the driver. "We've changed our minds. Can you take us to Inwood Park instead?"

Carlene braced herself as the cab made an abrupt turn onto a congested side street.

"We could look for TV work," Martin said, settling back. "Maybe you could audition for a soap."

"And play some up-and-coming starlet's grandmother? No thanks."

"You could interview for a network morning program, audition for a few cable shows, maybe go on *Celebrity Apprentice*—"

She glowered at him. "I don't need to grovel. I don't want to be in the spotlight unless I deserve to be there."

"But you have talent, and with that comes a responsibility—"

"I *had* a talent." Despite her intentions to remain strong, her chin quivered. "For six months I've dreaded this possibility, so I'm not going to harbor any delusions. I was an exceptional singer and a decent actress, but I'd be lucky if my reputation extends as far as the outer boroughs. No one in Hollywood is clamoring for my head shot. No one in network television even knows my name."

"They could learn it."

She snorted softly. "The market is already crowded with aging singers. I'm not going to force my company on anyone."

"You're too young to retire."

"Do I have a choice?"

"What else would you like to do?"

She pressed her fingertips to her temples. "I've never considered being anything but a singer. I never . . . I mean I don't think I ever had a choice to be anything else."

She closed her eyes as the cab jounced through a pothole. The doctor's announcement had floored her with its finality, but the news hadn't come as a complete surprise. For the last four months she had been warming up her lower register with scales and vocal exercises. But every time she approached the D an octave above middle C, her throat closed. No matter how hard she tried, she couldn't coax out any sound.

She groaned. "I should never have gone to that ENT. My coach said I only needed a few weeks' vocal rest, but that seemed too simple. So I had to go to the fancy throat doctor and he had to try a new technique..."

She blinked back a sudden rush of tears. Why had she thought surgery would help? Because she was hoping for a *better* voice, as if medicine could improve a God-given gift.

She wrapped her fingers around her agent's hand. "I'm sorry. I know you're trying your best to be supportive, and I appreciate it. But right now I'm not feeling optimistic."

He shifted to face her. "There's no reason this has to end your career. You take some time to think, and after you've come up with an idea of what you'd like to do next, give me a call. I'll help you get whatever gig you want."

She squeezed his fingers. "I appreciate the thought, but I'm not willing to sully the reputation I spent years building. I'm going to go back to my apartment, take stock of my situation, and maybe go for a walk in the park. That should clear my head so I can come up with a plan about what to do next."

"I'll always be here for you."

"I know you will." She squeezed his hand again. "You're not only a good agent, you're a good friend."

OTHER BOOKS BY ANGELA HUNT

Contemporary Fiction

The Fine Art of Insincerity

The Offering

Five Miles South of Peculiar

The Face

Let Darkness Come

The Elevator

The Note

The Immortal

The Truth Teller

Doesn't She Look Natural?

She Always Wore Red

She's in a Better Place

Unspoken

The Canopy

The Debt

The Pearl

What a Wave Must Be

Uncharted

The Justice

The Novelist

Passing Strangers

The Proposal

The Elevator

A Time to Mend

For a list of historical novels and children's books, visit
www.angelahuntbooks.com

www.ingramcontent.com/pod-product-compliance
Lightning Source LLC
LaVergne TN
LVHW040035080526
838202LV00045B/3355